T0123277

Turned On

"I appreciate your attempts to get to know me, so let me give you this. This challenge from you, this stubborn fight inside you, does nothing but turn me on." He waited until his words sank in and her eyes widened before continuing. "Your being pliant and obedient bores me. So you have a choice to make. Do you want to bore me or arouse me?"

She blinked. "How about I rip off your head and shove my socks down your headless corpse?"

Amusement grabbed him so quickly he couldn't help a quick bark of laughter. "Aroused it is, then." He slammed the door and crossed around the car to retake his seat. Oh, he couldn't keep her, but she was making that reality look bleak. Maybe someday when he took care of his problems, he could look her up.

Also by Rebecca Zanetti

IMMORTAL'S HONOR

By Rebecca Zanetti

LYRICAL PRESS
Kensington Publishing Corp.
www.kensingtonbooks.com

LYRICAL PRESS BOOKS are published by

Kensington Publishing Corp.
119 West 40th Street
New York, NY 10018

All Kensington titles, imprints, and distributed lines are available at special quantity discounts for bulk purchases for sales promotion, premiums, fundraising, educational, or institutional use.

Special book excerpts or customized printings can also be created to fit specific needs. For details, write or phone the office of the Kensington Sales Manager: Kensington Publishing Corp., 119 West 40th Street, New York, NY 10018. Attn. Sales Department. Phone: 1-800-221-2647.

Lyrical Press and Lyrical Press logo Reg. U.S. Pat.& TM Off.

First Electronic Edition: December 2021
ISBN-13: 978-1-5161-1077-3 (ebook)

First Print Edition: December 2021
ISBN-13: 978-1-5161-1082-7

Printed in the United States of America

Dedication

This one is for Donna, Jillian, and Liz—because sink or swim—the flock always protects each other. I love you three!

Acknowledgments

Thank you to the readers who've been with the Realm since the beginning, and those who have jumped in with this new era, starting with *Vampire's Faith*. I have many wonderful people to thank for getting this book to readers, and I sincerely apologize to anyone I've forgotten.

Thank you to my loving family, Big Tone, Gabe, and Karlina; as always, I love you and appreciate you so much.

Thank you to my hardworking editor, Alicia Condon, as well as everyone at Kensington Publishing: Alexandra Nicolajsen, Steven Zacharius, Adam Zacharius, Vida Engstrand, Jane Nutter, Lauren Jernigan, Elizabeth Trout, Samantha McVeigh, Lynn Cully, Jackie Dinas, Arthur Maisel, Renee Rocco and Rebecca Cremonese.

Thank you to my wonderful agent, Caitlin Blasdell, and to Liza Dawson and the entire Liza Dawson Agency.

Thank you to my awesome assistant, Anissa Beatty, for her excellent social media work as well as the fun with the Rebels.

Thank you to Writer Space and Fresh Fiction PR for all the hard work.

Thanks also to my constant support system: Gail and Jim English, Kathy and Herb Zanetti, Debbie and Travis Smith, Stephanie and Don West, Jessica and Jonah Namson, Chelli and Jason Younker, Liz and Steve Berry, and Jillian and Benji Stein.

Chapter One

Sam was so fucking finished with having no control. He looked at his right hand. Well, to be exact, he looked *through* his hand to see the ground wavering beneath his feet. His body was once again caught between dimensions, and the pain was starting to shred his self-control.

"It's only getting worse," Garrett Kayrs said, standing beside their motorcycles.

"No kidding." Sam coughed, blood dribbling down his chin. He tried to pull away from the vortex, shredding the skin on his arm. Bellowing, he broke all the way free and flopped on the torn cement.

Garrett sighed. "Here it comes."

Sam rolled to his feet and stared at the abandoned buildings around them. They'd barely made it to a safe place this time. Several crumbling apartment complexes seemed to hold their breath in an old, long-forgotten area about two hours out of Seattle. Someday the place would be revitalized, but right now, only rats and other vermin inhabited the condemned buildings. Heat rose in him, turning his veins red enough to glow beneath his skin.

"Shit," Garrett said, taking several steps back.

The fire rose through Sam's head, and he dropped to his knees. The building to the right exploded, shattering what was left of its glass windows. Smoke billowed an ominous gray, spiraling into the blue skies. The structure across the forlorn street detonated, throwing debris toward them.

Garrett ducked his head and crouched low.

Sam just watched. He felt the ripples from the explosions as if they came from inside him, which they had. They were part of him.

Sirens sounded, high and fierce.

He jerked his head and jumped to his feet. "What the hell?"

Out of nowhere, police cars and two SWAT vans roared into the vacant area. Helicopters hovered into view as well.

"Humans?" Garrett eyed several of the officers who jumped from their vehicles, took cover, and pointed weapons at them.

Sam's hand slid through the concrete to another place, and he grimaced as the pain pierced his brain. He struggled to free his hand before the humans witnessed the anomaly. This was crazy.

"Get down! Flat on the ground, arms spread," a male voice bellowed.

Sam tilted his head to meet Garrett's gaze. "I'm stuck at the moment, but you need to get out of here." God, he missed the days when he could teleport. "Go, G."

Garrett twisted his lip. "How bad?" He bent to look at Sam's arm, which was buried to the wrist.

"It'll take a few minutes. I'll have to go with them." He couldn't let humans see that he wasn't one of them. "We can't allow them to take us both. Go to the right of the metal building and get out of here." His friend would be burned, but the humans wouldn't be able to follow. As a vampire-demon, Garrett would heal soon enough. "I might need a lawyer. Keep your ear to the ground and track where they take my bike." He loved that bike.

"Down, now. We will shoot!" yelled a man from behind the SWAT van.

Garrett leaped for his motorcycle, jumped on, and spun away toward the burning building.

The humans launched themselves into action but weren't fast enough to stop him. Soon he looked as if he'd driven right into the flames. Sometimes Sam thought that was exactly what he wanted to do, but that was a concern for another day. "Don't come any closer," he yelled. Damn it. He had to free himself before they got close enough to see.

Grunting, he ripped his arm through dimensions, nearly puking from the pain. The world swirled around him, and he inhaled burning smoke.

Unconsciousness tried to possess him. He took a quick inventory, head to toe. The vibrations had subsided, so it should be safe for humans to be around him for a little while.

"Get down!" the same male voice yelled. "Now, or we will shoot."

Sighing, he shifted to his knees and then followed directions until he was flat on the crumbly cement, his arms out. His head rang and he longed for a beer. Or a keg.

The officials were quick and efficient in cuffing him and dragging him to his feet, even though he stood at least four or more inches taller than the biggest guy. They read him his rights, and he blocked them out as the helicopters flew away.

Then the blackness took him.

Hard and fast.

The last thought that filtered through his mushy brain before his body went limp was that control really was an illusion.

* * * *

Dr. Honor McDoval watched the interrogation through the one-way mirror.

"Is it just me, or is he the hottest thing you've ever seen in real life?" DHS Agent Bill Smith said by her side, file folders in his good hand.

"If you like the desperately wounded and pissed off type," Honor murmured, studying the subject. He sat facing them, lounging in the interrogation chair, his expression bored and his body apparently relaxed. She knew better. Even through the cement wall and reinforced glass between them, she could feel his pain. His fury. This was something new.

Her interest was piqued against her will.

"I do like that type. Joe was often cranky, although I don't miss him as much as I thought I would when he ditched me for that foot doctor," Bill muttered, saying the word "foot" with a slight sneer.

"You're better off without him," Honor said, patting his arm.

Bill nodded. "Thank you for coming in on this." He was short and blond with a wrestler's body. Strong and sturdy. "I know you're taking a break from consulting with DHS, but this guy..."

Yeah. This guy. "How's your arm?" Honor asked, keeping her focus on the man in the interrogation room, who was currently ignoring the agent yelling for him to cooperate.

Bill glanced at the sling on his left arm. "Healing. I start physical therapy next week. Have I thanked you for saving my life?"

"About a million times." Honor shook her head. "I didn't save your life."

"You got intel from the coconspirator that stopped me from running into a building set with bombs." He looked at his sling. "Almost in time." His grin was contagious.

She smiled. "I'll try to do better next time. If there is a next time." She'd spent too many hours helping interrogate people, internalizing their pain. "I'm not sure I can consult any longer." Plus, she really had to get out of town. Her own consciousness was unraveling, and if she tried to explain the situation to anybody, even to a good colleague like Bill, they'd find a padded cell for her.

Maybe she was crazy.

Bill checked his hip against hers. "You deserve a change, and you've worked hard to open your own clinic. Have you decided on which office space yet?"

"Not yet. I'm leaning toward the one near the river, although it's more expensive." She was ready to help people one-on-one and use her odd skills for good, to go deep and ease people, while she still could. For years, she'd been preparing for this, and she was ready.

"I like that view," Bill agreed. "But you have to branch out and let people know how good you are, okay?"

She swallowed. "I will." After losing her parents, she'd shut herself off a little bit, privately exploring her abilities but hiding them from most people. "I'll stay in touch, too."

"Good. Have you talked to Kyle yet?" Bill asked.

"No." She absently ran her right pinkie over the ring finger of her left hand. Her now naked ring finger. "He's supposed to get back after midnight, and we're meeting for breakfast before I go on walkabout."

"So you haven't told him?" Bill asked.

She shook her head, her stomach hurting at the thought.

Bill chuckled. "Man, I hope I never piss you off. Yeah, he's the bad guy, but still. You're giving back his ring and then leaving town, and the moron has no clue."

She fought a grin. Upon learning that her fiancé had taken his sexy new accountant with him on his business trip, and upon said accountant sending Honor naked pictures of her weekend with Kyle, the ring had lost all meaning. She'd cried enough for that loser. "The worst part? I feel better with the ring off."

"I never thought you two fit," Bill agreed.

There was no fit for her. She was too...weird. She just didn't feel things other people apparently did. She and Kyle had seemed like a good match, and she'd liked him before he'd turned into a cheating asshole. "I'll miss the ring, though," she mused.

Bill burst out laughing.

Honor chuckled, finally letting go of that dream. She was fine alone and was excited about her new career path away from subterfuge and lies.

The officer inside the room slapped a hand on the table and his companion jumped, but the prisoner didn't even twitch. Instead, his gaze lazily shifted to the mirror, meeting hers. Well, that was impossible. But he did look exactly where she stood.

"Wow," Bill breathed.

Indeed. The man's eyes were a sea green with a fierce tint of... gold? Just around the irises? His shoulders were too broad for the chair, and they narrowed nicely to his waist and long legs. He had to be around six-five or six-six, with black hair, thick and wavy, that curled beneath his ears. His bone structure was brutally cut, sharp with muscle and masculine strength. Everything about him was harsh angles and barely contained energy that most people probably couldn't see. Right now, he was staring at her.

Bill shifted his weight. "I don't think I ever really understood the term 'male animal' until right this second."

Honor nodded. "Agreed."

The two agents shoved away from the table and stormed toward the door.

The prisoner tilted his head, still watching her. Or himself in the mirror. She reminded herself that he couldn't see her.

"You're up," Bill said. "Thanks for coming in, again. I know you want to flee town tomorrow, and you totally deserve the vacation you have planned."

"I'm ready to take a break away from here and explosions and fires and bad guys." She stared for one more beat at the prisoner. "Though I'm glad you called." There was something about the cuffed man that drew her. Oh, she didn't like her unusual gifts, and until lately, she'd been able to hide them, but this guy was a challenge. Even for her. "I'll send you a postcard from Ireland. Or Iceland. Or wherever I end up." She was ready for a walkabout, and it was time to write that book she'd always wanted to start, before she went completely crazy. Then she'd open her new office and make a fresh start.

The door opened, and the nearest agent shook his head. "This one hasn't said a word. I'm not sure he's even there. He did pass out when we first caught him."

"Probably from the localized blast pressure," Bill said. "Those two buildings exploded fast."

Honor took a deep breath. "I'll see what I can discover." She moved efficiently past the agents and into the room, shutting the door behind her. Energy struck her so quickly, she took a step back before she could stop herself. Then she breathed deep and forced her body to move into the electric field generated by the prisoner.

She'd never felt anything like it.

Drawing out a chair, she sat. It was still warm from the other agent's butt. "Hi. I'm Dr. Honor McDoval."

For the first time, the prisoner reacted. His upper lip twitched.

She settled more comfortably in the chair. Her skin electrified, and her breathing stopped for a moment. This was odd.

"Sam." The guy looked down at his hands, which were secured by cuffs to a bar set into the table. "I suppose these are for your protection?" His voice was a low rumble, slightly gritty.

She wet her lips. Why did she have a feeling he could get out of those if he so chose, but he just hadn't bothered? "Yes."

"I won't harm you, Honor." His gaze ran over her features, and in the dim light of the interrogation room, his eyes darkened to the viridian patina of a lost sunken ship of old. "You're a special one, aren't you?"

She cleared her throat and forced herself to remain in place. "I sometimes consult with Homeland Security, but I'm not an agent."

"Why you?" he asked softly, that gritty tone licking over her skin.

What in the world was wrong with her? She lifted one shoulder. "I'm good at it. Reading micro expressions, noticing nuances that nobody else sees." It was the best she could—or would—explain it. "Do you want to tell me why you blew up those buildings? Homeland has been tracking you for the last month, and it seems you've destroyed plenty of real estate. But you've been careful not to hurt anybody. That makes you a good person." She kept her voice level. Soft and encouraging.

His bark of laughter caught her off guard. "Oh, baby. You're wrong on both counts."

Chapter Two

Sam's head still rang from the blast, and his arm felt like snakes had sunk fangs through every tendon, but he couldn't stop staring at the female. She was stunning. Curly black hair fell beyond her shoulders, and her full lips, lightly painted a glossy pink, would give any male ideas. Her skin was a light brown with warm golden undertones.

But her eyes. Those eyes went beyond a human female's. Oh, she was human, but her enhancements glowed bright in her eyes. The color was an iridescent dark topaz he'd only seen in nature once, in a stone worn as a pendant hanging between the breasts of a queen. Intelligence and kindness glimmered in the depths of her gaze.

She tilted her head. "Do you mind speaking with me?" Her voice was soft and calm, betraying both intelligence and a slight, very slight, Oklahoma accent.

"I very much would like to speak with you," he said, meaning every word. For the moment, he was balanced, so he could let down his guard.

"Good." She clasped her hands on the table. Her nails were painted a light pink, and several silver rings decorated her long fingers. "Why did you blow up those buildings?"

"I didn't." Probably. Oh, the energy had gone through him, but since he hadn't controlled it, he wouldn't take responsibility.

She withdrew her hands. Good interrogation tactic. "I can't speak with you if you lie to me."

"I won't lie to you. Ever," he vowed. Their interaction would be brief, despite her draw. But he could at least promise her that.

She lowered her chin and angled her head slightly to the side. Air brushed across his neck, along his jaw, and up into his brain.

He paused. "What are you doing?"

"Watching you."

No. She'd done more than that. He leaned toward her, and she instantly leaned back. "What are you?"

Her eyebrows arched. "I told you. I'm a consultant."

He centered himself completely and scanned her, letting her essence fill him for a moment. Female. Enhanced human female. Not yet mated. For a second, she'd felt like a witch or a demon destroyer messing with him. But she wasn't. Just a very talented human female who'd apparently found an avenue to use her gifts. "How long have you known you were different?" he asked. Most Enhanced human females either ignored their gifts or explained them away.

She blinked. Just once. "We're all different." Then she shifted uneasily on her chair, bringing attention to her full breasts. She was dressed appropriately in a light gray suit, but she had a healthy figure, and when she moved, he couldn't help but notice. "If you didn't ignite those two buildings today as well as the others during this month, then who did?"

"I don't know." Also the truth, because if he could figure out where this energy to create fire was coming from, he'd get rid of it. "Sorry."

"That's okay." She angled her body toward him again, rewarding him for speaking with her. She was good at this. "Who was the man who rode into the fire? Was he the one who planted the explosives?"

"No," Sam said softly.

She reached for his hand and gently placed hers over it. "He couldn't have survived driving into that building, Sam. I'm so very sorry for your loss. Were you close?"

Her touch was warm, generating energy that crackled between them. He grinned. "What can you get from a touch?"

She straightened. "Excuse me?"

"You shouldn't lie to me, either," he said, lowering his head and leaning just a little closer to her. She smelled like the mountain laurel flowers, sweet and wild, that grew in sacred places. "That's the deal. I talk to you and you talk to me." He'd allow her some control over the situation because this was her job and he was in cuffs. But a guy had to have limits.

She allowed a smile to curve her lips, once again drawing his focus to her mouth. "I'm good at my job, Sam. While I might not understand how, I can read expressions and feel…tension. I guess. I don't really know. But you seem like a decent man, and I'd like to help you. Help me to do so."

"Okay. Let's go rapid fire," he said, flipping his hand around and grasping hers as much as the cuff would allow.

Her quick intake of breath held more than surprise. "Rapid fire?"

"Yeah. Favorite color?"

"Pink," she said. "You?"

"Violet blue." The color of his niece's eyes and the reason he was in this mess right now.

Honor nodded. "Why do you blow things up?" She tried to extricate her hand.

"I don't. If I never see another explosion or fire again, I'd be content." He held her palm where he wanted it. "Do you think you're psychic?"

Her grin was spontaneous this time. "No. Are you compelled to start fires?"

"God, no." He'd never wanted to kiss a woman more, and wasn't that a pisser? He was leaving soon. "How about empathic?"

"No." She sighed. "I don't think so." She looked charming and at ease, which made the slide he felt against his brain a bit of an insult.

He mentally shoved her out.

She drew back on the chair, surprise lightening her eyes.

"You okay?" he asked.

"Yes." Now confusion cluttered the brightness there.

Oh, she knew she had skills, even if she didn't understand them. Apparently she was willing to use them. "Can you read minds?" Would she tell the truth?

"No." She shook her head. "Sorry. Nobody can read minds."

He sensed she was telling the truth. Many demons could read minds, and they could plant pain and excruciating scenes inside minds, but she wasn't a demon. "Man, I wish I could get to know you," he said, truly meaning it. This time he let her remove her hand from his.

"Then let's get to know each other," she offered. "If you work with me, I can help you."

He was tempted for no other reason than he wanted to know more about her. Unfortunately, from the sound of heavy footsteps down the hallway that she couldn't yet hear, he knew he was about to get sprung.

* * * *

The door opened and Honor jumped. Bill walked inside, his blond hair ruffled and his brown eyes pissed. Behind him came another behemoth of a man. This guy wore a tailored gray suit, Italian loafers, and a white dress shirt beneath a silky blue tie. His hair was messy around his ears in a way no over-the-counter product could create, and tinted glasses veiled his eyes. His briefcase probably cost more than her apartment.

Plus, he was huge. Just as tightly packed with muscle and as tall as Sam.

"What's going on?" Honor asked.

Bill snarled. "Orders from higher up. Way higher up. We have to let him go."

The newcomer stared at her, his head cocked to the side. "Hello." His tone was dark and hoarse.

Who the heck were these people? These overly large and way too muscled men? Tension rose in the room with a hint of something she couldn't grasp. Something beyond her experience that felt... powerful. And dangerous. "What do you mean we have to let him go?" she asked, forgetting the fact that she wasn't really a part of "we." She'd just gotten started with her interview.

Bill shrugged. "We have our orders, and they come from the top."

She stood to face the new guy, acutely aware of Sam straightening in his seat. Then she tilted her head back, way back, to glare at the guy. While she was almost five foot ten, he towered over her. "Who are you?"

"Who are any of us?" The new man smiled, revealing a dimple in his left cheek.

She narrowed her gaze.

Bill moved past them both and uncuffed Sam. "If another agency is working in the area and disintegrating buildings for no apparent reason, we'd really appreciate a heads-up. The task force we've put together for this op has been costly in both time and expenditures."

"We'll do better in the future." Sam stood, his gaze remaining heavy on Honor. "It was a pleasure, Dr. McDoval."

But she hadn't gotten what she needed. She always found the solution to every puzzle, and she hadn't come close with Sam. The few seconds she'd tried to read him, tried to figure out the pattern of his brain, to see if he was lying, weren't long enough. So she pivoted, putting her body between him and the door. "Who are you?"

His smile was slightly lopsided. If she hadn't been studying him so closely, she wouldn't have noticed. While he stood a good eight or so inches taller than she, he stayed a foot away, almost as if he didn't want to intimidate her. "I'm a guy who's wishing we could've met under different circumstances. *Much* different."

"I know you had something to do with those explosions, and we're going to find the body of your accomplice," she said, irritation igniting through her system.

"There's no body," Sam said, almost gently. "I don't know what your people think they saw, but nobody rode into a burning building today." The way he gazed into her eyes felt personal. Deeper than most people could even think of going inside her head. "I wish you the best, Honor."

She didn't want to move out of the way. There was something about him she couldn't nail down, something that had never happened to her. His allure was magnetic, and the hunger to solve the puzzle he represented shocked her in its intensity. He was a criminal, probably an arsonist, and yet, he had connections inside the agency. Or even above the DHS. What did that mean? Who was he? What was going on?

His smile widened. "I can almost hear your brain working." Then he did step into her space. "Let it go. Trust me." He inhaled deeply and then motioned for her to move to the side.

She did so, her skin prickling with an unnatural heat. He smelled like a mystery. A masculine one with hints of smoky copper or the pleasant aftermath of burning cedar planks. Probably because he kept blowing up buildings. "Let me help you." She didn't know why, and she didn't know how, but there was no doubt in her mind the man needed assistance.

His supernaturally green eyes softened. "If only you could."

"Let's move," the other guy growled. Like really growled.

She jumped and then took another step away, keeping her focus on Sam. "This is a mistake. You've been trying to keep your compulsion to create fire from harming anybody, but that will change. Luck has been on your side so far, but you know luck wanes, right? You will kill somebody, Sam." Was that even his real name? Doubtful. "I can tell you don't want to hurt anybody. You'd never kill anybody."

One of his dark eyebrows rose. "You're misreading me."

Huh? As in he didn't want to harm people or that he'd never killed anybody? "What do you mean?" she whispered, caught in this oddest of moments.

"Now." The other guy had apparently had enough. His bark this time echoed through the room, but Sam didn't even twitch. "This can't happen and we need to go. Knock it off, Sam."

So his buddy called him Sam. Could be part of the act. Were they CIA operatives? That was the only thing that made sense, but it didn't feel right. Oh, they were deadly—she knew that from just being in their space for a few minutes. But the CIA didn't fit.

Bill must've had the same thought because he spoke from the doorway. "Who are you people?"

"Nobody you need to worry about," the other guy said. "We're leaving."

Sam turned to the door.

For the first time in her life, Honor acted on instinct. She grabbed his arm with both hands. Her nails dug in. "You can't go." What was wrong with her?

Sam stiffened and looked down at her hands. Heat blasted down his arm, beneath his shirt, and burned her skin. Something crackled. She cried out and stepped back.

Bill rushed to her. "What happened? Are you okay?"

The pain instantly disappeared, and she looked down at her palms, which appeared fine. Then she lifted her gaze.

Sam's jaw snapped shut. "Shit."

Chapter Three

Sam threw the empty beer can across the Grizzly Motorcycle Club main clubhouse, pacing even faster than before. A light rain pattered outside, fogging up the multitude of windows in the party room, which was now empty save for the three of them. "I can't believe this."

Garrett sat at the bar with a coffee mug of bourbon in front of him and watched the can dent the wall by the door. He'd been quiet since his appearance as a CIA agent to effect Sam's release from DHS. Upon returning to the Grizzly club grounds, he'd torn off the gray suit jacket and loosened the tie so that it hung at an odd angle around his thick neck.

Bear McDunphy lounged on a leather chair with a bottle of scotch in his right hand. The president of the club was well over six feet tall and broad, with shaggy brown hair and honey-chocolate eyes. Danger cascaded off him, and that was when he was relaxing with friends. "You're paying for that repair, Kyllwood." He tipped the bottle back and drank half the contents, sighing afterward. "You know, in the years you've been a Grizzly, I don't think I've ever seen you lose your temper like this." He sounded merely thoughtful, apparently not caring that there was now a four-inch hole in his wall.

"That's because I don't lose my temper," Sam bellowed, reaching for another beer on the wide bar. "Ever."

"Humph," Bear said, his tawny gaze unperturbed. "Good thing the rest of the club is out on an overnight ride. It's been tough enough keeping them okay with having vampire-demons as brothers. Your always calm facade has helped." He jerked his head toward Garrett. "Unlike Kayrs."

Sam took a deep breath and tried to subdue his racing blood. He had become a member of the motorcycle club to keep an eye on Garrett, who was hell-bent on riding his bike over a cliff these days. Picking an immortal club full of bear shifters had seemed like a good idea when Garrett had wanted to join one, but now Sam wondered if they'd both been dropped on their heads as kids. What had they been thinking? "I'm telling you, something happened when she grabbed me in that interrogation room."

Garrett sat on a tall stool, his legs easily reaching the ground. Disgust crossed his face, and he kicked off his expensive brown loafers, revealing gray socks with holes at the toes. "Who wears crap like this? My feet are killing me." He rested his back against the burnished wood of the bar. "I felt it—in the interrogation room."

Bear cocked an eyebrow. "The woman?"

"Enhanced," Garrett affirmed. "Like seriously Enhanced human female."

Definitely. There were human females in the world who were Enhanced with supernatural gifts, and they could mate an immortal male, unlike un-Enhanced humans. Some believed the Enhanced humans were related to the witch nation, while others believed that they were actually a species of their own. Sam had never given it much thought.

Garrett shook his head. "I couldn't get a sense of Honor's gifts, but maybe she's a psychic? Or talented empath? Not sure, but she gave off strong enough vibrations that I felt her upon entering the building."

Heat rose inside Sam in a way he didn't like. Filling his chest and billowing out. He'd die for Garrett, and he'd most certainly kill for him. They were brothers in every sense of the word, and he'd protect him just as he would his blood brothers Zane and Logan. But he did not, for one second, appreciate Garrett feeling Honor's vibrations. So he kept silent.

Bear finished off the bottle and then wiped his mouth. "Check your palms, Sam. Any mating mark?"

Sam's head jerked so fast, his ears rang. Then he looked down at his palms. Immortals with demon blood carried a marking in their genetics. Usually made up of the first letter of their surname, it appeared on their palm much like a tattoo, and they transferred it to their mate upon performing the mating act. His palm was clear. "No." Thank the gods. He couldn't take a mate.

Bear shrugged. "Then what's the problem?"

Sam looked at Garrett. Maybe he was just losing his mind faster than he'd thought with all the dimensional disturbances lately.

Garrett's metallic gray eyes narrowed. "Something did happen between Sam and Honor in that room. I don't know what, but there was an energy, and it was hot. Something hurt her hands, but then she was unharmed without a mark on her. I can't explain it."

A sliver of relief filtered through Sam's anger. He wasn't going crazy. Well, about this, anyway. "I felt it, too."

Bear kicked his monstrous boots out and crossed his ankles. "With all the weird shit you're dealing with right now, maybe that's just part of it and you should let it go. You know. Go back to figuring out why your body keeps getting caught between dimensions and then, I don't know, blowing everything up?"

"I don't know what's happening," Sam said. "I've moved between dimensions before, as I've told you, and it hurt. Yet now I keep getting stuck in other worlds for some reason. What's worse, I keep feeling this energy that I can't control, and then fires erupt around me. Fires lead to explosions. We're just lucky nobody has been harmed—yet."

Garrett cut Sam a look. "Maybe it's time to bring the Realm and demon nations in?"

In other words, call Garrett's uncle and Sam's brother. "No," Sam growled. The Realm was a coalition of immortal species, and they were closely aligned with the demon nation.

"Agreed," Bear said. "I like having you two here, but the second it's Realm or demon business, you have to go. You know that. The Grizzlies are content staying off the radar, and I ain't changing that, despite my obvious fondness for you two."

"You threw me down a cliff yesterday," Garrett snapped.

Bear flashed his teeth. "Yeah, but I made sure there was water at the bottom. Kind of."

Garrett scrubbed both hands down his face. "The Realm is also busy trying to find all of the suddenly missing Enhanced human females. The Kurjans are taking them faster than we can save them, and my gut aches all the time. Something is happening."

The Kurjans, a white-faced, sun hating, deadly immortal species were their natural enemy, and they were starting something big, kidnapping Enhanced females. The campaign had to be stopped.

Sam didn't have the time or patience to deal with either male right now. "I need to go for a run. Just hold tight until I get back." Hopefully he'd gain some perspective before his head exploded.

"Good idea," Bear said. "Although I guess I should tell you that I'm bringing my witch in on this."

Sam closed his eyes and counted to ten. Frankly, it was surprising Bear hadn't asked Nessa for help before now. "Okay, but we all know she still works for the witch nation, or the witch badass security force, or whatever," Sam muttered. "The witches hate the Seven. We've kept her out of this so far to protect her."

The Seven was a group of immortal males who were supposed to protect the world from the deadliest member of the Kurjan nation, and Garrett was a member of the Seven. Sam and Garrett hadn't told anybody why they'd joined the motorcycle club, basically because Garrett was convinced it was the only way to find his true mate because of dreams he kept experiencing. The only issue that would now be different was that Sam's problems would be known.

Bear's eyes morphed to the color of burnt honey. "I need to protect her. Right now, you're causing fires and explosions, and I want her to be on the lookout. In addition, witches are the only ones who can control quantum physics, alter matter, and create plasma, so maybe she can help. Either way, she knows something is going on with me; her patience has ended with my so-called uncommunicative nature, and I'm not dealing with a pissed-off mate because you can't control yourself."

That was fair.

"Okay. I'm going for a run and will be back in a couple of hours." Sam didn't like lying to his friends, but he needed to figure this out on his own. He turned and walked outside into the gentle evening rain, loping into a jog as he took his phone out and dialed a number.

"Sam? What's up?" Chalton Reese, the Realm's best computer expert, answered immediately.

Sam squinted rain from his eyes. "I need a favor. An address— just between us. It's personal, not business. I'm just horny," he lied, wanting to keep Honor under the Realm's radar. Chalton would believe him, so he would not waste time trying to figure out why Sam wanted the number. The need to get to her, the craving to see her again, made him speed up.

As his body fell into a rhythm, he ran even faster, his mind spinning back to the fateful day, eighteen years ago, when he'd voluntarily gotten himself into this mess.

The thing was, he'd do the same thing again.

Sam looked down at the beautiful baby in his arms, and darn if his little niece didn't look right back, her eyes a deep blue and showing a wisdom way beyond her one month of life.

He grinned.

She grinned back, her pink lips curving.

"You're a special one, aren't you, Hope?" he murmured, carefully holding the baby in her little pink blanket. She smelled like powder and innocence.

She gurgled.

His gaze ran unwillingly to the deep blue markings on both sides of her fragile neck, marks that set her apart as one of only three prophets his people would accept. Why her? His chest heated and his ears rang. The danger of the future wouldn't come for her. He wouldn't let it. "You're safe. I promise," he vowed.

"That's the truth, brother." Zane dropped into the chair next to Sam and set two longneck beer bottles on the table in front of them. He'd had a month to recuperate from a virus after the cure had been found in his child's blood. Hope's blood.

"Isn't saving our people enough?" Sam muttered, keeping his voice cheerful for the baby's sake. "Does she have to carry the prophecy mark on her neck as well? It's too much." He lifted her up and looked right into her violet-blue eyes, noting that she seemed to be reading him at the same time. Then she smiled and gurgled again.

"Agreed," Zane said, kicking back in his chair.

Sam turned his attention to his older brother. The brother who'd saved his life more than once while they'd been kids, and the demon who'd just become the king of their entire nation. Thank God he had his mate at his side. Janie Kayrs was a force to be reckoned with—and loved. She was the sister Sam hadn't realized he'd ever be fortunate enough to have. "How's it going?"

Zane took a rare moment to relax. His black hair hung to his shoulders, and his green eyes blazed in a sign of the good health that had returned quickly after receiving the cure from a virus created by the Kurjans to kill them all. His shoulders were wide and his muscle tone already back. "It's going." His gaze landed on his daughter. "She's the priority. I don't like the marking any more than you do, and I mean to protect her from it. If she wants to be a prophet in a few hundred years, then fine. If not, then Fate will have to find another way."

"Agreed." Sam glanced at the markings on both of his brother's hands. The mating markings. "I wonder."

"Yours will be a K for Kyllwood, as will Logan's," Zane said, rolling his eyes. "I wish you'd gotten the first initial, but we both knew I'd be the demon king. Man, I hate being called king." For their people, the marking a demon passed to a mate was always the first initial of their last name. Only the true and destined demon king ever had a different marking—the first letter of his first name. Zane had the markings of a Z on both hands; no doubt, Fate had been making a strong statement.

"Better you than me." Sam reluctantly handed the sweet baby to his brother. "I have a meeting but will be back for dinner. I promised Janie I'd make my peanut butter chicken and rice dish." Only his family was aware he enjoyed cooking. The rest of the world didn't need to know anything about him.

Zane took his daughter and snuggled her against his powerful shoulder. "What's your plan, Sam? I could use a liaison with the other nations, and you'd be good at it. The job would allow you to travel and have some fun, but it'd be nice to have you covering my back while you did it."

"You've got it." Even if Sam had been inclined to refuse the job, he wouldn't do so if Zane needed him. Family was all that mattered.

"Good. Thanks." Zane patted Hope's back while she snuggled into his neck. His hand looked broad and strong across the baby's tiny body, holding her so carefully. She snorted, and her body went limp in sleep.

Sam grinned. "Do you ever remember sleeping like that?"

Zane held the baby close. "No. We slept with one eye open at all times, remember?"

"Yeah." Sam sobered. They'd been in danger from their uncle from day one, and Zane had eventually killed him, thus becoming king. "It'll be different for her."

Zane's eyes blazed. "Damn straight," he whispered.

A car sped by, throwing rainwater to hit his face and bring Sam out of his memories. He glared at the driver, and a bush caught fire at the side of the road. Sighing, he stopped running and moved over to stomp it out.

Things were getting worse.

This close to Honor's house, maybe only three blocks away, he could feel her. His blood heated, and he darted back into a run. He needed to get to her. Now.

Chapter Four

Sam reached Honor's house, which was surrounded by deciduous trees and landscaped rocks that probably required little maintenance. He stopped running and settled against a dripping wet tree, content to keep watch for now. He was probably going to die soon—this was no time to court a woman—but he could at least figure out the mystery of Honor McDoval.

His body slowly relaxed, and he flashed back to those moments after Hope was born that had changed not only his life but his destiny.

After leaving Zane, Sam had moved through headquarters and then stepped into the office where the two existing prophets awaited him. "Hi."

"Hello." Prophet Lily sat in a floral-covered chair, drinking from a teacup. "Thirsty?"

Sam shook his head. "Sorry I'm late."

"Time is merely an artificial construct." She'd captured her thick blond hair in a braid, and with her long skirt and demure blouse, she looked like a lady of old. Hell. She was a lady of old, even though she appeared to be twenty-five. The prophecy marking her neck did little to detract from her beauty. "Please, sit."

Sam clocked the male standing silently near the window. "Hi, Caleb."

Caleb nodded, his prophecy mark darker and more jagged on his neck than Lily's. "Sam." His bizarre multicolored eyes remained unreadable. Tension cascaded over Sam's arms as he headed forward and sat in a sturdy leather chair across from Lily's dainty one. "Listen. I know you're both prophets like my niece, but I'm fine with her living her own life for a few centuries, as is Zane. If you want to talk to my brother about his daughter, going through me isn't the way to do it." He kept his voice respectful because Lily was a lady. Although she'd been known to throw her teacup at a patient's head once in a while if he was being a moron.

"Don't blame you," Caleb muttered, his body big and broad, a gun and knife clearly visible in his leg sheaths. He stalked over and dropped into a chair that matched Sam's. While there was another floral-decorated chair in the room, it would probably break if he tried to sit in it. "There should be a choice about whether somebody wants to be a fucking prophet."

Lily rolled her eyes, put her cup on her saucer, and placed both on the delicate chair by her arm. "I would choose to be a prophet, Caleb."

"I wouldn't," the warrior said mildly, watching his mate closely. "If I could get us both out of the deal, I would."

Lily smiled, and warning showed clearly in her intelligent eyes. "Let's keep our family squabbles to ourselves, shall we?"

One side of Caleb's mouth twitched. "You're cute when you're being a smart-ass, mate."

Sam cleared his throat. "If you two want me to leave..."

"No." Lily set her small-boned hands in her lap. "There's an... issue. Caleb and I discussed it, and we've come to you first."

"Instead of Zane?" Sam asked, kicking back in the chair.

Lily swallowed. "No. Instead of Logan or Garrett."

Sam stilled. Logan was his younger brother, and Garrett was Janie's. "Excuse me?"

Caleb shook his head. "This is a bad idea."

Lily's mouth tightened. "It's not our decision to make." She pressed a hand against her forehead. "We only have part of the puzzle, but even so, I feel we need to do something. Don't you understand?"

"No," Caleb said.

Sam straightened. "Enough, please. What's going on?" Heat flushed through his torso in an ominous warning.

Lily lowered her hand. "There's no way to sugarcoat this, and I don't have a full picture, but it appears that Hope is not only a prophet but the Lock as well as the Keeper."

"The Lock and the Keeper," Sam drawled. "That sounds a little weighty for a seven-pound baby, don't you think?" He was already getting pissed, and there was no doubt Lily hadn't given him the bad news yet. Or she hadn't explained it, anyway. "What's a Lock or a Keeper, and are you sure you haven't been reading too many fantasy novels?"

Caleb shook his head. "You've heard of the Cyst?" At Sam's raised eyebrows, he growled. "I've been having dreams, too."

Sam slowly nodded. "I've heard of the Cyst but never met one." Supposedly they were the spiritual leaders of the Kurjan nation, which had just gotten its butt kicked in a war with his people. "Are they reaching out for diplomacy?"

Caleb's snort wasn't humorous. "No. Long story short, centuries ago, a group of seven vampire-demon hybrids created a prison world outside of this dimension to hold Ulric, the Cyst leader. The asshole killed one hundred Enhanced females in a ritual that made him truly immortal. He can't be killed from outside his body, so the Seven tossed his ass in a world completely separate from this one."

Sam didn't have time for this. "So Ulric is off this world. Who cares?" As a demon who could teleport across the globe, it was easy for Sam to understand that some folks could probably travel through dimensions to other places.

"Well, he's probably going to make it back here someday," Lily said gently. *"The Kurjans won't rest until he does. At that point, the only way to kill him will be by enacting another ritual, one that was made possible the day he killed the Enhanced females and became immortal."*

Caleb smiled for the first time that evening. *"He can only die by ingesting a combination of the blood of the three Keys and the Lock, because one of the slaughtered Enhanced females, a witch, tainted her blood to cause this weakness before he killed her."*

"Nobody is taking Hope's blood," Sam growled.

Lily held up a hand. *"That's not our current issue. A prophet has always been the Keeper of the Circle, which is where the ritual will happen. It's a dangerous job with a lot of power. Hope can't be both the Lock and the Keeper. It's too dangerous, and even she can't handle that much energy, not to mention the ritual to cement the Keeper to the Place."*

"Another ritual?" Sam asked.

Caleb shifted his weight. *"According to the ancient texts we've read as well as some psychic dreams Lily has had, the ritual is very similar to the one the Seven males went through years ago. It's painful and there's a ninety percent chance of death."*

Sam's nerves fired. *"I'm not letting her go through anything like that."*

"I know, which is why we came to you," Lily said softly. *"The Seven members include one of your ancestors, and one of Garrett's. We believe that certain bloodlines survive the ritual better than others, so we're asking you first and then Logan and Garrett."*

"I already attempted the ritual to become the Keeper, but it wouldn't take. Wouldn't even begin," Caleb groused. *"Apparently the Fates want me to remain a prophet, and they should've asked me first."*

Sam took a deep breath. *"You're telling me that I need to undergo a ritual that will probably kill me in order to protect my family."*

"Pretty much," Lily said.

"What if it doesn't work?" Sam asked.

"It has to." Her eyes blazed a deep blue. "There's no choice. We can't let Hope undergo it at her age. She'd die."

Sam rolled his neck to keep his temper from exploding wildly. Why wouldn't Fate leave them alone? "I'll do it."

Caleb nodded. "Just think of the good news. If you survive the ritual and become the Keeper, you'll be in perfect control of the entire situation."

Yeah. That was the plan. "Let's do this," Sam said. There was no need to involve his family or let them know what he planned. Might as well start protecting them now. "I hope it works."

Caleb stood. "Hope is all we have. Tell Zane we need you for backup on a diplomacy mission. The ritual has to take place between dimensions, and Lily knows of a place. If you die, I'll tell him why. If you don't, then there's no need for him to learn anything about this."

Sam stood. "Agreed." It was good he'd be able to control this situation.

"Um, Sam?" For the first time, Caleb looked serious. "This is gonna hurt. Forces beyond imagination will rip you through dimensions, and predators will come at you from every direction. Your chances of survival aren't great."

Sam flashed him a smile. "They never have been, Prophet."

He returned to the present, standing outside Honor's home, already feeling her energy. His entire body heated and then calmed. He could control this reaction.

There was no choice.

* * * *

Back at home after a goodbye dinner with several of her friends, Honor finished rolling two more pairs of socks into her overstuffed suitcase. She'd changed into a plain white T-shirt and blue sweats, keeping tennis shoes on so she could load her car.

She'd drive down the coast and stay along the ocean until she reached San Diego. Afterward, she wasn't sure where to go. Probably Scotland? It didn't matter. She'd stored up airline points for years and was ready to use them. She looked over her checklist again. Her plants had been moved to her friend Maisey's house, her mail had been forwarded to her accountant, and all her services for the house would be shut off the next day.

She was packed—and ready to go first thing in the morning. In fact, she'd meet Kyle for breakfast, return his square-shaped diamond ring, and then head off into freedom.

When she'd cleared her mind and had enough of an adventure, she'd return and start that clinic she dreamed about. The one where she helped people by using her odd abilities instead of trying to trap them in lies.

Why was her brain continuing to return to the mysterious Sam? Humming to herself, she strode from her bedroom to the kitchen of her two-bedroom townhouse in a perfectly manicured neighborhood of young professionals. While she'd waved to her neighbors once in a while, she knew nothing about them. Someday she'd like to live in an area where neighbors shared keys, just in case somebody was locked out. Where kids played in the street and left their balls in everyone's yards. Where people maintained green yards and not rock formations that took zero maintenance. In the meantime, this worked for her.

But she was restless. Had been for a while—even before Kyle had shown his true colors. Plus, the dreams were getting stronger; it was time for a vacation. Everyone should take one once in a while. Sometimes she wondered if she was going crazy, and that's when time at a beach became necessary. She could live with that solution.

The muscles in her palms twinged, and she rubbed them against her legs. What had Sam done to her?

It didn't make sense. She'd grabbed his arm, felt the fabric over his skin, and then had experienced a flash of fire. But she wasn't burned, so what had he done? And how had he done it?

There must've been some sort of chemical on his clothing. Unfortunately, there hadn't been time to take samples. It figured he'd have such chemicals, considering he had blown up those two buildings.

He'd been telling the truth when he'd spoken to her, but it was only the truth as he believed it to be. If he were insane or guided by some other power only he could hear, then he would've thought he was telling the truth. But there was no question he, and the man who'd burned up in the building, had created not only these explosions but the other ten that had occurred during the last couple of months.

She'd had to let him go. Rather, the DHS had been forced to release him. By whom?

Sweat dotted her brow. Had she left the heat on too high? It was autumn, and a mild one at that. Rain pattered softly against her windows, the tinkling sound peaceful. She walked into her small kitchen and took out a glass to fill with water. She drank the entire amount and felt somewhat better.

Smiling, she moved to wash the glass, and fire erupted from her fingers.

She cried out and dropped the glass, shaking her hand wildly. Nothing. Blinking, she turned her hand over to study the palm. No fire, no burn marks, no...nothing.

She was losing her mind. It had finally happened. Even so, a residual pain throbbed through her pinkie finger.

The atmosphere around her wavered. Sparkles popped. She backed away from the sink, her heart pummeling her rib cage until it hurt to breathe. The air was sucked away from her, leaving a vacuum. She gaped like a trout out of water and instinctively planted both hands over her ears.

The sliding glass door on the other side of the round table was ripped open, the lock protesting with a loud scratch. A hulking form rushed inside. It took a second for her eyes to clear enough to recognize him. "Sam?" she whispered.

Bubbles popped all around her.

He leaped over the table and picked her up, barreling through her small home into the bedroom.

She screamed and fought him, sucking in air as fast as she could, trying to fill her bruised lungs. Panic grabbed her, replacing thought with pure instinct. To fight and flee. Her fist connected with his neck while she kicked her feet, but he didn't seem to notice. Holding her easily, he grabbed her top mattress with one hand and pivoted, shoving it against the door.

An explosion echoed from the other room.

"What did you do?" She punched him again, squirming in his arms, so panicked her brain wouldn't work.

He grunted. "Stop hitting me." His voice was a low growl, barely human.

Think. She had to think. The man held her easily, and she was no lightweight. Her best move, only move really, was to get free and run. Fighting him was a losing proposition. "Okay," she said, trembling against his chest.

"I won't harm you." Holding her aloft, he shoved the mattress out of the way and opened the door, peering into the hallway. His arms were unyielding around her, and his chest felt as if he was wearing a metal shield. The strength in him was surreal. And terrifying.

She tensed. If he released her, she'd run.

He cautiously stepped outside the room and then into the hallway, twisting his torso to prevent her head from hitting the doorframe. Then he moved back into the kitchen, where smoke billowed from the counter by the sink.

She gasped. Her paper towel roll was on fire. She started to struggle again.

He went to the sink, turned on the water, pulled out the faucet, and sprayed water until the flames sputtered out. Burned pieces of paper towel wafted around. Then he reached across the sink to open the window—still holding her.

"Put me down," she snapped, fear riding her hard.

He set her on her feet. "Don't run. You won't make it."

The open back slider, damaged with the lock mechanism hanging off the edge, was her only bet. Her muscles tensed to run.

Sam planted a hand against her upper chest with his fingers extending to her neck. He pushed her against the counter, which pressed uncomfortably against her butt. "I told you. Do not run." His eyes blazed an unfathomable green, and at the moment, anger glowed in them.

"What did you do to me?" She clutched at his arm, her nails drawing blood. "What did you put on me? What kind of chemical?" It hadn't rinsed off in her earlier shower, and even now, she couldn't feel anything. What kind of substance reacted with paper towels to cause a fire?

"No chemical," he said, looking over his shoulder toward the bedroom. "Your suitcase is packed already. Good."

Her heart hitched.

Chapter Five

This was a complete disaster. Sam took stock of the kitchen, making sure the flames had been extinguished. What had he done to her? How had that brief moment passed this curse to the female? The energy still roiled through him, promising more fire, so he hadn't gotten rid of the power. He'd only shared it.

Why now and why her?

Her terror thickened the smoky air around them. Reassuring her of his good intentions wasn't helping, and since she obviously had a brain, nothing he could say would help.

Especially since he was about to kidnap her.

The woman had a decent left cross, but she was dainty at only five ten or eleven. Those curves of hers had filled his arms in a way he'd remember in his dreams, but right now, he had to get her to safety. Or at least to somewhere they could find safety and rid her of this shitty curse he'd passed on to her. He had no choice because he had to get back to covering Garrett's ass and couldn't leave her alone to deal with the fire. He could protect her...only if she was close by.

She glared at him.

"Here's the deal." He kept his voice low and as soothing as he could, considering his throat was burning again. "We need to leave here, and you have to come with me until we figure this out."

Her eyes widened and then flared. "I'm not going anywhere with you. Let me go and get out of here. I'll give you the count of sixty before I call for help."

He frowned. It was a decent offer—but a stupid one. "If somebody is trying to kidnap you, and you want to reason with them, don't even mention you are going to call the authorities." Just being this close to her was having the oddest effect on his blood. For the first time in months, his blood pressure began to calm. To steady. "Lie and say you won't tell anybody."

She shoved him as hard as she could, without effect. "Thanks for the tip. Now get out of my house."

He smiled. Couldn't help it. "You're a scrappy little thing." As well as gorgeous when angry.

She pushed again. "I'm neither scrappy nor little. Get out of my house, Sam. Now."

"Agreed." Tension still popped in the air. The fire wasn't finished unless they took their energy elsewhere. "Do you have everything you need in that suitcase?" he asked.

"No." She gave up fighting and stood straighter, projecting her next move.

"Kick me and you'll regret it," he grumbled.

Her stunning brown eyes widened.

"Suitcase? Ready?" he snapped.

Slowly, she shook her head. "No. I was just trying to find a good place to store extra clothes. I'm not going anywhere. In fact, Homeland Security is expecting me for a late and very secret meeting tonight to discuss your case and all of the explosions. I'm going to be tardy if I don't leave right now, and then DHS will be looking for me immediately. So go. It's your only chance."

Man, her pink lips were full...and enticing. He couldn't keep a slight grin from tipping his mouth. "For someone who detects lies, you really suck at telling them, sweetheart." Holding her in place, he yanked his phone from his back pocket and reached for hers on the counter. He pressed speed dial.

"Good evening, Sam," Nessa McDunphy answered politely, sounding like the powerful leader she'd become even before mating Bear and moving her operations to the Pacific Northwest. "Hi," he answered, not using her name just in case. "I need a favor. Dump this phone for me, would you?" He trusted that Nessa could get the number easily. "Everything. Phone calls, messages, and emails if you can get into Honor McDoval's email account from just this information. She works for DHS, so there are probably safeguards in place."

"Are you trying to insult me?" Nessa asked.

"No," Sam said, meaning it. Nessa was a female one never wanted to insult. Ever. "I apologize."

Thunder rolled outside in both locations.

"That's better," Nessa said. "Where are you? Bear said you went for a run, and there's a heck of a storm coming. I'll send someone to fetch you."

"I have a car." He'd noted one in Honor's garage, already gassed up, with provisions for a long drive.

Nessa paused. "All right. How about you tell me what's going on before I do this dive? You know I don't like going in dark. That always creates more problems than it prevents." Her mate obviously hadn't informed her of Sam's problems yet.

"She's a woman, Enhanced, and I can't get her out of my mind," Sam said. All of it was true, and Nessa, being a romantic, would probably run in the wrong direction with it.

Her slight gasp proved it. "Oh, Sam. You bet I'll help. I've been so worried about you."

Honor had listened and apparently decided on a course of action. She opened her mouth, no doubt to scream for help. Sam pressed his free hand against her lips, cutting off all sound but being careful not to bruise her. Her eyes widened, and she subsided.

"Thanks," Sam said, shutting off the call before anything else went wrong. Then he removed his hand. "All right, gorgeous. I'm giving you one chance here. We get your suitcase, take it in a composed manner to your car, and get out of here before anything else blows up. Fight me, and you'll ride in the trunk. Got it?" He didn't want to scare her, but he could feel the tension around them ratcheting up again, even though he was calmer than ever.

The atmospheric turmoil was coming from her, and he had to squire her into another environment as soon as possible. It was a lesson he'd learned the hard way. Once he changed the atmosphere in a place, he had to leave or more explosions would occur.

It felt like the same thing was happening with Honor.

She blinked. Once and then again.

"I'll take that as a yes." Releasing her shoulder, he grabbed her hand and turned for the bedroom. "We have to hurry."

* * * *

In what seemed like seconds, Honor found herself in the passenger side of her own car, the seat belt strapped securely around her. The suitcase was in the trunk, and the bag of munchies she'd already packed was in the backseat. "This is kidnapping."

"I'm aware," Sam said, driving sedately through her neighborhood with the windshield wipers softly smoothing away rain. "If it helps, I'm sorry about this entire situation."

"Oddly enough, that does not help," she muttered, looking outside for anybody. If she saw a person, she'd shove open the door and scream. As usual, the entire subdivision was quiet at this hour with most urban professionals long since asleep. Okay. She often dug into the minds of criminals and witnesses for Homeland Security, and she could draw on her skills now. "Sam? Is that your real name?"

"Yes." He drove her silver Arteon out of the neighborhood and headed for the interstate.

She took a deep breath. "It's a nice name. Family name?"

He angled his head to look up at the rolling clouds. "I don't think so. It's just a name, and my mother seemed to like it."

Anticipation licked through Honor. "Your mother? Is she still alive?"

"Yes." Sam accelerated and then increased the windshield wipers' speed in response. "She's very much alive."

"Mine isn't," Honor said. If she could get him to see her as a person, she might stand a chance. "I lost both of my parents when I turned twenty, and I don't suppose I've been the same since." The world flew by outside.

Sam glanced her way. "I'm sorry about that. How did they pass?"

Pass. Oh, that was such a bland word for the horrific reality. "They were murdered by a serial killer."

Sam jerked and looked at her again. "Seriously?"

She nodded. "Yes. A monster named Jack Forester murdered several couples over a two-year time frame. He broke into our home, killed them both, and then ate all of the food in the fridge. He got into a shootout with the police but survived and is spending the rest of his life in prison." She'd never gotten the answers she'd wanted from him, although he probably couldn't have given them. Killers often didn't have a good "why."

"I'm sorry about that, Honor." Sam sighed, and his massive chest moved with the sound. "Is that why you became a profiler?"

She almost smiled. "I'm not a profiler. I'm a psychologist, and DHS asked for help with a case two years ago. I helped. They've called me in several times since as a consultant, but I'm not an expert on the criminal mind. It just seems that I, well, read people well?"

"It's more than that and you know it, but we don't have to discuss your gifts if you don't want." His voice remained gentle and calm.

She was getting through to him. Good. Exposing her pain was difficult, but she'd do what she had to in order to survive this. All she needed was an opening to get free. "Sometimes I wonder why them. They were good people. Mom taught second grade, and my dad taught world history and was the high school football coach. They were...everything." Her chest hurt.

Sam sped up to pass a couple of logging trucks. "I really am sorry. We lost our father when we were young, and it was difficult." His hands were imposing on the steering wheel.

They were getting somewhere. "We?"

He paused. "I have two brothers."

Good. She had him talking about important things. Did he love his brothers? Hate them? Was he indifferent? She couldn't get a full read on him the way she normally did. What did that mean? Was he a true sociopath? Psychopath? She forced a smile. "I can tell, just from meeting you, that you're the oldest." He was definitely a take-charge person, even if he was criminally insane.

His cheek creased. "Nope. I'm the middle one."

Her eyebrows rose. He was the middle child? She would've bet anything against that. "You're not typical," she murmured.

He shrugged. "We might be. My older brother is type A and a natural leader, whether he likes it or not. My younger brother is on the wild side and takes risks I'd advise against. I'm the steady one."

Her mouth gaped open.

He must've caught her expression, because he burst out laughing. It was brief but a deep and intriguing sound. "Keep in mind that you haven't met them."

She never would, either. If they really existed. She centered herself and partially turned to face him, fully studying him. His body was relaxed, without any micro expressions that might show he was lying. Or think he was lying. The guy might live in a totally different world inside his head, and she couldn't forget that. Regardless of his deep laugh, muscled body, and out-of-this-world good looks. Why did bad boys have to look so sexy? The question was, just how bad was he? She tried to tap into his mind with her mental fingers, to read his brain wave patterns, but he kept her out. He had impressive shields. "Why do you blow things up?"

"I don't," he said, his focus returning to the traffic on the rainy road.

Shoot. She'd pushed too fast. "Tell me about your brothers."

"I already did. Do you have siblings?" He reached over and turned on the defogger for the front window.

"No. I always wished I did," she admitted, sliding back into personal matters. He wasn't ready to talk about whatever was happening. "What's it like?"

Sam rested his left arm on his door and drove with one hand, apparently relaxing even more. "It's the best and the worst. We've had to protect each other, and with that comes stress and responsibility. Our enemies are everywhere."

Her skin prickled. Was he paranoid? Delusional? "Do the enemies have anything to do with the explosions?"

"I assume so," Sam said, switching lanes.

She kept an eye on their route. "Where are we going?"

"Somewhere safe." He finally exited the interstate and drove down a long ramp to a stoplight at the bottom. A set of outlet malls were silent to the left, while to the right, there were gas stations, fast-food joints, and a grocery store.

It was now or never. In the smoothest motion she could manage, Honor unclipped her belt, shoved her door open, and sprung out of the car.

Chapter Six

Sam hadn't expected the action. Honor hit the wet gravel and rolled onto the grass, coming up fast to turn and run.

Damn it. He jumped through her open door, tucked his head, and somersaulted to his feet. He ran after her, fury catching him around the throat.

The woman could run. She dodged and wove, making it to the arterial street before he caught her. He manacled one arm around her waist and slung her over his shoulder in a smooth move, turning and running full bore back to the vehicle at the stoplight. No cars were behind him yet, which was why he'd chosen this exit from the interstate.

She kicked and struggled on his shoulder, spitting expletives even he hadn't heard put together in his lifetime.

He dropped her back into her seat. "I don't think that's anatomically possible." He secured her seat belt again, his hair dripping rainwater onto her chest. Then he leaned in until their gazes were an inch apart.

She shrank back, her chest heaving.

"I don't want to put you in the trunk, but I will," he growled, letting the beast inside him make an appearance. "I've been gentle with you so far, and I mean you no harm. But I'm taking you where I'm taking you, and there's not a thing you can do about it. Either get on board, or the rest of the ride is going to be very uncomfortable for you." The idea of trapping her in the trunk made his gut clench, but he'd do it.

Fear glimmered in her eyes because she wasn't a moron. Even so, her jaw set at a stubborn angle that both impressed and intrigued him. She looked beyond him at the lights of the fast-food places, and then her lips turned down.

"Nobody saw us," he confirmed. The rain increased in force, plastering his hair to his head. Even so, he stayed right where he was since the exit ramp remained deserted. "I appreciate your attempts to get to know me, so let me give you this. This challenge from you, this stubborn fight inside you, does nothing but turn me on." He waited until his words sank in and her eyes widened before continuing. "Your being pliant and obedient bores me. So you have a choice to make. Do you want to bore me or arouse me?"

She blinked. "How about I rip off your head and shove my socks down your headless corpse?"

Amusement grabbed him so quickly he couldn't help a quick bark of laughter. "Aroused it is, then." He slammed the door and crossed around the car to retake his seat. Oh, he couldn't keep her, but she was making that reality look bleak. Maybe someday when he took care of his problems, he could look her up. Of course, she'd probably be around a hundred years old by then.

He drove onto the main road and turned left, headed toward the mountains.

Wet grass covered his shoes and made his ankles itch. Even so, he hadn't been this calm in months. The longer he was around her, the more he felt like himself again. They drove for nearly an hour before he spoke. "How are you feeling?"

She started. "Excuse me?"

"Right now. How are you feeling?"

"Extremely angry," she said, her hand clutching the door handle. "I don't know what your game is, but kidnapping me and then expressing concern won't work. I'm too smart to be brainwashed."

Nobody was too smart to be brainwashed. "I'm not playing games with you." For the briefest of seconds, he considered telling her the full truth. That would be treason on so many levels, but he didn't much care about immortal laws. Unfortunately, giving her such knowledge would only put a bull's-eye on her back, and he couldn't do that to her.

Barely noticeably, she reached for her seat belt, and her body tensed.

He sighed. "If you jump out of the car now, you'll harm yourself. I'm about done with this, Honor."

She looked at him. "Oh yeah? You said that you won't lie to me, and you also said you wouldn't hurt me. So I'm feeling all right about defying you."

He turned off the road onto a private lane clearly marked as such by the Grizzly Motorcycle Club. "I said I wouldn't harm you. Hurting you is on the table."

She jerked. "Are you nuts?"

Sighing, he reached over and pinched her arm.

She yelped and rubbed her bicep. "What in the world is wrong with you? Why did you pinch me?"

He'd barely touched her. "Don't be a baby. I was showing you the difference between harm and hurt. I won't cause you harm, but if you don't start behaving yourself, I have no problem enforcing my rules with a little bit of hurt."

She partially turned to face him. "Are you kidding me? You're going to pinch me to death?"

He grinned. She really was funny. "No. I'm not going to pinch you to death." Then he turned to face her, the road in front of him memorized so well, he didn't really need to pay attention. "But here it is, gorgeous. I'm trying to help us both as well as the people around us, and I need some space and time to do that. The uncle who raised me was a bastard on all levels, but he did impart several lessons that have served me well. One was that every action has a consequence. Don't make me teach you that." He looked back at the road, searching for the turnoff into the mountains.

Her breath quickened. He could hear it. "Are you threatening me?"

"Yes."

Her chin dropped, and the vibrations cascading off her weren't from fear. No. They were anger, and they made his skin prickle.

While he appreciated the fact that she wasn't terrified of him, even if she didn't realize it, he needed her to behave so she didn't blow herself up. He drove across a handmade bridge over a small creek and parked next to a cabin set against an outcropping of rocks. The shed to the side was only big enough for his two bikes, not the car. "Now that we're on the same page, we're here."

* * * *

She could not figure him out. He'd caught her too fast after she'd gotten free. Was he some sort of athlete? The strength with which he'd tossed her over his shoulder had caused all sorts of flutters in her abdomen before her brain kicked in. Was she already getting brainwashed? Identifying with her captor out of necessity? For a quick second, she shut her eyelids.

When she reopened them, the cabin was still there. The structure was dark and indistinct in the rainy night, but if she squinted, she could see better. Rough logs had been shaped to form the home, and the weather had darkened them to a rough gray. "I'm not staying here."

"You are." He opened his door and crossed to the trunk, taking out her suitcase.

She released her belt and pushed open her door, slamming it loudly. The sound echoed back from the rocks behind the cabin, but nothing else stirred. How far were they from other people? She kept her focus on the cabin and tried to study the surrounding land through her peripheral vision as the rain slashed at her, molding her white T-shirt to her full breasts.

Only lurking trees, high and dark, stood guard around them. The creek flowed quickly, no doubt to a larger river. If she followed the creek to the bigger tributary, she could find her way down to a town.

"You're hours from anywhere," Sam said, carrying the case toward the cabin. "It's dark and the storm is getting worse."

Her skin chilled. She moved to follow him.

His shoulders visibly relaxed, and the second he planted a shoe on the narrow porch, she launched herself into action. She barreled around the car and straight for the forest, running along the creek and plunging between two trees. Then she made a sharp left toward a group of boulders, zigzagging rapidly as she moved, being careful to avoid following a straight line.

The wind picked up, punishing her along with the chilly rain. She lowered her chin and ran full out, not caring where she went but systematically going in the opposite direction from the cabin.

A healthy fear propelled her, giving her additional strength and speed.

She tripped on a branch and went down. Pain flared along her arm and hip, but she jumped up and kept going, keeping as close to the creek as she dared.

Her foot snagged on tree roots, and she halted, her arms windmilling to keep her balance. Sucking in air, she put her back to the tree and listened.

The blood rushed through her head, making her ears ring. She breathed through her nose, trying to concentrate. The wind whipped tree branches around, and pine cones pummeled the rushing water, clopping against rocks. Rain pinged on the mud puddles and the pine needles around her.

No other sounds emerged.

She quieted her breath, perfectly hidden against the ponderosa pine with its top branches scraping the swollen underbellies of the rapidly moving clouds. Her hair dripped into her face, and she wiped it away, her hands wet from the rain. Had he not followed her?

Maybe not. Confusion caught her unaware. So far, he hadn't hurt her, and there had been that odd fire from the chemicals she couldn't find. Yet he'd kidnapped her, and they were alone in the middle of nowhere. She did not know him. Any woman with a brain would flee, get to safety, and then figure out all of the oddities.

Tension spiraled through the trees, tightening her muscles. Her legs trembled. She had to get a bead on him before she moved. If she couldn't hear him, then he couldn't hear her.

Where was he?

She couldn't see him, and she couldn't hear him…but she felt him. He was there and he was close. How was he moving without making one sound? She shivered and not just from the angry rain. Even if she didn't know of his problems, and even if she hadn't been kidnapped by him, she would've recognized Sam as a predator in a world of prey. There was something dangerous and otherworldly about him, and if he wasn't a fire-burning psycho, she'd be fascinated by him.

She wiped her face off again. All right, she *was* fascinated. But right now, she had to reach safety.

Gingerly, she moved away from the sanctuary provided by the tree, no longer running out of control. Now she moved swiftly but kept her senses fully tuned to the forest around her. If he made a sound, she'd catch it. She moved between trees, deliberately shifting away from the water to confuse him. It'd be smart to double back, but she needed a hint of his location first so she didn't run right into him.

He'd left the keys in the car, so if she could just get to it, she'd stand a real chance of getting free.

Now that she'd slowed down and was no longer running out of pure panic, she could think clearly. Okay. If she put the creek behind her, she could slowly make her way back to the car. There was no need to hurry. It was more important that she stay out of his range. The clear tenor of his voice echoed through her head, promising that he would hurt her. As far as she was concerned, hurt and harm held the same threat.

She sidestepped a series of bushes and kept moving, as steadily and as quietly as she could.

"You're not bad at this," he murmured.

She jerked to a stop to see him leaning against a tall tamarack. His eyes glowed through the night brighter than any wild animal's. She took a step back.

He stretched almost lazily.

She gulped in air and tried to calm her breathing.

"I'll catch you. Run all you want, backtrack at your leisure, follow the creek…it doesn't matter." He pulled car keys out of his pocket and jangled them in the storm. "Get to your car. Sit there. Try to hot-wire it." A pine cone fell to his shoulder and bounced away from the hard surface. "Tire yourself out all you want, Honor."

She looked around at the darkened forest as the storm beat against her, feeling vulnerable and out of her depth. "When did you find me?" Where had she gone wrong?

"I never lost you, sweetheart," he said, his voice soft. Dangerous.

She shivered in the cold, her mind spinning. So she did the only thing she could. "I choose none of the above." Lowering her head, tucking her chin to her chest, she rushed him.

Chapter Seven

Sam was never caught off guard, but when the woman lowered her head and slammed into him, shock stunned his entire system. He pivoted and put her ass against the tree so she didn't hurt herself. She struggled against him, kicking and punching, and he let her work the energy out of her system. Finally, her arms dropped, and she panted wildly.

As gently as he could, he smoothed the heavy hair away from her wet face. "You done?"

Fire lit her eyes. "Not even close," she snapped, belying the weariness blurring her features.

Damn but he was starting to really like her. "Listen. I know I'm coming across like a huge, overbearing asshole, and I understand you have no reason to trust me, but there's nothing I can do about that right now." Not without putting her in even more danger than he already had. The woman was cunning and brave, and that was as a human. What would she be like as an immortal mate?

As soon as the treacherous thought wandered through him, he quashed it. She was an Enhanced female who could mate an immortal, but it couldn't be him. Definitely not him. Although, she was a temptation. His gaze dropped to her full, lightly pinkened lips. Would she taste like strawberries?

She punched him in the ear and then shoved her hands against his chest. "Is this when you hurt rather than harm me?" Her voice was breathless.

"I'd rather cut off my arm than do either," he said, giving her the truth, even as pain echoed in his eardrum.

Then, damn if all the saints didn't curse him, she looked up at his mouth. Interest lingered in her gaze before she veiled it. At least this attraction wasn't one sided, although it had to be confusing to her. Humans didn't trust their instincts the way they should.

Hers were telling her she was safe with him, or she would've tried a different tactic than punching him in the head.

He leaned in to her, noting her sharp intake of breath. Then he scented the air between them. No fear. A boatload of adrenaline, excitement, and curiosity. As well as anger. Yeah, that was between them as well. "Are you finished running through the woods, or do you want to keep going for a while?"

Her chin lowered. "If you're not the bad guy, as you say, then let me go."

"I can't right now," he murmured. "I will as soon as it's safe, though."

"Safe for whom?"

He rubbed a smudge of dirt off her chin. "For everyone. That fire in your house didn't just happen, you know. You're in danger, as am I, as is anybody near us." The wind shifted direction, so he moved his body to protect her better from the slashing rain and forest debris. A pine cone hit him in the back of the neck. "Don't tell me you've already forgotten about the fire or convinced yourself that it didn't happen."

"No. I remember the fire." Confusion mingled with the anger in her topaz-colored eyes. "What I don't understand is how you made that happen. What did you put on my skin, and why couldn't I wipe the substance off? What was it?"

Based on her knowledge of science, that conclusion wasn't a bad one. "No chemicals." Lightning zapped the area by the rocks, zinging the scent of ozone through the forest. While he'd easily survive a lightning strike, as a human, she would not. "Time's up, beautiful. We're taking refuge in the cabin and now. You walking or do you want to be carried?" He'd love to get his hands on her again, even for a short time.

Another lightning strike hit, this one closer.

She jumped. "I'll walk." She shoved him again, and this time, he stepped back.

"Good. Follow me." Without waiting for more agreement from her, he took her hand and started back toward the cabin. He could see in the dark, unlike her, and he steered her away from loose branches and torn-up roots. The rain increased in power, and he shielded her the best he could until they arrived at the cabin. This time, he kept hold of her as he strode onto the porch and to the door, opening it and gently nudging her inside.

She stumbled but righted herself. "You had time to bring in my suitcase, turn on the lights, and start a fire before you ran after me?" Her voice sounded lost. Confused.

"Yeah." He'd promised not to lie to her. So he shut the door and then moved to put another log on the fire. "I'm a good tracker." Maybe she'd be satisfied with that explanation.

She rubbed her hands down her wet arms.

He turned and got his first good look at her now that they were out of the storm. Her hair curled wildly, and with her makeup washed off, she looked pure. Beautiful with her tawny skin and those topaz eyes. Her clothing was...wet. The white material of her shirt clung to her very full breasts, and the sweats outlined her thigh muscles. Heat rose through him, singeing his ears. Desire glided along his skin, inside his torso, landing torturously in his groin. Hard. He coughed and cleared his throat, willing his suddenly raging dick to behave itself.

She sneezed.

The sound propelled him into action. He lifted her suitcase and delivered the heavy bag to the only bedroom before returning.

"Go in there and change into something warm. I'll heat tea and then we can talk."

She hesitated and then followed his directions. When she reached the doorway, he spoke.

It was only fair to give her warning. "There's a sliding glass door in the bedroom. Feel free to make use of it and run back into the storm. I will find you and bring you back here. It's dangerous out there, Honor," he murmured.

* * * *

Honor stepped inside the room. "It's dangerous *in* here," she said, shutting the door. She leaned against the smooth wood and took several deep breaths. Okay. This situation was beyond her experience. What did he want from her? What kind of game was he playing? None of it was making sense. When she didn't show up for breakfast with Kyle, would he call the authorities? Or would he realize she knew about his cheating and figure she'd just left him?

If nothing else, she knew she couldn't count on Kyle. She was on her own.

She sneezed again. Catching pneumonia and dying wasn't the way to go. So she quickly changed into jeans and a thick blue sweater along with plush socks. Then she searched for a weapon, but there wasn't anything useful in her pack. She looked around the bedroom.

The bed was larger than any she'd ever seen, and it was covered by a comfortable-looking plaid bedspread in greens and blues. Twin bedside tables flanked the bed with a dresser to the left. To the right, a sliding glass door did, indeed, lead out to a deck that extended to the rocks. Outlines of chairs, a table, and maybe a couple of stools were visible in the pouring rain.

She hustled toward the bed tables and rummaged through them, only finding odds and ends. No weapons. She looked at the rickety dresser. Hurry. She had to hurry. So she tiptoed over and went through the drawers, just finding jeans, T-shirts, socks, and boxer briefs. Warmth flushed her as she rifled through Sam's personal belongings. What was wrong with her?

"Honor?" he called from the other room. "All my weapons are in a closet on the other side of the kitchen. Not in my drawers."

Heat lanced into her face. Lacking any other option, she stood and strode toward the door. There had to be a decent knife in the kitchen. If she could arm herself, she could force him to give up the car keys. Her head held high, she moved into the small living room, which held a sofa, one chair, and the fireplace. An alcove by the door contained different motorcycle boots, tennis shoes, and leather jackets. A couple of loose socks were on the floor by the fireplace, and the room smelled like warm woodfire and dust.

"Thirsty?" Sam stood in an L-shaped kitchen on the other side of a counter, complete with two chairs on her side. He'd tossed his wet shirt onto the kitchen table and stood there in wet jeans and bare feet. Nothing else.

She swallowed.

His chest was wide and muscled, which she already knew from when he'd carried her. But seeing it was something else. Talk about a cutout of a perfect male body. Too bad it belonged to a kidnapper. Two steaming earthenware mugs were in front of him, and he liberally poured bourbon into one. "Want some?"

"No." She angled toward the barstools, her gaze scouting the kitchen. Wooden counter, closed cupboards, stove top, oven, and microwave—all dingy white and at least ten years old. The place was definitely a bachelor pad. Where were the knives?

"The knives are in the drawer by the sink," Sam said, setting down the bottle.

She paused.

He grinned. "Saw you looking."

She smoothed her hair away from her face, noting that the heavy strands were starting to dry. "How many women have you kidnapped?" If there had been others, they would've done the same thing as she, looking for weapons.

He rolled those dark emerald eyes. "None. You're my first." He lifted the mug in a toast.

Her legs wobbled.

"Seriously. Stop being afraid." Now he sounded frustrated. Turning, he opened a drawer and revealed his strong back. A jagged tattoo covered his left scapula in a series of barbed lines that formed an intricate circle. A scary one. He turned back and slid a large knife across the counter. "Here. If it makes you feel better, take this."

Her hand trembled, but she reached out and clasped the wooden handle. The blade glinted in the soft light.

"Feel better?" he asked, tipping his glass to his mouth.

"Not really." She tightened her hold and held the knife away from her leg. "I don't understand." Was this some sort of weird game?

If anything, his gaze softened. "I know."

Her key chain, the silver one with green gems at the end, stuck out of his front pocket. If she could just get to it...

He pointed to a stool. "You look exhausted. Sit down."

"No. Now it's time for you to tell me what you want," she said, setting her stance.

"That's fair." He finished his drink. "I want you to slowly concentrate and see if you can create fire again. If you do, try to stop it."

That was crazy. "I didn't create fire." How far gone was he?

"Just try," he murmured, watching her.

"Fine." Maybe if she proved she couldn't make fire, he'd let her go? She squinted at the counter and tried to make flames.

He cocked his head. "What are you doing?"

"Trying to make fire," she muttered. "What does it look like I'm doing?"

He lifted one broad bare shoulder. "I don't know. You look constipated."

She slid her gaze up to his. "Seriously?"

His grin was almost charming. "Yeah. I think you should start small." He dug a napkin out of a drawer stuffed with different types—mostly from fast-food joints. "Try to burn this."

Oh, that was ridiculous. If she could gain his trust, then maybe she could get those keys. At some point, he'd get tired, and as far as she could tell, there was only one bedroom in this quaint little prison. She lowered her head, pretended she was Superman shooting lasers from her eyes, and shot.

Nothing.

The napkin sat there, right where Sam had put it.

Her head hurt and her nose felt stuffy. "No luck."

He sighed. "Yeah. Well, it was worth a shot."

The idea that he believed she could make fire with her brain was terrifying. What other illusions did he hold? They were alone, in the middle of nowhere, and she couldn't get free. Her stomach cramped.

A log in the fire fell over, and flames spit out, pushing open the grate. Another log tumbled out onto the living room floor, scattering embers.

"Shit," Sam said, hurrying around the counter toward the fireplace.

She didn't have a choice. Holding her breath, she stabbed him as hard as she could in the lower back. He hissed and fell, blood pouring from the wound. "Sorry," she cried out, grabbing the nearest stool and swinging it at his head. The metal impacted with a nauseating crunch, and she darted forward, snatched her keys from his jeans, and ran for the door. "I'm sorry, sorry, sorry," she panted, ripping the door open and running into the storm. "I'll send help. I promise." God, she hoped she hadn't killed him.

Chapter Eight

Unconsciousness captured Sam for the briefest of seconds, but it was long enough for the woman to get to her car and spin out of the clearing. He groaned and lifted himself to his knees, having to reach around to wrench the knife out of his kidney. Growling, seeing double, he yanked his phone out of his pocket, nearly dropping it thanks to all the blood on his hand.

"It's too late to be calling. What the fuck do you want?" Bear snapped, sounding sleepy.

"There's an Arteon driving way too fast away from my cabin with a human female at the wheel. Stop her. Everything is at stake." Sam dropped the phone and forced himself to stand, sending healing cells to his colon. Not in a million years had he thought she'd stab him in the back. Fury crackled down his body, and flames erupted on the sofa.

Shit.

"I'm not a witch," he muttered, rolling his neck and wiping blood off his temple. There was no way he should be able to light his sofa on fire just with his temper. He reached into the cupboard beneath the bar for the fire extinguisher, taking care of the sofa. He sent more cells to his head to heal his pounding headache and then moved to step into his motorcycle boots.

He ran through the last few minutes, swore, and picked up his phone to dial Bear again.

"What? I'm going right now," Bear snapped.

"Don't hurt her," Sam said.

Bear growled. "You said everything is at stake."

"Don't even think of hurting her, Bear. Just stop the car before she gets to the main road. That's all." Sam barely kept from threatening the shifter, which wouldn't get him anywhere.

"Fine. I'll just stop her. Probably." Bear hung up.

Even at top speed, Honor would only be halfway to the main road by now, and hopefully she was being somewhat careful in this storm. She could just as easily wrap the car around a tree as reach the road.

Sam would have to get to her before Bear did anything stupid. If Bear shifted, he'd reach her long before anybody else, but at least he'd keep Honor from telling anybody about the kidnapping.

What in the heck had just happened? Sam was always so prepared, his brothers often ridiculed him. How had he let one small human nearly take him out? It was crazy. Yet somehow, he'd trusted her. Her soft eyes and quick brain. Oh, he'd been a moron.

He walked right past the jackets hanging near the door. Right now, his body and temper were too hot to wear any other clothing, so he crossed out of the cabin and hustled into the storm as his kidney healed along with the rest of his injuries.

She'd actually stabbed him in the back, hit him with a stool, and left him to die.

He had to admire that in a woman.

The chilly rain felt good on his skin, and steam rose around him. He ignored it and loped into a jog, making sure his body was repaired, before increasing his speed and running all out along the now muddy road. The lump on his temple slowly receded, and soon he was at full health, his boots splashing up mud and water onto his ripped and soaked jeans. While he appreciated the woman's ingenuity, he couldn't let her get away with it this time.

She'd put herself in danger by driving so crazily, and she'd put herself in peril by forcing Sam to call in Bear. Bear was the leader of the entire bear nation, and while he appeared to play it fast and loose, he held a tight rein on protecting his people. He'd never allow a human to threaten them. Ever.

Sam ducked his head and ran faster. What had he just done by calling in Bear?

* * * *

Honor's wet hands slipped on the steering wheel, and it took her a second to realize it was blood and not rainwater covering her fingers. Metallic fear filled her mouth. She'd never stabbed anybody before. But they'd been at a deserted cabin in the freaking woods…and he'd kidnapped her. What choice had he left her? What if he died? She'd call for help the second she reached safety. *Drive. Just drive.*

She pressed the gas pedal, flying through the storm. Rain splattered the front window along with pine needles, and she flicked on the wipers. Her lungs struggled to keep up with her panicked breathing.

Okay. She was safe. It was okay. The mantra repeated itself inside her head. All she had to do was find a phone.

Slowly, her heart rate returned to almost normal. Even if Sam had somehow gotten up, there was no way he could follow her now. As soon as she reached a phone, she'd send the authorities out to help him.

She took another deep breath. The tires threw mud up, but she had no problem staying on the road. Something moved in the trees, catching her eye. Her mind spinning, she looked closer. Nope. Just darkness and trees. She was losing it. Her shoulders trembled, and cold slithered through her. Shock. She was going into shock. Swallowing rapidly, she leaned over and turned up the heat.

Three bears bounded out of the trees and skidded across the road.

She shrieked and slammed on the brakes. The car hitched and then spun, kicking up more wet mud. She wrenched the wheel to correct and then slid to a stop.

The bears looked at her. The hugest one was in the middle. He remained right there, opened his mouth, and yawned.

The other two bears scampered off, leaving just the biggest one blocking her way.

Honor stared at him, her heartbeat echoing in her head. She waited. He was right in the middle of the road and didn't seem inclined to move. Rain bombarded him, turning his brown fur a darkish red. His ears twitched, and his golden eyes seemed to focus on her. He was solid muscle and looked like he could take out a tank.

She had to get out of there. Her hands prickling, she tightened her grip on the steering wheel, looking in the rearview mirror. Only an empty, dark, wet road lay behind her. Okay. She could handle this. Her mouth had gone dry, but she tried to swallow anyway.

The bear remained in place. Even though he was sitting, powerful muscles played beneath his fur.

Maybe her headlights had captivated him somehow? She gingerly reached forward and turned them off. Rain continued to lambast her car, and in the darkness, for the briefest of moments, there was only her and the bear. With the lights off him, he was only a dangerous shadow in the middle of the road.

What should she do? Holding her breath, she reached for the knob and flicked the lights back on. Maybe she'd startle him into leaving.

He blinked several times but didn't move.

Oh, this was crazy. She didn't have time to deal with an insane bear. Should she honk her horn or try to drive closer to intimidate him? She bit her lip and gingerly pressed the horn. No sound came out. Darn it. Taking a deep breath, she planted her hand on the horn, and the sound blared across the forest.

His right ear twitched.

Irritation pricked her, and she pressed harder this time, keeping her hand on the horn.

He waited a couple of beats and then stood to his full height on two legs and growled, showing a full mouth of sharp teeth. The fur rose along his back, puffing out.

Crap. She'd made him angry. "Sorry," she whispered, releasing the horn as if she'd been burned.

He roared again, this time louder, looking like he could rip the car apart if he so chose. Could he? What if he rammed her? Bear against car? Right now, she wasn't sure she'd win.

She had to get out of there. Lights and horn didn't work. There was only one other possibility since she couldn't go around him. The trees were too thick on both sides of the road, as if he'd chosen the perfect place to stop her. Which was impossible. She gently stepped on the gas and rolled toward the animal.

He dropped to all fours, staring right at her.

It was silly, but she swept her hand out wildly. "Get out of the way," she whispered, trying to wave him away.

He cocked his head, and one of his ears twitched.

She continued toward him at a slow roll. Why wouldn't he just move? The car kept moving toward him, and when she was about three feet away, he lifted to his full height again, roaring wildly. She slammed the brakes again. A slightly hysterical laugh bubbled up from her chest. "Get out of the way!" she yelled, about to lose it.

He dropped back down and snorted, looking even more powerful and dangerous this close.

Her door was ripped open, and a strong hand yanked her into the storm. She yelped and slipped in the mud, pivoting as she was planted against the car, her butt to the back door. Sam loomed over her, fury cascading off him in waves.

Her mouth gaped open even as pine needles scattered against her side. "Sam."

"Yeah. I cannot believe you stabbed me." In the storm, his eyes looked more black than green.

She shook uncontrollably and looked down the empty roadway. "How did you get here?"

"I ran," he growled.

There was no way. Not only had she stabbed the guy, but nobody could run that fast. "I don't understand."

He shook her with restrained violence, not hurting her but definitely scaring the crap out of her. "You pierced my kidney and my colon. That was a kill strike."

She shoved him, unable to stop herself. "You kidnapped me. What did you expect?"

"I didn't hurt one hair on your head." He towered over her, the heat of his body warming her despite the storm.

"Yet," she yelled, no longer thinking clearly. The bear growled and she shook her head, spraying water, looking at the animal who seemed to be watching the entire scene. This was truly insane. "You have a bear for a pet? One who can block the road?"

The bear looked at her like she was nuts. Then, in front of her eyes, his fur receded, his snout narrowed, and soon a muscled and very naked man stood in the rain. His hair was shaggy and the same color as the fur, and his eyes were a pissed off honey brown. A tattoo of sharp talons covered his left bicep and shoulder, looking like part of a dragon. Was the rest on his back? "Pet? Do I fucking *look* like somebody's pet?" he snapped.

Her brain shut off. Completely. She was pretty sure Sam caught her before she hit the ground, but at this point, she no longer cared. Unconsciousness was a decent place to land.

Chapter Nine

The smell of burnt fabric was the first thing that caught her attention. Then a thrumming headache that hurt down to her neck. She remained perfectly still, listening.

"She's awake," a low voice all but growled.

"I know. Give her a second," Sam said, his voice familiar at this point.

She opened her eyelids to find herself on a blanket on Sam's sofa. Early dawn light had begun to filter through the windows. How long had she been out? That was the first time she'd ever fainted. "What smells like burned cotton?"

"Burned cotton," Sam said dryly. "The sofa caught fire, and I had to use the extinguisher."

She pushed herself up, noting a knitted blanket between her and the charred remains of the sofa cushion. Sam stood by the fireplace, his form long and lean as he rested against the wall. Her mind reeled through the events of the night. "Did you drug me?" How could he have? She hadn't accepted the mug of tea from him. So, she purposefully turned to stare at the man sitting in the only other chair in the room.

He was the guy who'd been a bear. Now he wore ripped jeans and nothing else, his eyes a curious honey-brown and his shaggy hair rapidly drying. His chest was wide and just as muscular as when he'd been an animal. "Hi. I'm Bear."

She snorted and then caught herself.

He rolled his eyes. "Fine. I'm Beauregard McDunphy, but everyone calls me Bear. If they want to live."

She shuddered. "I saw you."

"Yeah. I saw you, too." Bear cut a look at Sam. "I might've let my temper loose a little bit, but that doesn't change the situation."

Sam lost the lazy look in his eyes. "You're the one who outed yourself. I had things under control."

Honor shifted her weight. "Am I the situation? Because I, um, saw you turn from a bear into a man?" Her mind reeled. She'd seen it, but how was it possible? This was too weird.

"Yes," Bear said, his expression unfriendly. "See, people, as in *human people*, don't get to know about us."

"What happens if they do?" she whispered, her voice shaking even as her brain fought to convince her that none of this was really happening.

Bear studied her for several moments. "Either we make them one of us, or we kill them." He spoke as if discussing what to bring to a picnic.

"Oh." She looked at the door. Did she have a chance of making it out to the forest with the two of them watching her so closely?

Sam shifted his weight, following her gaze. "You're kidding, right?"

She looked away, and unfortunately, her focus landed on the bloody floor. Her stomach lurched. She looked back up at Bear. "You shifted from a bear into a man. So shifters exist." Sure, she'd read books with shifter heroes, but those were fiction. Not reality. Although, most myths were based in fact.

"Apparently," Bear agreed, still looking like he might want to take a bite out of her.

She looked up at Sam. "Are you a shifter?"

Bear snorted. "If he was a shifter, he would've gotten to you first."

Sam rolled his eyes. "I had a punctured kidney and colon, in addition to a concussion. Give me a break, Bear."

"Sure." Bear held up his hands. "Fine. Just don't go burning down my guest cabin here."

When in doubt, act calm. She clasped her hands in her lap. "You mentioned making people who know about you...one of you. You can turn a person into, a, well..."

"Shifter?" Bear said helpfully.

Her mouth went as dry as any sandy beach.

"Nope," Bear said. "You can't be turned into a bear, so please don't faint again. Fainting creeps me the hell out. Promise you won't do it anymore."

Numbly, she nodded.

"Good. Here's the deal. A shifter can mate an Enhanced human such as yourself, thus giving you immortality but none of the cool shifting stuff." He grinned, showing wicked canines. "Isn't that awesome?"

"Enhanced?" she asked weakly, ignoring the mention of mating.

"Yep." Bear cut a gaze toward Sam. "What is she?"

Sam shrugged. "I don't know, but she's strong. From what I've been able to discern, she seems like a cross between a demon mind destroyer and an empath. Meaning, she can glide into minds and measure truthfulness. Although she doesn't seem to realize how good she could be."

"A human lie detector? Very cool." Bear looked her over, his gaze appraising.

Panic seized her, but she kept her expression placid.

"You're terrifying her, Bear. Knock it off," Sam said. "Honor, you're safe. Ignore him. He's happily mated, and if his mate knew he was in here scaring you, she'd rip off his ears."

Bear frowned. "Are you threatening me, Kyllwood?"

"Yes," Sam said simply. "Be nice."

"This is me being nice," Bear exploded, jumping to his feet and pivoting to face Sam directly. "Do you have any idea the shitstorm I've been handling by having you and Garrett Kayrs become Grizzly members? The shifter nation is two farts away from war with the Realm because they haven't destroyed the dickhead Sevens, and since I allowed you two here, we've been facing internal war. *Garrett is a Seven.* How the king allowed that to happen, I'll never know. The canine shifters won't even speak to us—and don't get me started on the dragons."

She had no clue what any of that meant, but even so, Honor cringed away from the anger. Canine shifters? Dragons? They were real too?

"I know," Sam said calmly. "I really do, Bear. We appreciate the refuge, and if I could get Garrett to leave, I would. But this is the only safe place for him until he finds what he's looking for."

"He's looking for something that doesn't exist, and you know it. Fate is messin' with him. I thought you were the voice of reason until you started setting my world on fire. Literally. Do you think I haven't noticed you and Kayrs sneaking off and coming back smelling like burned-out buildings? I'm a fuckin' bear."

"I know you're a fuckin' bear," Sam snapped, shoving off the wall. Apparently his limitless patience had just run out. "I gave you my word that the moment the Seven became a problem for you, we'd be gone. It'll kill Garrett if I force him to leave, but I'll do it if that's what you and the Grizzly Club need."

Bear dropped his head. "He's not going to find her, Sam. You know it, I know it, and even the Fates know it. Whoever's shoving that dream into his head, and don't think I haven't looked for a rogue demon around here, is doing it on purpose. The guy is barely holding on."

Honor couldn't stay silent any longer. "Demon? There are demons? From hell?"

"Yes," Bear said just as Sam said, "No."

Sam glared at Bear. "Would you please stop talking? Every sentence you speak just gets her in more danger. She knows too much already."

Bear's jaw went slack. Then he smiled, and it wasn't a nice sight. "She's full in, brother. Knowing about us gives her a hundred percent knowledge, as far as we're concerned." He glanced at Honor and shook his head. "Besides that, she is seriously gifted. I can feel her vibrations from five miles away. It's a fuckin' miracle somebody else hasn't already found her and locked her down hard."

A pit the size of Toledo dropped into her stomach. Locked her down? "Um—"

"I know," Sam said, looking at her. "Even if she agreed to forget everything you just made sure she knows, she's a beacon."

Bear's cheek creased. "So."

Sam leaned back against the wall, crossed his arms, and stared at Honor. "So."

Honor didn't know what was going on, but she knew she probably wouldn't like it. "Since you've done your best to enlighten me, Mr. McDunphy, I feel I can ask some questions. From what you've said, there are humans and shifters in this world. Shifters are either bear, canine, or dragon. These people can mate humans and then everybody is immortal."

Bear grinned. "You forgot feline. There are fuckin' feline shifters, too."

"Of course," she said quietly, her mind melting away. "I mean, if you're going to have people turn into animals, you'd want to have lions and panthers and so on." She swallowed. "Do all bears have potty mouths like you?" She had no clue what words were coming out of her mouth at this point.

He laughed, the sound low and rich. "Yeah, pretty much." He looked at Sam again, and most of the tension in the room dissipated. "She's funny and seems a little nutty. Maybe she's a fairy."

"She's human," Sam muttered.

Fairies? "Fairies are real, too?" she whispered.

"Yup. They're nuts," Bear said cheerfully. "Sam's younger brother is mated to one. She's okay, but I like crazy people, so I might be biased."

Honor shook her head. "Am I having a psychotic break?" She slowly turned to look at Sam. Of course she had separated from reality. Nobody was that masculine and good looking. "Or did you somehow dose me?" There were powerful psychedelics that could explain a break like this.

He ran a rough hand through his still wet hair. The dark mass curled around his ears, matching his fierce eyebrows. "I know this is a lot, but you can handle it. Of course, you've always known you had gifts, so it's time to stop pretending that you don't. Once you accept yourself and realize that you're normal for an Enhanced human, then you can accept the rest of it more easily."

"What's the Seven?" she asked.

Bear lost his amusement. "That's a great question and one we'd all love to have answered."

Sam remained tight lipped.

This was all so freaking weird. "What's the Realm and who's the king and who's Garrett Kayrs?" she asked in rapid succession.

Sam was the one who finally answered. "The Realm is a coalition of immortal species, the king is the guy who's in charge, and Garrett Kayrs is his nephew as well as the guy you met yesterday. He came to get me released from DHS."

She wanted to stand, but her legs felt too wobbly. "You're a member of the Realm, but you're not a shifter? That means you're an immortal." The idea wasn't as farfetched as it would've sounded yesterday. It would explain his supernatural strength and speed, as well as the fact that his body had healed already from the would-be fatal knife wound she'd given him. "What are you, Sam?"

Bear gestured in the air as if there was no choice but for Sam to talk.

Sam's eyes darkened to the deep green of pine trees battled by a storm. "I'm a vampire-demon hybrid."

Her body went numb. Or maybe that was her brain. "Right. You're part vampire and part demon. Sure. That explains a lot." Her voice sounded…funny. Hollow and distant.

"You're losing her, Kyllwood," Bear said. "Give it to her. Come on. We need to get past the bullshit phase of this and actually come up with a plan that doesn't involve me killing both of you."

Sam moved then, right into Bear's face. He had about an inch or so on the shifter, and they both had muscle and testosterone to spare. "I'm about done with you having fun here. I told you to stop scaring her, and that includes any and all threats against her life. I mean it, Bear. I'm pissed off and ready to throw you through that wall, and a part of me thinks you want that to happen."

Bear smiled and didn't move back. "It's about time. I get so sick of you being so calm all the time. It's like you're glacial ice when the rest of us are burning. Well, until recently. I want to know what's going on with these fire trips you've been taking."

"If I knew, I'd tell you," Sam ground out through gritted teeth.

Bear's eyebrows rose. "You really don't know?"

"No. I'm having a fire issue and we're trying to figure it out." Sam's voice was so hoarse, he sounded more like an animal than Bear.

"Huh." Bear angled to the side so he could see Honor. "Hey. Human lie detector. Is he telling the truth?"

Her mouth dropped open, and she quickly shut it. "Uh, yes. I think so?" What did she know? "Sam? I don't want to be a vampire." The idea of sucking blood made her want to puke.

His sigh was long suffering as he moved toward her then dropped to his haunches. His heat wafted over her along with that unique scent of burning copper. He was still taller than she. "You can't be turned into anything." Slowly, twin fangs, sharp and deadly, dropped from his mouth. They were as real looking as knives or an animal's sharp teeth and nothing like what she would've imagined. Then he retracted them. "You okay?"

She nodded, because really, what else could she do?

Bear clapped his hands together, and she jumped. "All right. Well. There's only one solution here, and I'll leave you to it."

"Solution?" she whispered.

"Yep." Bear made it to the door. "Right now, you're as vulnerable as a chicken in a wolf den, lady. You're gonna have to mate, and Kyllwood has made a claim. Good luck." He opened the door, revealing a rainy morning.

Her hand went to her throat. "Does mating have to be consensual?"

Bear's eyebrows lifted. "No, but it's the only option. Don't you want to be immortal?" He jerked his head at Sam. "Bring her on the ride tomorrow."

Sam winced. "Bear—"

"I need you," Bear said quietly. "Garrett's found the love of his life once again, and it'll go to crap like always. I'm having an internal Grizzly Club issue with a few members, and I can't cover him completely."

Sam blew out air. "Then we'll be there."

A ride? She wasn't going on a shifter motorcycle ride, for goodness' sake. "I—I can't mate," she said, her voice rising. Though she didn't know the specifics of mating, she could guess. Her mind spun and then decided to shut down for a while. "I'm still engaged to somebody else."

Chapter Ten

Sam drove along the interstate, keeping the heat on in the vehicle in case Honor had caught any sort of cold while running from him through the woods. After Bear had left, she'd taken a shower before changing into dark jeans, a white sweater, and brown leather boots that seemed to lengthen those already long legs. He'd given her space to work through everything she'd learned.

Her mind was still spinning so fast he could almost hear it.

He passed a school bus. "We're going to come up with a game plan for this breakfast, and since we'll be there in about thirty minutes, how about you tell me why you're engaged but not wearing a ring?" He'd kept quiet as long as he could. The idea that she was taken was fuel injecting an unhealthy heat through his entire body. While Bear was wrong that Sam had made a claim, he sure as shit didn't like the idea of Honor being engaged.

Her hair was in wild curls down her back and her makeup understated, giving her an untouchable appearance. She looked at him, her eyes beautiful but tired. "I was going to break up with Kyle on my way out of town this morning. For my first vacation in much too long."

Sam paused. "Wait a minute. You were going to end an engagement and then just leave town?"

"Yes." She plucked at her jeans. "He's a psychologist, and we worked together for six months, then started dating. It was comfortable, usually. He accepted my oddities, and it was nice that somebody did."

"You're not odd. You're Enhanced and exceptionally gifted," Sam growled, his voice lowering to demon hoarse.

She looked at his mouth and then quickly away. "Well, I didn't know that. Plus, I found him restful to be around, if you know what I mean. I guess his brain patterns are so calm that I stopped trying to read him. Shouldn't have."

"Why?"

She blushed. "It's a little embarrassing, considering my job. Apparently Kyle has been out of town having an affair with his accountant, and when I found out, I was sadder to lose the ring than him." She shrugged. "I don't think I'm cut out for relationships."

Not with a dickhead named Kyle who cheated on her. Sam fought a grin. "Does this guy have any idea you're about to drop the hammer?"

"I don't know," she said quietly. "His girlfriend sent me pictures of them together, so she might've told him. But when he confirmed breakfast last night before you, um, kidnapped me, he didn't mention anything." She shook her head and looked out the window. "I really don't understand people. I mean, I think I do, because I'm good at my job. But then I don't. I was engaged to a guy I didn't know, and now I'm hanging out with vampires, demons, and shifters."

"Thanks for telling me." Sam took her hand.

She looked down at their hands. "When we're together, your energy is different. Not together. I mean, when we're in the same vicinity as each other, your energy smooths out."

He gripped the steering wheel, knowing full well what her admission had cost her. She was working on her gifts, and to do so, she had to admit she had them. He liked the idea that she was beginning to trust him. "That's intriguing. Tell me more."

Her expression lightened. "Okay. So, when I watched you in the interrogation room, your energy was all over the board and, well, heated. Then I entered the room, and you seemed to calm.

I can't explain it, but I could feel it. If I concentrate...I might be able to see it."

That made sense. "I've been having trouble with fire, as you know. I can't control it. In fact, it seems that I've passed the problem on to you, but then I burned the sofa after you took off last night." He already had several theories about that, but he wanted to see her mind in action. She was intriguing and sexy to start with, but when that brain kicked in, she was incredible. "What do you think?"

"I don't think my reading your brain patterns will help with the fire situation." She gestured with both hands, causing her breasts to lift beneath the snowy white sweater. "I need more information. Do other demons or vampires have problems with fire? With creating explosions?"

"No," he admitted, taking the next exit and driving down the ramp to an area with several shopping malls, gas stations, and restaurants. He looked for the right one. "It's a long story and more info than you probably need."

"That's bull," she said.

He turned toward her. "Excuse me?"

"You heard me," she said. "So far, from what I can tell, you have a problem, and nothing has helped. Until I walked into the room and you were able to share the problem with me. Have you noticed that no fires or explosions have occurred when we're in the same vicinity?"

"Yes," he said. "I figured that was temporary, though."

"Then in order to help you, I need the entire story." She squared her shoulders as he parked in front of a diner. "After I deal with Kyle. I'll be right back."

Interesting. She'd misread him again. "Right. I'm not letting you go in alone."

She paused in the midst of removing her seat belt and turned to face him. Her scent filtered through the car, and his body woke right up. "I'm not your responsibility, Sam."

"Baby, you've got that wrong." He opened his door and crossed around to open hers. "Let's do this and get on the road with the shifters. You haven't lived until you've gone on a ride with a bunch of insane bears."

She faltered and then accepted his hand. "Surely you're not on board with Bear's bizarre thoughts?"

He helped her out and then shut the door, escorting her to the diner. "Bear only seems crazy. The guy is usually on track." They walked inside, and he clocked Kyle in a second. Tall, dark hair, brown eyes. Fit and wearing a casual T-shirt with jeans, sitting in a booth facing the door.

Sam put his hand to the small of Honor's back and propelled her beyond the other booths.

Kyle looked up, surprise on his clean shaven face. The guy was probably good looking to most.

Sam showed his teeth.

* * * *

Okay, this was beyond awkward. Honor slipped inside the booth across from Kyle as Sam followed her, and she couldn't help but compare the two men. She was only human. They were both good looking, but Sam's animal magnetism all but squeezed out any appeal Kyle might've had. He was also bigger, stronger, and sexier. But hey, the guy was a vampire-demon hybrid, so it probably wasn't a fair contest.

"Hello." Kyle held out a hand. "I'm Kyle Longboard."

"Sam." Sam accepted the hand, his bigger. The shake was quick and apparently painful to Kyle, based on his indrawn breath.

He looked at Honor. "Honey, what's going on?"

She delved into Kyle's brain, her mental fingers tapping along the waves. Man, he still seemed honest, but subterfuge lurked just beneath the surface in a series of rougher bumps that didn't belong in his thought patterns. "I shouldn't have let my guard down," she muttered. This was all too much, and yet, she didn't have the energy to really get angry. She needed some serious sleep. When was the last time she'd pulled an all-nighter? She couldn't remember.

"Honor?" Sam prodded her, his gaze remaining squarely on Kyle.

Oh. She forced herself out of her thoughts and drew the ring from her pocket; then she pushed it across the table. A twinge of regret caught her. The diamond really was pretty, and she did like things that sparkled. "Here's your ring. Good luck with life." She looked at Sam. "I'm ready."

Kyle jerked. "What? Wait a minute." Anger infused his eyes, those brown eyes she'd thought were so intelligent. "What is going on?" He glared at Sam. "Would you please excuse us?"

"No." Sam didn't move.

Honor sighed. After the last twenty-four hours, this just didn't seem like the big deal it had yesterday morning. "Listen, Kyle. I know about your accountant or girlfriend or whatever."

He blanched. "I'm so sorry. It was a one-time mistake, and I'll never do it again." He looked at the ring sparkling on the table. "You've been so busy at work, and I've been so stressed. I just think we need to work things out. The two of us—alone."

So his cheating was her fault? Right. Not. She looked at him, not feeling much. That was just sad. What had she been thinking? "It's okay, really." As she said the words, she realized she meant them. "I was lonely and figured it was time to get married, and you seemed like a good candidate on paper, and I felt at peace around you. I don't know. I guess I was hoping there'd be romance and all of that in the future, and I didn't take time to really think about what I was doing."

Sam cut her a look. "Daaaamn."

She giggled. Then she sobered. What in the world? She wasn't a woman who giggled. But she'd been up for way too many hours and was getting punch drunk.

Kyle gaped. "You don't love me?"

It was hard to feel sorry for him considering he'd spent the weekend wrapped around a big-boobed blonde. "I don't think so.

I thought I did, and I really did like you, and as a kisser, you're not bad." She nudged the ring closer to him. "But it wasn't love. Obviously it wasn't for either of us, or you wouldn't have screwed your accountant."

Sam coughed under his breath. Or maybe that was a chuckle. God, she was tired.

Kyle reared up, something akin to panic crossing his handsome face. "Is it because of this guy?"

She partially turned to look at Sam. "No. He's another whole boatload of problems right now." When that made Sam grin, she felt all gooey inside. "But I bet he's a heck of a kisser. Better than not bad."

Sam leaned toward her. "You need some sleep, gorgeous."

"Now just hold on a minute—" Kyle started.

She was so done with this. "No. Listen. We dated, had fun, got really drunk one night, and then got engaged." Frankly, she wasn't even sure how it all had happened, and they'd only been engaged for two weeks. She'd gotten caught up in the moment, and that could happen to anyone. She would've called it off eventually anyway. "Then you showed up with the ring, I started thinking about babies and all of that, and it was a mistake. You know it, I know it, and the big guy here definitely knows it."

If anything, Sam saw her better than anybody else had her entire life. Even so, she wasn't going to be forced into mating, and he'd all but said he agreed with Bear on that. He was right that she needed sleep. He was wrong that she needed to go on a motorcycle ride with a bunch of bears to figure out her life.

Sam was bigger than life, and he'd already proved that if he wanted her in one place, she'd remain in that place. Would he force her to mate? While he seemed kind, at least to her, he hadn't changed his course of action when he thought he was correct. No matter what she'd said. The guy had kidnapped her and refused to let her go. She shivered.

"Well?" Kyle said. "I've put too much into this for you to just walk away."

She jerked. "Crap. Sorry. What did you say?"

Sam burst out laughing this time, and the sound was a low rumble of pure pleasure.

She shivered in response.

Then Kyle made the colossal mistake of grabbing her wrist.

What happened then wasn't a surprise except for the speed with which it happened. Sam manacled Kyle's wrist, yanked him from the booth, and put him squarely on the ground. Kyle made a sound between a yelp and a screech and then went silent.

Sam looked down at him. "Don't ever put your hands on her again." His voice was low with threat, and any humor that had lurked in him was long gone. In its place was a firm, raw, and deadly resolve that was more frightening than yelling. Or anger.

She saw him. Really saw him this time. That calm exterior of his hid a nature she hadn't come close to understanding. This was a primal being who would absolutely force her to mate in order to protect the shifter nation—maybe to protect her. He was smart, sexy, and immortal. Somebody she couldn't take on and win.

She needed time and distance to figure out this new reality without him in her space. Without him dictating her future.

Her throat went dry, and she scooted from the booth, grasping the ring and gingerly leaning over to put it on Kyle's heaving chest. "Maybe the accountant will like this. It really is a pretty ring, Kyle." Then she stepped away. "Sam? I need to use the restroom and will meet you at the car." Then she turned, forced herself to walk slowly, and entered the restroom beyond all the booths.

There was a window next to an old-fashioned powder room. She only had seconds to make it.

Chapter Eleven

Sam stood by the car, enjoying the crisp day. The rain had stopped, leaving the scent of clean autumn air all around him. He dug his phone from his back pocket as Kyle drove away.

Nessa answered. "Hey, Sam. Glad you called. Do you want Fireball or an Irish whiskey in your flask for the ride?"

"I'm easy," he responded, watching the diner door. "Do me a favor and do a deep dive on a Kyle Longboard, would you?"

Nessa paused. "Sure. Why?"

"He was Honor's fiancé, and I'd like to know more about him." Sam's instincts thrummed, but it could be because Kyle was an ass who'd just grabbed Honor.

"Sure. Is he a vampire?" Ness asked.

Why wasn't that door opening? "No. He's human, but there's something off about him. Maybe. Maybe not. I just need to make sure. Thanks and I owe you." He clicked off and slipped his phone back into his jeans pocket. Was Honor okay? Perhaps the breakup had been more difficult for her than she'd shown. He strode back into the restaurant, making it to the ladies' room. He knocked. "Honor?"

Nothing.

He paused and reached out with his senses.

Nothing.

He opened the door, and yep, a window was open next to a little makeup area. He grinned. He couldn't help it. Then he took out his phone and pressed a series of buttons. Honor was moving swiftly toward Seattle. She must've gotten a cab or Uber.

He couldn't blame her. The mating talk had probably freaked her out, which was understandable. Though he'd wanted to trust her, he wasn't a moron, so he'd stuck a tracking device in her purse. Good thing too. He dialed Nessa again.

"What? Give me a second, Sam. I'm not even at a computer," Nessa complained. "Plus, I have a big-assed bear as a mate, and he's growling all over the place about this ride. You'd think Fireball would be good enough, but no, today he wants tequila. For Pete's sake. I'm the leader, I mean I *was* the leader of the most elite fighting force in the world. Do I seem like a bartender to you?"

"No," Sam agreed, knowing full well she was still on the job. "I need a different favor. Would you trace Honor's credit card usage for the last day or so?"

"Sure." Nessa clicked off for a few minutes and then returned. "Um, she has a reservation for a bed-and-breakfast down the coast in Squall's Cove. Are you guys going there instead of on the ride?" Her voice quieted. "You need to come on the ride. Bear is about to kill Garrett."

Sam turned and strode out of the restaurant to Honor's car. He could catch her right now, but she needed to learn a lesson about trying to escape him. "We're coming on the ride, but I need Bear to switch the route. We'll still get to the campground but will take a slight detour. It'll be a nicer drive along the ocean anyway. I'll send you the coordinates. Thanks, Ness." He clicked off and dropped his bulk into the car.

Heat flared along his arms.

Taking several deep breaths, he tried to control the fire. Something pulled at him, and his leg dropped into nothingness, so cold he nearly yelled. Instead, he tried to drag it back to this dimension. Something bit his ankle. He bellowed and freed himself, bleeding profusely. There were sharp bite marks through his jeans. He rapidly started the engine and roared away from the curb, flipping through different maps he'd memorized and taking a sharp left toward what used to be an industrial area. "Call Garrett," he barked at the phone.

"Yo," Garrett answered, sounding lazily content.

"You alone?" Sam asked, swerving around a couple of minivans.

Bedclothes rustled. "For now. What's happening?" Garrett went from calm to full alert in a second, his voice sharpening.

"Fire. Problems." Flames exploded beneath the dash. "Meet me here as soon as you can." He rattled off an address and then sped up, taking a corner on two wheels. Hopefully Honor had decent insurance. Smoke filled the interior of the car, and he rolled down the windows, going so fast the outside was only a cement covered blur.

Finally, he whipped to the end of an abandoned area and stopped in the middle of what used to be a parking lot. Then he tumbled out of the car, staggering a few feet before an explosion ripped through the air behind him. The force threw him several yards, and he flew fast, landing flat on his face. Pain burst through his skull.

Swearing, he flipped to his back and sat up to find Honor's car engulfed in flames. Metal and other debris rained down, still burning. He took a deep breath and then looked around. His left shoulder felt broken, so he sent healing cells there as well as to the bite mark in his leg. Whatever had bitten him had used poison to thin his blood, and his leg was already turning numb.

An abandoned factory loomed to the left, its steel walls crumbling, and its windows all burned out. Graffiti marred what remained. He reached out with his senses to ensure that nobody was inside. Nope. Empty save for rodents and a couple of wild cats. He wiped blood off his face and sent healing cells to his broken nose.

The cement around him was cracked, revealing several pieces of rebar sticking out. It was a good thing he hadn't landed on one of those. The air shimmered next to him, trying to draw him in. Damn it. He forced himself to his feet and moved away from the opening, knowing if he got stuck again, the pain would be excruciating. He stayed close to the fire, for now, feeling he wasn't going to set anything else ablaze. The fire burned, wild and free.

The sky was blue and calm, so there was no rain to help put it out.

The engine blew, throwing the hood into the sky. It landed hard near the factory.

Garrett finally drove up in a black truck, jumping out and tossing a fire extinguisher at Sam before turning to extract another. Between the two of them, they had the fire out within a few minutes; only smoldering smoke still billowed into the sky. "Let's get out of here just in case the human authorities catch wind of the fire." He looked down at Sam's leg. "You okay?"

Sam nodded. "Something bit me from another world. It was a good one, too. The healing cells struggled." He tossed the extinguisher in the back of the truck and crossed to the passenger side, wanting to heal his shoulder while Garrett drove.

Garrett jumped inside, rocking the entire vehicle. "Where's Honor?" He sped away from the scene of the fire.

Sam drew his phone clear to read the screen. "On her way down the coast. Probably jumped on a bus."

Garrett shot him a look. "Want me to head that way?"

"No. We'll catch up to her on the ride." Sam put his head back and shut his eyes, having to fight the pull through dimensions.

Garrett was quiet for a few moments. "Sometimes I forget what a bastard you can be," he murmured.

Sam double-checked his injured shoulder and then sent healing cells deeper into the muscle. "What do you mean?"

"You know exactly what I mean. You're cold, man. Methodical and exact, just like a knife." Garrett turned on the heat.

"She's gotta learn," Sam said, his leg itching now. What kind of creature had bitten him?

Garrett cleared his throat. "Learn what? That she can't get away from you? That's going to scare her."

Sam opened his eyes. "She needs to be scared." He sat up as Seattle flew by outside the vehicle. "I don't have the luxury of coddling her right now. She's in danger, and not just from Bear and the shifter nation. Her power is strong, and probably even more so since we interacted and she caught the fire, for lack of a better explanation. She needs to be protected, and I can do that. It's that simple."

"Are you going to mate her?" Garrett asked.

The words shot straight to Sam's groin. It was a question he hadn't allowed himself to ponder. Mate? "No mating mark." He held up his right hand. The marking that showed when a demon had met its mate was absent from his palm. It was surprising and oddly disappointing.

Garrett snorted. "Please. Your system is all screwed up, thanks to what's happening to you, and besides, you're such a control freak that a marking won't appear unless you allow it. Now answer the question." The youngest Kayrs warrior looked large and formidable in the truck, and right now, he was in a good mood.

Sam eyed the kid who'd become as close as a brother to him. "She has to be willing. Currently, she's not. So I'm not going to worry about it." He couldn't think about mating right now. If the woman would just stay where he wanted her, they'd both have time to sort things out.

"Fair enough." Then Garrett grinned. "This is going to be a good ride. I can feel it. I think I might've found her, Sam. For sure this time."

Sam barely kept from wincing. "You've thought that about twenty times during our stay with the Grizzlies." Each time, when Garrett was proved wrong, that he hadn't found his mate, the fallout had been ugly. "How are the dreams?"

"The same." Pain and uncontrollable anger rippled through the cab. "I'm on a bike, on a ride, and she's behind me. I feel her. She's wild and strong and so solid it hurts to breathe. Then she's ripped away, and I'm alone with a knife in my heart." He grunted. "Sometimes I don't sleep for weeks, and I know that's bad. Since I met Juliet last week, I have hope."

Sam wasn't going to take that hope from his brother. "Just keep in mind that the dreams might be false. It's entirely possible that an enemy, and we have many, has found a way to drive you crazy."

"That's not it," Garrett said softly, his voice hoarse. "I can't explain it, but I know that's not it. This is real. The dream is as intense as if I experience the reality of it every time. It's like having the most important person in the world, the one who holds your soul, ripped away from you with great pain. Each and every time."

Sam's gut hurt. He'd do anything to protect Garrett from that pain. Right now, all he could do was support him and be there when things turned to shit, as they usually did. "Okay."

"Okay." Garrett turned toward the Grizzly property. "So. Honor. Is she going to wear your colors on the ride?" Different clubs had different colors, and a woman wearing a color was left alone by males.

"Yeah, Garrett. She's definitely going to wear my colors." That was as much as Sam would admit right now.

Garrett grinned. "You might as well just plant your mark on her ass the first night. You're already lost, and you don't even know it, brother."

"I know exactly where I am," Sam said evenly. That was part of who he was as the sounding board for his brothers as well as their allies.

He always knew exactly where everybody was at any time. He glanced at his phone again, reading the screen. Including Honor.

Chapter Twelve

Honor was feeling mildly triumphant, if a little sleepy, as the driver dropped her off at the quaint bed-and-breakfast on the coast. At least she'd caught a couple hours of sleep during the bus trip to town. The Pacific Ocean rolled loudly below the cliffs, while blazing red and yellow leaves fluttered all around the front area of the white clapboard building with a wraparound porch. Now all she needed was about eight hours of sleep, some meditation time, and a piece of paper to create lists. Then she'd be able figure out what to do with Sam, with her new knowledge about the world, and with her life.

Electricity ran down her arms—again. She caught her breath, trying to control the sparks. A flash of fire burst from the nearest bush, burning quietly. God, she couldn't control it. What should she do? Moving over, she stomped out the fire. It was the third one of the day, although so far, she'd been able to rapidly extinguish each fire.

A rumble echoed down the quiet street that rapidly turned into a roar. She pivoted to look at the road and saw a multitude of motorcycles headed her way. Mostly black cycles, all manned by riders in leather.

What in the world?

Oh, crap. Her skin tingled and her ears rang as she caught sight of Sam on his bike, leading the procession of more than a dozen other motorcycles. Then the rest of her tingled as well.

He looked big and dangerous on the cycle, his green gaze cutting across the distance to land on her. His black leather jacket was open, revealing a dark T-shirt stretched tight across his powerful chest.

Her legs wobbled with the urge to run, but his expression froze her in place.

In that second, she realized two things. First, he'd obviously placed some sort of locating device on her. And second, he could've caught her at any time but had decided to wait until she thought she'd found safety. Anger filtered through her along with a desire that almost hurt. Her breasts felt heavy and her thighs soft, and she'd never in her entire life felt more feminine. More *female*.

He stopped at the curb, only a couple feet away from her. Then his gaze caught on the few remaining embers among the burning leaves. Anger exploded within his eyes, turning them a surreal silver streaked with emerald. "Get. On." Fury rode his tone.

She blinked. Her mouth opened and then shut. She lowered her chin.

He shifted his weight, and the motion was a threat. She couldn't swallow. She couldn't breathe. He looked at her, so much command in his gaze that her body moved without her mind kicking in. If she didn't get on that bike, he was going to put her on that bike. She knew that with everything she was.

She reached him. "Um."

He grasped her arm and twisted his torso, sitting her firmly behind him. "Not now. Don't say a fucking word right now." His gaze remained on the extinguished fire. Then he handed her a helmet, and she put it over her head without argument. Maybe now wasn't the time to talk.

Grabbing her hands, he secured them around his waist, patting them into place. She held on, turning her head and forcing her body to relax. There didn't seem to be much of a choice.

She bent her legs and set her boots behind his, holding on, her heart racing. She'd never ridden on a motorcycle before, and this close, she could finally touch his spectacular body. The feeling of his hard torso against her chest, the touch of his rippled abs beneath her hands, and the rumble of the machine between her legs nearly threw her into an orgasm. She had to fight the brief spasm and return to reality.

His already solid body went rock hard.

She stiffened. He'd felt that. He knew. She tried to pull her hands away, but he set his palms over hers. Hard.

She gulped.

Then he drove away from the curb and they were flying. Fast and wild, totally free. Exhilaration filled her, and she held on, her head thrown back with pure pleasure. There was no feeling like it. Anywhere at all.

She allowed herself nearly an hour of just enjoying the ride before she began to take notice of the bikes around them. About half had women riding behind the driver, and those stayed in the middle of the pack. Up ahead and behind, and even to the sides, single riders drove. Mostly male but also a few females riding solo.

Bear rode to Sam's right with a petite woman, probably half his size, holding on to his waist. Her long, curly black hair flowed down her back, and she held tight, with her face tilted to the sun. Hey. She wasn't wearing a helmet; nor were many of the other riders. Were they all immortal?

Honor turned to the left to see Sam's lawyer, or buddy, or whoever he pretended to be. Garrett Kayrs. He rode steadily, his body relaxed, with a buxom brunette holding on to his waist, her fingernails a light pink. She also wore a helmet, so she must be another human.

Energy flowed through Honor, calm and sure. Oh. The impending feeling that she was about to cause a fire was gone. She closed her eyes and reached out with her senses, finding a solid wall of safety in front of her. Around her. Her essence mixed with Sam's...all flowing easily. No disturbances. No explosions and no flames.

Desire filled her senses, winding around them both. His body remained taut, and she sensed tension rolling off him, stronger than anything else. She dug her fingers into his abs, caressing each ridge. Each hard-as-stone ridge.

A low sound rumbled back to her.

Had he growled?

She couldn't help herself. Holding her breath, she swept her fingers beneath his waistband, touching the bare skin at his waist. His heated skin.

Her throat was parched. Her head ached. Her entire body pulsed with need.

She lost track of time.

Finally, Bear signaled something, and the group moved en masse off the interstate and down an exit, driving through a quiet neighborhood to a vacant park, bright with fallen red and gold leaves. The bikers all parked along a curbed area, and Sam pulled up and cut the engine.

Her ears still rang, and her body still pulsed.

In one impossibly smooth motion, Sam twisted his torso, hooked her around the waist, and lifted her off the bike so that she straddled his hips, her breasts crushed against his chest. He ripped off her helmet and threw it over his head, dismounted, and marched toward the trees.

Then his mouth was on hers.

* * * *

Sam took her mouth with all the pent-up frustration of the last few days, hoping someone caught the helmet. He filled both hands with her spectacular ass and strode toward a stand of trees he'd clocked the second they'd arrived. She tasted like strawberries and honey, and he kissed her harder, finally taking what he wanted.

She tunneled both hands through his hair, kissing him back, her body gyrating against his. He kept going until the only sounds around them were wind and the rustle of leaves beneath his feet. Then he settled her back against a tree and slowly released her lips. He let his mouth wander along her jaw, over one high cheekbone to her ear, where he nipped the shell and then bit down on the lobe.

"Sam," she whispered, clutching his hair.

Yeah. One of the sweetest sounds ever. Her voice was soft with need and her body one rigid line of hunger against him.

His cock tried to punch through his jeans. He lifted his head, scouting the area with every sense, making sure they were safe.

Then he looked at her. That glorious hair fell in curls down her shoulders, and her eyes shimmered with a mixture of shocked innocence and sultry need. The combination drove his lust hotter than any fire. Her sweet lips were a brighter pink from his kiss.

She blinked, her legs spread around his hips, her core against his. Shouting came from a distance, but he didn't care. Not at all.

He lowered his head so he could capture her gaze. Keeping it, he kissed her again, wanting more of her. She tentatively slid her tongue against him, and any self-control he'd planned to maintain blew into pieces. He dove into her mouth until the entire world narrowed to the two of them and his blood pounded through his veins. Honor. So fucking soft and sweet and defiant. Yeah, he liked that about her, too.

She bit into his bottom lip, and it was all he could do not to rip her clothes off and take her on the bed of leaves. He growled low, and she shivered in response. Good to know. Then he kissed her jaw, and she tilted her head to grant him better access. Taking full advantage, he scraped his fangs down her delicate neck while plunging one hand inside her jeans.

Her gasp and body jerk spurred him on, and he found her, lightly pinching her clit. She went off like a rocket, hot and fast, crying out his name.

He kissed her again, swallowing the sound. It was for him. Only for him.

A set of bushes exploded next to him, and he jumped away, keeping her safe.

The soft sound of surrender she made when coming down nearly killed him. He removed his hand and set her shirt back in place. "Hold on." He set her down and turned to stomp out the fire, careful not to burn his ankles.

She looked at the smoldering ashes.

He reached for her. "We're going to figure that out." They couldn't be starting the world on fire.

Her doe-soft eyes cleared. Surprise appeared on her face and then embarrassment.

"No," he growled, moving his face to within an inch of hers. "You can be pissed, you can be surprised, you can even be so hungry you beg, but there's no embarrassment. Not between us. Got it?"

She slowly nodded. Even so, she looked bewildered. Endearingly so.

He slid his arms around her waist to make sure she'd completely gained her balance. "You hungry?"

She stilled. "Hungry?"

"For food." He hid a smile. Getting her off balance had just become his favorite pastime. "Bear stopped so we could have a snack."

"Oh." She moved across the leaves and tripped, eyeing the now burned bush warily.

He reached for her hand.

She pulled back. "Everyone will know…that we, um…"

He tugged her toward him, willing to wait all day if she needed time. "You're riding with a bunch of bear shifters. Half of them are off getting naked in the woods right now."

Her peel of laughter caught him off guard and made his already hard dick pound with a need so great even his ears heated. "I hadn't thought of that." Her eyes sparkled. "I was looking for an adventure, and I guess I've found one. But I'm calling the shots on my future. Don't forget that."

"Right." He led her out of the trees toward where Nessa had already stockpiled a picnic table full of treats for those few who hadn't suddenly disappeared into the trees.

A partially burned tree was next to her with a fire extinguisher at its base. Sam winced. So that explained the yelling. He'd started a fire on his way through.

One thing at a time. "You need to eat something, and then we're going to ride for a while longer. Keep up your energy, baby. I haven't even started with you yet."

Her quick indrawn breath made him smile.

Again.

Chapter Thirteen

Honor sat on a blanket beneath the boughs of a generous pine tree, munching happily on a sandwich. A turkey, ham, and salami sandwich that was probably the best one she'd ever tasted. Nessa was amazing with a picnic basket. During the long ride, they'd stopped three more times for bathroom and food breaks, and she and Sam had stuck to the food except for the first time—and they hadn't started any more fires. Her body still hummed, and she wanted to ask what he'd meant by not being through with her.

Oh, she knew what he'd meant. It was a little embarrassing that the stolen moment in the trees had resulted in the best orgasm of her life. The guy had barely touched her. But she still wasn't sure what mating entailed. It was time to stop admiring the man and get some answers. After dinner.

Folks bustled about, preparing tents for the night. Sam had set down the blanket, handed her a sandwich, and told her to sit tight. Her legs were tired from riding all day, as was her body, so she'd complied.

Now she watched him cross back and forth by a glade of cottonwoods, a cell phone to his ear. Again. During their brief stops, he'd taken a call from his brother Zane, who turned out to be the demon king. Zane needed an update on Garrett as well as advice about some sort of treaty with a vampire group out of

Montana. Then younger brother Logan called, needing advice about an upcoming meeting with the witch nation as well as help dealing with a crazy-assed fairy named Mercy who apparently Sam adored because he always took her side.

Sam had called his mother to check in on his younger sister, who was trying to date a dork named Bobby. His advice was to allow said sister to date the dork, because it would only last an hour. His sister was too smart for dorks. But in case she wasn't, Sam had advised that somebody named Paxton should check Bobby out and scare the shit out of him if necessary—and to keep Daire away from Bobby to avoid some sort of internal war. She was still guessing who Daire might be.

Right now, Sam was talking to another king. Honor knew this because he'd started the last sentence with, "You might be the fucking king, but you have your head up your ass right now. Stop and think, Dage."

Huh. She reached for her open bottle of tea and drank some down, cooling her throat. Fascinating. Absolutely fascinating.

Garrett whistled from over by a stand of trees, gestured, and waited for Sam to point toward Honor. Then Garrett hefted a large pack over his massive shoulder and headed her way with the cute brunette trailing behind him. She carried a backpack and picked her way carefully across the grassy way.

"Hey," Garrett said; they'd formally met again during one of the other stops.

"Hey," Honor replied. "Sam's talking to a king."

Garrett nodded. "My uncle. Sam runs interference sometimes." The brunette was still out of earshot.

"He does a lot more than that," Honor murmured, her gaze moving back to the hybrid pacing by the river.

Garrett paused and focused on her face, his gaze appraising behind his tinted glasses. "You caught that, did you?" His perusal was more than casual, as if he was seeing her for the first time. A slow smile tipped his lips.

She returned the smile. "Most people don't?"

Garrett shook his head. "Not even close. He's the middle brother sandwiched between an older brother who's a king and younger one who's destined for something big that I can't go into with you. Most folks don't look beneath the surface and think Sam's the peacemaker. The wanderer and the...other brother."

She laughed out loud. "Only because that's what he wants them to think."

Garrett lifted his chin. "You're not just a pretty face with Enhanced gifts, now are you?"

Heat flooded into her face. The hottie thought she was pretty? Man, she was a dork. "Sam's awfully good at this, right?"

"Right." Garrett gave her the full force of his smile, and it was something to see. Then he winked before turning to the brunette who'd just caught up to them. The pretty woman had disappeared into the trees with Garrett at every stop during the day and now sported whisker burn across her chin as well as a very sleepy and satisfied smile. "I don't think you two have met yet today. Honor, this is Juliet, also affectionately now known as Doc Julie. She's new to the group."

Ah. So she didn't know about shifters and vampires and the rest? Honor was on the inside of this one, apparently. She nodded to show that she'd understood.

"Juliet, stick with Honor for a couple of minutes, would you? I'll set up our tent." Garrett took Juliet's arm with the gentlest looking of touches and settled her with Honor.

"Sure," Juliet said, extending her legs on the blanket. She'd piled her burnished brown hair up on her head, and in the waning twilight, her skin glowed a soft peach. She filled out her pink shirt like it had been made for her. "Thanks, Garrett." Her voice was sweet and slightly tired. Then she handed over the small backpack. "Garrett mentioned you didn't have clothes, and I have an extra set. We're about the same size."

That was sweet, but Honor's butt wouldn't fit in that woman's jeans. She could probably borrow a shirt, though. She shifted her weight. Should she start working out more? Then she flicked the bad thought to the embers. She was fine with her body and her many curves. She settled back with her tea, noting that Sam checked on her periodically as he spoke.

His attention made her insides go all squishy. She sighed.

Juliet chuckled. "Right? I can't believe these guys are real."

In a way, they weren't. Not in the human world. "Garrett seems like a nice guy," Honor offered. At least when he wasn't pretending to work for the federal government to spring possible arsonists. Was that only the other day?

"Oh, he is." Juliet crossed her legs and stretched her back, rolling her neck. "This is the craziest thing I've ever done. I mean, I met the guy last week and now I'm on one of those motorcycle rides like you see on television shows?" Her eyes widened, and she really did look like a princess. If Garrett's uncle was a king, then his dad was probably a prince, which made Garrett a prince, too?

Honor chewed the inside of her lip as she pondered. "Yeah, me too."

Juliet paused. "I wanted to get you alone for a minute, and I meant to do it before now."

Honor's interest was piqued. "Why's that?"

The woman turned and met her gaze directly. "When we picked you up earlier, I wasn't sure you were willing to come. Then when you went into the trees, you seemed pretty willing. But I need to make sure you want to be here. If not, we're leaving."

Honor's heart warmed. "I want to be here, but I appreciate your concern. You're a nice person." It was good to know that the sisterhood existed even in the middle of nowhere. She didn't get any odd vibrations from Juliet except tired ones, so she stayed out of her head, as was only polite. For now, she had some things to figure out once Sam stopped fixing the world. For one thing, did immortal really mean immortal?

Juliet fiddled with the bottom of her shirt. "Have you done this before?"

"No." Honor burst out laughing. "I am so far out of my comfort zone that I don't even see the shore." What she did see was Sam Kyllwood in all of his pacing glory as Bear tossed a leather jacket at him from quite a distance and Sam caught it easily with one hand, not pausing in his discussion on the phone.

Juliet chuckled. "That makes me feel better, less like an idiot. This has been so much fun."

"It has," Honor agreed. Once she'd decided to go with the flow and enjoy the moments, her entire body had relaxed. She could control her future while still exploring the present. Life was so much bigger than she'd realized. "Why are you called Doc Julie? It's a cool nickname," she said.

"Oh." Juliet rubbed her calf. "I'm a veterinarian, and I work at Base Mountain Vet. Garrett brought in a baby fox with a broken leg last week. I just moved from Portland to take the job, and my boyfriend didn't want to do the long-distance thing, so he pretty much dumped me." Her face turned a lovely shade of pink. "I've only known Garrett a week, and today we…"

Honor patted her hand. "One thing I've noticed about this group is that there's no judgment. If you're having fun and you feel safe, then why not?"

Juliet smiled. "Yeah. Why not?" When Garrett finished setting up their tent, he motioned her toward him, his gaze intent. "Seriously. How is he real?" Then she stood. "One of the women from a different camp came over to talk, and she said there's a shopping mall only ten minutes away. Let's go tomorrow. I forgot some items, and you need clothes."

"Sounds great," Honor said. Good. She needed thicker socks, for one thing.

Juliet set off, headed for Garrett at a pretty fast pace. He caught her, lifted her high, and then ducked into the tent with her. It was set against the trees some distance from the main group, which was probably a good thing.

Sam tucked his phone in his pocket and loped toward her, looking like a panther in his element. "How are your legs?"

"Time for the Honor compartment, huh?" she asked, lifting her head to better see him.

One of his dark eyebrows rose. "Excuse me?"

She grinned. "You. Everything in compartments and you check them off one at a time. Must be my turn." The guy had a strangle hold on control in a totally calm way.

"Right. This is for you. Wear it." He tilted his head, just studying her. Then he tossed the leather jacket next to her. The back design was of a grizzly bear that looked as if it was rolling its eyes. Script above the bear said GRIZZLY MC and the font below it said PROPERTY.

She studied the logo. "Property?"

He shrugged, the last rays of light streaking out behind him and putting his hard-cut face into shadow. "It's MC lingo. Most of the clubs at this ride are human, and they have their own rules. Wear that, and nobody will harass you."

She ran her fingers across the wild design, ignoring the "most are human" bit. "I'm not wearing this."

"Up to you." He reached for the pack next to her and drew out a tent. "But you will get hit on and pestered, and the later the night goes, the drunker everyone will be. Especially the humans."

She looked over at him, suspicion filtering through her. "You're being awfully agreeable."

"I'm an agreeable guy." He started placing metal spikes throughout the tent material, his movements smooth and efficient.

"No, you're not. You give that impression, but it's just another way you do what you do." She looked around and noticed that most of the women were wearing leather jackets. "In fact, I think you're being so agreeable because you know I don't want to be hit on and will probably end up wearing this."

His quick flash of a smile stole her breath. It was as close to an admission as she'd get, and she knew it.

"Dude, you're fun to watch. For a second, I thought you were the man behind the curtain," she murmured.

"For a second?" He efficiently lifted the now put together tent and looked around for a spot to place it.

She stood to help him, although he didn't seem to need it. "Yeah. You're the guy *in front* of the curtain. Not hidden, not quietly pulling strings, just right there holding everything together. You manage everyone without seeming to do so and are so tough you told off two kings within the span of an hour. While I have no idea how powerful kings are in this new and crazy immortal world, that had to take balls."

Apparently he found the right spot, because he set the tent down against a rock outcropping with trees on either side. "This'll do," he murmured.

She pushed him. Right in the ribs.

He looked down at her. "What?"

"Enough, Sam. I want to know everything. Why are we accidentally creating fires when we're apart from each other, or when we're too close to each other, what does enhancement mean, why are we on a ride with a bunch of bears, and are you going to try to force me to mate?" She put her hands on her hips.

Then that very green gaze slammed into her. His full attention. "Is that all?"

Her legs wobbled. "No. I want to know just how long you think you're going to be able to hold this all together and still keep up that calm facade? While you're shielded and I can't tap into your brain, I'm not clueless. I can feel the effort all of this is costing you, and at some point, you're going to explode. You know it, too."

Chapter Fourteen

Only years of training kept Sam on his feet looking mildly interested. The woman had just rocked his brain. What the hell? Nobody peered beneath his surface. Not a soul saw what he didn't want them to see. Except her.

He didn't want to be seen. It made his job—his jobs—too difficult. Right now, he was barely holding it all together with both hands.

She frowned. "Enough. This is my life, and I deserve some answers."

The woman wasn't wrong. He motioned for one of the prospects to bring his stuff over, and the young bear, a kid named Lake, hustled to do it, placing everything by the tent. "What do we have?" Sam asked quietly.

Lake stretched his thick neck. "Looks like ten different clubs, all just out for some fun. Eight human, one lion, and us. No rivalries or anything big going on, and the lions don't want to interact. They're from Nevada and are just here for a ride and a goodbye to autumn—so they're pretending we're not here, which works for us. We're settled farther east than the other camps, and forest land extends beyond us. Scouting showed nothing near, so we're secure."

Sam nodded. "Bear?"

"In a decent mood right now but it's only Thursday night. He should be pissed off and tired of being around people by noon tomorrow." The kid flashed a smile. "Nessa will keep him calm through tomorrow and probably we'll have a good party tomorrow night, but we'll be headed out Saturday like usual." He cut a look toward Garrett's rocking tent and sighed.

"Thanks," Sam said, ignoring the movement of Garrett's tent.

"You bet." Lake spotted a couple of human females lounging near a picnic table. "Now. It's time to be a good ambassador for our people." He chuckled and took off at a slow stroll toward them.

Sam fetched the blanket from under the tall pine, set it near the tent against the rocks, and dug out a rare bottle of Midleton Pearl whiskey and two glasses before gesturing to the blanket. "I hope you appreciate good Irish whiskey."

"Let's find out." She moved gracefully to sit on the blanket.

"Yes, let's." Sam sat and opened the bottle, quickly pouring. "Our mom mated a witch enforcer, Daire, who sends me the good stuff once in a while." He held out the glass. "Sláinte."

"Cheers," she returned, sniffing the glass and then sipping. Her moan was one of pleasure that shot right to his cock.

He tipped back his drink, letting it steal his breath for a second. He refilled his glass and topped hers off. "Okay. To answer your questions. Enhancement means that as a human female, you're special. You might be a slightly different species from human, or you might be cousins to the witches, but nobody really knows. What it means is that you have extra gifts and can mate an immortal, which would then increase your chromosomal pairs, ultimately giving you immortality but not changing you in any other way."

She blinked. Once and again, her pretty brown eyes wide. Then she tipped back the rest of the whiskey and coughed several times. "Is immortality real immortality?"

"We can be killed by beheading and possibly with fire," he said. When she remained quiet, he continued. "We're riding with a bunch of bears because Garrett is plagued by nightmares in which his mate is torn off his bike, and he loses it. Now he's obsessed—he has to ride all the time, and I'm covering his back while Bear's doing the same. Bear goes on these rides because he's learned that human MC clubs don't try to infringe on his territory after they see what a badass he is. Then he doesn't have to kill anybody, and that makes him happy. So while he growls about it, there's a benefit to him in attending these parties."

"He does like to growl," Honor said, holding out her glass.

Sam refilled it to the top. "Okay. So next question, and I can't answer all of it. Here's what I can say. There's a ritual coming up with Seven immortals, including Garrett and my younger brother Logan, in order to kill our worst enemy, an immortal we'll call the Big Bad for you. You don't need to know more than that. The Seven are pretty much prophesized to die during the ritual, as is my young niece Hope, and I agreed to be something that is unfortunately called the Keeper. It's a fucking stupid name."

"The Keeper?" She barely kept the skepticism out of her tone.

"Yeah." He finished his whiskey and poured more. "As far as we can tell, I'm supposed to create a place between dimensions for this ritual to take place."

"Well, of course you are." She wobbled a little on the blanket but sipped more of the rich whiskey. "If one is going to be a Keeper and create a circle for a ritual, then one should absolutely do it between dimensions. What good would a ritual be in one dimension?"

Amusement took him along with desire. God, she was cute. "Exactly," he said, enjoying the banter. "Why do you assume it's a circle?"

"What else would it be?"

He chuckled. "That's a good point." It was nice to talk about all of this with somebody. With her. "So, I agreed to be the Keeper, which involved being dragged through a bunch of dimensions and nearly dying a few times, resulting in the very sexy marking on my back. At least, I've been told it's sexy." He couldn't help but tease her.

She set her hand on his thigh, nearly blowing his head off. "It is sexy, Sam." Her voice slurred a little, and she lifted the glass to finish the drink. "I like Irish whiskey."

"Who doesn't?" He followed suit and refilled their glasses. "A few years back, a whole boatload of crap rained down, and the immortals' ability to teleport was destroyed." God, he missed teleporting. It still felt like he'd lost a limb. At her raised eyebrows, he continued speaking. "Yeah. Many demons could move from one place to another in a blink. It was exceedingly convenient, but now the paths have been shut. Somehow."

"Ah." She licked her lips.

He shoved down a groan of need.

"So you can't create your circle because you can't teleport," she said wisely, her eyes unfocused. "Well, that would explain why you're somehow creating fire and explosions. You have energy that has nowhere to go. What about me?"

"I don't know," he admitted, resting back against the rock and giving into temptation by tugging on her curly hair. Her hair was amazing. The heavy texture and tempting curls felt like heaven against his fingers, so he started to play. "You're taking this very well."

"I'm drunk," she blurted out. "Plus, I'm tired. I've only slept a couple of hours in way too long."

He nodded. "Got that. Best I can guess, with your enhancement, you read vibrations from people and also have the ability to smooth them out. You've used it to coax confessions and find liars, but I think you're naturally helping me. How you ended up with the problem as well is beyond me, but I'm guessing you took it on without knowing. I think." It was the only explanation he could come up with.

"Oh." She took another deep inhale of the drink and then sipped delicately, her pink lips closing over the glass in a way that tortured him more than she'd ever know. "You've almost answered everything." She looked down at her glass, and a light peach color filtered across her cheekbones.

He set a knuckle beneath her chin and lifted her face to meet his gaze. "I would not force you to mate. Ever." It was important she understand that fact.

Even intoxicated, her eyes showed how intelligent she was. "What does mating entail?"

"Sex, a good bite, and the transfer of a mating mark from the demon's hand to his mate," he murmured, fixed on her eyes but wanting her mouth.

She chewed on her bottom lip. "Thinking logically, why wouldn't we mate? If it would make me safe and maybe help you out with the fire problem, why not do it and then just go our separate ways? I wouldn't mind immortality, really. I've been thinking about it."

He rubbed a thumb across her mouth, forcing her teeth to abandon the sweet flesh of her lips. "Mating is forever."

Her frown was lopsided and adorable. "It can't be."

He grinned, watching his thumb on her soft mouth. "It is."

"No." She shook her head. "You told me that your mom is mated to a witch enforcer, whatever that is. I mean, who wants to enforce a bunch of witches?" She gestured with her graceful hands. "Back to the subject. The way you talked…he's not your dad. This Daire with the very good whiskey is not your father."

The woman was too smart. "True," Sam allowed. "Our mom is a demoness and our father was a vampire who died a long time ago. When a mate is dead, it's possible to negate the bond by exposing oneself to a particular virus that was recently discovered. Our mom took the virus and later mated Daire. Nobody knows the power of the virus, and there's never been an instance of a matehood being broken when both parties were living. So mating is forever. Period."

"Oh." She finished her drink. "Well, then."

"Yeah. You need to trust me, Honor. We'll figure out a way to keep you safe." How he could make that happen without mating her, he didn't know. But he was Sam Kyllwood, and he got things done. He'd figure it out.

She wobbled some more, clutching his thigh to keep her balance. "You said you wouldn't mate me against my will."

"I promise."

She frowned, her gaze still unfocused. "I know you wouldn't rape me, Sam. Duh. But let's be honest. You are you."

Well. That was intriguing. He skimmed his fingertips down her neck, feeling the blood rushing through her veins. "Meaning?"

She blinked. "Meaning that you take advantage of situations when you decide it's necessary. What if you decide it's necessary to mate me? You're very charming, and you kiss like a god. After what happened earlier, you know I want you. So much that it's kind of terrifying. You don't know what it feels like to have the best orgasm ever up against a tree."

He coughed out whiskey. "That was your best orgasm ever?"

She threw out her hands, nearly dislodging his glass. "Yes. Can you believe that?"

"No." That was just sad. He'd needed to remedy this situation. If his cock could nod, it would have right then. He shook his head. Life had gotten too weird, but he was enjoying this moment of relaxing with her. He never let his guard down—he had to get a grip. Maybe one night with her would give him perspective. Or a permanent hard-on for her for life. Who knew? "I bet I can do better."

She swung a leg over his and set her sweet ass right on his groin.

Fire crackled down his arms, and he quickly squelched it.

"Cool." She planted her hands on his shoulders and leaned in to press her lips against his. "I would like to do that again. But no mating. No matter what. You have to promise me."

"I can't." He spoke against her mouth and then kissed her, going as slow and gentle as he could with her on his pulsing cock.

She drew back. "I knew it."

He wouldn't make a promise he might not be able to keep. She'd read him right. Damn, she was smart.

She squinted as if having trouble making him out. "Okay. Then let's make a deal. Promise me that no matter what happens between us tonight, you will not mate me tonight."

That he could do. "Sure."

Her lopsided and tipsy smile was the cutest sight he'd ever seen. "All right." She leaned down to kiss him again.

He tangled his fingers in her hair, drawing her head back. Her soft gasp of surprise and need nearly undid him. "Not tonight, baby."

Her mouth turned down. "Excuse me?" She sounded haughty in her drunkenness.

Yeah, the gods were trying to kill him. Or torture him at the very least—and he'd spent hundreds of years being tortured in dimensions where time moved differently than it did here. This wasn't fair. Her curvy body was ripe for the taking, and she was more than willing. "You're drunk and exhausted, gorgeous." It hurt to say the words. "We need sleep, and you need all your faculties. If you wake up sober and still want me, reach over and say so." With his luck, she'd wake up and want to make a run for it. *Another* run for it.

"Boo," she said, surprising him.

He laughed, for the first time relaxing even though his balls felt like they were rapidly turning a horrific shade of blue. "You're killing me, Honor."

Her smile was sweet. "Well, that's something, then."

Chapter Fifteen

Honor stretched awake, her lower back protesting from the long ride the day before. She turned her head in the sleeping bag to see Sam's bag empty, an indentation still on his pillow. Rolling onto her back, she took stock. Besides the slight backache, she felt fine. Her head was okay despite all the alcohol. Maybe the good stuff didn't cause hangovers.

Memories of the night filtered through her brain. She'd thrown herself at the huge hybrid, and he'd been a gentleman. She sighed.

The sounds of life could be heard through the tent. Somebody laughing, a grill firing up, motorcycles roaring in the distance.

She definitely needed to use the facilities. She'd slept in her shirt, but she needed to retrieve her jeans and then go shopping. Drawing them on, she unzipped the tent, poking her head outside to see a nice fall day.

Juliet spotted her from a few yards away and made a beeline with a cosmetic bag in her hand. "Hey. I was going to hit the showers. Want to come?"

"Yes." Honor pushed out of the tent, stood, and stretched. Her stomach growled, and she noted Nessa beneath a wide blue tarp manning several grills at once and issuing orders to the prospects around her to get a move on. First a shower, and then she'd see what she could do to help. "You're a godsend," she said to Juliet.

Juliet laughed and pointed toward a trail between a couple of leafy trees. "The bathrooms and showers are this way. Then we can eat breakfast and hit that mall. I need some new tennis shoes and you need everything else." She nudged Honor. "Even though you're here willingly, it was a surprise, right?"

"Yep." Honor slipped on her boots and headed for the trail, crunching leaves as she went. "I don't suppose you have an extra toothbrush in there?"

"I actually do." Juliet tripped along behind her. "I bought a bunch of travel items for this trip, and there are two toothbrushes folded up in the kit."

A sprawling pond lay to the right where several people were swimming and goofing off, shouting from the cold. It was way too chilly for the pond, so Honor didn't even consider it. Crazy people. She hurried toward a large wooden building, smiled at a couple of other women coming out, and hurried inside to use the restroom before washing her hands and returning outside to Juliet. "Thanks for waiting." She smiled at the young woman, noting tension coming from her. "What's wrong?"

"Nothing." Her eyes said otherwise. "The showers are over here."

Honor grasped her arm. "Juliet."

The woman rolled her eyes. "I don't know. Garrett is fun and wild, but it felt like he was... I don't know, disappointed this morning. Like..." She lifted her hands helplessly.

Like he was looking for an immortal mate and couldn't see what a great woman he had in front of him? Honor sighed. "These guys are way too tense—I wouldn't take it personally. For now, let's shower and then we can go pummel him with rocks or something."

Juliet grinned. "Good plan." She led the way to a shower area with separate and surprisingly nice stalls.

They showered, handing the shampoo and conditioner over the top. Then they moved to the sink area for teeth and then the mirror area, where Honor borrowed eyeshadow and some lip balm. Juliet's base was too light and her blush the wrong color, but Honor didn't use much makeup, anyway. She added a little product to her hair. "I really appreciate this."

Juliet's stomach growled. "I'm starving. Garrett didn't let me get much sleep last night." Pink colored her cheekbones. "Maybe he does like me and I'm just looking for problems where there aren't any."

"Sure." Honor led the way out and stopped short at the sight of Sam emerging from the pond, water sluicing over his hard body. "Oh. My. God." Heat slammed into her abdomen so fast she nearly doubled over.

Juliet giggled. "Guess he skipped the showers and jumped into the pond? At least he's wearing swim trunks."

Yeah. They were black and molded to his body the way Honor had wanted to be the night before. His torso was sculpted steel, his abs were solid rock ridges, and even his thighs looked powerful. Water slicked his black hair back from his angled face, and in the soft morning light, his eyes held the mysterious depths of genuine emeralds. The darker ones.

Right now, they were fully focused on her.

Juliet gasped. "All right. Well, I'll meet you at the picnic area," she whispered. Then she turned and hurried toward the trail.

Honor swallowed over the lump in her throat and moved toward him, her legs working independently of her brain. She soon reached him. "Morning."

"Morning. How are you feeling?" The tension rolling from him stole her breath.

Aroused. Horny. So achy in her tender parts that she was going to get a stomachache. "Good. No hangover. How are you, um, feeling?"

He just stared at her. Then he moved. One second she was on her feet and the next up in the air and secured against his front, her thighs naturally clamping onto his hips for balance. He kissed her, hard and deep, not holding anything back. Diving in, he deepened the kiss, tasting of coffee and butterscotch. Heated thrills coursed beneath her skin, and she returned the kiss, for once not caring who was around. He set loose a part of her she hadn't realized existed.

While his mouth worked her, his strong body carried them away from the pond. His skin was wet against her, and droplets of water plopped from his hair onto her face.

They reached the tent and he bent, carrying her inside and zipping it up. Then he just looked at her.

She panted, on her back, so much need filling her she couldn't breathe. Slowly, he settled one knee to her side and flattened his hands over her stomach. Which was so *not* close to being flat like his. "Sam, I—"

"You're perfect." He slid those broad and way too heated hands up and over her breasts, his eyes shooting silver through the green again.

Shouting came from outside the tent from what sounded like a boisterous game of tag.

She paused, mesmerized by the sight as well as the feel of his palms against her. Just lying on her, gently placed, they nevertheless held weight. Power. He definitely had it. As if appeasing himself, just playing, he slowly curled his fingers around both breasts, filling his palms.

The sound he gave was a growl...a dangerous one.

Laughter pealed outside from the area of the grills. She jumped. "Sam. Everyone will know."

"I don't give a fuck." He tightened his hold, shooting sparks of desperate, erotic need to her core. He paused, looking up at her face. "Do you?" A wet lock of hair fell onto his forehead, doing nothing to tame the harsh angles of his indomitable face.

"No," she whispered, telling the truth. She was way too far gone.

"Good." He straddled her, releasing her breast after a quick squeeze that had her seeing stars. "You gonna be mine today, Honor?"

"Yeah." Even her breath felt hot.

"Yeah," he repeated, his hands going to the button on her jeans. He whipped them out of the way along with her panties, working her shirt and bra so quickly, she was naked before she knew it. "You about killed me last night." Leaning over, he sucked a nipple into his mouth, hard and fast.

She cried out, trembling. He was killing her right now, and he'd just gotten started. She scraped her palms up his chest, pressing hard to feel the strength. He sucked harder, and a quaking started just inside her.

"No." He released her. "Oh, you're earning this one." The dark tone shivered over her, nearly impelling her body to disobey him.

She cupped the side of his neck, feeling energy. Raw, untamed, dangerous energy flowed from him. Tingles clawed through her, heated and demanding.

He kissed her, taking whatever he wanted. She held him tight, wanting more. Wanting everything. His taste, his energy, his strength. All of it. "Sam?" This was beyond her experience, and a small part of her tried to find reason. Sanity.

"All right. Just one." With those four little words, he slipped a finger inside her, twisted his hand, and rocketed her off the sleeping bag.

The orgasm blew threw her with the force of a charging animal, creating rippling waves that only hinted at the storm to come. She quieted, her eyes wide. "How do you do that?"

"It's you." He nipped her ear, not so gently.

Man, she loved that. "No. It's you."

He removed his finger, leaving her empty. "Maybe it's us."

The ache inside her pulsed to her clit, forcing her to move against him. "Enough foreplay?" Never in her life had she needed anything so much as she did him inside her. She cupped him through the swim trunks, and damn if her hand didn't get hot. He was big and ready to go. "Sam." It was more of a plea than a demand.

He vibrated against her, and a feminine power she'd never experienced filled her. Quick moments later, the trunks were across the tent and he was levering himself above her, slowly penetrating her. His gaze remained on hers, the silver fanning out through the green and circling it. She'd never seen anything like it. "I—"

"Just feel, baby." He took his time, his penetration unrelenting but slow.

She moaned from the delicious pleasure. "Wait. We didn't use—"

He nipped her nose. "Immortal. Don't have anything, can't give you anything, and only mates can procreate." He licked her mouth until she opened for him, and then he dove in, kissing her hard. She reacted instantly, digging her nails into his shoulders, arching against him.

The second she did, he shoved all the way inside her.

She cried out, into his mouth. Then she panted, her body shaking. With shock...and need. He was freaking huge, and her body had to adjust. A lot.

Tension rolled from him, around them, but he paused. Waited for her. Then he lowered his head again to possess her mouth, taking her out of the moment. Letting pain move to pleasure. So much pleasure, and she wanted more. She *needed* more. So she bit him. Hard.

He cocked his head, and his eyes darkened. "Be careful."

She didn't want careful. Or gentle. Or him being the way he would with any breakable human. She wanted *him*. He didn't get to hold back now. So she tilted up, taking more of him while digging her nails into his hard flesh.

"Don't," he growled, the sound vibrating between them.

"Do," she countered, clenching her internal muscles around him. "Too late, Sam," she whispered. "You can't hold back."

The muscles in his arms bulged as he held his weight off her and leaned down, his nose nearly touching hers. His eyes had flashed all silver, burnt with dark edges. "You're human. Let me control the pace so you don't get hurt."

"Forget that," she whispered right back, moving her hips in a tiny circular motion. Did his eyes roll back in his head?

"Last chance, little human," he growled against her, his arms seizing on either side of her. "I mean it. One more move like that, and I'll fuck you until you can't walk for a week. Losing control will be absolute. I'll make you beg, baby. I promise. Give me a damn second and then we'll do this right and easy."

A spasm of raw sexual electricity zipped through her. She didn't want easy or right. The compulsion was more than physical, and what they could reach would be beyond her imagination. She knew it. "Oh yeah?" she whispered, catching back a moan. "You beg. *Baby*." Then she clenched hard, twisted her hips, and slashed her nails into his chest.

He sucked in air. The atmosphere stilled.

Oops. Lesson one. Don't challenge the immortal.

He growled, ripped his cock out of her, and flipped her onto her stomach. She gasped just as he forced her onto all fours and yanked her head back by the hair. "You're gonna scream," he said, shoving inside her with one hard push.

The game outside got louder, and it sounded like somebody plowed into a tree.

She arched her back and sucked in air, overcome. Then he started to pound. Hard and fast and wilder than any thought, he hammered into her, only one strong hand on her hip keeping her from careening right thorough the tent material. Live wires uncoiled inside her, and she flew away, the world sheeting white.

The orgasm stole her breath, and she came down, whimpering.

The hand in her hair twisted, turning her head so his mouth could bite her earlobe. "Not loud enough. Again." His voice was a raw growl, and he hadn't paused a bit. If anything, he powered even harder into her, taking all of her.

The second orgasm rushed in with an edge of pain. Just an edge that she rode until her body softened.

Somehow taking even more of him.

"Better," he whispered, his heated breath at her ear. "Not quite, though."

She whimpered.

He chuckled. "Nope. Not enough." Releasing her hair, he grabbed both of her hips, partially lifting her and changing his angle. She cried out.

"There we go," he panted, pistoning deeper inside her, his hands controlling them both. He went for so long, she could only try to breathe, and then she was climbing again. Fire, heat, lightning all combusted inside her, and she fought it, frightened of the edge that was so close.

"Now. You go now," he ordered, lifting her even more.

She exploded, screaming his name. Ecstasy surged over her, through her, inside her. She spasmed wildly, her fingers clutching the sleeping bag. The wild waves seemed to last forever. Finally, tears flew down her face and she went limp, blinking rapidly. He dropped her down to all fours, bent over her, and pressed his face to her jaw, jerking with his own release.

Silence descended. He let her go flat and limp on the sleeping bag, withdrew from her body, and settled at her side. Then he brought one hand down on her ass. Hard. "Don't challenge me."

Against all rational thought, she burst out laughing.

Chapter Sixteen

Sam accepted a beer from Nessa and stared bemused at the five trees that had caught fire while he'd had sex with Honor in the tent, having no clue they were blowing things up around them. "Sorry about that."

Nessa shook her head. "We managed to take care of it, but when we go to the store later, we need more fire extinguishers."

Huh. Sam shook his head. "I didn't even realize we'd done that."

"You were busy," Nessa said wryly.

Sam would not blush.

A German shepherd barked once and ran full on for him, snagging his beer bottle and running behind Nessa. He watched, bemused.

"Roscoe, damn it," a British human male yelled, stomping toward the food tent.

Sam pivoted to cover Nessa.

"Get out here now," the Brit barked as the dog emerged and tossed the empty bottle at Sam's feet.

Sam shook his head. "Your dog drank my beer."

"Sorry about that, chap," the British guy said, looking tough and sleek in dark jeans and an even darker jacket. "I'm only watching him for a friend and we're on a bit of a hunt. We just stopped at the park so he could relieve himself, and he caught wind of the beer. Bastard has a problem."

The dog wagged his tail happily.

The Brit glanced at the smoldering trees. "I have a fire extinguisher in my car if you need it."

"We're fine, but thank you," Nessa said, smiling at the dog. "Don't worry about the beer. He's a special one."

"You have no idea. Sorry about the beer." The Brit turned and loped toward the parking area as the dog cheerfully followed.

Sam accepted a second beer from Nessa. "Cute dog," he said. He took a deep drink and then caught sight of Garrett scowling at a couple of prospects, who were horsing around near a dartboard stuck to a tree. "Ah, shit."

Nessa tilted her head to look beyond him. "Here we go again. Take care of it, would you?" The witch might have been half his size, but she had no problem issuing orders when she wanted.

"Maybe they all want to fight," he offered.

She looked up at him, her eyes narrowing. Her very blue eyes with a hint of fire in them. "Samuel, you know I can throw as well as quench fire these days, right?"

When a century-old witch used your full name, you listened. Even if said witch was tiny with a pert nose. "Yeah. Okay." He glanced over his shoulder at his tent, which was still zipped nicely up.

Nessa snorted. "Anybody could cause fires. She's still in hiding?"

He grinned. "I took her a sandwich for lunch, but she has to be getting hot in there. I think it's more the decibels than the fires." Although the fall weather was pretty mild.

"I'll take care of it. We're supposed to go shopping in an hour, and I know she needs clothing," Nessa said. "Go handle Garrett. I'm not in the mood to see blood today."

Fair enough. He snagged another beer and strode over the uneven ground while keeping an ear open to the other camps. A club called Psychos was having problems, if the sound of fists hitting faces was any indication. The human club was at the far side of the party park, so he wasn't going to worry about it yet. If ever. Probably never. He reached Garrett and handed over the sweating beer bottle. "Nessa says no blood today."

Garrett accepted the brew. "Come on."

"Nope. Walk with me."

Garrett turned away from the other two and strode by Sam's side toward the thick trees. "Fine. Has Honor come out of the tent yet?"

"No," Sam said, but if he knew Nessa, Honor would be out soon.

"The female has some lungs on her," Garrett observed.

Sam tipped his bottle and drank half of the contents. "I might've gotten carried away."

"You nearly started a forest fire." Garrett chuckled. "I like her. She's smart."

That she was. It was rare for Garrett to comment on Sam's choice of a date. "Where's your date, G?"

Garrett glanced back at his tent. "She's taking a nap. I might've kept her up too late last night." He rubbed a hand through his thick hair, for the moment looking just like his father. Cranky. "Do you like her?"

Sam paused. "Um, yeah. I mean, I haven't had a chance to really talk to her, but she seems nice. She's a vet, which means she likes animals and that she's smart. The question is whether or not you like her."

"I do." Garrett looked down at his right hand and flipped it over to reveal his calloused palm. "No marking, though."

Through the years, Sam had exhausted himself talking about the dreams, whether they were real or not, and whether Garrett was trying too hard to find a mate. The woman might not even be born yet. Garrett was young, still had centuries to mate. So Sam just finished his beer.

Garrett paused near a tree and drank his beer in two gulps. He turned to survey the area. "You feel them?"

"Yep." Sam had clocked the two lions tracking them the second they'd moved toward the forest. "One's a female."

Garrett angled toward the forest. "They're probably just curious. The Seven is such a mystery to everyone, and even we don't know all of the details." He tugged on his dark shirt just as Nessa apparently coaxed Honor from the tent across the way. He chortled. "I have never seen a woman blush that hard. Man. That's gotta hurt."

Sam turned and barely kept from laughing. He should feel bad, but his body felt too good. It was the best he'd felt in years, and it wasn't as if he hadn't warned her. Plus, they were in the middle of an MC ride for adults only. He could hear several couples going at it right now from different directions.

"The throes of ecstasy notwithstanding, you're more relaxed than you've been in years," Garrett observed. "It's hard to put my finger on it, but it feels like her energy balances yours, when you're not blowing things up?"

Sam nodded, watching Honor move with Nessa toward a blanket set beneath a tree over by the grill and food supplies. "Yeah. Except when we're both lost during, well, sex, she can balance out the fire and flames for me and tension for others. She's a good lie detector, it seems." When Honor sat down, Nessa all but forced a bottle of prosecco into her hand.

"You keeping her?" Garrett asked.

"No." Sam straightened and forced himself to pay closer attention to the lion shifters slinking around in the forest. "Final battle, danger, the Seven, and all of that mess."

Garrett ducked his head. "The Seven are supposed to sacrifice themselves, not you."

"How do you know that?" Sam cut him a look.

Garrett shrugged. "I guess I was hoping. Why haven't you ever told anybody else about the ritual you endured? Just me?"

"Why should I?" Sam asked. "It is what it is, and here I am. It was the only way I could keep Hope, Logan, and you safe."

He'd undergone the ritual to learn how to manage travel between dimensions, and if he was the Keeper, he could prevent the ritual from happening in the first place.

"Destroying the ritual circle won't help," Garrett said wearily. When Sam stiffened, he rolled his eyes. "Please. I know you're a control freak and you think you can just keep us all from having to endure the ritual, but this is bigger than one place, bigger than all of us. You know that, deep down. So why not find happiness when you can?"

Sam shook his head. "If that ritual takes place, we'll all make a sacrifice. That's what I know." Then he started withdrawing from the conversation. "Besides. A mate always comes first. I can't place anyone first right now." With his life? Even if he prevented the ritual, he'd never be able to put a mate first. Fire crackled on his arm. He sighed.

"Looks like your reprieve was temporary," Garrett noted.

"Yep." It wasn't a surprise. The demand of the circle or the dimension it was in or maybe freaking hell was too strong. This was only more proof that Sam shouldn't lock down the sexiest woman he'd ever known.

Honor deserved better.

* * * *

Honor could just die. She leaned against the tree and drank the champagne split, cooling her heated body.

Nessa quietly handed her another one. "You really have to relax. So you were having a good time. Who cares?"

Honor looked at the woman. "We started the place on fire." Nessa had long black hair, unique blue eyes, and a peaches and cream complexion. As well as the slightest Irish brogue. "Sam is very good in bed."

Nessa burst out laughing, and the sound was musical. "One would hope so, considering your reaction." Today she wore a light blue sweater over jeans and kick-ass black boots. Her hands settled in her lap. The neck of the sweater slid to one side, revealing a huge, healed bite mark. Only part of one. Was the other part on the other side of her shoulder?

"What bit you?" Honor whispered.

"A bear." Nessa grinned. "So. Sam says that your skills are in reading people, looking for lies, and finding a person's essence."

Honor sipped the second bottle, eyeing the pretty woman. "I guess. I mean, I'm learning rapidly what I can do, but it's mainly with him. With other people, I've kind of been able to tap into the patterns of their brain waves, which has helped to find knots or bumps in the waves, which has indicated untruthfulness before. It's harder to read you immortals. Why do you ask?"

Nessa cleared her throat. "Read me."

Honor pursed her lips. What a wonderful opportunity. She settled in, just like she would with a human. "Okay. I'm going to ask you questions. Give me a couple of truths and then a lie."

Nessa grinned. "Fun."

"What's your favorite color?"

"The green of Ireland," Nessa said softly.

The tapestry of Nessa's brain waves remained smooth and well spun. Truth. Honor tilted her head. "How old are you?"

"One hundred and twenty-five," Nessa said.

Honor blinked. That was another truth. Holy crap. "That's awesome." She ran through possible questions. "Okay. Why does Bear have a dragon tattooed on his back? Right in the center of the animal is a cool Celtic knot. What does it all mean?" She'd seen the entire thing earlier when he'd jumped into the pond.

"He had a stuffed dragon as a kid," Nessa said.

Honor studied her. Wide eyes, soft tone, but the oddest vibration about her lips. The tapestry of brain waves unraveled a little in the middle and then stitched back together. "That was the lie." She delved deeper, somewhat surprised when Nessa let her. Subtly, Honor glided into her mind. "You feel that?"

"Aye."

"Can you shut me out?" Not that Honor could read minds or anything, but still, she was in there.

Nessa smiled. "Yes. I could make it hurt, too. But I won't."

This was so freaking weird. But kind of fun, too. "What do you want, Nessa?"

"Keep reading me. I want to know what you find," Nessa said, her eyes sparkling.

Honor followed the vibrations of that thought, surprised when her focus slid down the witch's body to her abdomen. Maybe a little lower. The essence there hit her full force. "Oh my."

Nessa leaned toward her. "What did you get?"

Honor moved closer. "You're pregnant?" she whispered. "I can sense an essence, and it's different from yours. Separate but very close by?"

"Yes." Nessa grasped her hand. "Here's the deal. Immortals have shields that keep us from using ultrasound or anything like that. I already feel health from my womb, so I'm not worried about that. I'm not worried at all, but I'd love to know what I'm dealing with. A shifter or a witch? Boy or girl? Just give me a clue here. I'm going out of my mind with curiosity—I just want to know something about him or her. Just a little something." She kept her voice low and soft.

Delight filled Honor. What a fun task. "Does Bear know?"

"Not yet, but he will soon. He'll be able to scent the baby, so I probably only have a couple more days of, well, this." She gestured around the clearing.

Honor frowned. "What do you mean? Is there some weird ritual with immortal babies that you have to be on bed rest or something?"

Nessa laughed, the sound happy and free. "No. No weird ritual. I'm just mated to an overprotective bear who'll go into full lockdown protection mode the second he finds out. I love him, but he can be a pain sometimes. My people have fought wars while pregnant, but he won't pay any attention to that." She pursed her lips. "Although I would like to remodel my office, and he'll go along with anything that keeps me out of the field and happy. So there's that." She grinned, happiness all but flowing from her.

"Okay." Honor kept hold of her hand. "Explain this a little to me. You asked if the baby would be a shifter or a witch, but shouldn't he or she be both?"

"Kind of," Nessa said, stretching out her legs and crossing her ankles in those incredible boots. "With immortal species, we exhibit one true nature. Like with Sam. He's part vampire and part demon, but in his case, he's much more of a demon. Not that it matters, but each nature has different skills and gifts, and I'm so anxious to know this little one. So excited. It's actually difficult for immortals to become pregnant, and it can take centuries. I'm thrilled."

Honor kept her hand, her heart warming for her new friend. "Okay. I can't guarantee anything, but I'll sure give it a shot." She leaned her head back on the tree and closed her eyes, centering herself with a couple of deep breaths. Then, feeling slightly like a dork but still having fun, she reached out with her senses to Nessa's abdomen.

A fluttering sensation tickled her senses. She gasped. "Oh, this is awesome." Why hadn't she ever thought to try this before?

"What?" Nessa asked, her hand flipping around to hold Honor's.

"Just the little one in there. Okay. Let me concentrate." She kept zeroing in, making sure she stayed just outside of the little bubble she perceived and didn't cause any disturbance. "All right. I'm getting an energy...let me think." She let the energy flow along with hers and tried to think back over the last few days. "Just like...you but a little more energetic. Maybe softer?"

Nessa sighed happily. "A witch? A little baby girl?"

"I think so." Honor kept her eyes shut and moved her focus around; then she stiffened. "Oh. Um, okay."

"What?" Nessa's voice rose.

Honor settled. "Another energy. This one all bear. Just like him. Full on, erratic, powerful. The girl is powerful, too, but this is more…basic. Both pure. Oh, it's a boy."

Nessa chuckled. "Figures. Twins are rare, but witches do have them every once in a while."

Something, a sense of something else, pulled Honor deeper in. She breathed out, her brain fuzzing.

Nessa tightened her hold on Honor's hand. "You went still. What's going on? What's wrong?"

Honor tilted her head and focused on the swirling essences as they combined and then separated and then moved together again. Her eyelids flipped open to see Nessa staring at her, worry in her sapphire-colored eyes. "Um, how about triplets?"

Nessa's jaw dropped. "What? No. That's so rare."

"Huh. Well, you've got three very distinct essences in there, Nessa." Honor chewed on her lip. "I didn't recognize the third. He's kind of like Bear but different. Sharper and way more intense? He runs hotter, too?"

Nessa released her. "Come on." Then she grinned. "I can't believe it. Triplets. A bear shifter, a witch, and a dragon shifter?" She laughed full on. "Life is crazy, right?"

"A dragon shifter?"

Nessa smiled. "Bear has dragon blood but is definitely a bear shifter. That's why he has a dragon tattooed on his back. Oh, he is so going to freak."

Truth.

Chapter Seventeen

Sam lounged against the wall and answered texts at the interior entrance to a department store inside the mall. Garrett had been waiting impatiently with him until Sam had sent him over to the hotdog place to grab some food, and Bear was studying a series of tennis shoes through a shop window with a bag full of new fire extinguishers at his feet.

Juliet emerged from behind a display of sweaters just inside the store. "We're almost done. Sorry about the wait. We found the cutest sweaters for Honor—you're going to love them."

"Great," Sam said, digging out his wallet and tossing a card to her. "Use this, would you? It's not Honor's fault she's in the middle of nowhere and needs clothing." He would've given the card to Honor, but there was no doubt she would've refused. Heat spread through his arms, and he calmed himself, fighting the fire.

Juliet caught the Amex black card and whistled. "Sweet." Then she turned and hustled through the throngs of winter sweaters.

His phone rang, and upon seeing it was his sister, he answered. "Hi. What's going on?"

"I've so totally had it," Clarissa exploded. "I'm sixteen, Sam. That's practically an adult. Dad is all over me about Bobby, and he's not so bad."

Sam's foot felt as if it was on fire, so he sent healing cells to his toes. "That doesn't sound like Daire. He's usually pretty reasonable. What happened?" He could almost see her rolling her pretty green eyes.

"Like Dad never got drunk and drove a car into a tree. Geez. Come on. We're kids. Bobby is really sorry for it."

Sam straightened. "Were you in the car?"

Silence.

Ah, damn it. "Sweetheart, I've got a lot going on right now."

She sighed. "I know, but you're always the voice of reason, and I need your help. They've totally grounded me. It's not like we were having sex or anything."

Sam winced and tried not to heave. "I wasn't saying that I wouldn't help you, just that my time is limited and I have to cut right to it."

"Oh. Okay. What does that mean?" she asked, sounding so young that he wanted to hug her.

"It means that if you're still dating Bobby when I get home, I'm going to rip off his head and use it as a projectile to kill all of the bees' nests Mom missed," he said reasonably.

Her gasp was a cute mixture of shock and anger. "Sam!"

"Rissa, the guy was drunk and drove a car into a tree...With. You. In. It." Sam looked up to check Garrett's progress with the food. "If you ask me, he's lucky to still be breathing. How did Mom keep Daire from killing him?" Or for that matter, their mother from killing him. Their mom was probably twice as dangerous as anybody he'd ever met.

"Dad is out of town right now, but he's still bossing everyone around by phone," Clarissa admitted. "Mom thinks I'll come to the right conclusion on my own, whatever that means."

Sam shook his head. "Do you care about Bobby?"

"Yes!"

"Then tell him to leave town. It might be brave to date a girl who has a witch enforcer for a dad and a demoness for a mom, not to mention three hybrid older brothers who've been in war before, but to put that girl in danger? That shows a serious lack of mental capability. Get. Rid. Of. Him." Sam's other foot started to burn. "Or I will. Gotta go, sweets. Love you." He hung up.

Honor, Juliet, and Nessa came out of the store, all carrying a multitude of shopping bags.

Bear moved away from the shoes, and Garrett returned with a couple of food bags in his hands.

Honor marched up to Sam and handed over his credit card. "I can buy my own clothing. But thanks." Her sweet smile softened the rebuke.

"We done?" Bear asked, the frown on his rugged face suggesting that they were done.

Nessa nodded. "Juliet is getting a migraine, so we need to go back."

Juliet had paled a little. "My medicine is back in the tent. I'm sorry about this."

"Let's go." Bear took the packages from Nessa. "Buy anything fun?"

The witch cocked him with her hip. "You'll have to see later."

Sam reached for Honor's bags, but she drew them away. "I've got them." Hmm. Independent little thing, wasn't she?

Juliet put her hand to her forehead. "Oh, crap." She blinked several times. "Do you guys mind if we pop into the pharmacy? I saw one at the back of the mall. I need something now."

Garrett handed the food sacks to Sam and took her shopping bags, sliding an arm over her shoulders. "No problem. Come on—there's a shortcut right here."

Honor walked beside Sam and winced.

"You okay?" he asked, fighting the urge to take her bags.

"Yes," she replied.

He looked down at her hand. "What the hell?" Slight burn marks marred her thumb and wrist.

She winced and leaned toward him to whisper, "I don't know. The fire has returned, and I'm not sure why. You?"

"Same." Irritation clawed at him. Had having sex just opened the floodgates for the fire and the dimensions? They had to figure this out before she really was harmed. "Let's get some ointment at the pharmacy." Garrett and Juliet walked outside, and Sam held the door open for everyone before following.

In a second, he realized his mistake.

They were in the back area of the mall with a truck and trailer in front of them. Warning zinged through the air. "Take cover." Sam grabbed Honor and yanked her behind him just as twin squads of Kurjan soldiers came around the trailer from each end, all armed with deadly weapons pointed at the group. Twelve against four, and Bear was already pushing Nessa behind him, growling furiously.

Twelve against three.

The passenger side door of the truck opened, and a Cyst general emerged. He smiled, showing sharp-as-razor canines. "Afternoon." His gaze encompassed the entire group. "Now would be a good time, Juliet."

Sam partially turned to see Juliet holding a glowing green gun against Garrett's neck.

Well, shit.

* * * *

Honor's body shook uncontrollably, and a cold sweat broke out over her skin. Her hands felt numb. What were these people? The two squads wore military-style clothing with silver medals and many weapons, but she'd never seen anything like them. Most had black hair tipped with red, while others had red hair tipped with black. But their faces. Stark white with purple or red eyes. She forced herself to deal with reality and not pretend this wasn't happening. How could they be real? They were all nearly seven feet tall and looked impressively fit. Horrifyingly dangerous.

In the midst of this terrifying horde, their obvious leader stood out. He was bigger and broader than the others, and one strip of white hair bisected his scalp in a braid that extended down his back. His eyes were a light purple tinged with red rims. There was no doubt he was in charge.

Slowly, Honor turned her head to look at Juliet with the weird-looking green gun pressed up against Garrett's neck.

She couldn't move. Terror caught her hard as tension hit her from every direction.

"What's the plan here?" Sam asked, almost casually.

The white-haired guy flashed yellowish teeth with sharp fangs. "We want the Kayrs. That's it. We go, no fight, you all live."

Garrett smiled. "Sure. Sounds like fun. I'd love to vacation with the Kurjans and Cysts."

"No," Sam said. "Not happening...General."

So the medals were some sort of military designation. The general didn't seem put out by the denial. Instead, his shoulders went back. Then his head tilted. His sharp gaze shot right to her. He inhaled.

Sam growled.

The general's chest filled. "What do we have here?"

Honor fought the desperate urge to run.

"My, but she's a strong one. I apologize and must implement a new plan. I want the Kayrs *and* the Enhanced female. We're making a collection of them, you know," the general said.

Honor shuddered.

"Garrett?" Sam said calmly.

"Yep," Garrett answered.

Then Sam partially turned, looked at Juliet, and smiled.

The woman's eyes widened, and she screamed, dropping the gun to grab her head and fall to the asphalt. Before Sam could take advantage, two soldiers jumped onto the trailer from the other side, shooting arrows. The arrows rapidly flew through the air, slicing through Bear's neck as he began to charge. Blood spurted in every direction, and he dropped to the ground.

Nessa screamed, the sound full of fury and pain. Fire hovered over her arms, pulsing and waving in different colors. Her hair blew back as her chin lowered, and she threw balls of plasma so quickly they looked attached to each other.

At the same time, Garrett and Sam rushed forward, knives and fists slashing.

Honor slid to the side, grabbed Juliet's discarded gun, and rolled to her feet, firing at the soldiers up on the trailer. They seemed to be the biggest threat right now. One fell off the other side, and she set her stance, continuing to fire at the other one. Every time she squeezed the trigger, a line of laser flew out, somehow turning solid as it struck the soldier's body.

He jerked with every hit but didn't fall.

She twisted to the side and changed her angle, aiming for his eyes instead of center mass. She hit him right between, and he finally went over the other side.

Then she backed up, trying to cover both Nessa and Bear.

"Go to the right," Nessa yelled at her mate. "You're hurt. You have to shift."

His head hung down, showing gaps in his trachea. His growl was furious as he turned to lumber down the side of the building.

Honor's stomach lurched, and she ran toward him, providing cover so he could escape. Garrett was battling three soldiers, Sam four, including the general, while she and Nessa attacked the others with a volley of fire and lasers.

Two soldiers darted forward and picked Juliet up off the concrete. Blood flowed from her ears and eyes, and she kept screaming a high-pitched wail of raw pain. What had Sam done to her? They carried her away from the melee and around the trailer. An engine ignited, and then they were gone.

The air shimmered. The earth stilled. Many yards away, Bear shifted from human to grizzly. A blast of power flew toward them, and Honor instinctively ducked. It still slammed into her, sending her senses reeling.

He lifted to his full height, his neck still injured, roaring with a raw fury that sent spikes of terror through Honor. She sidestepped closer to Nessa, carefully firing at the enemy while avoiding Sam and Garrett, who fought wildly with movements too fast to track. It seemed everyone had guns but were choosing knives. She apparently couldn't kill with the gun, but she could maim.

Nessa nailed one soldier full on in the face with a spiked plasma ball, and he flew into the trailer, dropping unconscious. A soldier next to him ran forward and tackled her into the wall.

Bear went berserk. He lowered his head and charged, wrapping his powerful jaw around the soldier's neck and snapping his head right off. Growling, huffing, Bear threw the head toward the fighting soldiers.

Honor's legs went weak.

The animal turned into the fray, slashing with sharp claws and cutting with deadly teeth.

Sam flipped a soldier over his shoulder and followed him to the ground, stabbing a sharp blade into his neck. Another soldier rushed him.

Honor dropped into a shooting stance and fired, slowing the guy down.

Sam turned and stared at him. The black-haired guy stopped, and his eyes widened. He clapped both bony hands to his ears and screeched. Sam turned his attention to the next Kurjan, slashing with his knife. He was so fast and so deadly, she barely recognized him.

Two more heads rolled away. Then two more. Soon it was one on one, and Bear was heaving over by the trailer, blood still flowing wildly from his wound.

One of the enemy soldiers retrieved a gun from his pants and turned, firing wildly at Nessa.

"No!" Honor yelled, jumping in front of the pregnant witch. The laser pierced her leg, and pain exploded through her. She cried out, falling hard, blood gushing from her.

The soldier fired again, hitting Nessa several times.

Honor tried to crawl toward her.

Time stopped. Sam turned, looked at her, and then inhaled. He flipped the knife around in his hand, twisted, and stabbed the general in the eye, neck, and groin in a methodical strike that was as cold as ice. He hit the other eye and shoved down, pinning the enemy to the ground. In battle, he was unbeatable. Fierce and cold. Then he ran to her, his eyes wild.

Another two heads rolled.

Garrett followed him, the enemy put down for now. "How bad?"

Sam pressed his hands against her thigh, and she gasped, pain filling her. "Bad. Artery." He studied Nessa. "You?"

Blood flowed from Nessa's wounds, and the witch looked like she was in shock.

Garrett moved for Nessa, easing her back against the brick. "Close your eyes and concentrate on healing." Blood trickled from his jaw, but he ignored it.

Sam unbuckled his belt and wound it around Honor's leg. "This is gonna hurt, sweetheart."

Honor whimpered and instinctively tried to move away, but Sam held her in place. "Nessa? Can you make fire?"

"Yes," the witch ground out, pain wafting from her. Fire traveled down her arms to her hands.

"Only if it doesn't hurt you," Sam whispered, blood flowing from wounds on his face and neck.

Nessa moved forward, her eyes wide, her neck bruised, her eyes dazed. "I'm sorry." Then she pressed the fire to Honor's flesh, cauterizing the wound. For one beat, there was only smoke. And then pain.

Agony ripped through Honor's body, and she stiffened and screamed. Then she passed out.

Cold.

Chapter Eighteen

On the way back home to Grizzly Club territory, Sam's shoulders relaxed slightly as the rest of the Grizzly riders roared up behind him on their bikes. It had taken them an hour to catch up after tearing down the camp, and now he had backup. Okay. He drove the truck that held Garrett and Nessa in the backseat, while Honor lay on the front with her head in his lap. He'd taken off her jeans and boots, covering her with a blanket. She'd been out cold the entire time.

Nessa was stark white and had closed her eyes, going deep to heal herself. It was odd that the witch was having trouble, but maybe she'd taken more bullets than Sam had thought. Garrett watched her carefully while also scanning for enemies outside the window. He visibly relaxed when the motorcycles caught up.

Tingles popped through the cab as they all tried to heal their wounds.

Sam turned his head to see Bear in animal form, winding his way through the trees to one side of the road. He had to stay out of sight and only emerged once in a while. His neck looked raw, and he looked furious, but he couldn't heal himself in human form.

Honor shifted next to him and then awoke with a shocked whimper.

Sam's gut clenched. "Don't move."

Ignoring his order, she turned her head and then gingerly rolled onto her back, pain cascading from her. Heated, sharp, jagged waves of pain.

"As soon as we can, I'll stop and find you a painkiller," he promised.

She looked up at him, her hair spread over his lap and thighs. "Ouch."

He tried to grin for her but failed. Along with anger, pride filtered through him. "You're good in action, sweetheart. Where did you learn to shoot like that?" Man, she'd been impressive.

"With the agency," she murmured. "Even though I was just a consultant, I took any training they offered. Those laser guns?"

"The bullets turn to metal upon impact," he confirmed.

She shivered. Probably from shock.

He turned up the heater.

Garrett leaned forward and looked over the seat at her. "You doing okay?"

"Yeah," she said softly, her voice sounding pained. "Is everyone else all right?"

"Think so," Garrett said.

Honor stiffened. "Nessa? Is she okay? Where is she?"

"Right here," Nessa said wearily, finally opening her eyes. Pain filled them.

Sam stiffened. "Ness? What's going on? Why aren't you healed?"

Honor pushed herself up and wavered on the seat. "The babies?"

A tear slid down Nessa's face. "I don't know. I can't tell."

"Babies?" Sam asked, a boulder dropping into his gut.

"Affirmative," Nessa said, her voice shaking. "Triplets. Bear doesn't know." More tears slid down her smooth cheeks. "I can't feel them. I was shot in the abdomen, and I can't feel them."

Honor reached her hand back. "Let me see. Let me try."

Sam grasped her arm. "What are you doing? Hold still."

"I will." Honor swayed and then turned to kneel on the seat. "Come toward me."

Garrett helped Nessa move forward, his eyes a sizzling, panicked gray.

Honor pressed her hands to Nessa's abdomen and shut her eyes. Sam put one hand to the small of her back to stabilize her, driving with the other hand.

Honor jerked. "Pull over. Right now, Sam."

He released her, grabbed the wheel, and barely made an off-ramp, skidding through the stop sign at the bottom and heading toward a forested area. He quickly parked near a copse of trees as Bear lumbered out, still in bear form. "What's happening?" Sam asked.

"I need to get back there." Honor tried to climb over the seat.

"Whoa." Sam grasped her hips and handed her over to Garrett, who settled her next to Nessa and then stepped out of the truck, guarding the door.

Bear edged closer.

Honor put both hands back on Nessa's abdomen and closed her eyes.

Bear shifted from animal to human, his hair shaggy and blood still flowing from a wound in his neck. "What the fuck is going on?"

Nessa wiped away tears. "Triplets but something is wrong." She looked at Honor. "Can you feel them?"

Honor breathed deep. "Yeah. Two of them are hurt." She angled her head as if listening, and her fingers started to tap on Nessa's stomach. "They're all mixed up, and there is pain." She leaned back, her eyes somber.

Nessa grabbed her arms. "Do something. Please."

Honor straightened, confusion blanketing her features. "Do what? I'm not a medical doctor, Nessa."

Nessa lowered her chin and power flowed through the cab. "No, but you can get in there. You're the only one who can, so help them." Tears slipped from her eyes. "Please, help my babies."

Honor inhaled shakily. "Um, okay." She straightened her shoulders. "All right. We can do this." Gently, she placed her hands back on Nessa's abdomen, thoughts scattering rapidly across her stunning face. "Sam? Did I see you attack Juliet with your brain?" She kept her voice soft.

"Yeah," Sam said, jumping out of the truck and circling around to open Nessa's door. "Why?"

"I need you," Honor said. "Can you go into brains without harming?"

"Yeah." He reached out to hold her shoulder, trying to help her balance. "Tell me what to do."

Honor exhaled, her eyes still shut. "The dragon baby is healthy. He's trying to heal his siblings. I need you to help." She opened her eyes, and they were a supernatural brown. "I can repair what's wrong, and Nessa, you send healing cells. We can do this." Sweat poured down her face.

Sam opened up his mind, and pain instantly slashed into his brain. He accepted it, trying to pull the hurt out of Nessa. Three heartbeats filled his head, one fast and two slow. This was crazy.

"You can do it," Honor whispered. "I feel you. Just give me some of your strength."

Nessa cried harder but closed her eyes. Healing cells all but popped in the air around her.

Bear crowded in, holding on to her knee, careful to stay out of Honor's way.

"There we go," Honor said, turning pale. "We've got the witch. Now just help me slide along her little brain. Don't go in. Just glide."

Sam was accustomed to going full in with his demon mind control, so he sought Honor's essence, found it, and just added power. They eased along.

"Good," Honor whispered. "Now clear a path next to me. Right there."

He gently probed around, and a blast of heat nearly knocked him out of the moment. "Whoa."

"It's the dragon." Honor closed her eyes. "Let him heal the other two. We just have to keep his brain waves strong and intact, while Nessa sends more healing cells."

This was the most amazing thing Sam had ever felt. Three small, fragile lives were fighting so hard. The dragon's essence held unimaginable power for a baby, and he fought relentlessly for his siblings.

"They're getting wound up," Sam said, lacking a better way to put it.

"I know," Honor said quietly. "We have to save them."

Bear reached in and smoothed Nessa's hair off her face. "I can feel them. They're strong."

Too strong. Whatever they were doing to save themselves would have repercussions, but Sam didn't stop. Saving them was all that mattered.

"I have the bear and am calming his essence," Honor mumbled. "He's hurt. His leg." She gasped and opened her eyes to Nessa. "Was that you?"

The witch opened her eyes, which were a pain-filled dark blue. "No."

Honor kept her hands still in place. "I think it was your little witch. She packs a punch. She healed the leg." She blinked several times, her vision clouding. "They were like three little calm lights before. Now they're full-on beacons." Then she fell back, and Bear barely caught her before she slid to the rocky ground.

Sam slowly withdrew from the three little minds.

Nessa looked at him and then at Honor. "They're okay?"

Honor's hand shook when she pushed her hair away from her face. "I think so. They need to rest, as do we. I'll check in on them later."

Bear lifted Honor into the driver's seat, and she scooted toward the other door. Then he jumped into the backseat and lifted Nessa onto his lap. "Triplets?"

The witch set her head at the crook of his neck. "Yeah."

Sam shut their door and crossed to retake the driver's seat as Garrett sat behind him. He quickly drove away from the forested area and caught up to the motorcycles, his head spinning and his body wanting to shut down. Not yet. Not just yet.

Honor scooted over and lay down, setting her head on his thigh and sighing. "Those soldiers. Who? What?"

Oh. Yeah. She didn't know his world. The woman had jumped right in so quickly, he'd forgotten that fact. It was good she wanted to talk. "The white-haired male was a Cyst general. They're the spiritual leaders of the Kurjan nation, our enemies. The other guys were Kurjan soldiers. All immortal and just another species."

She yawned, no doubt exhausted. "Why did they want Garrett?"

Garrett snorted from the backseat. "Could be a bunch of reasons. Now they want you, too."

Anger shot through Sam so quickly his throat heated. His tongue burned. Yeah, Honor was on their radar now. "One thing at a time. Juliet was a plant, which means they might know about your dreams. That you're looking for a mate." His gaze caught Garrett's in the mirror. "Don't get pissed, but did she give any indication?"

Garrett's jaw clenched so hard, it probably gave him a headache. "No. Nothing. I didn't get one hint of subterfuge from her."

Sam looked down at Honor's pretty brown eyes. They were filled with pain at the moment. "What about you?"

"No," she said. "I didn't try, though. We had a couple of conversations, but nothing she'd lie about, so I didn't catch anything. Wasn't looking."

Yeah, neither was Sam. It was good to have something to concentrate on while both Bear and Nessa tried to heal themselves and their little family. "Garrett, you met Juliet when you found an injured fox. That had to be a setup." Which meant the Kurjans were making a move, and they didn't mind doing it in Grizzly territory. They'd also chosen a female who was Garrett's type.

Buxom, smart, and pretty. He'd always liked full-figured women, and Juliet was stunning.

"Now they have human females assisting them?" Nessa asked, pressing a protective hand to her flat belly and not opening her eyes.

"Makes sense," Garrett muttered. "They've been kidnapping Enhanced females for years, and we haven't rescued enough of them. Juliet was probably just trying to survive. She did keep trying to get me to bite her, which I thought was odd, since she supposedly didn't know I was anything but human. I figured it was just one of her kinks."

"Did you?" Sam asked.

Garrett shook his head. "No. Isn't one of my kinks."

The last thing Sam wanted to discuss was his brother's kinks.

"Why do they want Enhanced females?" Honor mumbled.

Protectiveness seized Sam's entire body. "Doesn't matter."

"Sam." She looked up at him.

He didn't want her to worry, but maybe understanding the situation would help her. "Three possible reasons. One, they want mates. Two, they want to duplicate the ritual that caused all of this and create a super immortal, and sacrificing Enhanced females is part of the ritual. Three, they want to enact some plan we can't figure out to end all Enhanced mates. Forever."

Honor's eyelids fluttered shut. "I hate all of those reasons," she mumbled. "Every one of them. That sucks."

Sometimes the woman just nailed it. Sam sped up, noting clouds rolling in from the west. "Agreed."

They drove in silence all the way back up the coast to Grizzly territory, and the woman slept the entire way, save for when he awakened her to eat a quick meal of fast-food burgers. After that, he let her rest, hoping her body could heal itself. Nessa and Bear had healed themselves by the time they ate dinner, but nobody was sure about the babies.

Dusk came and then night before they finally reached home. Sam dropped Garrett off first and then wound through the territory to Bear and Nessa's sprawling log home. He whistled when he saw a figure waiting on the front porch.

Nessa breathed out happily.

The male ran for the truck and opened the back door, pulling Nessa into his arms.

"Flynn!" she cried out, snuggling close. "You're here."

Honor jolted awake. "What's going on?"

Sam sighed. "The dragons have arrived. Just what we need."

* * * *

Bear finally healed the wound in his lower back as Sam turned the truck and drove off with the talented human female. The woman knew how to aim a gun. He grabbed his half brother in a hard hug.

"Dude. Clothes," Flynn protested, hugging him back.

Bear leaned back, his entire body exhausted. "I have jeans on. That's all you get." It was lucky Garrett had had an extra pair in the truck. Bear's neck still ached, but it would heal. "What the hell are you doing here?"

His brother had longish black hair, glittering black eyes, and a sharply delineated bone structure. The guy all but screamed *dragon.*

Flynn eyed Nessa. "Well, I guess to congratulate you? Dragons are so few in the world that we know instantly when a new one is coming. The air shifts around the planet."

"You're so kind to come check on us." Nessa was still too pale. "Can you sense anything?"

"No," Flynn said. "Why?"

She sighed. "Let's go inside. You must be hungry. I know I'm starving." She took Flynn's hand and tugged him up the steps.

"Mate?" Bear said mildly. "I believe we need to have a chat."

Nessa kept tugging Flynn to the door. "We have company, Bear."

"Nessa." He put bite into the tone this time.

Flynn looked over his shoulder, amusement softening his features. "I hope I didn't let the rabbit out of the hat, so to speak."

"Funny," Bear snapped. It was a little-known fact that dragon shifters turned into bunnies at first, when they were kids. "No. I discovered my mate was with child while we were being attacked by a Kurjan squad. Three of them, actually. The news that one is a dragon should please you, Flynn. Figures."

Flynn lost the smile. "Kurjan squad? What's going on?"

"Long story." Bear stomped up the steps and motioned them both inside, where he lifted his tiny yet deadly mate against his chest and then set her gently down on the plush sofa she'd insisted they place near the fireplace.

She settled herself. "The babies were injured, but I feel like they're okay now."

Bear put his hands on his hips. "I couldn't sense them before, and now, they're like cyclones." He was grateful to his soul that they were all alive, but he couldn't help wondering what kind of effect there would be from the healing offered by a powerful demon, a deadly witch, and a way too talented Enhanced human female.

No doubt her sparkling blue eyes saw right through his bluster. "They'll be fine. So long as they're alive, we can handle anything," she said.

Yeah, they could. "Why didn't you tell me?"

She plucked a string on her jeans. A bloody string. Yeah. That was why.

He nodded. "You're right, sweetheart."

She jerked her head up. "I am?" Her smile was too sweet.

"Oh yeah. Because you're locked down now. Completely." It made no sense for him to be the alpha of the entire bear nation and not be able to protect his mate and their children. He didn't give two shits that she was a witch leader who could command a force of thousands. She was his.

She rolled her eyes but apparently knew better than to argue right now with blood on her jeans. Oh, he had no doubt she would later.

Flynn shook his head. "I am never getting mated." He clapped Bear on the shoulder. "If it helps, I'm not getting a sense that anything's wrong."

"It helps," Bear said, his chest finally relaxing.

"Good." Flynn looked around. "I went through the information you sent and have some ideas."

Nessa's dark eyebrows rose. "What information?"

"About whatever's going on with Sam," Bear admitted. "It has to do with fire, and I figured a dragon might have a different take on the situation. I would've explained this to Sam, but I'm sure Honor needed sleep."

Nessa's eyes filled. "I think she saved our babies, Bear."

Everything inside him softened. He plucked Nessa off the sofa, sat his ass down, and settled her on his lap. Holding her. Right where she belonged.

She pressed a hand to his chest and kissed his jaw.

He kept his expression bland, but the soft touch slammed right to his heart. She'd captured it the first moment they'd met, and that hadn't changed through the years. If anything, she'd taken over the rest of his soul. It was fine with him. She could have all of him. "What are your thoughts, Flynn?"

Flynn watched them carefully, an unreadable light in his dark eyes. "If Sam's having trouble with fire, I need to know why and how. A demon-vampire hybrid shouldn't have any fire capabilities. What don't you know about him?"

That was a great question. "There's a good chance he won't reveal the entirety of what's really happening." Bear had always suspected that Sam had something to do with the Seven and their grand plan to hold some stupid ritual and kill a Cyst leader someday, and he didn't like it one bit. "If he doesn't tell me, they're gone." When Nessa started to object, he tightened his hold on her. "No. I've been at the edge of my patience for a while now, and I'm done. I'll explain this to them and then they can decide what to do. Their future is in their control." He wasn't going to let any threat near his mate and unborn babes. Nessa had to know that.

She sighed.

He snuggled her close, inhaling her sweet scent. "So a dragon shifter, huh? Male or female?"

She settled herself against him. "Don't freak out."

Female. He was having a female dragon daughter. His half sister was one, as well as being a witch, and she was as wild as the wind. He tried not to groan.

Nessa chuckled and kissed his neck again. "No. According to Honor, whom I believe, we're having a dragon son."

Huh. A dragon son. It was a good thing Flynn was willing to visit and thus offer flying lessons. "This is fantastic."

"Yeah," she whispered. "I think we're also having a witch daughter and bear son."

Bear studied her lovely face. His heart filled. "That sounds like the perfect trio."

"Yep." She kissed him again. "Things are about to get interesting."

Chapter Nineteen

Sam carried Honor inside with the blanket securely around her and settled her right in bed. Then he leaned down and looked at the burns. "At least the bullet went all the way through."

She studied the raw burn marks. "In movies, vampire blood can heal people."

He grinned. "Yeah." In fact, it wasn't a terrible idea. "Usually my blood would kill a human, but since you're Enhanced with serious power, we could give it a try. A small try." Plus, the fact that they'd had sex and already mixed fluids didn't hurt. His fangs dropped, and he ripped open his wrist. "Take just a little."

She looked at his blood, shrugged, and then licked him like a cat.

His cock nearly burst from his jeans. He forced desire down.

She sat back, her face filling with color. "Oh," she whispered, the sound throaty.

Fire lanced down his arms, and he stepped back, keeping her from the flame. Pain flared beneath his skin. He growled. This was a fucking disaster.

Slowly, the wounds on her leg mended.

His eyebrows rose. "Well. That worked."

Delight filled her eyes along with caution as she looked at his now burned arms. "I feel so much better. The pain is gone."

"Good to know." He slid in beside her. "Let's get some sleep and figure everything out in the morning." He needed to heal his arms as well as a nagging cut on his ankle that still hadn't mended. "Deal?"

"Deal." She snuggled her sweet butt into his groin and almost immediately dropped into sleep.

He held her, comforting himself with her even breathing and heart rate. Too many emotions bombarded him at once as he relived the attack, and he needed to shut it all down. So he concentrated on her breathing, matching his to hers, and soon fell into sleep. Healing cells surrounded him, fixing everything that hurt. For now.

In that moment, he was transported from this world into another one, reliving the ritual he'd endured eighteen years ago. Some of it good, some fascinating, some downright painful. Different dimensions, all unique.

A burst of fire started following him, trying to burn him alive. He'd been here before.

He leaped through portals between dimensions, looking for escape wherever he went. If he could keep moving, he'd be okay. If he stopped, he was dead.

The fire propelled him, and he shot through an ice age, his skin freezing. Flames came for him again, and he turned to the nearest portal, jumping.

The stupid force was herding him.

He paused just as a wide portal opened in front of him, the interior dark. The pull was incredibly powerful. He looked down to see his bare feet skim across a black rock. One with eyes. Surprise jolted him just enough that he let down his guard and went flying into the abyss.

He landed hard on a beach at nighttime. Or maybe daytime wherever he was. He turned his head and coughed out sand, rolling to his feet. Liquid, an insidious black goo, slid up the sand and then receded, just like waves in an ocean. Trees of spiky nails rose around him, and in the distance, something screamed. Two moonlike orbs shone down, one tinged blue and the other orange.

No wind whistled through the trees. The only sound now was the slap of liquid on sand.

Then tension. A crack of the atmosphere. A hint of power that had Sam turning toward a rock cliff farther down the beach. He sharpened his focus and loped into a run, his senses wide open for any danger. Fire flowed along his arms, and in this place, the flames didn't burn. They rode with him, gleefully flaring orange with a deeper blue hue.

He reached the cliffs and looked up. They rose so high he couldn't see where they ended in the night sky. Or the day sky if this was all there was.

The skin at his nape prickled, and he paused, turning toward the vast almost-ocean. A glimmer caught his eye. Something shiny. He stepped closer to the liquid, his toes sinking in the goo.

Mist spread out in front of him, just a few yards from shore. He looked down to see a wide, flat rock floating in the liquid. Shrugging, he stepped gingerly on it, watching the flames brighten on his arms. Huh. He looked around, spotted another rock, and followed the path into the mist. Every time he stepped onto a new rock, the fire brightened, filling him with more power.

Nothing hurt. For the first time in a while, not an inch of his body hurt.

He reached a platform of rock and stepped onto it, walking along its length, going with instinct that he didn't want to fall into the goo. The mist parted, swirling around him without affecting the flames. Now they danced down his legs and wound around his toes, tingling but not burning.

What was this place?

He reached the end of the platform, and the mist cleared. A figure stood on a shoreline about twenty-five yards away across the liquid.

His head went back, and his shoulders straightened. A growl erupted, coming straight from the animal deep inside him. "Ulric," he said, eying the distance between them. If he could just get across the water, he could... What? What could he do? The bastard was immortal, untouchable from the outside. Only the right ritual could destroy him.

Ulric stood with his legs braced, scars covering his ancient face, his white hair glowing in the meager light. Then he cast a look to Sam's right.

Sam slowly followed his gaze, catching sight of another platform, this one holding a tall blonde with stunning light eyes.

Her red lips slowly curved. "Sam Kyllwood. Now that makes sense."

He rocked back. Shit. He'd seen pictures of her. "Yvonne." Ulric's fated mate. His Intended. For now. "This isn't a dream." Damn it to fuck.

Ulric stepped closer to the muck, his body vibrating, his eyes a pure, deep amethyst. "Come closer," he whispered.

So even the Big Bad was afraid of the goo. Good to know. Sam cut a look at Yvonne. "Come here often?"

She smiled and clapped her hands together. "I'm brought in every full moon. The timing is probably a coincidence but maybe not? Anyway, so good to meet you, Kyllwood. You're the Keeper. God, we've wondered. This totally makes sense." The human woman was supposedly a brilliant scientist who'd been with the Kurjans and the Cyst for years, holding herself pure for Ulric's return.

Sam flashed his teeth and hid his anger. Nobody was supposed to know he was the Keeper. "You're getting a little long in the tooth, lady. Who's the next Intended? Has she already been found?" It was a rotten thing to say, but Yvonne had tried to kill more than one of his friends' mates over the years.

Surprisingly, it was Ulric who answered him, his voice deep with ancient power. "The time is coming soon. I feel it. I'm almost free of this prison world, and what a ritual we'll have. Unfortunately, you're not the prophesied Keeper. You won't be there."

"You know, that's the dumbest name I've ever heard," Sam drawled, ignoring the threat. "Keeper? Seriously?"

Flames lit up behind Ulric, somehow glittering in his eyes. Which was impossible, but hey. There it was. "You're a child, Keeper. Such a child."

Age wise, compared to the thousand-plus-year-old immortal, probably. "Yet I'm the one who's going to end you."

Yvonne wore a long white dress with diamonds sparkling everywhere. It hugged her perfect figure and looked mystical and mysterious. Yet her gaze was sharp. "You can't even save yourself, Sam. Have any problems with fire lately?"

Ah, damn it. "Nope. Why?"

She smiled. "The circle is calling to you. Don't you feel it?" She shook her head. "It's only going to get worse, but I can help you. Only me."

"How's that?" Sam kept them both within sight, knowing the female would like nothing better than to slice off his head.

Her voice lowered to a purr. "Find me and find out. Until you do, the fire will burn and the dimensions will drag you between time. Might even tear you apart, and then Fate would have to find another Keeper. Maybe that pretty woman who shot so well earlier today. Saw the video—that was some impressive power."

"She died," Sam said flatly.

Yvonne's tinkly giggle was out of place in the hollowed-out world. "No. Honor McDoval is very much alive. Did you think we wouldn't be able to identify her? Oh, we're making plans now."

"You'll fail," Sam said darkly.

Yvonne stepped closer to the edge of her platform, causing Ulric to tense on the shore. "You could always mate her. Though...the fire will burn her up in a way I wish I could see." She angled her head. "Any cute little demon mating mark?"

Sam calculated the distance between them. It'd be tough, but he might be able to leap to her platform with a full run.

"I didn't think so," she murmured, her voice echoing all around them. "Can't get it up for her, huh? Too bad. It would've been fun to see that much flame." She waved a hand in the murky air. "Not that it matters. Ulric is correct. You won't live long enough to perform the duties of the Keeper. Even you must know that."

Sam turned and strode to the far end of his platform.

"Where are you going?" Yvonne called. "We're not done."

He flipped around and ran full bore across the platform, ducking his head and pushing off at the end.

Yvonne screamed and turned to run.

Sam landed, his toes touching her platform. He burst forward, tucking and rolling before coming up to rush the woman. In a split second, she disappeared. Sam windmilled to a stop before plunging off the other end of the rock. He breathed out and fire licked along his lips.

Ulric sighed, the sound slithering over the ocean. "I can't let you kill her. Not yet, anyway. She's good at her job."

Sam partially turned. "Her job?"

"Supposedly she's made it so we can endure the sunlight of Earth," Ulric said. "Can you imagine? After centuries upon centuries of not being able to stand in the sun, now both the Kurjans and the Cysts can enjoy the heat."

It was, unfortunately, true. "She's lying to you," Sam said. "Sorry about that. You can't go into the sun. Now, why in the world would your Intended lie in such a way?"

Ulric's face contorted, and flames burst up from the beach around him. "How dare you." His voice thundered, and ripples flared in the goo. His nostrils widened, and then he calmed, his chin lowering. "Oh, Kyllwood. The things I'm going to do to you." He flicked his wrist, and a portal opened.

Sam stiffened in preparation, but instead of the portal pulling him through, a body crashed down onto the platform he'd just vacated.

"Darn it, Ulric." Hope Kayrs-Kyllwood pushed herself to her feet, wearing a cute cami-short sleep set. She looked around, and then her blue eyes widened as she spotted him. "Uncle Sam."

Oh, hell. The flames on his arms grew hotter along with his temper. "Hope." His niece was eighteen and had apparently visited Ulric before this. "How about you tell me what's going on? I'd just freaking love to find out how you know Ulric here." He had to keep his head involved rather than his temper.

She looked fragile but her voice was strong. "I was drawn in two weeks ago, the day after I turned eighteen. I'm safe here, Sam." Her blue eyes burned through the mist, and with her brown hair in a ponytail, she looked young and breakable. "You know I'm the Lock."

"You know you're the Lock?" he muttered.

She rolled her eyes, looking so much like her mother that he could only stare. It was as if Janie stood there for a moment. "Of course I know."

Ulric snapped his teeth together. "Shut up, female. I didn't bring you here so you could have a family reunion."

Hope slowly turned to face the immortal. "Did you just tell me to shut up?"

Ulric puffed up like a predator of old. "You—"

"You shut up, you old bastard." Hope lowered her head, her eyes more violet than blue. "I've been here three times, and that's all I need." She stretched her arms, and fire lanced along her skin.

"Hope!" Sam yelled.

"I'm fine. So are you." Her hair blew back, and she lifted her hands, sweeping them both out of the world.

Sam spun around and jerked wide awake in his bed in the cabin. Holy shit.

Chapter Twenty

Hope Kayrs-Kyllwood sat up in her bed, safe in her family home at demon headquarters. She flipped on her light and already had her phone in her hand when it buzzed. "Hi, Uncle Sam."

"Start explaining and right now," Sam barked.

She let out a startled laugh. Uncle Sam was the one who never lost his cool. "Ulric bounced me in two weeks ago and then two more times before I figured out how to control it. Tonight I imagined a shifting of the worlds with just enough power to alter my path and yours—he shouldn't be able to force either of us in again." She sighed. "But that won't stop the pull from other places, or the fire, so you'll keep getting burned and might find yourself drawn into other dimensions. I'm working on it."

Sam's voice scratched with irritation. "How do you know about that?"

"Dreamed about it," she said honestly. "Not sure if Fate is helping me out, but I can see what you're dealing with. Unfortunately, I don't know how to help you. Yet."

"Honey—"

"We can't stop it," she said gently, growing tired of everyone trying to protect her when some things just couldn't happen.

He was quiet, which was never a good sign. "You seemed... comfortable. Not scared. What do you know that I don't?"

Anything she knew would just create more nightmares for him. "I was terrified. Ulric is more than an immortal—more than even what the ritual made him." Killing him was going to be next to impossible, and the sacrifices that would have to be made were gut wrenching. And it still might not work. "I learned a long time ago not to reveal fear to a bully." Evil truly existed, and she wished she didn't know that fact. Her stomach hurt.

"I'll protect you from this," Sam said.

Her uncle was powerful—probably more so than he knew right now. More than she could figure out. "I know," she said softly because that was what he needed to hear. "Now. I'm safe at home, guarded from every angle, and you're safe now too. Let's get some sleep, and if I figure out anything else, I'll let you know. Please don't tell my parents. There's nothing any of us can do about this."

Sam started to argue as only a Kyllwood male could. So she faked a scratchy sound. "Oops. I'm losing you. Must be a tunnel somewhere." Then she clicked off, chuckling. At least Sam was usually rational. He'd think about the situation and come to the right decision in the morning. The sad fact was there was nothing anyone could do, and man, the Kyllwood family as a whole hated that very thought. For that matter, so did the other side of her family. The Kayrs family.

Sighing, she snuggled down in her bed again. It had taken a full week of meditation to figure out how to close the gap so Ulric couldn't get her, and now she was tired. So freaking tired.

She drifted into sleep and immediately found herself in a cheerful world with light pink sand, a bubbly blue ocean, and a clear, aqua-colored sky.

"Ah, darn it," she muttered, sinking a foot into the clean sand. She'd already done her job and messed with Ulric, so why couldn't she get a decent night's sleep?

The time of Ulric and the ritual was coming soon, and more of this crap was going to happen.

Well, at least now she knew she could once again visit the good dreamworlds. Since she'd turned eighteen and had been briefly subjected to Ulric's whims, she had avoided other dreamworlds. Gut instinct told her they were available now, though they hadn't been for the last few years.

Did she have any power here? She sat on a rock warmed by two suns and then flicked her wrist.

Her friend Paxton Phoenix immediately took form, standing up to his ankles in the water. He looked around, caught her gaze, and frowned. "Are you kidding me?"

Hope laughed, swinging her foot back and forth while making sure she wore clothes. Yep. Blue shorts and a white tank top.

Pax wore black shorts and a gray tank top that showed off his new and rather impressive muscles. His black hair hung shaggy beneath his ears. His eyes had always been blue, but as he'd gotten older, a silver sheen had metallicized the color. "I thought you had to be sleeping near me to get into these dreamworlds." Yep. Though he was only a few months older than Hope, he'd already perfected that vampire-demon hybrid growl when he was annoyed.

"Your mean little control plan worked for three years," she murmured. She didn't know why, but in her youth, she'd only been able to visit dreamworlds if Pax had been nearby. For a year after they'd last slept in the same room and visited a dreamworld, Pax had stayed away at night. Then he'd just stayed away almost all the time. It felt good to see him now. Odd little tingles fluttered in her abdomen. They were just friends. Best friends. Her body seemed to be confused. "How have you been?"

"Good." He walked out of the water, and she had the thought that he'd gotten even taller than the last time she saw him—which was nearly a year ago. Sure, he'd emailed, but his messages had lacked personality. They were almost a report on what he was doing and seeing.

She looked way up at his face. "You missed my party." The family had thrown her a big eighteen-year-old bash.

"Just got home last night," he said, scouting the area.

The ping to the heart shouldn't hurt, but it did. He used to call her the second he got home from one of his trips with his uncle. How long was he going to be mad that she hadn't wanted to date him when they were fifteen? Irrational anger slapped through her. *"I can send you out of here, Pax. Just say the word."*

His head turned toward her at the same time that his chin lowered, giving him a predatory look he'd never had before. *"Don't even think it."*

She blinked. Once and again. Maybe a third time. Those tingles full on exploded inside her. She swallowed and looked at him. Really looked at him. Long gone was the chubby, good-natured kid whose one goal in life was to protect her. In his place stood a hybrid warrior. One with an edge she hadn't noticed in others his age. He was young, but his eyes held an ancient wisdom and always had. *"So you didn't miss me at all."*

"I missed you every second," he returned, his chest wider than last time. Cut muscles formed down his arms, and he even had ripped abs now. Somebody had been working out. *"But you made it clear where we stood, where we'll always stand, and I needed some distance."*

"Three years is a lot of distance," she exploded, kicking sand at him. *"You about over your snit now?"*

He stilled. Then he moved toward her, all grace and muscle, the clumsy kid gone. Her heart did some jumpy thing in her chest, and he kept coming until he towered over her, blocking out both suns.

This was new. She looked up into his determined eyes, and her mouth went dry.

He slowly, deliberately, planted both weighty hands on either side of her hips on the heated rocks. *"Snit?"*

She lifted her chin to meet his gaze. *"You going all vampire dominant on me here, Pax?"* Her voice only shook a tiny bit. Why was this sexy?

*"You don't understand dominance if you think this is close,"
he murmured, his gaze dropping to her lips.*

"Well, this is uncomfortable," a male voice said.

*Hope jumped and twisted to see her Kurjan friend Drake
emerge from the trees with his cousin, Vero, at his side. She'd
been meeting with Drake in dreamworlds most of her life, but his
cousin was a new addition to the group. Drake was the prince of
the Kurjans, and he was going to help her find peace for all of
their people. He had to.*

*Pax only turned his head, remaining in place. "You have got
to be kidding me. Did you call them?"*

*"No," Hope murmured, taking inventory. In three years, Drake
had gotten taller and broader, and his green eyes had a light
purple rim around the irises now. His hair was all black with no
red, so he could almost pass for human. Vero, at his side, was still
a little chubby, but at sixteen or so, it looked like he was hitting a
growth spurt as well. Kurjans were taller than any other species
usually. "But if we're back in the dreamworlds, it makes sense
that they are too." The dreamworlds belonged to all of them. As
did the responsibility to avoid the wars to come. They'd always
been able to meet here—the Kurjans and her people.*

*In fact, her mom and dad had met in dreamworlds before getting
mated in real life.*

*Both Drake and Vero were in black cargo pants with matching
shirts. But their feet were bare on the sand.*

*Drake tilted his head. His features were angular and sharply
cut. "How about you take a step away, Phoenix? I'm not liking
you that close to her."*

Hope's eyebrows rose. This was new.

*Vero cleared his throat. Last time, three years ago, he'd looked
terrified. Now he just looked uneasy. "Why am I here? Again?"*

*Drake didn't take his gaze off Hope. "We're training in Iceland
and sharing a tent. When Hope brought me in, you must've jumped
on board. By the way, you talk in your sleep."*

Vero nudged him. "I do not."

Drake rolled his eyes. "I'm not asking again, Paxton."

Pax flashed his teeth. "Come closer so we can discuss it."

Time for a distraction. Hope waved her hand, and a loud splash echoed.

"You have got to be kidding me," Libby yelled, stomping furiously out of the water. All gazes turned to her. She wore a small white cami set, showing off her long, toned legs. Her blond hair was wet and her tawny eyes sparking. "I'm a cat. A feline. Stop dropping me into the freezing water." She stomped up the beach, paused, and then her face cleared. "Hope!" She made a beeline for Hope and hugged her, elbowing Pax out of the way. Then she turned and jumped at him. He caught her and they hugged. It had been too long since any of them had met in person. This was as good as it was going to get, though. The shifters were withdrawing from the Realm, so Libby no longer lived at headquarters.

An uneasy feeling filtered through Hope at the sight of her friends' embrace. She loved Libby and she loved Pax. Why shouldn't she love the sight of them together? She shook herself out of it. "So. The gang is all here." Then she paused. "Maybe. Let me try one more thing." She centered herself and thought really hard about her cousin, and like a dream, he materialized right next to Vero.

Hunter Kayrs, true to form, looked slowly around the scene, taking in each of the participants, and then squared his shoulders. He was sixteen, looked twenty, and had the king's stamp so hard on him there was no doubt of his lineage. "Why the hell am I in a dreamworld?"

It was a little off-putting, really. Nobody seemed happy to be in her dreamworld. Hope frowned. "I figured we'd have our first official meeting of the coalition that's going to save the world."

Hunter sighed and strode toward her, past Libs and Pax, to stand by her side. Flanking her. Protecting her.

She shook her head. Sometimes the guys just didn't get it. "What are you doing?"

He cut her a look that was all Dage Kayrs. "I'm the only male here who isn't planning to better himself by mating you. I must be your muscle in this charade."

She ignored the first part of his statement. Her muscle? Yeah, Hunter was built like Dage, powerful and strong. But he was a scientist and much more comfortable in a lab than with a gun, although he was a crack shot. "I don't need muscle."

"Too bad. You drag me in here, I'm doing my job," Hunter returned. He lifted his chin at Libby. "Hey, Libs. Long time no see. You might want Hope to find you something else to wear." His gaze remained respectfully on her face and not the wet and see-through outfit.

All the male gazes turned to Libs. Hope winced. Libby now stood in white shorts and a pink tank top. Not see-through.

Hope straightened on the warm rock. They might as well get everything on the table now. "Nobody here is planning on mating anybody."

"I am," Drake said quietly. "Your parents met in dreamworlds, and you and I have as well. You want peace? The path toward peace is always the joining of a couple to bring species together. You're eighteen and old enough to make the decision now. I'm ready."

Her mouth dropped open.

Paxton partially turned, putting his body between them. "No."

"Not your decision, hybrid," Drake said.

"Wrong," Pax said, the muscles in his back vibrating.

Drake smiled, and the sight wasn't pleasant. "You finally making a claim, Phoenix?"

"Yes," Pax said quietly.

Libby shot a look at Hope, her eyes wide.

Hunter groaned next to her.

Hope couldn't speak.

Drake lost his smile. "You smell that? On the air. That scent?"

"I do," Paxton said. "Smells like war." He clapped his hands. Hard.

Hope sat straight up in her bed, wide awake, her heart thundering.

Holy crap. A quick glance at her phone showed that Uncle Sam had called three more times. She groaned and flopped down, pressing a pillow to her face. It was all too much.

Her window opened, and Paxton jumped inside her room.

Chapter Twenty-One

After grabbing a bottle of whiskey, Sam walked outside to sit on the cabin steps beneath the eaves, watching the rain punish the earth. The moon pierced through different cloud openings, showing pine needles scattered every which way.

"Can't sleep?" Bear and Flynn strode up, both sweating, obviously having been out for a run.

"No." Sam handed over the bottle to Bear, who plopped down on one side of him while Flynn did the same on the other. Great. Now he was flanked by a bear and a dragon. Life had gotten way too weird. "How are the babies?"

"We have a couple of healers with Nessa now, and so far, everything seems okay." Bear tipped the bottle and took several deep gulps before handing it over to his brother. "We've been trying to figure out your fire problem."

Sam stretched his legs to the rough ground. "Any luck?"

Flynn took a drink and then wiped off his mouth. "Not really. Fire is an element, so if we could find someone with the earth's gifts, maybe a mate for you, it might balance the fire."

The female sleeping in his bed wasn't one with the earth. "How did I infect Honor with this fire problem?" Sam could feel the brothers cast a look at each other behind his back. He groaned. "Knock it off. What have you determined?"

"Try me," Bear said, holding out his arm. "Try to transfer the fire to me like you did Honor. Or a part of it, anyway."

Huh. Wasn't a horrible idea. Sam grabbed Bear's wrist and tried to force flames into it. Fire lit his arm, burning him.

"Ouch." Bear jerked free.

Sam snuffed out the flames, which took more energy than he'd expected. "Sorry."

Bear rolled his neck and held out his arms, looking constipated. Nothing happened. "I don't feel the fire."

Flynn leaned forward to study his brother across Sam's body. "Nope. No fire there. Not even a hint of a fire. So that means..."

"There's something special about Honor," Sam mused. Something besides her being brilliant, gorgeous, and kind. "Flynn? As a dragon, can you quench either fire? In Honor or me?"

"Nope," Flynn said, his voice rough. Probably from spitting fire all the time. "I can't quench it, but if I mated Honor, I could control her fire. We'd need that connection for me to exert any power over her." When Bear turned to look at him, he shrugged. "Little-known dragon fact. The females don't like it, but it's how we've evolved."

The idea of Flynn mating Honor shot irritation through Sam, and flames erupted from his fingertips. "Shit." He aimed them at the wet ground, where they were squelched.

Bear clapped him on the back. "Well, that's an answer. What if Sam and Honor mated?"

Flynn clenched his jaw. "I don't know. Maybe they could control each other's fire and find a balance, or maybe they'd just blow things up all the time. My gut says that they'd be safer if they were mated. Also, the only reason folks can't teleport any longer is because the dimensions around us, around this world, are out of whack because of what the Seven did to imprison Ulric. Or how it backfired, anyway."

Sam sighed. The dragon was not wrong. "I went through multiple dimensions during a secret ritual I took part in. It seems the fire has followed me."

Flynn studied Sam, his gaze going deep. "The fire in you is much more dragon than witch for some reason. Tell me about this ritual."

Sam rolled his ankle to make it pop. His skin still felt sore from an earlier burn. "Eighteen years ago, I went on a little journey off-world that took a few centuries, and I was bitten by something that looked like a dragon." Well, with three heads and seven legs, but close enough. "My body was on fire for a good thirty years, since time moved differently in those worlds, and then it all went away."

"A weird infection that has lain dormant all these years. Why now?" Bear growled.

Flynn shook his head. "Because of the Seven. They screwed the laws of physics by creating three prison worlds, one to contain Ulric and two to house his guards. The latter have fallen, which has had widespread repercussions we're just figuring out. Only Ulric's prison world held."

Sam jumped. "What do you know about Ulric?"

Flynn's eyes glittered a deep black in the night. "Dragons know more than you think…or want. We arrived too late to stop the initial ritual in which Ulric murdered one hundred Enhanced women, but we helped the Seven and the witches to create the prison worlds. I'm afraid we're at fault here too. It was a mistake. One that's causing more disturbances than just your being plagued by fire." He stretched out his legs as well. "We've been trying to get to Ulric ever since then, hoping to kill him off-world. We could never find him, and now, as you know, nobody can teleport."

Sam shifted his weight. "Even if you found him, you couldn't kill him."

"No, but if we blew up his world in a way that guaranteed he'd never make it back here, good enough," Flynn said. Then he winced. "Your new affliction is a warning. If we mess with physics and other worlds any further, what will happen to this one? We're all connected, and it's beginning to look as if Ulric's world has to fall on its own like the other two did. Even so, we might be in a crapload of trouble."

Sam wished he could just go back and beat everyone who'd created this messed up situation. "I've met Ulric." He gave them the whole story.

Flynn frowned. "The fire didn't burn you in his world?"

"No." Sam scrubbed both hands through his hair. "I think the reason I passed some of my fire problem to Honor was because she was open to it. She tried to dig inside me to find the truth. The unique element here is her. There are probably very few people I could infect."

"Or she's your mate," Bear said, going right there. "It might be as basic as that."

Flynn nodded. "Agreed."

Sam held out his palm. His very empty palm. "No mating mark." The idea bothered him, and it shouldn't. He didn't want to mate.

"So?" Bear said, reaching for the bottle again. "You're all sorts of screwed up right now. Fire is actually coming from your fingers. Maybe the mating mark is just struggling to make it through."

"Or maybe you don't want to see the mating mark," Flynn said quietly.

Sam snagged the bottle from Bear and drank rapidly. "That's crazy," he said, wiping his mouth.

Bear reached for the bottle again. "Why wouldn't he want to see a mark? They totally fit together."

"Well, not really," Flynn countered. "She's modern, he's not, although he puts up a good show. Add in the dragon fire, and he's not nearly as mellow as he appears. Although that's not why he refuses to see the mark, is it, Sam?"

Sam cut a look at the dragon. "Have you been studying me?"

"Of course," Flynn said.

Well, that wasn't disconcerting or anything. Sam sighed. "I'm not afraid of the mark."

Bear growled. "Stop talking in riddles. What's wrong with the mark?"

"Nothing," Sam said, shrugging. "I'm sure I'll have a nice *K* on my right hand someday."

"Oh," Bear muttered, finally clueing in. "Huh. I didn't think of that. One *K* is good. Two *S*'s for Sam would be...bad."

Yeah. "Two *S*'s would mean I'm stepping up as demon leader and Zane is going to be dead." Sam shook his head. He'd do anything to protect his older brother. "Logan wasn't worried about it, but...I've had dreams. For years." He'd never admitted it to anybody. "Both hands with an *S*."

Bear handed him the bottle. "Dreams often don't mean anything. It could be Fate messing with you or just bad dreams. We all get them."

"Yeah, but sometimes dreams come true," Sam said softly. Unfortunately.

A scream from inside the cabin had him springing off the stairs in a heartbeat.

* * * *

Pain clawed at Honor's leg, digging deep. She screamed as something wrestled her from the bed. "Sam!" Her leg was out of sight and freezing cold. Where was her leg?

Sam barreled into the room followed by Bear and a huge dude with black hair. The dragon? He looked different in the light.

"What has you?" Sam slid on his knees to her, grasping her upper thigh.

"I don't know." Tears streamed down her face, and she kicked her invisible leg, barely seeing a circle around it. The force grew stronger, hauling more of her inside that circle. She screamed and scrambled for purchase, both hands going to Sam. She dug her hands into his bare torso, trying to climb inside his skin.

Sam released her leg and yanked her in front of him, plastering her back to his chest and holding tight. "Pull back. Pull!" he ordered.

She kicked uselessly with both legs, fighting hard, panic giving her strength. Her missing limb wasn't functioning properly. Too cold. "It feels like my leg is freezing," she whimpered. "It's going numb. I don't understand."

Sam looked over his shoulder. "Flynn?" he barked.

As one, Flynn and Bear moved. Bear leaped across the bed and linked his arms through Sam's, giving him better purchase.

Flynn ran around the other side of Honor and settled on his knees, pushing his face nearly into the circle. It sucked him in, and he growled, sinking surprising claws right through the wooden floor to balance himself. Then he opened his mouth, wider than any human could, and roared fire into the abyss.

Heat flashed along her leg. She gasped. "Better."

He did it again, and her leg started moving. "Don't want to burn you," he muttered, his eyes flicking to reveal oval shaped irises.

"One more time," Sam ordered, hauling her back against him.

Flynn leaned down and turned his head, blasting fire into the abyss.

Her leg warmed, and she kicked more wildly.

"Now!" Sam yelled.

Flynn grabbed her waist while Bear and Sam pulled back. At the last second, Bear released them, and Sam twisted to the side, propelling her toward the door.

She flew across the room, her leg free, and smashed into the wall with her forehead.

"Shit." Sam was right there, turning her over, looking down into her eyes. "You okay?"

"No." She pressed a finger to the painful lump that was already forming and then scrabbled to sit up, looking down at her leg.

"What just happened?" She rubbed her thigh, which showed several indentations and the raw remainder of frostbite. Tears slid from her eyes as panic all but choked her. The outer layer of skin on her leg came off in her hand, and the pain arrived a few seconds later. She gasped and then whimpered before startling herself with a shriek as damaged nerve endings tried to awaken.

Sam's fangs dropped, and he sliced into his wrist. He held the blood to her lips, giving her no choice but to drink. She took several deep gulps, and then he removed his hand. The taste was the same as before. Slightly metallic and a little bit spicy. Bubbles burned down her throat and then spread heat out to her extremities as if she'd drunk a supernatural hot toddy. The second the blood cells hit her injured leg, angry pangs of raw pain took her.

She cried out, whimpered, and turned to bury her face in his solid chest, her body shaking.

"It's okay." His broad hand ran down her spine, offering comfort. "Just give it a second. Damaged nerves and skin actually hurt worse to heal than an organ. You've got this. You're strong and brave." He held her tight, his body warm and solid, his words reassuring as they tumbled out of him into her thick hair.

After the pain came more numbness and then nothing. She sniffed. Slowly, she lifted her head to look down at her leg. The skin had healed. Gingerly, she bent her knee and then extended her leg again. No pain.

She breathed deeply, her heart still thundering. Then she remembered the two other men in the room. She was dressed in a short T-shirt and light pink panties. "Um."

The dark-haired guy grabbed Bear. "We'll meet you in the other room." They hurried out.

Her body settled except for the lingering effects of Sam's blood. Her nipples hardened to sharp rocks, and her clit pounded. She tried to shove arousal away. "What just happened?" She twisted to look up at his face, unwilling to completely let him go yet.

He looked down, his eyes darker than any real emerald. "Put bluntly? A portal to another place opened, and your leg was forced through several dimensions to it. If you'd been alone, your whole body would've been dragged through, and it seems like it was a cold place. Very."

Her mouth gaped open. "That's impossible."

"So are vampires, demons, shifters, and dragons, baby." He didn't want to scare her, but she needed to understand the danger involved. "I could go into the science of it all, but it's pretty boring. You understand the gist of it, and that doesn't change anything, really."

Her body trembled as her brain tried to catch up. "Will that happen again?"

He cradled her, his back against the wall. "Yes."

Her ears rang. "Does it happen to you?"

"Kind of. Since I used to be able to teleport, I can control it better and get free. Sometimes I let my guard down and get hurt," he admitted. "But I can heal myself quickly."

She settled more comfortably on his hard thighs. Desire pounded through her body, in her veins. For the love of all that was holy and good. She'd just had a body part yanked through dimensions and almost frozen off, and she was aroused? That immortal blood of his had some power. Where was her brain? "What now? What do we do now?"

He kissed her mouth, shocking the hell out of her. Then he leaned back. "There's only one choice. We're going to mate, and then you're going with Flynn to Fire Island, where you'll be safe."

Whoa, what? She tried to unpack that entire sentence. "No."

He kissed her again, this time harder. "Yes. That's the end of the matter, Honor. Wrap your head around it." With that, he stood, set her on her feet, and patted her ass. "Get dressed. I'll meet you in the living room." He opened the door and shut it quietly behind himself.

She stared at the closed door. "Seriously?"

Chapter Twenty-Two

Sam finished making another pot of coffee and glanced outside where the sun was finally trying to make an appearance through the clouds. Bear and Flynn overwhelmed the sofa, coffee mugs in hand, staring at the fire.

Bear finally shrugged. "I don't know how to force the mating mark on a hand. I do know it can be done because you demons have had so many arranged matings through the centuries."

Flynn nodded. "I think you just do it. Like imagine it, and then the thing appears." He took a deep drink of his coffee. "I'm not comfortable forcing her to Fire Island, Sam. Before you get all insistent, let me remind you that humans who see the island… remain on the island. We're shrouded from the rest of the world on purpose, and if I take her there, she's staying."

"She won't be human any longer," Sam countered, pouring two mugs. "She'll be a mate, and as the ruler of the supersecret island, you can make an exception." Now that he'd made up his mind, his body was relaxed and his mind at peace. He and Honor had chemistry, and frankly, he couldn't get her out of his mind. She was smart, sexy, and resilient, and the image of her ducking, rolling, and then firing at those Kurjan soldiers—within seconds of finding out they existed—was downright impressive. "Ulric is going to be free soon. I know it, and my gut feeling is that you know it too, Flynn. If I die trying to kill him, then take Honor to the Realm, get her the virus to negate our mating bonds, and set her free." The woman would make good use of immortality. His heart felt a pang at the realization that he most likely wouldn't be there to witness it.

"What if you don't die?" Bear drawled.

Sam sipped thoughtfully. "Then I'll fetch her from Fire Island and figure things out. One problem at a time."

She stomped out of the bedroom, wearing black jeans and a light yellow sweater. "You're calling me a problem?" She marched right up to him, fire in those spectacular eyes. "I'm not your problem, ace. We are not mating just because you say so. It isn't going to happen." She punctuated her statement by poking him in the chest several times. Hard.

The female had misread him.

He grasped her neck, hauled her around until her butt hit the fridge, and then kissed her, not holding himself back. Everything he was, everything he'd endured, everything he'd ever be, poured right into her. She gasped, opening her mouth. He took advantage, diving in, not giving her a second of reprieve.

She whimpered deep in her throat, and he felt the vibrations through his chest, pressed against her. The small sound of surrender lit him on fire faster than any dimensional jump. Desperation to get closer clawed at him. He threaded his hand through her thick hair, loving how his fingers immediately became tangled.

No more holding back with her. Oh, he had let her see part of him before, but now it was everything. The choice had been made.

She moved against him, her full breasts against his chest, the apex of her legs hot. Welcoming. His. She dug her fingers into his chest, trying to get inside him, kissing him back.

Adrenaline and hunger roared through him, drowning out the rest of the world. Raw passion took him, and he streamed it right back into her, letting her feel real fire. She made little noises of need, gyrating against him, her body soft and so fucking sweet. The tension rippling between them almost pushed him over the edge.

"Enough, you two. Man. I didn't know you were gonna do it right here," Bear groused from behind them.

Honor jerked and panicked, trying to draw away.

Sam held her right where he wanted her. He released her mouth but not her neck, his nose nearly touching hers. Her pulse pounded against his palm. For a heartbeat, maybe two, he let her see him. The animal at his core, the one he so rarely gave free rein. The one determined to mark her for all time.

Her eyes widened, the pretty topaz darkening to a deep brown. Shock lurked there along with desire. Need and wariness. Smart girl.

"Hello?" The door opened, and Nessa entered with a duffel bag. "Since we lost all of the shopping bags in the fight, I brought more clothing from friends in case the stuff I left for Honor earlier didn't work." She paused, looked at them, and then glanced at the males on the sofa. "Um, what's going on?"

Bear lumbered to his feet and set his mug on the coffee table. "They're going to mate. It looks like right there at the fridge, so we should get going." He leaned over and kissed his witch. "You thought I wasn't romantic with our chase through the snow and then breaking the bed. At least we *used* a bed." He began to duck his shoulder as if to toss her over it and then paused, straightening and taking her hand instead.

Nessa sighed. "Bear. I'm not breakable. The healers all told me I need to spend time in nature and relax. I can't just stay in bed. I'm only pregnant."

"With triplets, and you've always been breakable, my heart." With that sweet statement, he moved toward the door.

Flynn stood too. "I have to call in. See you all later." With that, he jogged outside.

Nessa set her feet. "What a minute. I wanted to give everyone a quick update. Our security system has been attacked multiple times in the last few hours. They're pulling out all the stops this time. My electronic protections have remained in force, but you might want to consider destroying anything with GPS just in case. Not that your location isn't rather well known right now. But... missiles. Just to be safe."

The door opened again, and Garrett strode inside. "We've got intel from the Realm with notice of Kurjan bounties for Sam, Honor, and me." He tossed a printout of Honor's face over to Sam and then paused, looking at Sam's hand on her neck. "What's going on?"

Sam caught the piece of paper with his free hand. "I was explaining to Honor that we're going to mate."

Garrett smiled. "It's about time."

Nessa tugged Bear inside. "Honor? Do you mind?"

"Not at all." Honor edged out from Sam's embrace and moved toward the witch so she could set both hands on her abdomen. She closed her eyes and remained still. Her smile was sweet when she opened them. "They're okay. All of them."

Sam relaxed. "Good." That was the only thing that really mattered.

* * * *

Honor finished pouring two cups of coffee and took them out to the deck, where Garrett sat on the steps. Protecting her. Or was he watching her to make sure she didn't make a break for it? The second Sam had made his pronouncement, his brother had called and insisted upon a teleconference. Sam's brother...the king of the demon nation.

She handed the mug to Garrett and sat beside him on the rough-hewn steps. "Are you here making sure I stay here?"

"Yep." He took the cup, inhaled the steam, and then took a drink, staring out at the trees surrounding them. "I also wanted to avoid the big teleconference right now. Wasn't in the mood."

She didn't blame him. This was good. He was somebody she could get on her side, once she figured out what her side might be. "You and Sam are tight?"

"We're brothers. As close as brothers, anyway." Even Garrett's profile was rock solid and strong. "When his brother and my sister mated, we became family. His younger brother, Logan, and I are the best of friends, and when I joined the Grizzlies, Sam came with me. We're solid." He cut her a look, his eyes metallic gray. "He'll be a good mate. The best, actually."

They all talked about mating like it was normal. In her world, only animals mated.

"Garrett. Happenstance put Sam and me in the same place and gave me this weird fire and dimensional problem." She blew on the coffee. It was too hot.

He snorted.

She paused. "What?"

"Fate happened. You know, my dad is probably the deadliest warrior alive today, and he totally and completely believes in Fate." Garrett took another drink. "Figures people who don't are just fighting themselves for some reason. Why are you fighting it?"

She blinked. "I don't believe in Fate."

"Ah. Okay. Let's come at it another way."

"No. Let's talk about you." She sipped gingerly. Yeah, good coffee with a hint of cinnamon. "Let's say you found your mate."

Garrett sighed. "Let's say I finally do, although I'm getting tired of looking for her. She'd better have a damn good reason for being so hard to find."

A quick look showed he wasn't kidding. "Um, all right. What if you find her and she doesn't want to mate you? Is it like a proposal that goes wrong?"

"She'll mate me," Garrett said, his voice low.

Wow. Force of nature or what? Honor settled more comfortably on the hard steps. "Okay. Forgetting the fact that I haven't made up my mind yet, I have some questions, and you're here, so you get to answer. What about this final ritual you all keep talking about? Sam was saying he wouldn't mate me because you're all probably going to perish, but now he's changed his mind because we're in danger if we don't mate. So let's talk about you. If you meet the woman you believe to be your mate before the ritual, are you going to mate her? Even though you think you're going to die?"

"I'm mating her the second I can lock her down," Garrett said, his voice a low growl. "This ritual may take place next year or it may take place in a millennia. I don't know. What I do know is that my mate is out there, unprotected, and I'll damn well put her where I can keep her safe, even if I die the next day."

"Here I thought Sam was a control freak," Honor muttered into her cup.

Garrett flashed a smile, watching a squirrel climb up a tree. "I'm not a freak. I just like control, and I take it. My mate will not only understand that fact but appreciate it."

Honor took a big drink of the coffee to do something with her mouth other than argue with him. "Are you a bunch of centuries old?" It would explain the attitude.

"No. Zane, Sam, Logan, and I are from this century. We're quite modern for our people."

She couldn't tell if he was joking but had a sinking feeling that he was not. "Wow."

He finished his coffee and turned to look at her, his gaze unreadable. "We're not humans. We don't date for two years, wonder if there's someone better out there, waffle around, and then have a party with a preacher and a piece of paper from the state. We're immortals with enemies who want to separate our heads from our bodies. When we find a mate, we keep her. Now. Not tomorrow when it may be too late. Sam would never force you to mate, but you need to let go of your human training and stop and think about what you really want. Decide, forgetting all about rules and conventions. What do you want?"

She looked away. "I don't feel things like other people. I mean, I think, consider, mull…. I'm a thinker."

"Sam's dead. You'll never see him again," Garrett said. The instant pain was shocking, especially since she knew it wasn't true. Still, her chest hurt.

"There you go," Garrett murmured. "Love's a construct that people spend their lives trying to nail down. You can say it, you can experience it or not, but what you just felt right then was real. It was more than love, and you could have that with Sam."

His words made sense. She grinned and nudged him with her shoulder. "So, if I mated, would I end up totally gorgeous?"

"You're already totally gorgeous," he said easily. "You'd still be you, just with some extra chromosomes so a bullet couldn't kill you. Or any illness."

Heat filtered into her face. He said she was gorgeous. "This is the best girl talk I've had in a long time." Speaking of which, if she was going to get rid of her GPS and phone, she needed to check in with several of her friends first and let them know she was all right.

"I'm good at girl talk," Garrett drawled, his odd metallic eyes sharp.

She chuckled. "What if your mate is just like me? I mean, come on."

His eyebrow rose. "Just like you? You're great. Why wouldn't I want a mate just like you?"

Okay. Now he was being sweet, and she was starting to like him as a buddy. "I mean, independent. You want a woman to just fall in line. Most of us won't."

He shook his head. "It's my job to make her fall in line. I want her independent until I don't."

"Man, I hope I get to meet your mate," Honor murmured.

"Me too." Garrett frowned again and turned his head, straightening.

A minute later, Nessa came down the path, flanked by two massive men who looked like they could turn into bears. How did humans miss seeing what they really were? Nessa rolled her eyes. "Sorry about the entourage. G? Nice try getting out of it, but your presence is requested for a little family meeting, teleconference-style. I'll keep Honor company, and the hulking badasses here will protect our bodies." She grinned at Honor. "I hope you have decaf."

Chapter Twenty-Three

Sam settled back in his chair with a beer in his hand, staring at the monstrous screen taking up the entire wall. There was no doubt this was Nessa's setup and not Bear's, even though Bear was manning the controls so they couldn't kick him out of the room. It was apparent the shifter had reached the end of his patience, and Sam couldn't blame him.

Garrett loped in, grabbed a beer out of the fridge near the door, and moved to sit next to Sam. He looked at the various faces on the screen—all members of the Seven. "Hi, Logan."

Logan grinned, his green eyes blazing. "Find your mate yet?"

"No." Garrett twisted the cap off his beer. "She'd better have a good explanation."

Logan burst out laughing.

Sam nodded to the rest of the Seven members—Ronan, Quade, Ivar, Adare, and Benny. Add in Garrett and Logan, and they were the Seven. Soon demon king Zane Kyllwood took shape on the screen and then Dage Kayrs, King of the Realm.

"It's a power meeting of what-the-fuck proportions," Bear muttered to nobody in particular, his huge body overwhelming the chair a tech usually used. He had both a bottle of whiskey and a beer close to his elbow, and irritation all but cascaded off him.

Zane leaned toward the camera, his backdrop unidentifiable. "Hey, Sam. Want to tell me why there's a Kurjan bounty on Garrett's head as well as yours? It reads dead or alive, and we have bounty hunters sniffing around town. Want to explain?"

"Of course," Sam said calmly to his older brother. "I know the Seven has worked in the shadows for the last several centuries, but I think it's time to bring in both Dage and Zane— as well as myself."

"You?" Dage asked. "You're a member of the Seven? That's not in my intel."

Sam didn't want to know the extent of the king's intel. "No. I'm the Keeper," Sam said.

"The what?" Talen Kayrs, Dage's brother and Garrett's father, leaned into camera range.

Dage sighed. "You were supposed to stay in the background."

Garrett rolled his eyes. "Right. Was there anybody here who thought my dad would stay out of this?"

Sam cleared his throat. "Nobody else. It all stays here. I'm the Keeper in charge of the place of the ritual."

"The Keeper?" Talen asked. "That's a fucking stupid name." His eyes were an irritated gold shot through with green.

Zane's face went stony. "How does one become the Keeper?"

"The ritual is similar to becoming a member of the Seven," Sam said.

"What did you do?" Logan burst out. "You went through that ritual without saying anything?"

"So did you," Sam reminded his younger brother calmly. Before Zane could also blow up, he lowered his chin. "The prophet who died was the former Keeper. The duty would have been transferred to Hope when she became a prophet. At the time, she was only a baby, and the ritual would've killed her. So I did it."

Shocked expressions met his proclamation. Most of the warriors watching were related to Hope in some way, and every single one of them would've done the same. As would the members not of blood relation.

"What has changed?" Zane asked softly, his eyes a swirling green.

Sam took a deep breath. "Excuse me?"

"Only one reason you start telling all, Samuel," his older brother said. "Something has changed. What is it and what do we do about it?"

Yeah, his brother knew him. Sam had debated on whether to tell all, but since Hope's life was at stake, he was done with keeping secrets. The males on the screen and in the room could be trusted. "I'd like everyone to remain calm while I speak." Though he could only look at the camera, he tried to focus on Zane. "I was dragged through multiple worlds the other night and ended up seeing and speaking with Ulric. I know all of you, whether you admit it or not, know who Ulric is, so let's all admit that." Several voices erupted, and he held up a hand. "Here's the more important news. Hope was there too."

"Hope? As in, gee, I hope things go well?" Zane growled.

"No. Hope as in your daughter," Sam confirmed. "Ulric figured out a way to tap into some sort of portal, and he brought her to his prison world a couple of times. Somehow, she closed the portal for both of us. Or she said she did. I believe her."

"Wait a minute." Zane moved closer to the camera. "You're telling me that my eighteen-year-old daughter has been jumping through dimensions and meeting with a sociopathic bastard who wants to kill her as well as all Enhanced females. Is that what you're telling me, Sam?"

Perhaps this had been a bad idea. But if he had a daughter, he'd want to know if she was meeting with a thousand-year-old psycho. "Yes."

Now dead silence met his words.

"We need to lock her down," Talen growled. As a grandfather to Hope, he'd do it himself if they didn't talk reason to him.

Sam shrugged. "Where? He got to her in the middle of demon headquarters. There's nowhere to put her, Talen." Even so, he watched his brother. Zane's fury could be felt through the screen. "Don't be angry with her. She had no choice, and she did a good job protecting herself. Protecting both of us."

"She had a choice about not telling me any of this," Zane snapped. "A big-assed choice."

"What would you have done?" Garrett asked quietly. When Zane turned the look of death on him, he held up a hand. "She's my niece and I love her, Zane. But what could you have done? Even if you slept on her floor, she would've been gone."

Sam grunted. "I didn't just call us together for the hell of it. It's time to do this thing. If we could close those portals, then we can open them too. I say we bring the bastard home where we can control where he is and what he does. With a massive amount of pain if necessary."

"How?" Zane asked.

"I don't know," Sam said. "But I'm being pulled through dimensions while being burned by fire I can't completely control, and my mate is inflicted similarly. I believe our combined energy could do something. That we could somehow get to Ulric."

"Mate?" Zane asked, his chin dropping.

Sam cut a look at Garrett. "I might've forgotten that part."

Garrett grinned, even though stress lines fanned out from his eyes. "Sam met his mate. Her name is Honor, she is Enhanced to the nth degree, and she's a gorgeous badass."

"Thanks, G," Sam said congenially.

"You bet," Garrett said.

"Enough!" Zane slammed his fist on the stone table in front of him, and the thing broke in two. "From the intel I've gathered, you need all three Keys and a Lock to make this ritual happen. You have two Keys and no Lock. Right?"

Logan scratched his neck. "Hope is the Lock."

Then Zane lost it. Not a little. Not loudly. But death glowed in his eyes, and a quick look at Talen and Dage showed similar rage. Garrett tried to stop the oncoming train. "Why do you think we signed up for this gig? Seriously. Logan and I have planned since the beginning to protect her at any cost, and once we realized Sam is in this too, the three of us have been ready. Jesus. Do you really think we aren't doing everything we can to keep her safe?"

"Including us is necessary to keep her safe," Dage bellowed. The king so rarely lost his cool that the earth kind of shifted when he did.

"We are including you," Garrett yelled back. "You're here now, and there's not a thing you could've done before right now. Hell. You want my take? There's nothing we can do now that you *do* know. You're right. We don't have the last Key. We don't have a place for the ritual, regardless of Sam's shitty Keeper title. And we don't know how to kill the bastard. Our situation is no different now than it was last week or last year or last fucking century. Yet now you know. Feel better?"

Sam elbowed him.

Talen leaned in. "Yeah. I feel better." His glare at his son held heat. A boatload of it. "We don't keep secrets like this, son. Ever."

Garrett met his father's gaze evenly. Man, they looked exactly alike. "I took a vow. It wasn't signing a piece of paper, Dad. It was in blood and bone...and it hurt. Bad."

Talen's jaw hardened.

Sam got it. He didn't have kids, but he did have a younger brother, and the idea of him being in that kind of pain pissed him right off. "I'm not saying we have a place for the ritual or the Keys. I'm not saying we can bring Ulric here and kill him right away. What I am saying is that we might have a chance to bring him home. We don't have to kill him right away. But if he's here, we can lock him down and learn how to kill him."

Logan scratched his head. "He's dangerous even from a world far away. How dangerous would he be here? We don't know. He obviously has unbelievable powers."

Sam rubbed the scruff across his jaw. "Yeah. I thought of that. Any action is a risk, but I thought we should all make the decision together."

"That's a nice change," Zane said, heavy on the sarcasm.

Sam had expected it, so he didn't reply.

Garrett tipped back his entire beer and set down the bottle. "Regardless, somebody should speak with Hope. We need to learn everything she knows about the portals and what she did to prevent Ulric from taking her or Sam again. Once we have all the facts, we can make a decision."

Sam scrubbed both hands down his face. "Honor and I will work together to see if we can open up any of these portals or if they're just going to keep trying to drag us in. I'm hoping once we mate, we'll be able to control the pull."

Zane straightened. "Don't be mating for convenience. I want more for you than that."

"I like her," Sam said. "I might even love her. It happened fast."

"It always does," Talen agreed.

Garrett eyed him. "I'm not sure she has agreed as of yet."

"She will," Sam said, keeping his expression calm.

Logan grinned, but strain showed in his smile. "So you got your marking. Just a plain old *K* like mine."

Sam smiled. "No double *S*'s. Sorry, Zane. You're keeping the crown." The empty feeling in his gut was one he'd keep to himself. The marking would appear any minute, now that he'd made the decision. It had to.

Zane exhaled, obviously releasing his anger. "Congratulations. Can't wait to meet her, and you'd better call and tell Mom. Sooner rather than later. I'm done with secrets in this family." He looked into the camera. "Talen and Dage? Since you're just a couple of miles away, would you like to join me for a family meeting with Hope?"

Sam groaned. "Don't triple-team her, you guys. Just talk to her and be gentle. She can't help being prophesied or whatever."

Zane showed his teeth. "Oh, if my baby girl is mature enough to zip through dimensions and take on psychopaths without so much as a heads-up to her father, then she can handle speaking to her dad, grandfather, and uncle at the same time. Let's make it after dinner when she returns from shopping with Janie and Cara. And yes, I have ten guards on them right now."

"As do I," Talen growled.

Zane nodded. "Good." His screen went black.

One by one, the members of the Seven disappeared from view.

Garrett took Sam's beer and drank the entire thing down. Then he looked at Sam. "Well, I guess there's a bright side here."

Sam looked at the empty bottle. "What would that be?"

"Neither one of us is Hope Kayrs-Kyllwood."

Chapter Twenty-Four

Hope Kayrs-Kyllwood walked wearily into her bedroom around midnight, her ears ringing and her temples aching. Oh, her family would never yell at her, but the tension between Zane, Talen, and Dage, also known as Dad, Grandpa, and Uncle, had made her skin itch. She shut the door and then gasped as she saw the male lounging on the floor by the window, his long legs extended. "Pax."

His gaze raked her. "You okay?"

"How did you know?" She kicked off her tennis shoes and went to plop down next to him.

"Your dad called me earlier this morning and asked if I knew you'd met with some psycho named Ulric." Pax put his arm around her shoulders and tugged her into his nicely muscled body. "Unfortunately, I did *not* know you'd been meeting with psychopaths in dreamworlds."

She shut her eyes and let him hold her for a moment. They'd been best friends her entire life, and sometimes it shocked her how badly she needed his quiet strength. Especially at times like this. "Don't be mad. I've had enough held-back-male outrage for the evening. I feel so terrible."

He shifted and pressed a kiss to her forehead. A soft one, but his lips were firm. And warm. A surprising shiver wound through her body. "You should. Secrets like that aren't good."

She lifted her head, looking into those silvery blue eyes that became deeper every year. As did his voice. He sounded almost more demon than vampire these days. "I don't feel bad because I kept a secret from them. I feel horrible that now they know everything, well almost, and there's not a thing they can do about it. Don't you see? Their feeling helpless is the worst thing ever."

"Secrets are the worst thing ever."

She rolled her eyes. Darn warriors. From ancient to only eighteen, they were all just overbearing jackasses sometimes. "Did you tell my dad that I took you into the dreamworld?"

"No, but only because he didn't ask," Paxton said. "I wouldn't have lied to him."

Was it odd that Paxton hadn't told him? She looked out the window, where autumn rain fell softly. "I'm surprised they're not in here right now asking what you're doing in my room."

"I must've missed the sensors and guards," Pax said quietly, shrugging and nearly unsettling her. "They don't know I'm here." He reached behind his back and drew out a small box wrapped with newspaper. "Happy late birthday."

She smiled and reached for the box, happiness bubbling through her. "Paxton." Then she quickly unwrapped it to reveal a necklace with a stunning pink stone. "Pink quartz?" It was roundish with a few rough spots, held by a sparkling silver chain.

"Yeah." He took the necklace. "For luck and protection. It's all natural, not polished or shaped. There were ones with cool shapes, but I wanted natural for you, and this one is ancient. It's smooth from the passage of time, and I found the chain at a small jewelry store during my uncle's last trip to study butterflies. Well, butterflies and bluebirds." He clasped it at her nape.

She touched the stone. "Thank you." Oh, it was so pretty. She sighed. "I was hoping to be able to travel with you next time and see a little of the world, in addition to maybe getting my own apartment. That's put on hold now. Obviously."

"Obviously." He leaned his head down to hers. "At least you're taking college classes, right? I mean you graduated already from college, but are you taking graduate studies?"

"Yes, and I'm already bored. I've been studying the geometrodynamics of cylindrical systems to try to figure out these dreamworlds and how to navigate them, but humans don't know as much as we do. The witches are mad at the Realm, so I can't study with them at their universities, unfortunately."

Paxton stiffened. Then, in a surprisingly smooth move, he lifted her to face him on his lap.

"Pax," she protested, her hands going to his chest. His hard, cut, grown-up chest. A warmth flushed through her, catching her off guard.

He cocked his head. "I've never asked you for much."

Unease swept over her, along with a pulsing need that she wasn't sure how to handle. So, he was sexy. She'd always thought he was good looking. Now there was an edge to him that was all the more appealing. But she never wanted to lead him on or hurt him. The future was too unclear. "I know."

"Then I want a promise. No matter what." His eyes glowed a deeper blue with a silver rim around the irises now. "If you are forced into a dreamworld, any dreamworld, you call for me. Bring me in. We both know you can do that now, and I really don't understand why you didn't invite me along when Ulric called you."

"I promise." It was an easy one to make. "If Ulric ever gets me in again, I'll reach out to you." Years ago, she'd told Pax about Ulric, so he knew the basics. She chose to ignore all the posturing he and Drake had done the other night in the dreamworld. For all they knew, any of them, her future did not include being a mate to anybody. Even so, her gut told her she'd someday have to choose between them. She told her gut to shut up. "So you're not mad at me any longer?"

"I was never mad at you." He threaded his hand through her hair, watching the strands fall across his knuckles.

"Pax." Her voice shook a little.

His gaze returned to hers. "One kiss? You have to live a little before you fight the ultimate showdown with a deranged millennia-old psychopath, right?"

She grinned, partially laughing. There was some truth to that statement, and man, she was curious. "One kiss, but it doesn't change anything. We're best friends for life, no matter what. You can't be mad at me and turn away, even if I end up dating a dragon shifter from the seventeen hundreds. Promise."

"I promise." His dark gaze dropped to her lips. "If you end up with a dragon, I want a front-row seat. You don't like to fly."

She licked her lips.

His eyes flashed.

Then he lowered his head, his hand twisting in her hair, and he kissed her.

* * * *

Paxton slipped back inside the home he shared with his uncle and jogged downstairs, moving through a hidden door to a cement-walled space where three men waited for him. The leaders of the Defenders, as they'd finally chosen to call themselves.

His uncle Santino sat at the head of the table, his white hair and midnight-black eyes revealing his lineage as a purebred demon. "Well?"

Well? His lips were still tingling from kissing the girl of his dreams, and he had a hard-on that might kill him. Were blue balls a real thing? "Everyone is in the loop." Pax drew out the remaining chair and sat. "Both kings, Talen, and even Bear McDunphy now know almost everything Hope does about Ulric and the ritual, which isn't enough, frankly. Also, Sam Kyllwood has confirmed to his family that he is the Keeper of the Circle, and as predicted, he's starting to unravel."

Charles Fralep, a demon older than even Santino, leaned forward. "Are they aware of the twenty Enhanced females kidnapped last week?"

"I don't know," Paxton said. "It would surprise me if they didn't, but—" His phone buzzed and he looked down to see Zane's face on the screen. "Hold on."

Santino leaned back and flipped a switch so Paxton could answer the call without interference. Otherwise, the bunker remained off the radar, which was exactly how they wanted it. He hit the button a couple of times when the light wouldn't go out. It finally did.

"Hi, Zane," Pax said easily, as he'd done for years. "What's up?"

"We have a series of kidnapped Enhanced females from the Utah area, and I'm sending in two squads to rescue them. They're at a Kurjan holding area—we think. I want you to get some on-the-ground experience since you're back in town for now. Are you ready?" Zane asked.

"Yeah. I'm ready," Paxton said, his gaze meeting his uncle's. If Zane had any idea how much on-the-ground experience he already had, he'd be shocked. As well as seriously pissed off.

Papers rustled across the phone line. "Good. We're nailing down their location and trying to bring in some locals. Wheels up in thirty minutes. I'll see you here." He ended the call.

Paxton clicked off.

Santino reached behind himself and reengaged the security. "That's good. He trusts you."

"He has always trusted me," Paxton said, still feeling the slight weight of Hope sitting on his lap. Torturing him. "I don't like the idea of lying to him, but I get it. They don't know what we do, and telling them wouldn't help anything."

Fralep patted his flat belly, his white hair in a buzz cut that made his black eyes stand out. "I think we go with the first plan. How close can you get to Sam Kyllwood? Intel says he's in Grizzly Club country."

"I could get right next to Sam," Paxton said. He hadn't actually been studying butterflies with his uncle for the last few years as everyone thought. He'd done things that still made him sick at night, but war was riding the wind, and such things were necessary. "I still disagree. Killing Sam is the wrong move." Not to mention that it would destroy Hope, which negated the whole reason he had become a spy or whatever the fuck he was these days.

Henric Jones tapped his long fingers on the table. Unlike the other two, he was a hybrid with more of a vampire look. Brown hair, metallic eyes, broad body. "Sam Kyllwood is well trained and dangerous. You sure you could kill him?"

"Yeah," Pax said softly. "Most people couldn't, but he knew me as a kid, and he trusts me. I could get close enough to take him by surprise. But again, killing him is the wrong move."

Henric shook his head. "Kyllwood is falling apart, and his disintegration could bring Ulric back before we're ready. Kyllwood was never meant to be the Keeper, and the ritual he undertook was as much of an abomination as the one members of the Seven endured. The rightful Keeper will be chosen by Fate the second Sam Kyllwood goes down."

"Fate chose Hope in the first place," Paxton snapped. "When she was just a baby, and she would've died from it."

"Maybe she was supposed to die," Henric said quietly. When Paxton reared up, he held out a hand to stop him. "Think about it. She's not natural. There aren't supposed to be female vampires, and she's not stronger because of it. She gets human illnesses, as you know. Perhaps her destiny was fulfilled upon her birth and that's all she had to give. Perhaps by making her both a prophet and the Lock, Fate saw a way to finish her circle."

Paxton leaned into the male's face, fury tightening his spine. "I do hope you're not suggesting we take out Hope." Sam Kyllwood wasn't the only one Pax could get to—he knew every entrance and exit to Henric Jones's house.

"No," Henric said. "I am not suggesting that. I was merely making an observation and pointing out the fact that Sam Kyllwood isn't supposed to be the Keeper."

"Yet, he is," Uncle Santino murmured. "I'm with Pax. If we take out Sam, then another Keeper will be chosen, and what if that person is a Kurjan? We would have no control or even access at that point. I say the risk of letting Sam try to figure out his problem is less of a risk than killing him. But we will vote." He gestured toward Paxton. "Thank you for the intel. Go get ready for your op, and I'll let you know of our decision."

Pax rose without a word, exiting the room and shutting the door. His heart pounded and his gut hurt. He trudged up the stairs as if he was a thousand years old, pausing when his dog ran toward him at the top. "Hi, buddy." He leaned down to pet the yellow lab mix. "Things are just getting more complicated."

The dog wagged his tail happily.

Oh, to be a dog. Life would be so much easier. God, Pax hoped they didn't vote to murder Hope's uncle. His lips still tingled from their kiss.

Sam Kyllwood had better get control of his gifts before it was too late.

Chapter Twenty-Five

Sam was just beginning to push open the door to his cabin when Garrett jogged out of the trees. He partially turned. "What?"

"Reports just came in of several Enhanced human females being kidnapped and held in Utah," Garrett said, his eyes glowing in the dark night. "The Realm and demon nations are on it, so we're going to hold tight. They don't need our help. My guess is that if there's one kidnapping campaign going on, there'll be another. When we find it, we'll go. You ready?"

"Always," Sam said. The Kurjans had been trying to collect Enhanced females for the last few years, and it was like playing whack-a-mole, trying to prevent the campaigns as well as rescue the women. "We need a better approach than we have right now, but I don't know what it might be."

"Agreed. I'll call you if we need to go." Garrett cast him a smart-ass grin. "Now get to the mating."

Sam barely kept from flipping him off and then ducked out of the way when the door opened wide and a lumbering bear shifter walked out of the cabin, snuffling. "Whoa."

"Sorry." Rody Flapper was a three-hundred-year-old shifter built like the solid base of a thousand-year-old pine tree. "I didn't mean to run you over. You're a good male." He patted Sam's shoulder.

"Bye." He sniffed a few more times and then leaped off the deck, shifting into a bear.

Sam ducked inside and shut the door. "You okay?"

Honor looked up from the sofa. The soft light fell over her high cheekbones, and her topaz eyes contrasted nicely with her lovely skin tone. "Hi."

"Hi." He shut the door. "What just happened?"

She shrugged. "Rody was having some problems getting in touch with his feelings about a few things and came to me for help. I wasn't able to get into his mind like I can humans, so I fell back on my schooling." She rubbed her jaw. "I need to do some more research into PTSD and also try harder to work with his brain next time. I just helped him to understand his feelings, which was what my psych degree was all about. Do grizzly bear shifters usually cry?"

"No." Sam shook his head. He had more important things to worry about, so he dropped into the adjoining chair. "Any problems?"

"If you're asking if I've created fire or had parts of my body pulled into other dimensions, then no. No problems." She set down the book. "We need to talk."

He'd rather just fuck, but he'd appease her. "Sure. No doubt you have questions about our mating." Not that the brand had appeared on his hand, because it hadn't. What was wrong with him?

"What if this fire thing that you passed to me is like a bug? Like some sort of infection?" She rubbed her eyes.

He nodded. "Could be. Or we're fated to be mated, and that's why you took on my problem. Or, with your enhancement, you take on everyone's problems but have been able to deal with that because they were all humans before. There are several explanations, and we don't have a solid answer, except to say that I haven't passed fire on to anybody else."

"Hmm. Well, I don't want to put anybody else in jeopardy, but we need to find out if we can pass it along. How about to a witch or dragon or someone who already deals with fire?" She kicked her feet out on the coffee table, putting them closer to the crackling fire.

It was a decent idea. He liked how her mind worked. "I already tried with both Bear and later Flynn with no luck," he admitted.

"Also, I'd like to continue exploring this relationship we've started, but I am not ready to commit for eternity. I like you, Sam. But I'm not ready to mate." She met his gaze evenly.

Should that hurt or piss him off? It did both. But she was being honest and she had every right to choose her own path in life. "Okay." He kicked off his boots and laid his head back, shutting his eyes. It had been a hell of a day. "The mating mark hasn't appeared yet, anyway."

Her soft indrawn breath surprised him. "Should I be hurt or insulted by that?"

He couldn't help the smile that crept across his face. "No. Chances are my system is completely screwed up by whatever is happening with the fire and dimensions and everything else."

"Or I'm not the right girl," she said softly.

He opened his eyelids. "I can't imagine anybody else being more right." He liked his life, and he liked himself. Yet sometimes, it would be so much easier if he had Garrett's attitude. G would just tell her they were going to be mated and to get on board. Of course, G would already have forced the mating mark onto his hand. This feeling of uncertainty was new, and it was beginning to tick Sam off. "Take your time and figure out what you want and need," he murmured. Of course, he was going to help her reach the correct conclusion, but everyone wanted a feeling of control.

He'd give her that.

Yeah, he was more like Garrett than he wanted to admit.

Even so…no marking.

Her chuckle swept over his skin and fired his nerves. "That has to be driving you crazy."

He let one eyebrow rise. "How so?"

Her grin was both impish and challenging. Quite the combination. "You know. You come across as totally chill while pretty much controlling every situation without seeming to do so, and you can't control this one? Your own hand and your own marking and your own body? It's a miracle you aren't accidentally burning the entire nation down."

Sometimes he *didn't* like how well she saw him. Irritation ticked along his neck. "You offering to help burn off some energy?"

Her smile slid right to siren range. "You up to it?"

A guy could only take so much of a challenge. He moved fast, tossing her over a shoulder and heading into the bedroom. Her peal of laughter unfurled the hard knot in his gut. She was a handful, wriggling and smacking him on the ass. By the time he flipped her onto her back on the bed, he was smiling, too.

"You're a brat," he murmured.

She propped herself up on her elbows, her hair springing around her shoulders. "What are you going to do about that?"

"Spank you or kiss you," he admitted.

Her eyebrows rose, and interest flashed across her expressive face. "Hmmm. I'm in the mood for only one of those items. Tonight, anyway." She really was a brat. "My leg is all healed, you know."

"I know." He grabbed her ankles and slid her toward him, causing her to fall back on the bed. She laughed again. He could listen to that sound every night for the rest of his life.

A sharp rap on the outside door had him growling. "Go away," he called out.

"Sorry," Garrett said. "Six fresh kidnappings out of Portland, and we're the closest team. The Seven is on the move, and if we hurry, we'll get there first. I called in a favor and have a copter waiting outside Grizzly territory."

"I can't go," Sam called out.

"Flynn is creating some sort of dragon tent around the place so fire can't get in and other worlds can't try to claim her," Garrett yelled back. "He said the protection can last for twelve hours, tops."

Sam shook his head. "I thought I felt something odd in the air." He leaned over and pressed a hard kiss to Honor's hip bone. "Looks like I have to go. Keep that thought. I'll be back as soon as I can."

"Help me up." She held out a hand, and he plucked her from the bed and stood her next to him.

He tangled a hand at her nape. "Be careful. If you feel any weird pull, call Nessa or Flynn." The force in the last journey through dimensions had been strong, so it shouldn't happen again for a couple of days, based on his experience. Even so, he didn't want to leave her.

"Go." She grabbed his hand and tugged him out of the bedroom and into the living area. "I'll get caught up on emails and calls to friends before we go dark, which rumor has it might happen. You go rescue those terrified women, and we'll pick up where we just paused. Who knows? Maybe I'll change my mind and want that spanking instead of a kiss." She nudged him with her hip.

Man, she was something. "I do like a smart-ass," he admitted easily.

"Good thing." She opened the door for him and paused. "Um."

He stepped outside, where Garrett waited to the side. At least six bear shifters lingered at the edge of the deck. "What's going on?"

Polly was the first in line. "Well, since you're headed out, we hoped Doc Honor would take some appointments. Rody was so much better after seeing her that, well, we figured we'd give it a shot." The hefty sow drew forth a bottle of red wine from behind her back. "I brought refreshments. Just need to figure a couple of things out. You know."

He had no idea. Know what?

Honor stepped to his side, her eyes wide. "I don't mind trying with all of you, but you have to realize I'm new at this. Well, not at the psychologist part, but at the part when I try to help you reach your own feelings. If you're lying to yourself, I'll know it and point that fact out. You might not want to delve into what we discover."

Sam straightened and looked solidly at Polly. They were friends. "Is this safe for her?"

Polly's brown eyes softened. "Absolutely. She's one of us now. Even if we don't like what we learn or feel, we like her. She'll be safe and protected. I promise."

Good enough. Sam looked down at Honor. "What do you think?"

She looked at the assembled group. "I'd like to help, but we'll need to do one at a time, and I can't give an idea of time frame. I think it'll vary by person."

Polly shrugged. "We're bears. Time doesn't mean a whole lot to us."

That was the truth. Sam looked at Garrett, who was studying a couple of bears half-hidden by bushes as if they were embarrassed to be there but didn't want to leave. "Huh," he mused.

Sam counted the bears—there were too many to counsel in one day. He did like the idea of Honor having cover while he was gone. "All right, but no matter who's left, this ends at one in the morning. Honor needs sleep. Whoever doesn't get answers can make appointments for tomorrow."

"You're being bossy," Honor whispered, her hand moving to his abs.

"Yes, I am," he agreed, not sure why she was pointing out the obvious. This was his cabin and his female, whether she realized it or not. That made her his to protect. Everyone watching them knew it too. There was no argument from anybody.

Polly grinned, revealing a crooked canine. "Also, not for nothing, but I'd go for the spanking first and the kiss second. Might as well get it all taken care of."

Sam's nostrils flared. How long had the bears been outside his cabin? He'd been so wrapped up in Honor that he hadn't sensed them.

"Good to know," Honor agreed. "I'll keep that in mind. In fact—"

He hauled her to him and kissed her. Hard. When he was finished, her mouth was rosy and her eyes unfocused. "Try to behave while I'm gone." Then he turned and followed an amused-looking Garrett toward the forest and weapons caches. He'd better get to punch somebody tonight.

Chapter Twenty-Six

Honor awoke to the feeling of a hand spread across her abdomen, a hard chest warming her shoulders, and a rock-solid erection against her bare ass. "Sam."

"Better be." He licked the shell of her ear. "You're in bed naked. For me?"

"Yeah. Figured you'd get the hint if you got home soon enough." The slightest streaks of dawn were filtering through the closed blinds. She wiggled her butt against his cock. "I guess you got the hint." She'd been alone for so long that it had been a shock to her system to have him always in her space. Then it had been a bigger shock when he wasn't…and she missed him.

He nipped her ear, and his hand moved up from her belly to caress her needy breasts. "How long were you up?"

"Till about two," she admitted. "Bears have a lot of issues, and with each new patient, I was able to go a little bit deeper into their brains. Bear shifter minds are different from human minds, and I had to learn new techniques. I'm getting there and was actually able to help a few of them." It gave her hope for her own clinic and what she could do there.

He pinched a nipple, and erotic streaks shot right to her core. "I told you to be finished by one."

"I disobeyed." Yeah, she knew she was poking the beast, but right now, parts of him were poking her too. She giggled. What the hell? She wasn't someone who giggled. Yet he made her feel light and young and free. "What are you going to do about it?"

He rolled her onto her back and covered her, pressing at her entrance. "Teach you who's boss?"

"Sure." She scraped her nails down his flanks and only then noticed the bruising on his neck. "You're hurt."

"I'm fine. Healing cells will get there." He leaned down and kissed her, pushing inside her. So big and full, and taking his time but not slowing.

She widened her thighs, her breath catching. Oh, she'd been dreaming about him and was more than ready, wet and soft for him. Even so, she could feel the tenuous hold he was keeping on his control. So she rolled her hips, taking more of him. Pain flashed inside her, and she winced.

His dark eyebrows rose. "You don't learn." Even so, he didn't halt in his invasion of her body, going at a slow and steady pace. He was so big and seemed to be taking her over. Completely.

"I'm not that bright." She grinned and shot both hands into his thick hair. His wet, thick hair. He must've showered.

"You're brilliant and you know it." He kissed her, going deep, continuing to stretch her internal walls with his cock.

She bit her lip against the exquisite pleasure tinged with a hint of pain. She liked that. Should she? "If I were brilliant, then I'd know what to do with you," she whispered.

His grin was wicked. "I'd say you're doing a fine job right now." With one hard push, he made it all the way inside.

She sharply drew air in her nose, her body kindling with a hungry energy. One only he could satisfy. She leaned up and nipped beneath his whiskered jaw, inhaling his fresh scent. "How was it?"

"Ugly." He leaned down and kissed her again. "Don't want to talk about it."

Right now didn't seem the right time anyway. "Okay," she whispered. "What do you want to do?"

He grabbed her hip, pinning her to the mattress with his strong body. His body covered all of her and then some, but he kept his bulk from suffocating her. Then he rocked his hips back and forth, watching her carefully.

Heat filled her and zaps of pleasure shot through her, from breasts to clit and back.

His grin was one of triumph and his gaze one of possession. Before she could question him or draw back into herself a little bit, just for a sense of self-preservation, he thrust.

Hard.

She mewled and gripped his warm body. Then he did it again, scraping his length along her internal walls and stealing any desire for self-protection. "More," she whispered.

He gave her more. Harder and faster, he filled her, covering her with raw strength. Bliss consumed her, and she tried to hold on and stay in the moment. "Go over," he whispered against her mouth.

She fought him. Fought falling over the edge and exploding. Just to stay in this moment of quiet, this moment of stretched tension, this moment of perfection. He hammered harder, watching her, challenge darkening the green in his eyes to something else. A color she couldn't identify.

Then he pinched her nipple.

She cried out, her internal walls clenching around his length, and exploded. Her body undulated against his, her breasts shaking, her body moving from the force of his.

He pounded harder, even as she came down and tried to catch her breath. "Again." It was an order.

"No," she protested, her body not listening to her. At all.

"Ah, baby." He kissed her, going deep, ending with a sharper bite to her bottom lip. "You don't get to tell me no." At that proclamation, one she would certainly argue about later, he changed his angle and hit her clit. Hard.

Her eyes might've rolled back in her head. The primal pleasure robbed her of all sense, all caution, all fear. She moved against him, needing more. *Demanding* it. Higher and higher she climbed, holding her breath, her entire body going stiff and still as she teetered on another edge.

He shoved her right over.

She screamed his name, shattering into too many pieces to count. The orgasm pummeled through her, sparking out, flying her into nothingness. Gasping, panting, her body still shaking, she let the last wave crest. Only then did she become aware of those glittering, all-knowing jade-colored eyes fixed to her face.

He'd watched her the entire time. "Sam," she whispered.

His face turned stark, determined. He pounded faster, deeper inside her than she would've thought possible. He held her in place, his body powerful, his essence wrapping around them like a shield. His jaw tensed, and he dropped his head to the crook of her neck.

Pain slashed deep into her flesh, and she cried out, her eyes opening wide.

He jerked against her as he came, groaning her name. Then his body slowly relaxed. He lifted up, and there was blood on his mouth.

She blinked. Her neck stung.

He eyed her and then leaned down, licking her entire neck. Warmth and numbness spread, and then nothing. He licked his lips and pressed a soft kiss to her cheek. Then he rolled to the side and planted a hand across her abdomen.

"You bit me," she whispered, her hand going to her perfectly healed neck.

"Yep. You taste like wild strawberries on a hot day," he murmured.

Well, that was sweet. Yet the idea that the same fangs that had pretty much decapitated an enemy soldier the other day had been in her neck made her tremble. Sam Kyllwood was as dangerous as dangerous got, even in this new immortal world she was learning about.

"Go to sleep, Honor," he said quietly, his breath at her ear. "We'll figure it all out in the morning."

Regardless of her spinning mind, her traitorous body just went right ahead and obeyed him. She was dreaming of puppies and lake cabins within minutes.

* * * *

Sam contented himself with listening to Honor's soft breathing for a while before sliding from the bed. He tugged jeans up over his hips and left the room, grabbing two beers on his way through the cabin to the front porch. He sat on the edge, watching the forest and drinking slowly. Two beers would help him settle down and return to bed.

He sensed Garrett before he saw him.

G ran full out by the river, a long line of angry male. His head was down and his legs pumping furiously. A human probably would only see a blur. He caught wind of Sam and pivoted, reaching the deck in minutes. "For me?"

"Sure." Sam held out the extra beer bottle. He had plenty more. "You okay?"

"No. You?" Garrett wore shorts and tennis shoes, and sweat rolled in rivulets down his hard-cut chest.

Sam shook his head. He was better after his couple of hours in bed with Honor, but not great. "I'm trying to figure out what happened and why, but I've got nothing." They'd rescued the six Enhanced females, finding that two of them had been tortured in every possible way. They'd been taken to a Realm hospital in Canada for help, and they'd need a lot of it.

Garrett sank onto the deck next to Sam. He took the beer and drank it back, setting the empty bottle next to him. "We've rescued many kidnapped victims, but they've never been used like that.

Hurt like that." Anger rolled with every consonant. "So it raises the question."

Sam nodded. "Yeah. This is something new."

"A psychotic rogue Kurjan soldier? One who isn't playing by their rules?" Garrett kicked out his legs.

"I don't know." The women had been too traumatized to speak; hopefully the Realm doctors would be able to get some answers. "We need to know who it is so we can take them out. Right now," Sam said.

"Agreed," Garrett muttered. "We also need to let the news out that this happened. If the leaders of the Kurjan nation have a rogue on their hands, they'll take care of it. I thought all of these poor kidnapped women were to be saved for Ulric." He sighed. "Or Jaydon, if we have that correct."

Jaydon was a Cyst general who might be trying to duplicate Ulric's earlier ritual to make himself invincible. The jury was out on it.

Sam finished his beer. "While I like the idea of an internal war within the Kurjan nation, we have to get this guy now. I agree. Let the news out. If Dayne has any intention of protecting the Kurjans from everyone else, he'll take care of it." Dayne had led the Kurjans for decades, and from what Sam understood, he was an asshole who wanted the Seven dead but didn't necessarily harm women in the way those two had been hurt. He hoped.

Garrett rolled his shoulders back. "All right. Enough of this. We did our jobs and will continue to do so. I had another dream."

"Same one?" Sam asked.

"I saw her."

Sam jerked. "You finally saw her?"

"Maybe not with my eyes, but I have a much better sense of her. It's like I saw her, in a way. My mate isn't human, Sam. For some reason, I would've bet my soul that she was an Enhanced human. But she isn't. She's an immortal—maybe witch or shifter—or even a demoness. Solid, full bodied, and strong." Garrett sounded almost dreamy. "I felt incredible power from her."

Sam paused. "Keep in mind the Kurjans have hacked your dreams. Or at least, they know you're having them. You can't trust your dreams, G."

"I trust my gut," Garrett countered. "For the briefest of seconds, I smelled the ocean. Not sure what it means, if it means anything, but at least it's something new." He hung his head, letting sweat roll from his thick hair to his knees. "I was thinking, maybe I'd talk to Honor about it? I know she doesn't read dreams or anything, but perhaps I'm missing something. I don't know."

"Sure. Why not?" Sam could still taste her blood, and it had been like drinking summer. "I bit her."

Garrett swung his head and looked up. "Seriously? Did you mark her?"

"No. If the marking had appeared, I would have." Sam held out his hand, looking at his empty palm. Was this what impotence felt like? Oh, he could get it up, but he couldn't control what mattered. The marking. "I want it to appear, Garrett."

Garrett sat up and leaned back on his elbows. "I've never heard of anybody not being able to make the marking appear, so there has to be something going on with you. It's kind of obvious with the fire and dimensions and all, but I don't know how to fix it."

Sam liked that Garrett's first thought wasn't that Sam was with the wrong female right now. "What if— "

"No. She's it. I can see you two together easily. She complements you perfectly. That's not it," Garrett said, his voice sure.

Sam agreed, but it was still nice to have his feelings confirmed by his best friend. "Then the problem is me."

"Yep. It's in your head," Garrett said easily. "Not sure how or why, but you need to figure it out. Like everything else around you, it's in your control." His phone buzzed, and he retrieved it from the pocket of his shorts. "What?" He listened. "All right. Thanks." Then he set the phone back and remained quiet.

"Well?" Sam asked, not wanting to know the answer.

"Two women taken from Boston, three from Los Angeles, and one from Indianapolis within the last twenty-four hours," Garrett said, a muscle working in his jaw.

Something was happening and soon. Sam shook his head. "Guess we'd better gear up."

"There's more," Garrett said, not looking at him. "The bounty for Honor has been tripled, so long as she's alive. They sensed her power the other day, and now they want her. Bad."

A low sound of denial erupted from Sam before he could stop it.

Chapter Twenty-Seven

There were at least ten bears waiting by the porch the next morning, even though the rain had increased in power and the wind had decided to get in on the action. The lights flickered. Honor peeked out the window as Sam handed her a cup of coffee and a bagel already made up with cream cheese and honey—her favorite. "You don't have to counsel anybody you don't want to," he murmured, sipping his mug.

She took a drink and looked him up and down. Man, Sam Kyllwood looked good in the morning. In fact, he'd made her feel good the night before. Her limbs were loose, and most of the tension had left her body. When he'd bitten her, she'd had the oddest expectation of feeling his hand against her hip. Had he wanted to mate her? They'd agreed to wait, so she wasn't sure how to ask. Oh, she would, but not until she figured out how she felt about it and what she wanted to say. "I like counseling people, and bear shifters sure have a lot of pent-up tension and emotion," she mused. "This feels right. I mean, while we're hiding out here, I like it."

He tensed just enough for her to notice.

She cleared her throat. "Speaking of which, how long do you intend to take cover here? I spoke with or emailed friends last night, so nobody is worried about me, but I do need to return to my life sometime." Not right now. Right now, she was on vacation in bear country with a male who could give multiple orgasms in one go-around. It was the best vacation of her life.

"I live here for now," Sam said, still watching the quiet shifters through the window. "I plan to keep living here and covering Garrett's back until he figures out what he wants or finds it, I guess. Unless Ulric gets free, and then I assume we'll go to war. Again."

She ate half of her bagel, kicking back on the sofa. "That was only half of an answer, Sam."

"I'm aware." He partially turned to look down at her, his eyes a lighter green this morning. "I don't have an answer for you. There's a bounty on your head, so you have to stay locked down until we can figure out what to do with it. In addition, you and I have some things to work on, and we need to stay in the same place to do it."

"What if I decide to go home?" she asked, mildly curious.

His frown drew both eyebrows down. "I'd go with you, but I'd need some planning time."

"To get somebody in place to cover Garrett?" she murmured. So he'd go with her? He'd choose her? That made her all squishy and warm inside. Did they have a chance at forever? Times like this, she felt maybe they did. Oh, she'd never been good with men or boyfriends, but Sam was different. In a very good way. The guy wouldn't let her push him away as she'd done with everyone else for years, and she was starting to rely on him. He was good and kind and so strong it hurt to look at him sometimes. But even he needed somebody. Could she be that somebody? "You'd need to protect Garrett before leaving." That was just sweet.

"As well as plan for you, sweets. You have a bounty on you, remember? That means round-the-clock security, and we'd need a force. The Kurjans aren't messing around." He surveyed her in the light jeans and blue sweater she'd found in the pile of clothing Nessa had brought. "I have a crew fetching clothing and such from your house right now. Should be here today."

That was sweet. "Thanks."

"Sure. If there's anything particular you need, let me know. It's a good crew, and I trust them all."

She started making mental notes. "I have a few things. I'll text them to you."

His phone buzzed and he looked down, scrolling through quickly. "Huh."

"What?" She ate the rest of her bagel, licking her fingers. It figured the best honey in the world would be found in bear country.

He slipped the phone into the back pocket of his jeans. "Intel on your parents' murder. I wanted to double-check that they were really killed by a serial killer and not the Kurjans or another immortal force that somehow knew about you."

She felt a chill. Right to the spine. "And?"

His voice softened. "They were killed by a serial killer. He targeted happily married couples, and your folks fit. The guy even confessed."

At least whatever she had going on hadn't gotten her parents killed. She missed them so much. "He's serving out his sentence right now. Sometimes it makes me so mad that he gets to breathe the air on this planet and my parents don't."

"I can fix that," Sam said, his gaze serious.

"Um, thanks. But no." She believed in the system and didn't need to go outside it.

Sam half shrugged. "It's your call. Also, a deep dive on Kyle, the moron ex-fiancé, showed that he's a harmless dumbass and not a threat to you. The guy has no connections in the immortal world." Sam leaned down and tugged a box of stuff from behind the counter. "After our raid, I hit an all-night shopping mall for you. It isn't much, but it's something." He pushed the box her way.

She set down her coffee. "I love presents."

"Good to know."

She slowly opened the box and nearly squealed. "Colored pens. A lot of them." She happily dug out several different sets of colored pens, a couple of notebooks, and then a sign that said:

The Doctor Is In. "Oh, Sam. This is all so nice of you." Her heart swelled inside her chest. Nobody knew her this well.

"I noticed the huge number of colored pens in your junk drawer when we were at your house, so I figured you liked to play with colors. Or work with them, I mean. The notebooks can be used for work if you end up keeping notes on the bears." He finished his coffee and set his mug on the counter. "The rain is getting thicker, and a storm is moving in, so stay here for the day."

She angled her head to look out the window, wanting to jump his bones again. He was so sweet and dangerous and hot all at the same time. The present he'd found was better than any jewelry could be, for her. She shook herself back to the day at hand. "Is there somewhere they can wait under shelter?"

"Why don't you set appointments first thing, so they can come back and not just hang out in the rain?" he muttered, frowning. "Although, bears aren't the best at time. It bothers them."

She wet her lips. "There's a whole community here, right? Maybe there's a place I could create an office that's not at our cabin. I mean, your cabin."

He grinned. "It's ours. Haven't you figured that out by now?" Snagging her neck, he leaned down for a hard kiss that turned soft and then firm and then deep. Finally, he leaned back. "Have fun fixing the bears, honey."

That was a sentence she never would've imagined hearing. She laughed.

* * * *

Sam ducked out of the cabin and into the rain. "She'll take you one at a time and might try to find office space later today." Then he turned toward headquarters.

"Sam?" A young female named Jellie caught him by the arm.

"Yeah?" He paused. In his experience, Jellie was pretty shy. Short for a bear at around six feet tall, she had light brown hair and dark brown eyes. Her skin was a soft pink, her nose pert, and her yellow sweater bright in the stormy day. "You okay?"

She slipped a pouch out of the front pocket of her jeans. "For you," she whispered.

He took the pouch, frowned, and looked inside. "It's a tea?"

"It's a poultice," she whispered, angling her body between him the rest of the bears. "For your problem."

He lowered his head closer to hers. "What problem?"

She turned beet red. Not crimson, not damask, but the color of ripe beets at the end of summer. "You know. Your problem." She drew out the syllables of the last word. "Put some on your hand during the day and the nerves will get activated." She patted his arm. "Oh. I think I'm first today. Good luck." She turned and ran up on the deck to the front door.

He slipped the pouch in his jeans and turned for headquarters. Seriously? Why couldn't everyone mind their own business? He strode quickly through the rain along the path to the main buildings and the mechanic's shop, going right past to the innocuous building that looked like a storage unit but actually housed an IT setup better than NASA had right now.

An older bear named Buck was coming out just as he was going in. "Oh. Hey." Buck clapped him on the shoulders, his beefy hand bigger than the Christmas platter Sam's mom used for ham. "Stop by our cabin later today, would you? Missy is making you a tea."

Sam's temples began to thrum like somebody was hitting them with hammers. "A tea?" he ground out.

Buck nodded, his eyes soft. "Yeah. It has Panax ginseng and zinc in it. You'll be right as rain in a heartbeat." Whistling happily, he strode off into the rainy trees.

Sam watched him go, drew out his phone, and looked up uses for Panax ginseng and zinc. Holy fuck. Seriously. "I don't have erectile dysfunction," he yelled into the woods. He was about to lose his temper. So he shook his anger off and strode inside, heading down to the basement and the main control room.

Bear, Nessa, and Garrett were already in place, looking at a map on a screen.

He paused. "Nessa? How are you?"

She looked over, her eyes clear. "Great. The babies are solid again—I can sense that much about them. But they do like to stay under cover."

So long as they were okay, Sam was happy with the outcome.

"There's no discernible pattern," Bear said, studying a series of green blips.

"No," Garrett agreed, frown lines cutting into his face. "Hey, Sam. We're looking at the most recent kidnapping locations."

Sam rolled out a chair and studied the screen. The locations appeared random. "So the question is, how are the Kurjans finding these females?"

Nobody had an answer.

Garrett shook his head. "We've been trying to figure that out for years. The Realm is doing a deep dive on each of the victims, but so far, nothing connects them except the fact that they're Enhanced and were ultimately kidnapped. The techs are also looking back the last ten years at missing women reports, in addition to the females we've saved and given new identities."

"We need to find where the Kurjans are taking and keeping these women," Sam said. He shook his head. "Something feels off about this, but I don't know what."

"I agree." Garrett said. "Also, as soon as we have a location on the missing women kidnapped yesterday, we're going in as the Seven. I have to warn you, the rest of the Seven are pulling away from the Realm again. They're too accustomed to working alone, and they're not happy we told Dage and Zane everything."

Sam shrugged. "Dage and Zane knew most everything, already. The bottom line is that if this ritual comes to pass, that is, if Ulric gets free, we're all going to need to work together. If only to save Hope."

Nessa looked up from a computer console. "We have another kidnapping happening right now in Seattle. A woman taken out of her apartment, and the roommate called the local authorities." Then she tapped her earbud and typed on the keyboard. "We might have another one out of Tacoma. Hold on."

They all stood. Sam needed to do something. Anything. "How about Bear and I take a squad to Seattle right now? Garrett, you and Lake take the Tacoma one. We have to stop them. Extra points if we get a Kurjan or Cyst back here for interviewing. We need answers."

"Good plan," Garrett said, shoving his phone in his pocket. "Flynn is creating another protective web around the territory for Nessa, by the way. He can make a new one every twelve hours, but it seems to tire him. For now, I'll grab a team and be ready as soon as we have information on Tacoma. Good luck."

"You, too." Sam turned and led the way up the stairs as Bear spent a moment with Nessa. At the top, he nearly collided with a nice lady everyone called Miss Lalla. Miss Lalla was an older bear with deep black eyes, long chestnut-colored hair, and twin dimples.

She stepped back. "Oh, good. Sam, I was wondering if you wanted to go to town with me tomorrow for my acupuncture appointment."

He smiled at her but kept moving toward the armory. "Do you need an escort?"

"No. Acupuncture is supposed to help with all sorts of conditions," she said, jogging alongside him. "The practitioner is human because we don't have one on the campus here, but he's very good. What do you say? I could make an appointment with him for you. You'll be in tip-top shape in no time."

Behind him, Garrett laughed loud enough he nearly got his head taken off.

Sam forced a smile as he yanked open the door to arm himself. "Thank you, but no. I've got this." Man, the Kurjans had better put up a good fight.

Sam needed it.

Chapter Twenty-Eight

Honor waited for her next patient to arrive, her mind on Sam. He'd been gone for several hours, and darkness was starting to fall. The door opened, and Garrett Kayrs walked inside, with two milkshakes in his hands. The wind blew in after him, scattering hail and more rain. It had stormed all day and didn't seem to be slowing.

"Hi," Garrett said.

"Hi." Honor accepted the milkshake. "This is nice of you."

He licked the top of his before it could melt down the side. "I figured you could use dinner."

She grinned and sucked gooey heaven through the straw. Honey and strawberries. Delicious. "Have you heard from Sam?"

"Not yet." Garrett frowned. "I would've gone with him, but we thought we had another kidnapping in Tacoma. That one ended up being a false alarm, and then it was too late to join in."

The guy sounded sorry he hadn't gotten to hit anybody. "So you came here?"

"Yes." He sat in the adjoining chair. "I figured it wouldn't hurt to have you tickle my brain." He blanched. "I didn't mean for that to sound sexy. At all."

"It didn't," she said.

He grinned. "Fair enough."

She sipped contentedly. "All right. What's up in that immortal brain of yours?" She'd learned quickly that humor and a direct approach worked best with immortals. No need to ease into it.

He drank more of his milkshake, which looked like chocolate chip. "I have these dreams, and they might be driving me crazy. They could be from Fate, they could be caused by an enemy somehow, or they could be my wishful thinking. I don't know. Dig into my brain and figure it out, would you?"

"I can try." She closed her eyes and searched for Garrett's essence. Strong and solid, slightly explosive. Yep. There it was. She delved deep, not going slow with him. There was no reason. He was wide open, which was impressive, really. An image came to her—him on a motorcycle, fulfilled. A weight on his back, slight and bright, all but surrounding him. Then it winked out of sight. Honor's eyelids opened. "Wow."

He stiffened. "Is it real?"

This was so far beyond her experience. "The vision appeared real, but that doesn't mean it is." She tried to think through the situation. "I feel like there's a ticking clock in your head. Has it always been that way?"

"Yeah," he muttered. "It's just life and destiny and all of that. What I need is for you to connect to her essence. Can you do that?"

"I have no idea," Honor admitted. "I'm not even sure how I'm connecting with yours right now, but I'm willing to try anything if you think it'll help. Close your eyes and think about her. Feel her. With everything you have." Never in a million years would Honor have imagined using her psychology degree and sixth sense about people like this. It was amazing and more than she could've ever hoped to do, and she didn't even understand it all yet. This kind of mental challenge excited her more than any other business opportunity she'd been offered. "You there?"

"Yes." His eyes were closed and his body relaxed. "I'm there. All thoughts and feelings. Dive right in, Doc."

She closed her eyelids and put her head back on the sofa, still holding her milkshake. Then she gingerly poked her way into Garrett's head. Though he was open to her, there was danger in what she was attempting. She'd had minds snap shut on her earlier that day, all by accident, and there was no doubt Garrett could inflict serious damage if he wanted. The thought occurred to her that she could, as well. Not that she wanted to hurt anybody.

"So, you're a really strong empath?" he murmured groggily.

"No. I don't feel your feelings. I clear the obstructions of lies from your brain so you can think and feel more clearly," she murmured. "All right. I'm there. Tell me what you think. What you feel. Both?"

He was quiet for a minute, his power all around her. He definitely held a breathtaking amount. "I feel her. Bright and light, substantial and strong. So fucking strong." His voice remained low and hoarse. "She's there and then she's gone."

Yeah. Honor caught that. "Slow down time, Garrett. The moment right before she disappears. Hold on to that."

She could sense his struggle, but she couldn't feel his pain. Although she could recognize that he had pain.

"She's too quick," he muttered.

"We're in your head. Your memories and your dreams," Honor said, guiding him. "Find that moment. Only you can."

He was so close. She gave him a little push, having no idea what he'd do with it.

"I'm there. Right there," he said. "She's behind me, we're riding the bike, life is so good. Then..."

Images and flashes of light exploded behind Honor's closed eyelids, and she gasped. "What is it?" She opened her eyes just as Garrett did the same.

He sat up, his jaw set and his eyes a morphing mass of metallic colors. Not just gray. "I had it wrong," he said.

She paused. "What does that mean?" She could only guide him. What had he found?

He shook his head. "The danger isn't around her. It's coming *from* her."

Oh, crap. "Your mate?"

"Yeah," he said softly. "I've been looking in the wrong places. Looking for soft and sweet like my mom and sister. That's wrong. She isn't human and she isn't soft."

"Where do you look now?" Honor asked, curious.

He stood and rolled his neck, looking as deadly as the storm raging outside the windows. "We'll see where, but at least I know to seek out dangerous and deadly. Sweet and soft aren't for me." He grinned, and the sight wasn't cheerful. "Thanks, Doc. You've taken the blinders off, especially since I finally know to start looking in the immortal world and not the human."

"Maybe, but I didn't get a feel for her," Honor protested. Before she could counter him or try to get him to go deep again, the door opened. Sam stood there, drenched with rain and covered in blood.

She jumped up. "Are you hurt?"

"No." Sam wiped blood away from his cheek. "We got the girl and had a hell of a fight. Sorry you missed it, Garrett."

"That's okay." Garrett moved for the door, slapping him on the back. "I got what I needed. You two have a nice night." The door shut behind him as thunder rolled above and lightning pierced the ground.

* * * *

Sam showered the blood off his body and healed the few cuts still remaining on his skin as Honor sat outside on the countertop, reliving her day for him. "So it turns out Polly has the hots for somebody and thought leaving honey on the guy's porch all summer was the way to go. I have to admit, I think she just needed some girl time and friendly advice more than my digging into her brain."

Sam washed out his hair. "Sounds like you had a good day."

"I did," she said. "Polly said I could tell you about her session, if I wanted, so I'm not breaking any rules by sharing. I also had nearly every patient leave either a concoction or some advice for you. Is this something we should talk about?"

It wasn't anything he wanted to talk about. "No."

"Okay," she said, her voice still cheerful.

He dropped his head to let the water sluice down his back. "They all like you and want to help. It's sweet, really." The entire bear nation seemed to want to make Honor an immortal. Frankly, it was surprising a couple of the bears hadn't made a play for her. He frowned. "Did anybody hit on you?"

"Three of them did," she said. "One made a pointed offer to mate and two tried gentle attempts to woo me. Do you think I'd make a good bear shifter mate?"

"No," he said, raising his head to finish washing the shampoo out of his hair. "I thought we settled this." He stepped out and dried off with a towel, tucking it around his waist. "We're courting and getting to know each other better, although we both already know what we want. We are mating." It was the first time he'd just declared it, but apparently she needed the words. "Understand?"

One of her dark eyebrows rose. "You're being bossy again."

"You like me bossy." He ran his fingers through his hair to comb it and loped into the other room to drag on sweats. "In fact, you're lucky I'm in such a good mood after a good fight." That was actually a true statement.

"What about your true calling, the final ritual, and sacrificing yourself?" she said, following him.

"Fuck that," he muttered, reaching for her and kissing her. Hard.

She leaned back when he allowed it. "Seriously? That's your answer. Fuck that?"

"Yeah," he murmured. "Don't know exactly when it happened, but it was probably at first sight. It's the way my people work. The ritual is going to happen whether or not I'm happy before it, and you're Enhanced and have to stay safe. More than that, you're head over heels with me and don't want to be because it doesn't make sense to your human brain."

"Head over heels?" She leaned back as far as his arm would allow, which wasn't much. "Really?"

He kissed her pert nose. "Yep. I can read you, even if you don't want me to." It was one of his skills, really.

She shuffled her feet, and he knew what she was going to say before she said it, so he beat her to it. "I don't know why the marking hasn't appeared, but it has nothing to do with my not wanting you."

She tilted her head. "I've been rubbing up against immortal brains all day. How about I take a spin in yours and we figure this all out?"

"I'd rather take a spin in you," he murmured, liking the feel of her against him. "Although I haven't noted your obedient agreement to my claim."

Her grin was cute and saucy. "You noticed that, did you?"

It was enough to give a guy a complex. First, his marking wouldn't appear. Second, his woman just wouldn't fall in line. He contented himself with rubbing an arm up her back. Shouldn't he be ticked about that? He wasn't. With a sweet and curvy woman in his arms, the one meant for him, he was having difficulty drumming up any other emotion but a combination of contentment and desire. That fight really had mellowed him out earlier.

She moved a little, for the first time letting uncertainty cross her beautiful features. To him, she was perfect. "My whole life my brain has been at the forefront. Even with my cool new calling, I use my brain and skills to help people, just like I would've as a shrink."

He filled his hands with her curvy ass, content to talk so long as he could play at the same time.

She gasped and then smiled, flattening her palms on his abs. At least they were on the same page here.

"Go on," he said, his erection aiming right for her.

She looked down, and her chuckle was needy. "When I get married or mated or whatever, I want it to be all feelings. All consuming, wild. Not because it's the smart thing to do, or because I'm in danger, or because I know what's right. I want to be so consumed that I can't live without you. You know?"

"You don't feel that now?" He was two seconds from making her feel a whole lot more than that.

She frowned, and even that was cute. Man, he had it bad. "I don't know. I feel a lot for you, more than I can even wrap my head around. I just haven't figured it all out."

He laughed out loud, happier than he'd ever been. "Let me get this straight. You want overwhelming passion and consuming love, but you need to analyze those feelings first so they line up and you can make a rational conclusion?"

She bit her lip. "I guess that doesn't make a lot of sense."

"No, but it's you, so take the time you need." He kissed her again, ready to take the time he needed. He'd rather have her smart and cautious than dumb and ready to jump in. He'd get her there. "Enough thinking. How about we feel now?"

She chuckled. "That's one rational conclusion I like. A lot." She rose on her toes to kiss him.

An explosion rocked through the storm outside.

Chapter Twenty-Nine

Honor gasped. In a microsecond, Sam went from teasing to cold. He lunged for the kitchen and secured a gun from a drawer, while tossing her behind him at the same time. His body was one long line of menacing threat. "Stay behind me." He edged toward the front window, peering out at the storm.

She could only hear rain and wind. Thunder roared loud enough to rattle the windows, and she jumped, gasping. Her head reeled as adrenaline swarmed through her. "What's happening?"

He nudged a curtain to the side just as another explosion bellowed louder than the thunder. "Two fires, small bombs—both aimed at the front of the cabin. The deck is on fire." He angled and got a better look outside. "They wanted to flush us out rather than hurt us."

Who would set bombs in the middle of Grizzly Club territory? She'd gotten to know the bears enough to understand that was unheard of...and crazy. "Is this a joke? Some sort of prank?" Her voice was so hopeful she wanted to wince.

"Doubtful." The lights flickered and then went out. From the storm or an attack?

Honor looked around the kitchen, her lungs feeling as if they were convulsing in her body. "Is there another gun?"

"Cupboard next to the stove. Keep your head down," Sam said, his body still as he studied the stormy world outside. He kept talking as she ducked down and crawled to the cupboard. "The front is a diversion, but we don't have a back door. They'll be coming in the bedroom window."

The words chilled her to her sock-covered feet. The socks he'd bought for her. She secured a weapon and scrambled up behind him, putting her back to his butt and pointing at the back bedroom. The only bedroom.

"I've got that. Get ready to run," he ordered.

She did so, calming slightly at his stone-cold tone. No panic, no worry. Just a hard-core command, and one she'd happily follow. "What now?"

"We go out and immediately right. There's a trail that can't be seen unless you know it's there. Follow me, and if you see anything move around us, go down. Fast. You can shoot even while lying on your belly." He looked at her, his eyes nearly black and completely glacial. "Do *not* jump in front of a bullet. Understand?"

Numbly, she nodded. That had been a one-time thing. Her hand shook around the weapon, so she held the metal with both hands. "I'm ready."

"If you see movement, shoot immediately," he ordered, his large hand moving for the doorknob. "It'll be the enemy."

"What if it isn't?" she whispered.

He slowly opened the door. "Anything out there is immortal. Just shoot."

Glass shattered in the bedroom. She yelped.

He dodged into the storm, his head ducked, already sending laser fire into the trees. She followed him, aiming for several blazing pine trees, where the flames were fighting a losing battle with the rain. Sam moved quickly, gracefully, across the deck to the right, keeping his body between the forest and her. She aimed to the side, hitting several trees and spraying bits of bark.

They reached the end of the deck, and he jumped down, continuing to shoot with one hand while lifting her by the arm with the other. His strength took her off guard.

Her feet hit the wet and muddy ground. A bullet flew past her and hit his shoulder.

He grunted, grabbed her, and started running. She ran as fast as she could next to him, while the rain pelted them. Her brain tried to dissociate and deny. This couldn't be happening. They were safe in bear territory. This wasn't happening.

She shook her mind into reality. This was happening. Time to act.

He dragged her through the trees onto a rough trail she hadn't noticed before. He scouted the area, trying to protect her with his body.

A Kurjan soldier dropped from a tree.

She jumped back, her socks sliding in the mud. Windmilling, trying to regain her balance, she fell flat on her butt. Pain ricocheted up her spine to her neck. Mud sprayed all around her.

Sam pivoted, nailing the soldier in the gut with a roundhouse kick. He advanced rapidly, shooting into the guy's face. The Kurjan hissed, his purple eyes wide, blood dribbling from his neck. Sam punched him in the eye, put him against a tree, and slammed his head so hard, the sound echoed like a watermelon bursting.

Without missing a beat, Sam turned and hauled Honor to her feet. "Run." He then turned, gun sweeping both sides of the forest.

Another Kurjan soldier, this one with red eyes, darted around a tree. Where had he come from? He kicked Sam in the knee.

Sam went down, spun, and came back up with a kick to the Kurjan's jaw. It shattered and the soldier howled in pain. Sam followed up with a punch to the solar plexus that pushed his entire hand into the Kurjan's gut. Sam pulled out what looked like a kidney, threw the guy to the ground, and smashed his already damaged skull with his bare foot.

Bile rose from Honor's stomach. She'd seen Sam fight, but she'd had no clue he was this deadly.

Sounds of running feet pierced the thundering rain.

She gulped and wiped rain and mud from her eyes, trying to focus so she could shoot. Anywhere.

"Forget it," Sam said, his voice clipped, blood spray across his bare chest. His gray sweats, now soaked with rain, mud, and blood, were plastered against his legs. "Just run. If you need to shoot, I'll tell you."

She fell into step beside him, ducking her head and trying to keep up. The rhythmic sound of helicopter blades wafted down through the punishing rain.

Then a spotlight flashed hot and bright in front of them. Bullets pattered down, splattering clumps of mud.

"Shit." Sam grabbed her arm and ducked between two trees, blood and rain commingling on his neck. He looked around, power steaming from him. "Hold on." Without waiting for her to respond, he whipped her onto his back with one arm. "Shut your eyes, go limp against me, and trust me."

The wind burst out of her chest when she collided with the solid wall of his back. She manacled her arms around his neck, clamped her thighs to his flanks, shut her eyes, and went limp against him.

Trusting him.

* * * *

Sam fired to the left, barely hearing a cry of pain before he ran faster, his bare feet kicking up debris. Honor held tight to him, her heart beating so hard he could feel it pulse against his back. He leaped between two trees, taking cover and trying to protect her from the branches. He'd gone cold. Rock solid, pure-crystal arctic cold. Later the heat and fury would come.

Now. Survival.

Two bears—in full vibrating fury mode—careened out of the forest to the left, jumping between him and the force coming at him.

He ducked his head, running as fast as he could, no longer worrying about the soldiers.

Everyone knew to protect the human. Hopefully her eyes were closed, because he ripped between a series of trees so fast, the outside world was just a blur, even to him. He emerged into the clearing in front of Bear's mechanic shop, where the alpha was issuing orders and looking more pissed off than Sam had ever seen him.

Shifter soldiers surged around him, some in human form with weapons and others in bear form, also with weapons. Claws and teeth.

Bear caught sight of him, the rain plastering his shaggy hair to his head. "Go through the office—door at the back is already open. Leads down to a tunnel to the safe room. Make sure Nessa is there and staying safe." He turned back to yelling at his people and giving directions.

Sam kept going, running inside the office of Bear's business and through the open doorway, taking the steps down four at a time. The tunnel was calm and cool with the earth surrounding them. Jagged slashes of silver gleamed in the rock, as well as a multitude of gun barrels and blades. Somebody had known he was coming.

He ran for almost a mile and then reached a solid steel metal door that was already opening. Inside were Nessa, a couple of computer techs, three pregnant women, and several children. The cavern was wide, with doors at each cardinal direction, and he'd entered through the east one. "You okay?" he asked Nessa as he helped Honor down. Her entire body was trembling.

Nessa watched a screen showing satellite feed of the area. She leaned forward, and her dainty finger hit a key on a black keyboard. A missile exploded from the earth and hit one of the three helicopters hovering over the forest. Metal exploded, fire reigned, and gravity took over. "I'm great." She looked over her shoulder, her eyes bright and pissed. "You?"

"Good. Honor's yours. Lock the door behind me." He hurried out. "Don't let any of those weapons in the tunnels loose until I'm free. Please." The door shut before he had finished speaking. Then he turned and ran, his feet not feeling the pain of the hard rock. Now that Honor was safe, he let the fury roar through his veins.

His home had been attacked.

He reached the office and ran outside, nearly colliding with Bear. "Where's Garrett?"

"Went east," Bear yelled, yanking off his shirt, an earbud in his right ear. "Forces attacked from the east and west, all on foot except for three helicopters. Now two," he reported.

A wisp of sound pierced the rain, and a second helicopter blew into a myriad of pieces, the bright flames bursting through the black underbelly of the angry clouds.

"One helicopter left," he corrected. "My forces are stronger to the west. You take east."

Sam turned and ran back the way he'd come, looking for a fight. Any fight. A punch of power hit him from behind, propelling him even faster. Bear must've shifted.

Two Kurjan soldiers met him at his deck, and he leaped forward for one while Garrett jumped from out of nowhere to take down the other. These were better seasoned than the ones earlier and gave a better fight. Even so, soon both of their heads rolled beneath the deck.

Sam stood, letting the rain wash away the burning blood. "You good, G?"

Garrett panted and wiped blood off his hand on his jeans. "Yeah. It's unbelievable. Attacking a shifter stronghold. This is war, right?"

Sam wiped rain out of his eyes. "Only if Bear reports it to the other nations." He looked around, but only grizzly bears met his sight. A pop sounded, and the third helicopter blew into nothingness. Nessa was dangerous with a satellite feed and explosives. Metal pummeled the forest, taking out a couple of trees. As the helicopter's remains hit the ground, the entire world seemed to shake.

He caught sight of a Cyst soldier battling with two fully formed grizzly bears. "That guy." He ran in, avoiding the claws and jaws of both bears. "He's alive. We need him that way," Sam yelled.

The nearest bear roared in displeasure.

Garrett moved to Sam's side. "He's ours, boys. You did a good job." Then he scented the air through the rain. "There's a squad of three coming at us from the north. They're all yours."

The bears turned and ran off, their muscles moving smoothly beneath their sleek fur.

The Cyst punched Sam in the head, and he saw stars as he pivoted. The solider started to come at him and then stopped cold. His purple eyes widened. He struggled but couldn't move.

Sam looked over at Garrett. "I'd forgotten you could do that."

Garrett shrugged, his attention solely on his prey. "I got more than stunning good looks from my father." A muscle ticked in his jaw, but otherwise, Sam wouldn't have been able to tell that Garrett had halted a century-old Cyst soldier just with his mind. "You want to mess with him?"

"No." Sam would save the demon mind attack for interrogation. "Let's just lock him down until the territory is clear."

"Copy that," Garrett said. "This was a helluva night. Did we lose anybody?"

Spittle and blood dripped down the Cyst soldier's pasty white chin.

"Don't know," Sam said. "I hope not."

Chapter Thirty

Honor picked up several broken mugs off the floor of Sam's cabin. The outside deck and part of the front wall had burned, while the window was completely shattered. The smell of smoke and blood filled the air, so she hurried outside to try to breathe. The storm had ended right around dawn's arrival, and the rain was on pause but no doubt would continue soon. She had to jump over a pile of burned wood to get to the muddy ground. At least her jeans, boots, and borrowed green sweater had survived the attack.

Sam stood near the tree line, kicking out the remains of a still smoking sapling. He'd changed into jeans and a dark T-shirt.

Bear strode through the trees, ignoring a burn mark down his arm. "Cabin?"

"Not bad." Sam crossed his arms and watched Honor pick her way through debris. "I can't believe this."

Honor reached him and kicked an ember out of the way. "Does this kind of thing happen often?"

"No," Bear answered before Sam could. "This is the first time we've been attacked on Grizzly soil. At least by the Kurjans." He angled his head to see a decapitated Kurjan body by the remains of the deck. "They might think twice next time."

Honor rubbed her chilly arms. Even though the storm had ebbed, a chill hung in the air. The promise of winter to come. "How bad was it, Bear? What are the injuries? Or deaths?"

"Several injured, only two need to be sent to the Realm hospital," Bear said, his eyes a deeper brown than usual in the early light. Anger rolled from him. "No deaths on our side, and we have a cleanup crew that should be here soon to take care of Kurjan dead. We've found four dead, not counting those in the helicopters."

Sam inclined his head. "Those probably survived. I saw a couple jump right before the explosions. They would've run the other way upon hitting the ground, just to go heal."

This was such a strange new world Honor had entered, but at least none of her new friends had perished. "This is our fault," she whispered, guilt stabbing her in the gut.

Sam swung his intensely green gaze toward her. "No. This is the Kurjan nation's fault. Period."

She shook her head, her stomach sinking. "They came for us. For me. We've put everyone in danger." She liked the shifters in Bear's compound and had found many friends already. The idea of them dying for her made her want to vomit. "We have to go."

He surprised her by nodding. "Agreed. Talked to Garrett, and we're going first thing tomorrow after helping with cleanup."

"The fuck you are," Bear snapped.

Honor took a step back out of pure instinct.

Sam merely lifted one eyebrow. "Excuse me?"

Bear's growl was all grizzly. "You're Grizzly Club members. Fully patched in, whether you're shifters or not. That means something and isn't for show, Kyllwood. If you think I'm letting the Kurjans attack us and force out two of our brothers"—his hard gaze cut to Honor—"and their females, then your vow didn't mean jack shit."

Sam turned only his head to stare at Bear. "You know me better than that."

"Yeah, I do. So we're not givin' the Kurjans what they want, which is you out in the wild swinging alone with Kayrs. We beat them back, and we'll do it again if the bastards come." Bear blew out air. "It was a good fight. My people needed one."

Sam shook his head. Then his phone buzzed and he drew it out. Bear unashamedly leaned over to read the face and then whistled. "You're on your own."

"Ha. We're brothers, remember?" Sam clicked the speaker phone. "Hi, Dage."

"What the fuck is happening in Grizzly country?" Dage yelled.

Bear snorted. "Hi, King. What are you talking about?"

Silence. Dead-heavy, threatening, violent silence somehow came through the line. Honor took another step back. Just in case a phone could blow up.

"Bear," Dage said. "Where is Garrett, and why isn't he answering my call?"

"Sent him to town with four other members of my club, to get supplies to fix up the place," Bear said cheerfully. "He's either not answering because he doesn't want to get yelled at, or more likely, he lost his phone. We had a bit of a skirmish here, just internal—good training. You'll be glad to know that he gave much better than he got and is just fine."

Sam rolled his head back as if a headache was looming. "We're fine, Dage. Nothing happened."

"I'm the king," Dage growled.

Honor nodded. Yep. He even sounded like a king. Power rolled from him.

Sam's lips twitched. "You're a good king. Great leader. Nice talk. See you later." He pressed the speaker button.

Honor gasped. She'd never met the king, but even she could feel the force that was Dage Kayrs. "You probably shouldn't hang up on the king. Any king, but definitely not that one."

Sam rolled his eyes. "He's just nosy. He'd already know if we were hurt." Then Sam concentrated on Bear. "What's your plan?

If you tell the shifter nation about this, then they'll want to know why we were attacked, and they aren't aware that Garrett is one of the Seven and that I'm, pardon the incredibly stupid name, the Keeper."

Bear wiped an ember off his arm. "Well, I've been thinking on that, and we've already had inquiries. Everyone owns satellites, Sam. There are no secrets." Stress cut into the sides of Bear's generous mouth.

Sam nodded. "My suggestion is to give them enough to appease them: Garrett is here and has a bounty on his head, which isn't a surprise, considering his dad is Talen Kayrs and his uncle is the King of the Realm. Let it slip that a rogue group of Kurjans tried to make a name for themselves and got their asses kicked."

Bear's alert gaze scouted the area around them. "That's a decent plan. No need to mention you, your lady, or Garrett's being part of the Seven. Yeah. I can sell that."

Sam's phone buzzed and he quickly answered it on speaker, not groaning this time. "Hi, Hope. What's up?"

"Uncle Sam? It's early here but I had a bad dream about you. You okay?" The voice was young and female—probably late teens? She sounded drowsy as if she had a horrible cold.

"We're fine," Sam said, frowning. "Why do you sound sick?"

The young woman sighed. "It's just a little cold. No worries. Love you." She hung up.

A muscle ticked in Sam's jaw. "That's a worry for another day."

"Agreed." Bear scratched his head. "What's on your agenda to worry about right now?"

Sam turned the full force of his gaze on Honor. "Tonight I'm going to mate my female and lock her down so this doesn't happen again."

Tingles exploded in Honor's abdomen.

Bear grinned. "Now that's a plan."

* * * *

Hope set her phone on the bed and fumbled for a throat lozenge on her bedside table. She sucked it, closing her eyes and settling the covers to protect her shivering body. This one must've come with a fever. She hadn't had a cold in over six months, so she'd hoped that part of her childhood had concluded.

Vampires didn't get sick. Neither did demons or shifters, and she had the blood of all three coursing through her veins.

Yet she did get sick. Oh, she tried to hide every illness from her family and friends, but they were all immortals, like her. They could smell an illness. Her eyes watered and she sneezed several times, grabbing a tissue from the table.

This sucked.

Even so, at least Sam was fine. The dream had been hazy and more than likely corrupted by her cold.

She let herself drift off to sleep. It was early in the morning, and she didn't have to be up for several hours. She purposely threw herself into a dreamworld with a lot of sun and warm sand. Vitamin D could only help at this point.

The heat instantly warmed her, and she plopped right down on the sand and leaned back against a warm rock. There. That was better. She could bring in a friend but wasn't certain she could hide her cold. Pax lost his mind every time she got sick, and it was nice to be babied by him, but she couldn't handle the stress and fear in his eyes. Libby was cranky this early in the morning, and Hope didn't need to deal with a cranky feline shifter. That left Drake, and for some reason, she didn't want him to know that she got sick. It was unnatural, and it was embarrassing.

She took a deep breath. Hey. She could breathe. Opening her eyes to watch the light blue water roll in, she took inventory. Interesting. She wasn't ill in the dreamworld. Good to know. Maybe she was just dreaming for real? She centered herself and sent out a call.

Drake appeared near the rocks, looking around. He spotted her, scouted the area again, and then loped her way. She watched him walk. He was taller than her dad but not nearly as broad. Not yet, anyway. His black hair was thick and reached his shoulders, and his eyes were a deep green. They could almost pass for human, but a stunningly vivid color whispered he was something else. He reached her and glanced down. "Is this how you see me?"

She took in the faded jeans and green tee that matched his eyes. "Yeah. What do you usually wear?"

He crouched and then sat beside her, leaning against the rock, extending his very long legs. "Normally black uniforms. They make it easy to do laundry." There was humor in the lightening of his deep voice.

She chuckled, so glad she wasn't sneezing. Not here, anyway. He waited a couple of beats. "Just us, then?"

She swallowed, suddenly nervous. "Yeah." For once, Paxton wasn't in her room when she'd made the jump to the dreamworld. "I take it you and Vero haven't crashed next to each other playing games?"

"No." Drake rubbed his hands down his jeans, showing a fresh cut on his wrist. "I'm actually not at home right now. Am elsewhere sleeping off a training exercise."

She grabbed his arm. "What happened?"

"Long story." He flipped his hand around and took hers. His wasn't as warm as hers, but it wasn't cold, either. "You are one tiny female." Gingerly, he felt her fingers. "So breakable."

"I'm tougher than I look." Tingles wandered over her skin and made her jeans feel uncomfortable. She was eighteen, she'd been kissed, and she'd even had some raunchy dreams involving Yoson An. But who hadn't? "Have we ever been alone together?"

"I don't think so," Drake said. "I haven't kissed you yet, so it's safe to assume we haven't been alone."

Her stomach clenched in an intriguing way. "Do you want to kiss me?"

"Yes." He kept her hand and continued watching the water roll in. "Why are you up so early?"

She tried to concentrate. The guy wanted to kiss her but then wanted to talk like everything was normal? Man, she was out of her depth here. Big-time. "I had a bad dream about my uncle Sam." And couldn't breathe because of a head cold, but there was no need to share that sad fact. If he did kiss her, he didn't need to be thinking of snot and phlegm. Maybe she'd just kiss him. Why wait for the guy to make a move?

"Uncle Sam?" Drake chuckled. "That's funny. The name, not the bad dream. Was it just a dream? Is your uncle okay?"

"Yeah," she said, leaning into Drake's side. It was sweet of him to ask. "I actually didn't see anything in the dream except that he was in danger. For all I know, he might've crashed his motorcycle or something."

Drake relaxed even more next to her. He must enjoy the sun here, where it couldn't hurt him. "This is nice," he said, confirming her thoughts. "While we can go out in the sun nowadays, we have limited time before our energy is depleted and we have to return inside. Hopefully we'll have a better cure soon. Vero is actually working on it. He's brilliant in the lab."

Yeah, enough small talk. She rose on her knees, turned toward him, and leaned over to kiss him.

He paused, sucking in a breath. Then he cupped her entire head and kissed her back, his lips cool and firm against hers. He went deep, making her close her eyes. Pleasure burst inside her. Finally.

Releasing her, he leaned back, studying her eyes. "Very nice, Hope Kayrs-Kyllwood."

It was better than nice. A sound echoed in the background, and he looked toward the trees. "I have to go, apparently. Bring me in earlier in the night next time, would you?" He smiled. "Let's do this again." Then he disappeared from sight.

She snapped her fingers, ending up back in her bed. Sniffling and with a headache.

Wow. She'd kissed both Pax and Drake within the span of a few days. They both were good kissers, and her body was all alive. She touched her lips.

"Where did you go?" Paxton appeared by the window.

She yelped and sat up, fumbling for the light. "How did you know?"

"Disturbance in the air." Man, he looked huge against her wall. Big and dangerous. His eyes narrowed. "Why is your nose red?"

She coughed. "No reason."

He was at her side in a second, smoothing her hair back. "You have a fever." Concern glowed in his eyes, and he drew her covers up to her neck. "Hope. I thought you were done getting sick." He wiped his knuckles across her cheekbone. "How are you feeling?"

She looked up at him, her body alive again. "Really confused, Pax." So darn confused. What now?

Chapter Thirty-One

"Get up," a male voice bellowed. "Roll call in twenty."

Drake rolled from his bunk, wincing at the cut on his wrist that refused to heal. He sent more healing cells there and quickly donned his uniform before taking care of business in the bunk's restroom. Then he loped between the tents to the central hub, where his dad was staring at a satellite feed. "Morning, Father."

Dayne looked over his shoulder. "Morning. Rumor has it you did a good job on the raid yesterday. Nearly decapitated a shifter."

Drake shrugged and drew out a chair. "Nearly isn't good enough, now is it?"

"No." Dayne looked back at the satellite feed. "We got a bead on the woman as well as Kayrs, but we couldn't get to them."

A servant, one of the few allowed to travel with attack units, deposited coffee and mugs on the table. Drake waited, but she didn't add any sweetener. Man, he missed Karma sometimes. She'd been kind and sweet and had always remembered the little things. There was no way she was happy with a vampire-demon hybrid. When he got the chance, after the dust settled, he'd go rescue her and bring her home. "You weren't expecting to be able to take them."

Dayne reached over and poured two mugs, his gaze remaining on the screen as the bears started to repair their territory. "No."

The cut on his hand finally healed. Drake took a mug and swallowed the hot brew. "Did it work? Did we flush them out?"

"Too early to tell," Dayne said.

The flap opened, revealing a gray and dismal Seattle day. General Jaydon strode inside, his neck bruised from a fight with three shifters the night before. His white braid still held a tinge of blood. "Well? Did we get the woman out of there? Honor. Even her name is perfect."

Yeah, it was a good name. "Nothing yet," Drake said, sparing his father the nuisance of answering twice. "I don't see the rush to grab her or any of these other women you keep seeking, General. Our great leader Ulric might not return home for a century." Man, Yvonne, Ulric's Intended, would be *pissed.* Well, she'd be dead by then. So maybe not.

Jaydon's eyes swirled deep red through the purple. "I don't answer to you, young one."

Dayne shot him a look.

Drake didn't twitch. "Actually, the Cyst do answer to us, since we're the ones collecting Enhanced women for you." Drake kept his voice civil. "I saw one the other day who looked terrified, fearing for her safety and her future. That was not part of the deal. We help you, and you take care of them." He didn't have the juice to take out the general yet, but he was getting there. Did the asshole know that?

"I do take care of them," Jayden snarled. "For now, just do your job. I'll make sure the three we have here are safely escorted to their new home. I assure you that a life of luxury awaits them there."

"It had better," Drake said softly, knowing full well he was threatening somebody he shouldn't threaten at this time. "Where is this paradise you talk about?" It pissed him off that the Cyst had secret holdings.

"None of your business," Jaydon muttered.

That wasn't going to do, but Drake would wait to speak with his father later. It was time to rebuild, and he was done taking orders from the Cyst.

Jaydon growled, and the floor vibrated. "Speaking of your job, have you accomplished anything?"

Drake still tasted Hope's sweet mouth, and his hard-on might kill him. "Yes. Hope doesn't understand our people or our reasons, but she trusts me." With good reason. He'd protect her.

Jaydon drew out a chair and settled his substantial bulk into it. "I want that woman. Honor McDoval. She's special."

Drake stiffened. "Why?"

"It's time I mated," the general said easily. "The power she has—I want it." He flattened his massive hands on the table. "Get me that woman, and the Cyst and Kurjans will be one again."

Drake glanced sideways. "Under my rule."

"Of course," Jaydon said, tilting his head as on-screen, the bears stomped out the remaining fires in the forest. "We are the spiritual leaders of the Kurjan nation. That is our role and our function. We lost both after the war, after so many of our soldiers died." He turned to face Dayne. "I wish for the old ways as badly as do you, my friend. But my first allegiance has to be to the great leader Ulric and his destiny. His plans must come to fruition, and we must get him home."

"We've never forgotten that," Dayne said, his eyes swirling a deep purple.

"Then we're in accord," Jaydon said. He flicked a glance at a computer tech typing away in the corner. "Why is Sam Kyllwood still breathing?"

Drake barely kept from reminding the general that Sam had been within their grasp the night before, and none of them had come close to taking off his head. "We're working on it."

Jaydon rolled his eyes. "Don't tell me. Aren't the concerned hybrid forces even able to do that job?" He snorted. "The Defenders. Only a bunch of scientists turned spies would even think of using such a stupid name. Next they're going to sew capes with an emblem."

Drake saw no reason to hide his grin. "Even so, they do have access to Sam Kyllwood through their youngest member, Paxton Phoenix, although I'm not sure he has it in him to kill Kyllwood."

Dayne looked at the tech, who was a young Kurjan soldier with thick red hair and spiky black tips. "What's our intel?"

The tech turned around, his eyes a light red with purple rims. "Our source said the Defenders took a vote the other night and have decided to hold off on killing Sam Kyllwood for two reasons. The first is that they don't want another Keeper of the Circle to be created without their knowing who it is—their fear is that it might be one of us."

"The second reason?" Jaydon asked.

The young soldier looked down. Many people had difficulty facing a Cyst. "Paxton Phoenix refuses to kill the uncle of Hope Kayrs-Kyllwood. Or he strongly argued against it. Our source is one of the ten members of the Defenders, but he wasn't in the room for the discussion with Phoenix."

Jaydon shook his head. "They don't even know we have a pawn on their chessboard."

Dayne looked at Drake. "Does the girl know you were on the raid last night?"

"Of course not," Drake said, refilling his coffee cup. "She's a sweetheart who loves her family and thinks they're the good guys. I see no reason to shatter that illusion. Hope deserves to be happy."

Jaydon's lip curled. "You sound like a human whelp, boy."

Drake had no problem meeting the general's gaze. "My future mate willingly comes to me in a dreamworld full of light and warmth. Yours is hiding out with bear shifters and the Keeper of the Circle. Whelp? I don't think so, General. I'd much rather be me than you right now." Especially since he could still feel Hope's hand in his.

Dayne cleared his throat. "Enough. General, we have to make some decisions. What if Bear McDunphy doesn't kick out Sam Kyllwood and Garrett Kayrs?"

"Then we go in and take the woman," the general said. "We need Kyllwood dead, and I'd like it if Kayrs died as well. That'd leave an opening on the Seven, and who knows how many will perish before they find another candidate. If Ulric comes home first, they'll be at least one down."

"Why don't we take out the entire Seven?" Drake asked, watching the bears again.

His dad finished his coffee and poured more. "If we could find them, we would. They've been spectacularly difficult to kill during the last century."

Drake wanted a piece of them and now. "It's unfortunate they don't see the beauty of Ulric's return. Why do they believe the lies of their ancestors?"

"It's who they are," his father said.

That was, unfortunately, a true statement. Drake scratched his head. "If Honor is as strong as you say, we'll need to get her before Kyllwood mates her. They've been together for nearly a week. I do wonder why he hasn't done so as of yet."

Dayne turned to his son. "What are your thoughts about Sam Kyllwood?"

Drake sat straighter in his seat. It was rare for his father to seek his counsel, but he'd begun to do so after his brother, Drake's uncle, had been killed. It was just the two of them now. "I think he's stronger than he should be," Drake said quietly. "He wasn't supposed to be the Keeper of the Circle, and taking that destiny on himself made him more powerful than he should be at this stage of his life. Add in the fact that he shares blood with a member of the Seven as well as Hope, the Lock, and he has to be taken out before the final ritual."

"What about sweetheart Hope?" the general asked, all sarcasm.

Drake flicked a piece of paper off the table. He kept his voice calm and his expression clear. "I'll protect her from as much of this struggle as I can. There are circumstances beyond my control, and life is full of loss. The point is easing her pain afterward." Which he could think of several ways to do, but that was none of the general's business.

Dayne nodded. "That's a good point. Before I forget, General, how many Enhanced females have you acquired?"

"I don't count them," the general retorted.

Why didn't Drake believe that?

Dayne shrugged. "Fair enough, but I have two soldiers who want mates. Shall I send them with you so they can choose?"

"No," Jaydon said. "I trust you, but the females' location must remain secret. There are too many holes still to be plugged in the Kurjan dyke, so to speak. These females must be protected at all costs." He leaned in. "Tell your soldiers to find their own mates." He stood and stomped out of the tent.

The tension dissipated. "How about we cut off his head," Drake said conversationally.

His dad snorted. "Keep that thought. For now, we need him."

Irritation tightened the nerves along Drake's neck. "I don't like it. Why is he hiding the Enhanced females? I understand we need as many as possible for the final ritual with Ulric, but that could still be a century away."

His dad looked at him. "What are you saying?"

"What if the rumors have truth in them?" Drake kept his voice low.

"That's crazy. Those rumors come from our enemies."

Drake shook his head. "Even so, what if? Have you kept track of how many females we've taken? What if Jaydon's planning to take Ulric's place and perform his own ritual to become immortal? It would be a travesty. Just something to think about, Father." He cocked his head. "If the general needs to be taken care of, I want the job." He'd like nothing better than to slide a blade beneath Jaydon's jaw.

Pride glowed for the briefest of seconds in his father's eyes. "All right. If I make that call, you're up."

"Good. I have a plan. He wants Honor badly." It didn't matter if the female had a last name. Kurjans did not have surnames, so she wouldn't, either. "I'll get her and force Jaydon to take me to where he's keeping the Enhanced females. Just to make sure everything is as it should be." Drake sat back.

His father's eyes gleamed. "All right. We'll go with your plan for the female. For now, we need to get to Sam Kyllwood. Are we in agreement about him?"

Hope's sweet face filtered through Drake's thoughts. How hurt she'd be when Kyllwood died. Even so, what were the other options? He nodded. "We're in agreement. Sam Kyllwood will die."

Chapter Thirty-Two

After fielding calls from two kings, a prince, his sister, and a couple of friends, Sam was done maneuvering the universe for his purposes. For now.

He lounged against a tree near the bear headquarters as the smell of grilled meat wafted through the damp air. Salads and other dishes had been placed on wide picnic tables. The bears were alive and celebrating, which meant it was going to be a wild night. He watched Honor interact with several of them, smiling and laughing. She'd made friends so easily. His chest warmed while his palm remained stone cold. What was wrong with him?

Apparently his mood showed, because not one bear approached him with mating advice.

Well, except Bear. McDunphy gave no fucks about anybody being cranky. *Like* found *like* in this world. "Hey." He handed over a longneck.

"Bear," Sam said, accepting the brew. "How are repairs coming?" He kept his gaze on Honor.

"On time. The sensors will be down for at least another day, but then we should be okay. We need to plan a ride." Bear's gaze zeroed in on Nessa, who was standing over by one of the grills.

Sam tuned in his senses to look for threats. "The ride. Retribution?"

"Yes." Bear lifted his chin in acknowledgment when Nessa looked up and smiled at him. She was glowing already, and power emanated from her, even across the distance.

Sam wanted that. With Honor. "Good." There was no chance the Grizzlies would let an attack go unanswered. "I have feelers out with the demon nation for locations of Kurjan strongholds."

Bear's rugged face cleared. "You're on board for an attack?"

Sam took a deep drink of the cold beer. "I'm a Grizzly Club member, Bear. They attacked us. Forget nations, forget shifters, forget the hybrids, the Seven, and all the rituals. At the end of the day, you were right. We're brothers, this is our club, and they made a colossal mistake in coming after us."

"Yeah." Bear straightened. "Damn straight." He finished his longneck. "If I have about fifty more of these, you might get an 'I love you, man' later tonight."

"Something to look forward to," Sam said dryly. Then his attention moved to a spot near the garage, where Garrett was making out with a female whose hair was streaked with bright green. Even through the distance, Sam could read her as a feline shifter. "Come on."

Bear snorted. "He found her in town. Her name is Claws."

"Clause?" Sam asked.

"No. Claws. Like nails and claws and danger. She's some sort of shifter bounty hunter." Bear's massive chest rolled with a chuckle.

Sam groaned. "He knows we have bounties on our heads, right?"

Bear shrugged. "Yeah, but she's not looking for you—is apparently hot on the trail of a feline shifter who robbed a clan in the Rockies. Nessa ran her background the second she arrived in territory, and she checks out. Although there are several state warrants out on her—apparently Claws likes to shoot people." He tossed the beer bottle across several yards to land in a garbage can marked "recycled." "But who doesn't?"

"Indeed," Sam agreed, irritation nevertheless trying to choke him. "Why couldn't Garrett's big breakthrough with Honor have been that he should be celibate for a few years?"

"Come on." Bear jerked his head toward one of the prospects, and the kid tossed a beer his way. He caught it and twisted the cap open. "Bad girls are good in bed, usually. Let the kid have some fun. Plus, the green in her hair is cool."

"Yeah. It is pretty cool." Although this was a mistake, like usual. Sam shook his head.

"Before I forget, a couple of the older female shifters have special teas for you. They swear by them," Bear said, not hiding a smile.

Sam growled. "It's not like I can't get it up, Bear. God. Tell your people to back off before I lose it."

"Already did, my brother." Bear clinked bottles with him.

Honor wound her way toward them, stopping several times to speak with people. She really did fit in. When she arrived, worry showed in her eyes. "Garrett."

"Saw him," Sam said, hauling her to his side. Where she belonged.

She rested her head against his chest, letting him take her weight. "I'm not sure. I think we did a good thing, digging into his brain, but now he's on a mission to find the toughest woman out there. Her name is Claws, Sam. *Claws.* She kind of looks like the woman he dreamed about? Now he says that the woman is hazy."

He tightened his hold. "I know. Garrett's a big boy, sweets. He can handle Claws."

She sighed, her breath warm against his shirt. "He really doesn't have the best taste in women. Doc Julie tried to get us killed, and now Claws asked if anybody here had drugs, because she'd like a nice buzz. The way I felt about his mate…"

Sam stiffened. "Bad?"

"Yeah. Dangerous and bad and there was a hint of pain. For Garrett." She shook her head. "I'm not sure what to do."

"You do nothing." Sam leaned down and kissed the top of her head. Her hair had dried thick and springy, and she looked young and full of life. He was going to keep her that way. Healthy and strong. Safe. "If Garrett's mate is an assassin or something similar, he'll take care of it."

She reared up. "Seriously? An assassin? Are you nuts?"

He grinned down at her. "My brother Logan and his mate met when she lured him out of a bar and kidnapped him, with the intention of killing him. They're very happy now."

Bear grinned. "And your mom met Daire by drugging him at an MC party and then robbing him. Didn't she drug him a few times?"

Sam chuckled. "Yeah. Good times."

"Has she robbed any banks lately?" Bear asked conversationally.

Honor jolted.

Sam rubbed her rib cage, where his hand hung over her fragile shoulders. "She doesn't tell me usually. Daire has a handle on it."

"You have an interesting family," Honor said, sounding dazed.

"Yeah. They'll do." Sam watched as Garrett tossed Claws over his shoulder and disappeared around the building. "At least he'll be in a good mood tomorrow. For Garrett, anyway."

Honor cried out, and pain pierced his side. From her. He looked down, and half of her left leg was gone. She paled. "Something has me."

* * * *

Honor shook with pain as sharp razors shredded her leg. What the heck had happened to Flynn's web? Apparently it only worked on the fires and not all of the worlds through dimensions. She grabbed on to Sam and tried to free herself. Nothing.

Sam lifted her with one arm and moved around her, his body shielding her from the rest of the party. "Hold on."

Bear moved to the side. "What is happening?" He looked around. "Stay cool. Keep it cool."

Sam reached down into the hole, keeping his hand on her leg. "Okay." A loud snap echoed. He growled.

Flynn immediately approached and took the opposite side of Bear. "I felt a disturbance." His eyes glowed in his coal-deep eyes. "What's happening?"

Honor trembled with pain and fought tears, kicking with all her might and holding Sam for balance. "I don't know." Whatever had her fought hard to get more of her, and she gasped, digging her nails into Sam's chest.

Sam hissed and swung her around, tearing her free.

She cried out and buried her face in his chest. Then he was moving. Wind whistled through her hair, touching her nape, and within a minute, they were back at their cabin.

He set her in the doorframe, which hadn't been fixed completely. "Don't look."

She looked and then bit back a scream. Her jeans were shredded, and several different-sized bite marks marred her flesh. She bled freely, and her toes had gone numb. "Sam."

"Hold on." He ripped open a vein in his wrist and pressed it to her mouth. "Drink. Now." His face was a hard mask of fury.

She drank, letting his sizzling blood trickle down her throat to her stomach and then spread warmth through her freezing cold body. Her wounds slowly mended. She went limp, tears still flowing down her face. "If you hadn't been there, I would've been pulled all the way in."

He brushed the tears off her face. "Guys? We need a minute."

Honor looked beyond them to see both Bear and Flynn, their faces set in anger and their eyes dark. "I'm okay."

"Not for long," Flynn said. "Nobody can create a web to fight that kind of power for long. I can only ward off the fire. You have to get this under control. Now."

"Minute. Now," Sam barked, his gaze remaining on her.

The brothers turned and disappeared back into the forest.

Sam lifted her, stepped up into the cabin, and strode to the fireplace, where he lit the logs while still holding her. Then he turned and sat on the sofa, cradling her. Warming her and making her feel safe. "Take several deep breaths, calm yourself, and then we'll talk. No hurry and no pressure on you. Let my blood ease you." His voice was soft and gentle, but tension rode each syllable. Hard.

She snuggled right into his chest, doing as he said. Her limbs felt lethargic and her mind buzzed from the rush of pain and then his blood. Finally, she started playing with the neckline of his tee. "I'm better." She kissed his neck.

"Good." He shifted her until she could look up and meet his green gaze. "It's time for you to dig into my head like you did Garrett's." His grimace was kind of cute. "I don't like the idea, but we have to figure out why the mating mark hasn't appeared, when all I want to do is mate you."

She had her own fears and insecurities about that. What if Fate had a different mate for him? What if she was just filler? "Okay, but I can't be completely objective with you."

"That's a good thing." He leaned down and kissed her nose.

She freaking loved it when he did that. He was so deadly, and she'd seen him kill faster than a thought, but with her, he was gentle. As far as she could tell, that side of him only came out with her and his family. Maybe Nessa, but she was pregnant with triplets. "We both have to accept what we find, Sam."

"I know." He settled his shoulders as if he was going into battle. "What now?"

She nuzzled her face against his warm neck. "Now you just relax and let me in."

He swallowed, and while his hold remained firm and solid, his big body relaxed against her. A large exhale moved her. "Okay."

Curiosity rode her, and she went in gentle with just a glide against his mind. Solid rock. She pressed her lips together to keep from chuckling. Then she tickled his mind.

"Hey," he murmured. "*That's* weird."

"I know." She kept it up until even his brain relaxed and then she glided right in. "Okay. I'm there. Tell me about the marking."

"Demons or hybrids have a marking, first letter of their last name, that shows on the hand. Usually right when they meet their mate, but sometimes later, and sometimes when it's forced there in the case of an arranged mating." Now he sounded slightly drugged.

The male really trusted her. She placed her hand over his heart and dug for images. Ah. The Kyllwood marking...on his brother. Logan? Yeah. She sensed Logan. Then another marking, this one of a *Z*. Zane? Oh. His first name because he was the king. Then another *K* and an *S*...images. Not real. Nightmares. She drew in his scent and settled herself. "Tell me about Zane."

"My older brother. He tried to protect us as best he could from our uncle. Always there." Sam's voice softened. "I'd die for him."

"You've spent your entire life trying to live for him," she murmured. "Helping and protecting both of your brothers. It's not easy in the middle, is it, Sam?"

He shrugged. "I'm good at it."

She slid deeper. "You are. But you're afraid."

"I'm not." His warrior ego flared hot for a second.

She kept her probing gentle. "Sure you are. Anybody who loves has fear. That's natural."

"Honor, I'm not afraid I'll get twin *S*'s on my hands resulting from Zane's death," he muttered.

"Sure you are. You're also a control freak, and the only way to make one hundred percent sure that doesn't happen is to not have a mating mark on your hand." Like, duh. But she didn't say that. "However, whatever your mark may be, that doesn't change Zane's destiny, does it?"

Sam sighed. "No."

There you go. She delved deeper. "Hey. What's this about me in there?"

"You?" He kissed her head.

"Yeah." Right there, with the marking, along with his really strong thoughts or feelings about Zane and being the king of the demon nation.

Her brain tingled. He explored the area inside himself with shocking accuracy. Better than anybody she'd worked with so far. Figured. She tilted her head to watch his face.

"Huh." He leaned back. "All right. Guess there's a fear that if we fully mate, I'll hurt you worse than I already have." He opened his eyes. "I gave you this problem with fire and dimensional pain. What if I give you more of it when we mate?"

"What if we cure ourselves?" she murmured. For the first time in her life, she went on instinct. Sam had drawn her out of her safe little world, where she protected herself and stayed alone, and now she had to take the final step. "If we remain like this and don't take the risk, aren't things going to just get to the point where one or both of us are dragged into some freezing cold, biting world?"

He lifted his chin. "Probably." He looked right at her. "Do you want to mate?"

Was that an offer? She hitched, suddenly nervous, and withdrew from his thoughts. She'd been thinking about this and could spend the next several decades still weighing pros and cons. Sometimes a girl just had to go for it.

"Yes," she murmured.

Chapter Thirty-Three

Sam rubbed a hand down Honor's damp back beneath his shirt as she snuggled into his side, falling asleep. His body was relaxed and his mind satiated. It had been one wild night. Dawn was just beginning to show beneath the blinds, and a chill filtered through the bottom of the bedroom door. He really should get the front door fixed so it at least, well, existed.

He stretched his legs and closed his eyes to scout for threats outside. The sensors weren't at full capacity yet, so he had to be vigilant.

The world was safe around them. He yawned and settled in to get a little sleep, ignoring the fact that the marking hadn't appeared on his hand. They'd had sex all night, she'd screamed his name, and he'd gotten lost in her sweet and curvy body.

But no marking.

Oh, she was right, and it was on him. Even realizing that fact didn't reveal a path for him to fix the problem. He forced the stress and doubts away and then drifted into sleep. The second he was almost there, the room spun. He growled and then careened through space and time, landing hard on his back.

Heat flared against his front and he groaned as he sat up. This wasn't a dream or a dreamworld—somehow, he was really here. At least most of him was in this place.

"Sam?"

He turned to find Honor next to him, sitting up on a red metal surface, her nose burning from the three red suns blaring at them. Only his T-shirt covered her. At least she'd drawn it on before falling asleep.

They floated above a sea of purple that seethed and spit up spiked steam. "Ah, great." He looked down at his boxer briefs.

Honor reached for his hand, the scent of her terror sharp on the slight wind. "Um. Are we dreaming? Is this a dream?"

"No." He held her closer, noting the dimensions of the metal sheet. It felt solid, but he'd learned during his ritual that illusions always gave way. If they plunged into the mess of liquid below them, pain was coming fast. "We might just be partly here, or it could be all of us. I'm not sure." Usually this sort of experience was a dream, but lately, with parts of their bodies being pulled into portals, it was possible they were actually here. Now he needed to get Honor away. He pinched her arm.

"Ow." She drew back, her eyes wide and slightly distorted by the strange atmosphere. "Why did you do that?"

"I was hoping to wake you up and send you home," he admitted. This was a disaster. He'd known better than to let down his guard, but after opening his mind to her and then having viorous sex for seven hours, he'd wanted to rest. "Okay. I need to think."

An animal screeched high and loud in the murky distance.

Honor jumped and scrambled closer to him. "What was that?"

Probably something that wanted to eat them for dinner. "Nothing. Don't worry about it—we're far away from it." Hopefully.

She gulped and looked down at the purple liquid. Curiosity lit her luminous eyes. "Are we in a different dimension?"

"No." He kept her close, waiting. Knowing it was coming. "We're three-dimensional beings, so we can only exist in a three-dimensional world." He looked for the portals. Not yet. "But we've traveled through different ones, probably, and here we are." Now he just had to get them back home.

She shook her head. "I can't believe this." Now she'd gone breathy. "I mean, how does this place even exist and we don't know about it?" He shrugged. "Your choice. It seems kind of obvious to me. There are worlds other than the one we live in." The mist parted, and the clouds started to move away. He looked up. "We're going to be dragged into different places, but hopefully it'll be fast. Hold on to me so we don't get separated."

She all but jumped on his lap. "How do we get home?" Her voice sounded shocked. Lost. Kind of intrigued.

"Instinct." It was the best he could explain. Of course, last time he'd jumped through worlds, he'd been undergoing a ritual to become the Keeper, and it had taken a couple of centuries. All that time was only many hours at home, though. This had to be different. He wouldn't allow Honor to face the pain he had. Ever.

Three portals swirled open above them, all dark, all hiding their secrets. "Gut?" Sam asked.

"Um, left one?" She held tight to him.

He shook his head. "No. Feel the vibrations. Reach out with those impressive skills and try to protect yourself." Before she could do so, the force started to draw them from the platform. He held her and maneuvered them through the middle portal.

This time, he landed on his feet with Honor in his arms. Sharp spikes rammed right through his heels to his ankles, and he growled. Pain flashed harsh.

Honor gasped and looked around, clinging to his neck. "Sam. Your feet."

"I know." He stood on a field of spikes with spiked trees all around them. A pleasant breeze wafted through the trees, smelling like chocolate chip cookies, and bright red butterflies meandered from spike to spike.

"What should we do?"

He sighed. "Just wait for the next series of portals. I'll send healing cells to my feet but can't really fix them until I get the spikes out."

He could, at least, neutralize the poison in the spikes. Apparently the butterflies liked the thick goo he could feel trying to kill him.

Three portals opened up above them. "Is it always three?" Honor whispered.

"Not always," he said, studying the dark voids. "Concentrate. Where do we go?"

She trembled. "Middle one?"

"No." He could feel danger and death in that one. "Left. This time."

* * * *

Honor would never be a world-class portal jumper. She'd chosen the wrong possibility about seventy percent of the time. "I suck at this."

"We all have different skills." Sam held her on his back as he healed bite marks down his torso. The thing that had come at them in the last world had looked like a cross between a tabby house cat and a fanged buffalo.

Honor set her head on his shoulder, her nose to his neck. It had been days. Or felt like days, but Sam assured her they'd probably only been gone a couple of hours. "Are we getting closer to home?" Earlier, he'd been able to feel a path home, but he hadn't mentioned it since.

"Yeah." He didn't sound sure.

Her stomach growled. They'd taken a risk and eaten some berries earlier, and she'd been farting since. At least they'd gotten some food.

One portal opened to the left, right beyond a red tree with pretty bright purple leaves. Just one?

Sam grabbed her wrists in one of his hands. "Hold on."

She clutched his neck, wrapping both legs around his waist. They tumbled up into the sky and then fell, zooming right through the portal, spinning end over end. She shut her eyes and just held on.

They landed hard, Sam on his feet, bouncing twice.

Cool air brushed her. She slowly opened her eyes to see a thick mist all around them. Below Sam looked like a pier of some type. Water, or a liquid thicker than water, bubbled all around, as if something gleefully waited for them to fall. She shivered.

He gently set her to the side. "Stay close to me."

"No problem." She all but plastered herself to his rib cage. "Where are we?"

Sam stood straight and tall, staring at what looked like a far shoreline. Well, not so far. But the mist made it difficult to see. "Ulric?"

"Ulric?" she whispered.

A figure strode out of a rock formation to the shore, and even she could tell he held tremendous power. He looked like the Cyst general she'd seen the other day, but he was taller, thicker, and somehow, more dangerous. His white hair bisected his scalp and ran down his back, and his eyes were a pure purple. Did they change color? She'd noticed that the eyes of most immortals did. Her knees shook and she pressed them together.

Ulric looked her over. "She's special."

Sam's body tightened. "Did you call us here?"

"Yes," Ulric said, his gaze licking over her like a tongue.

She pressed even closer to Sam, and he partially pivoted to stand in front of her. Even so, she ducked her head to look around him.

Ulric smiled, revealing razor-sharp canines tinged with red. Blood? "How about you leave the girl here?"

"No," Sam said.

Ulric tore his gaze away. "Keeper? It was difficult to get you here. The Lock did a decent job of closing portals, and I had to bring you the long way around. Sorry about that."

Tension rolled off Sam. "What do you want?"

Ulric shrugged. "Ideally? You dead. I can keep you spinning through worlds until a beast somewhere cuts off your head, and it looks like your female will go with you. I can't have you being the Keeper."

Honor pushed herself against Sam's side. Her head rang. Forever? Could they be trapped in these spinning and dangerous worlds for eternity? "Is it true? Do you really want to kill all Enhanced females?" Sam had told her the entire legend the night before, in between mind-blowing orgasms. "How does that make sense?"

Ulric didn't look at her again. "Your female doesn't know her place."

Honor straightened. "Right now, it's right here. Are you afraid to answer me?"

Sam's lip twitched. "Question, Ulric. Rumor has it one of your generals is trying to duplicate your ritual. He's certainly kidnapped more than a hundred Enhanced females, and based on my intel on the guy, he's more than prepared to sacrifice them all. Is it possible he could shield his entire body as you have?"

"No," Ulric growled, the sound vibrating back from unseen surfaces. "That's impossible. My people would never let that happen."

Fury rolled off Sam, but he remained calm. Even slightly bored looking. "Your people got their asses kicked in the last war, and the Cyst have risen within the ranks. You have a rogue general who's going to make you obsolete. You might want to concentrate on that sad fact." He slid an arm around Honor's shoulders and secured her closer to him. "Is the Intended just for you, or for whoever leads the Cyst faction? It's an interesting question, no?"

Ulric's too pale face turned red. An ugly red. "I'm going to make sure you last for a long time in these hell worlds, Keeper."

"You know, the name is growing on me," Sam said, all but vibrating next to her.

Ulric threw his head back and then stiffened, fixing his gaze on another platform not too far away. This one was vacant.

And then it wasn't.

A very pretty teenager stood there in jeans and a black sweater, her boots a matching black. She had long auburn hair and incredible blue eyes. Despite her petite size, she held an air of power. She looked around, turned her head, and sneezed.

Sam snarled. "Hope?"

This was Hope? The prophesied one? She looked like a normal teenager—maybe eighteen?

The young woman looked at Sam. "I felt you come here. Sorry. I thought I'd shut all the portals."

"You can't shut them," Ulric said, his voice deep. "I can always open them and pull the Keeper and his female through. The unnatural opens the door to opportunity."

Hope lifted her chin. "Yeah? Well, for now, fuck you." She clapped her hands.

"Wait!" Sam hissed.

Hope paused, even though a portal opened up above them. "What?"

He pressed closer to the edge and to her, holding on to Honor. "I have an idea. The ritual I underwent was unnatural, and because of that I caught something. Gave it to Honor."

"Because she's your mate," Hope whispered.

Sam nodded. "Agreed. Look what just appeared." He held up his right hand, revealing the stunning marking of a K surrounded by raw and bleeding lines. "There's only one way to get rid of the locator he has on me. You know it."

Hope paled. "That's crazy."

"The marking. It's here." Honor grabbed Sam's ribs. "What's crazy? What's happening?"

"It's the only way," Sam said quietly. "If it doesn't work, get Honor out of here."

Ulric bellowed, and the skies opened up to reveal a swirling mass of copper pain. He clapped his hands, and all three of them flew through.

Honor felt as if her soul had been shredded from her body.

Then, nothing.

Chapter Thirty-Four

Sam hit a spongy gray surface and rolled, keeping Honor with him. "Damn it all to hell," he muttered, landing on his back with her on top of him. A soft sun shone down, and he caressed her spine.

She blinked, looking dazed. "What happened? I thought we were going somewhere terrifying?"

"Hope tossed us at the last second, and we went through a different portal." It felt okay on the spongy material, and right now, nothing was stabbing or biting him, so he took a deep breath.

"Hope." Honor's eyes widened. "God. Where is she?"

Sam held her tight. "She's fine. I felt her spin off in a different direction, and she can get herself free of these worlds." Unfortunately there was only one way for him to do so, and now he was on his own without his niece.

Honor lifted her head and looked around. "She sent us to a nice world." She shifted against him, her eyes flashing. "You're aroused."

"You're on my dick."

A light pink wandered across her cheekbones. "Sam. We're in a world not our own, probably going to die, and you have a hard-on."

"Like I said." He pressed down on her sweet ass, pushing her core right against him. The woman didn't know him very well if she thought he was going to let her die in this place. In any place, really. The world settled around him, and the tension in his body slid away. The portals were far distant right now, and he was good with that.

Then he saw one. Up in the yellow-and-pink-striped sky, to the far right past clouds that appeared to have the silver lining on the outside, was a portal. A big, dark, locked portal. He grinned. Hope was good. Seriously good, and she'd done what he wanted. Yeah, he was buying her a new sportscar for her next birthday…if he lived to see it. Right now, there was a clear lock on the portal, one he sensed. One that would remain in place for a least a little while. Until he did what needed to be done.

He rolled up and looked around. It was a good world, not one of the hell ones. No danger lurked anywhere near. He bounced on the spongy gray ground. It extended as far as he could see, glistening in the full sun, which wasn't too strong. "I'm thinking this is a good place."

Honor reached to slide her hand over the sponge. "I like it here. I wonder how far we are from home?"

Home. He liked that she thought of their place as home. It was a good start. "I don't think distance works the way we think it does, even with our advanced knowledge of physics." Now that he'd made up his mind, his cock felt like it was about to break through his jeans for good. Down, boy. Now.

She reached for his hand, turning it over. "The marking. It's beautiful." She traced the jagged lines with her finger, and he was wracked by a shudder. "It appeared. Finally." Wonder filled her voice.

"Yeah. I stopped being a dumbass and stopped worrying about things I couldn't control."

"Who? You?" She leaned down and kissed the marking, and her mouth might as well have been right on his soul. "Not be able to control something? Come on. What is this false reality of which you speak?"

"Smart-ass." He pulled her toward him and kissed her, easing his pain with her sweet taste. For now. "We have a reprieve, and I thought I'd plant this on your ass. Or wherever else you want it." He'd freaking love to see it on her curvy ass. But if she wanted it on her back, he'd understand.

Her laugher pealed across the gray, spongy land, bouncing back. "Funny. Shouldn't we go home first?"

"No." He tapped her mouth. "We're doing this here, gorgeous. Decide where you want the marking."

Her eyes opened, and then she licked her lips. "We are not doing it here. We could get dragged out at any second. You're being crazy."

"I'm taking as much control as I can." He kept an eye on the nearly invisible lock on the nearly invisible portal up so high. "We're going back to meet Ulric, and I want you mated first. You won't have full strength or my gifts yet, but hopefully if you're hurt, we can heal you fast. Okay?"

"No." She stood on the bouncy surface, widening her legs to keep her balance. "We are not going back to see Ulric. Why would we do that?"

He brushed his knuckles down the side of her pretty face. "It's the only thing I can think to do. If I can hit him, I can leave this curse with him, hopefully. I caught it, gave it to you, and now I want it back." Mating would do that, he was fairly certain. "Then I dump the curse on him and we go home to no more fires or limbs being eaten by scavengers we can't see."

"That's crazy." Heat bloomed across her face. "Just nuts. You are not going to play tag with a zillion-year-old immortal god." The woman was a little bossy.

"He's not a god, and that's exactly what I'm going to do." There had to be a way to keep her in this world while he took care of business. If he died, hopefully his niece would be able to find Honor and lead her home. He trusted Hope to do that. "For now, you're about to get a marking on your flesh. Want to make it interesting?"

Anger, arousal, and curiosity flashed across her face in rapid succession. "Meaning?"

"I'll let you run." With the spongy ground, she wouldn't be able to go fast. "If you make it ten yards before I catch you, then we'll go with whatever plan you come up with."

She tilted her head. Acceptance of his challenge curved her lips. Oh, his girl liked a game once in a while. Good to know. "Four yards."

"Seven."

"Five."

"Deal." He held out a hand, and they shook.

She bunched her legs.

"Go," he whispered.

* * * *

Excitement surging through her, Honor turned and ran. Her feet sank into the squishy gray ground, but she lowered her head and ran full bore for the horizon. In his shirt and her light panties, she should feel vulnerable. Instead, she felt like a badass on a different world. One who could handle that world and the male behind her.

He caught her within two yards, twisted, and tossed her, keeping hold of her shirt when he did so.

She squealed and landed on her butt, flipping end over end on the soft surface, her bare breasts bouncing. Bounding up, she turned the other way to run, her laugher clipping through the pure air. Should this be fun? It was. Even so, her heart pounded and something primal rose in her. If he wanted her, he'd have to catch her.

Again.

Pivoting, she barely missed his outstretched hand. She jumped back, surprised by how far she bounced in the air. "You can't catch me." She landed, settling her stance.

His smile was all vampire. Or demon. Either way, all immortal. "I already did," he said softly.

Her breath felt hot, and her knees instinctively trembled with a warning to flee. "You going to give me all of you?" she whispered, ready to run.

"Without question." Silky and low, his hoarse statement shot right to her core.

She barely kept from doubling over. Instead, she edged to the side, ready to run.

He stalked her, all grace and danger. For a second, the tiniest of moments, she could only stare at him. The deadly beauty of him. It was too much. He was too close. His unblinking gaze, green edged with a silvery black, remained focused on her face.

Even so, she had to try. She bunched her muscles, but he was already on her, taking them both down to the porous ground. Then his mouth slammed down. Desperate, hard, forceful—Sam Kyllwood taking control, as only he could.

She moaned, need boiling the blood in her veins. Locking her hands in his hair, she kissed him back, taking everything he offered.

He kissed her deep, one hand around her neck, holding her in place. So much in one kiss. Promise and threat, hope and that ever present control.

Her tongue mated with his, and then because she was who she was, she bit his lip. Not gently. His blood tasted like power.

"You're a brat." He licked the wound clean, his hand sweeping beneath them to palm her butt and partially lift her off the sponge.

She panted at the friction, wanting to fight him but wanting him inside her even more. "I don't want to make this easy for you," she moaned against his mouth.

His bark of surprise erased her worry. "Easy? This has been next to impossible." He rolled to the side, flipped her onto her belly, and smacked her ass. "That's for making it so hard."

She laughed. Humor and need and more than that, a lot more than that, rushed through her. Was this love? Or was it just the love she could have with him? She wiggled her butt. "Do that again." He sucked in a breath and slammed his hand down again, sending searing heat right to her clit.

He chuckled and flipped her over again, covering her. "It's not a very good means of disciplining you if you like it."

"Then I guess you don't get to discipline me." She leaned up and licked his bottom lip. "Try something else."

He kissed her again, his hands at her breasts, kneading them. Plucking the nipples. Adding more than a hint of pain to the incredible pleasure only he could provide.

She gyrated against him, sweeping her hands down to push off his boxers. The man had survived multiple hell worlds wearing only boxers. Male. *The male.* He was not human. Not even close. "Now, Sam," she moaned, reaching for him.

He tweaked a nipple hard enough to make her yelp and then moved down her, his mouth finding her. Right where she wanted him. She flew off into another world in her head, orgasming so fast her ears rang. He bit her thigh, sinking his fangs deep. Then he scraped them across her more delicate flesh.

She gasped and held perfectly still.

"Finally. A way to get you to behave." He licked her, swirling his tongue across her clit.

She bit her lip to keep from crying out.

"You know I like you loud." He sucked the entire thing into his mouth, barely scraping his fangs along the sides. She blew apart, screaming, shaking wildly on the spongy ground. He let her come down. "Better. Much better." Then he turned her over.

She stopped breathing.

He drew her up on hands and knees before prodding her, sliding inch by inch inside her. So big and ready and impossibly hard. She dropped her head, willing her body to take all of him. Pain and pleasure and completeness took her, as his steady grip kept her in place. He didn't pause, and she stiffened, the pain increasing. He still didn't pause.

She quaked around him. His grip was unbreakable and his determination strong. "Sam," she murmured.

He tightened his hold and plunged inside her to the hilt, yanking her back into him. Shock took her at the suddenness of the pain, but she'd been wet and ready. Her body gripped his as if she'd never let him go.

"Honor." His mouth was at her ear. He slammed into her, fast, relentless, strong. She could do nothing but take all of him, and she screamed through another orgasm, sobbing his name.

He continued to pound. His fingers bruising her hips, his body bracketing hers.

Live coils unwound inside her, burning her skin, torching her nerves. She climbed even higher, held her breath, and then fell. The orgasm swept through her stronger than any force, and then his fangs slid into her neck, sinking into her bone. She stiffened, thrown into another climax, lights flickering behind her eyelids.

Fire blistered her butt, combining with all the other sensations. He groaned with his own release.

The world stilled. The slight breeze caressed her bare skin. She breathed deep.

He pulled out, leaned down to kiss the burning circle on her butt, and then stood, helping her to her feet.

She turned and snuggled into his chest, kissing him.

He bent and kissed her, his lips firm. "Get dressed. We're out of time."

She looked up to see a portal opening, its jaws wide.

Chapter Thirty-Five

Sam would give almost anything for a pair of jeans. Or a sword. He held Honor's hand, his mind retracing the steps Hope had taken to push him to this gray world. If he could do the same for Honor, at least he could keep her away from Ulric.

"Don't even think it," she said, digging her fingers into his hand. "Besides. You're not the only one with this infection. I have to touch Ulric too."

Sam straightened and took a deep breath. The gods owed him one. He brushed his fingers across her neck, closed his eyes, and dug deep into her for whatever this curse was. He caught it, a sense, and dug right into her brain for a kernel of fire that didn't belong there.

She gasped and fought him, but it was too late.

He forced the fire out of her and shoved the molten mass into his own center, mingling it with the weird lump that had existed inside him since he'd undergone the ritual. For the briefest time, while she'd shared the pain, he'd felt better. Stronger and whole. Now, it was all in one place and felt like poison inside him. But at least he'd gotten it out of Honor.

He didn't expect the punch to the gut.

He looked down at her. "Excuse me?"

She punched him again and then winced, shaking out her hand. "That wasn't right. You couldn't just take that…whatever it was. I felt it, and now you're in more danger than you were before."

"I know." He'd never lie to her. "But if the worst happens, you can't be dragged in again." When she tried to glide into his brain, he mentally slapped her back.

"Ow." She pressed a hand to her eye, glaring at him from the other one.

He shrugged. "Don't go into people's heads without permission."

"You just did," she exploded, stomping her foot with little effect on the springy ground. "This isn't right. I can't help you or protect you now."

Oh, she was so adorable and didn't understand a damn thing. "I protect you." There wasn't any need to go into it more than that.

Then he didn't have to because the portal opened wider and the air changed. He lifted her against his chest. "Hold on."

She did so, tucking her head beneath his chin. Her body trembled, and he held her tighter. "It's almost over." Then they were up in the air, spinning around. His stomach lurched, but he kept his eyes open. Blackness surrounded them and then a lighter gray, and they fell.

He tossed her to the pier and then bounced away, performing a series of flips in the air and landing in the purple water. Bubbles rose around him like acid, and he leaped out, falling onto burning-hot sand and rolling to his feet.

"Sam!" Honor yelled from the pier, standing and pressing her hands to her hips. She slid to the edge and looked frantically at the purple water.

"Don't even think it," he snapped, his voice echoing back at him hollowly. "It's acid, and there's something alive in there. Something that lives in pure acid."

Frustration wrinkled her face, and damn if she still didn't look like she was going to dip in a toe.

"I'm fucking not kidding," he roared.

She jumped back, her eyes wide.

Ulric strolled out from an opening in the rocks that Sam hadn't been able to see from the water. "Oh, Keeper. Did you have to make it so easy?" He reached out, almost casually, and punched Sam in the head.

Sam feinted to the side and dropped, coming up fast. He kicked Ulric in the neck.

The sound of his foot breaking preceded the sharp spike of pain up his leg. He hopped on the other one. "So the rumors are true," he grunted.

Ulric cocked his head, his eyes a swirling amethyst. "Yes. I'm impenetrable. You can't hurt me."

Oh, they'd see about that. Sam punched him in the eye, breaking three knuckles.

Ulric snarled. Then he kicked out, turning sideways. Pain ripped through Sam's ribs as several broke, and then he careened through the air to land on the hot sand. He grunted and rolled to his good foot. This was going to shit and fast. "Honor? I love you. I'm glad we mated."

"Love me? You seriously love me?" she yelled. "You don't love somebody and then put yourself in the path of a psycho immortal from hell."

"Your female has some lungs on her," Ulric said, circling him.

Sam rushed at him, looking for any weak spot. He settled on Ulric's lips, punching rapidly...and breaking several bones in his hand.

Ulric reacted by smashing his fist into Sam's left eye. The socket burst like a cracked egg.

Sam gasped, hopping back, half of his body either broken or numb. Liquid covered his face. Blood?

Ulric shook his head and strode forward. "You mated the Enhanced one?" He sniffed the air, pleasure blooming across his wide face. "Oh, she smells good. Did you taste her? Bite her?" He grabbed Sam by the hair and yanked him closer, razor-sharp fangs sliding down to his chin. "Do you know how long it's been since I tasted a female? Especially one with power like that?"

Sam gritted his teeth and punched out, hitting Ulric in the eye. His hand bounced off, and the bones in his wrist snapped apart. The pain nearly dropped him to his knees.

Ulric laughed. He scraped his fangs along Sam's neck and then reared back like a snake to strike, his mouth gaping wide open.

Sam punched as hard as he could into Ulric's mouth, mentally shoving the ball of fire out of his body and down into Ulric's. His nails scraped down inside Ulric's throat, and his fingers burned from the blood. He made it almost to the elbow and let go of the fire.

Ulric reared back, roaring.

Sam pulled his arm and hand out of the monster's mouth, fangs ripping into his flesh as he wrenched free. He shoved Ulric and then turned, praying his niece was still with them. "Now, Hope," he yelled, blood gurgling out with his breath.

A big blue portal opened and sucked him up, along with Honor, who scrambled to grab onto his arm.

Ulric bellowed furiously beneath them.

Then Sam landed on his bed in Grizzly Club territory, bounced once, and passed completely out.

* * * *

Feeling better after a night and another day of sleep, Honor fetched some fresh coffee from the temporary tent set up in the middle of Grizzly Club territory while everyone rebuilt. A bunch of work trucks were lined up to one side. Burgers were on for dinner but weren't quite cooked yet. She ran right into Bear.

He steadied her with both hands on her elbows. "Slow down. You're newly mated, and that takes a toll on your energy." His shaggy hair was somehow shaggier than ever, and sawdust covered his right leg. His eyes were a mellow honey brown. "Nessa is with

Sam right now, and she has confirmed that his niece, Hope, is safe at demon headquarters, so take a breath. Nessa will reassure Sam."

She did as he suggested, letting her body relax. They'd gotten home the night before, and Sam had been sleeping since. The air tingled all around him, and Bear had assured her that those were healing cells. "I'm going to kill him when he's all healed," she said, taking a drink of the coffee.

Bear burst out laughing and several people looked their way from the tent, surprise on their faces. "From what you said, Sam did the only thing he could—shoved his arm down Ulric's gullet."

A woman sauntered their way. Full hips, full lips, and a lot of wild blond hair. "Bear. Garrett told me to come grab dinner while he talked to somebody named King." The woman's voice was a low purr, and by the looks of things, she wanted to grab a taste of Bear. Her eyes were slightly off, kind of like a cat's. Was she a feline shifter?

Honor instinctively put her body between them. "Hi. We haven't met."

Bear sighed. "Honor, this is Sylvia, Garrett's…friend."

"Hi," Sylvia purred, her orange-red lipstick the wrong shade for her hair. By far. Her gaze went beyond Honor to Bear. "Rumor has it your wife is knocked up. That's tough on a guy. I could help if you want."

Honor's chin lowered. "What does that mean?"

"Exactly what you think," Sylvia said, winking at Bear.

Honor slid to the side. After that comment, there was no need for manners. "What happened to Claws?"

Bear lifted a shoulder, eyeing Sylvia warily. "Garrett ran her home this morning and returned with Sylvia here."

Great. Why in the world had Honor dug into Garrett's head? She had to do something about this.

Bear nudged her in the shoulder while staying slightly behind her. "You have to do something about this."

"I was just thinking that," she agreed. What, she wasn't sure.

Sylvia pressed her hands to her hips and stretched her back, pushing double D's against a plain white T-shirt that was cropped nearly to her bra. "What do you say, Bear? A quick knock one out?"

Holy crap. Had the woman just said that?

"No," Bear said with bite in his tone. "My...wife isn't the sharing type."

"She might never know," Sylvia said, her gaze licking along his body.

Bear took another step back. "Oh, she'd know, and you wouldn't like the results."

Honor nodded. She'd seen the witch throw fire, after all.

Garrett loped their way, tucking a phone into his pocket. "Where did you go? I thought you were bringing dinner?" He slung an arm over Sylvia's shoulders.

Honor shook her head. "She was propositioning Bear instead. Garrett, we really have to talk."

Sylvia reached out and tugged a piece of Honor's hair. "We could make it a threesome. Or four."

Honor shoved her, freeing her head. "You're in the wrong place, lady. This isn't a commune." She glared at Garrett. "Enough of this. Maybe your future...lady, is just dangerous to your heart. Seriously. Stop being a stupid asshole." It had only been a couple of days, but enough was enough.

Garrett's left eyebrow rose. "Little sister has some teeth of her own."

She gritted said teeth together. All right. Mating Sam did make Garrett her brother, and she wasn't going to let him make such stupid decisions. "Little sister is about to kick you in the balls," she snapped.

Sylvia ran her hand up Garrett's hard chest. "This isn't fun. Let's go back to your place."

They turned and headed back down the trail.

"Dude," Bear said, watching them go. "You really need to fix this." He turned on her. "And by the way, why were two of my most seasoned soldiers bawling like cubs earlier today?"

She winced. "Well, Sam was sleeping, and they came to the cabin for therapy. We went outside in the sun and worked through some feelings."

Bear shook his head, his eyes losing their mellow honey look. "Not again, Honor. It's like you turned on a faucet around here, and I'm done with the tears and getting in touch with feelings. Soldiers shouldn't have feelings, especially when we're planning an attack."

She tilted her head. "You know, maybe we should talk about that. About how *you* feel."

He threw up his hands and stormed off toward the grills.

A young female shifter approached her. The woman had to be in her late teens and had stunning brown eyes. "Um, hi. I'm Betty."

"Hi." Honor kept her smile in place. "What can I do for you?"

"Well, I don't know." Betty kicked a pebble. "I was hoping you could, I don't know, maybe help me talk to my parents about my going to college?"

Honor looked at the girl. "Aren't bear shifters allowed to go to college?"

The girl sighed. "Yeah, but I want to study the politics of nonviolent resistance as well as philosophy, and my dad just doesn't get that."

After meeting several bear shifters, Honor wasn't surprised. Especially since their people were about to go to war, from all indications. "I'd love to have a sit-down with you and your parents. How about tomorrow morning?"

The girl smiled, brightening her entire face. "Awesome. Thanks!"

"I can't promise anything except to facilitate a healthy dialogue," Honor warned.

"No prob." The girl all but hopped away.

Honor grinned and turned to head back to her cabin, where Nessa was slowly emerging from the door that had been erected that morning while Sam slept. "How is he?"

Nessa rolled her neck. "Seriously beaten up. It'll take him a few days to get back to full strength, but he's healing in sleep, so that's a good thing. Did you see the latest twit Garrett brought back?"

"Not only did I see her, she propositioned me. She also offered Bear a quickie," Honor said.

Nessa's eyes darkened. "Is that a fact?" The witch strode away, a multitude of energies dancing around her.

"Yep. That's a fact." Honor almost wished she could watch the action, but Sam needed her. He seemed calmer when she was by his side. She gingerly moved inside the cabin and shut the door, heading to the bedroom.

Sam shoved the blanket off his body, his movements restless.

Honor put her untouched coffee mug on the bedside table and slid onto the covers next to him, placing her hand on his heart.

He settled down immediately, his hand flattening over hers. Warmth and safety.

She snuggled her nose into his neck and yawned. Maybe a little nap wouldn't hurt. She fell asleep and woke up when it was completely dark, fell back asleep and woke up with the sun pouring inside. An entire day later? This mating business took some energy.

Sam was still sleeping, the air popping around him. His breathing was easy, so at least he'd fixed his lungs.

She slid quietly from the bed, used the bathroom, and went hunting for food. Man, she was starving. She reached the tent and dug through the sandwiches there to find a turkey one. Nobody was around the meal tent, so it must be mid-afternoon? She tore into the delicious meal, eating right where she stood. How was it possible she'd slept through an entire night and part of the morning without really awakening?

"Hi." A woman emerged from the trees and shoved a phone into a big blue purse over her shoulder.

It took Honor a second to recognize her. "Hi, Claws," she said, frowning. Wait a minute. Garrett must've taken Sylvia home that morning. Well, that was something.

Claws grinned and drew a beer out of the cooler. "I ran into Garrett this morning, and he brought me out for the day. Maybe the night." She leaned her head back and put the sweating bottle against her neck. "The guy is insatiable."

Honor held up a hand. "Don't want to know. Really." Yeah, she needed to fix this. Somehow.

Claws rolled her neck, looking Honor over. "What do you weigh, anyway?"

Honor stilled. "None of your business."

"But it is." Claws removed a Taser from her bag and shot the wires at Honor.

Electricity zapped through Honor, and she started to fall. Her chin hit the table, pain blew through her head, and then she dropped.

Darkness landed hard inside her brain.

Chapter Thirty-Six

Honor came to lying in the back of an unmoving truck. A canopy was above her, sealing her inside. Panic grabbed her, and she squirmed to the tailgate, kicking at it wildly.

It slowly opened, and strong hands drew her out.

She looked up at a young male. Beside him, Claws was counting out money—a lot of it. "What did you do?"

Claws smiled. "Sorry. Just business."

The male jerked his head. "Get out of here. You might want to leave the state. When Kyllwood finds out about this, he'll probably kill you." The guy didn't sound like he much cared.

Honor blinked several times, trying to regain her faculties. He had black hair, green eyes, and really pale skin. While he appeared similar to the soldiers from the other day, he also looked nearly human. "Are you a Kurjan?"

For answer, he lifted her and carried her to an SUV, where he put her in the passenger side, handcuffing her to the dash. Carefully, he secured her seat belt and strode around to the driver's side. Then they slowly drove away from the clearing.

Honor fought the cuffs. "Who are you?"

"Drake." He kept driving, his hands capable on the steering wheel.

The guy had to be, what? Maybe twenty? "How old are you?" she snapped.

"Eighteen, almost nineteen," he said, speeding up so that the trees flew by outside. He scented the air. "You've mated the Keeper. How unfortunate."

"Why's that?" She had to get out of the cuffs. Then she could run.

"He's going to die," Drake said. "You could always take the virus that negates mating bonds. We have some good soldiers looking for mates, and you have power. You could take your pick."

How lucky for her. Angling her head, she looked up at the cloudy sky. It wasn't raining, and the sun still illuminated the various formations.

"We can go out in the sun these days," Drake explained, going even faster. "For quite a while, actually."

She twisted her wrists in the cuffs, but there was no possibility of escape. "Claws works for you?"

"For today," he said. "We've made different attempts on Garrett Kayrs, and we saw him drop her off and figured he'd want her again at some point. We would've taken him out, but you were the better prize, and Claws was more than willing to help for the right price."

"I noticed," she muttered. "I take it she stole one of Bear's work trucks?" So at least the shifters would know how Claws had gotten her away from their territory. That was something.

He nodded. "The attack the other day was a diversion, a way to take out the shifters' sensors and hopefully much of their equipment. I'm sure your mate will come for you, and unfortunately, that's part of the plan, too."

Sam hadn't completely healed from his last fight with a Cyst psychopath. Honor tried to remain calm.

Drake looked at her, and now she could see a purple rim around his green eyes. "I need you to be quiet for a minute. I could gag you, but I'd rather not."

"Fine," she said. At the moment, he had the control, but she wasn't going to be in these cuffs forever.

He lifted his phone, took a picture of her, and then pressed a button. "Thanks."

A ringing came over the line. "Jaydon," a deep male voice answered.

"General? It's Drake. I just sent you a picture." Drake drove up onto I-90, taking her even farther from Grizzly territory. From Sam.

Quiet came over the line and then an indrawn breath. "Nicely done, Drake. I'll meet you at the temporary headquarters. You'll be rewarded for this."

Honor looked at the phone, her heart thundering. Her ears rang, and her adrenaline flowed freely.

Drake angled his head and passed a logging truck. "Tell me where you're keeping the other females, and I'll bring her to that location."

"No. Follow my orders," Jaydon snapped.

"No," Drake said easily, driving so fast the world became a blur outside. "You want her? Tell me where to bring her. Otherwise, I have a couple of friends looking for mates, and this one has impressive power. I'm not playing, General."

Honor struggled to concentrate and not panic. What was he doing and why?

Jaydon growled, and the sound sent shivers through her entire body. "Fine, but you've crossed a line. You'll regret this." He was silent for a moment. "She's unmated?"

"Yep," Drake said, swerving around a minivan. "Smells as pure as any male could want. Can't even scent the Keeper on her, actually. She's not talking, but I doubt they've been together. Not sure why." He looked in the rearview mirror and then scouted both sides of the highway. "She's hot. I wouldn't mind taking a shot if I didn't have other plans."

Honor fought to keep from kicking him in the face. Where would he keep the keys to the handcuffs? He wore jeans and a sweatshirt, so probably in the jeans pockets?

"Very well. We're on Salmon Island. The Cyst own the entire land mass. You'll need to be met at the dock," Jaydon said.

"We're a couple of hours out. I'll text when we're closer." Drake clicked off.

Honor struggled with the cuffs. "Where is Salmon Island?"

"It's probably one of the smaller islands in the Sound—my guess is close to Orcas Island but not too close. It's probably shielded so humans don't even know it's there." He zipped down an off-ramp and swung through a red light, barreling toward what looked like forest land.

"Where are you going?" Honor asked, trying not to throw up.

He slowed down. "I have a helicopter waiting."

So he didn't trust the general or the proposed dock pickup. Good to know. She searched for anything she could use as a weapon. "Fine. You used me to find out where he's staying. I get that. Let me go now."

"No."

She paused. He was young and he was strong. Could she get through to him? "Yes. I have been mated, and that means something. Jaydon, and I'm assuming he's the general I've already had the misfortune to meet, will just kill me when he finds out. Either way, I'm of no use to you. Let me go."

Drake drove through an archway of trees, speeding down a dirt road. "You have a lot of power, Honor. If you took the virus, you could negate the mating bond, and you could find a life. A good one with us." He took another turn. "Your choice of males isn't good. Upon learning of you, I interviewed your ex, a man named Kyle, about you. It didn't take much pressure to get him to tell me everything he knew about you."

She pressed a hand to her head. "Tell me you didn't kill him."

"I didn't. He wasn't worth it," Drake said. "Why did you choose him?"

"We just dated for a short time," she admitted, her mind spinning. "I mistook boredom for peace." While Sam wasn't peaceful, she felt peace with him—and she was never bored.

Drake drove faster. "You could find a good life with a Kurjan soldier."

She swallowed. "I want a life with Sam."

"Sorry. Sam is not supposed to be the Keeper, and we can't leave that much power in the Kyllwood family. He will die, and you'll be alone anyway. Let me help you." Drake slowed down and turned again, driving to a small parking area next to a shiny black helicopter.

She tried to glide inside his head.

He turned to face her. "Stop it," he growled.

"No." She tried again.

He shut down fast, expelling her abruptly. She cried out, her head jerking, her temples pounding. Her eyelids closed, and she struggled to keep her lunch in her stomach.

When she opened her eyes, he was watching her. "You shouldn't try to invade people's minds," he said.

She tried to swallow over the lump in her throat. The kid had some serious power. "You shouldn't kidnap people."

"Fair enough." He didn't smile. "Just a word of warning. Our people are different from the bear shifters. Our females don't have the freedom, nor do they want it, that you've enjoyed. Be careful. I could've hurt you just now, but I chose not to do so. The next soldier won't be as nice."

With that, he jumped out of the truck and signaled a pilot in the helicopter.

The blades started to turn.

* * * *

Sam stretched awake and winced as his barely healed ribs clacked together. He opened his eyes, feeling an empty place next to him. Where was Honor? He sat up, his instincts humming. Sending healing cells in every direction, he swung from the bed and dragged jeans on, huffing in pain as he did so.

Something was wrong.

He could feel it. His boots felt too small for his feet, and his arms protested when he pulled a shirt over his head, but he kept moving toward the door and shoved it open, revealing a gaping hole where his deck used to be.

Garrett barreled out of the trees.

Sam jumped down. "Where is she?" The air felt quiet and lonely around him. No sense of her.

Garrett's eyes were more onyx than metallic gray. "Nessa is trying to track her via satellite on the one system that wasn't damaged the other day. We just discovered that both Honor and Claws are missing."

Sam burst into a jog, turning for the headquarters area. "Claws?"

Garrett kept pace. "The Kurjans must've gotten to her. I'm sorry."

Sam didn't have time for sorry. "How long has she been gone?" He'd been sound asleep while his mate had been taken?

"About an hour—maybe more. We'll know when Nessa gets a bead on her." Garrett's boots crunched the leaves around them. "Honor is mated. She'll be protected until we get there."

Sam's ears heated. "She's a smart-ass and a fighter. No way will she wait meekly for rescue." His temper awoke, and he shoved it down with a cold ball of ice. He had to think rather than feel right now. "She doesn't know that they'll hurt her without an ounce of remorse."

"She's smart, Sam. We'll get to her in time."

They reached the clearing by the garage just as Bear and Flynn emerged, Bear fully armed and Flynn loading weapons as fast as he could.

Bear tossed him a gun. "Load up. Nessa found the trail and will send coordinates to us on the road. They headed north in a truck and just parked near a helicopter in Binbly's Forest. It's too late for us to blow it without harming Honor, so we have to let her on."

Flynn tore off his shirt and pants and kicked his boots to the side. "I'll get a closer visual and trail her." His eyes morphed to an elliptical green, and he turned, running full throttle down the road. His legs elongated, a tail emerged, he jumped forward. The air sparked all around him, and a fully grown black dragon flew into the sky.

"Holy shit," Garrett said, looking up.

Sam stalked into the armory and suited up, choosing more blades than guns. He was taking off heads today. When he walked out, a silver helicopter was landing where the bikes usually rested. "Whose?"

"Ours," Bear said, nodding at the pilot. "Bought it a couple of years ago and have had it locked down farther in territory just in case. Let's go." He tossed earbuds at them. "I can only afford to have the four of us away from the territory right now since most of our sensors are down. Can't risk another attack."

Sam shoved an earbud in, his chest feeling heated as he jumped in the back. "Nessa?"

"Yes," Nessa answered, and the sound of typing came over the line. "I have her. Helicopter headed north, but I don't know the destination yet. They may cross into Canadian airspace. I have Flynn, and he's almost there. He can mask himself from human detectors...ours too. But he's staying visible for me."

Good. Flynn was close. He'd make sure nothing happened to Honor.

Nessa cried out.

"What?" Bear bellowed, jumping into the helicopter.

"They just shot Flynn," she whispered. "Armed helicopter, and they must have sensors we don't know about. Nobody has sensors for dragons. God."

Bear paled but motioned for the pilot to take off. "Is he okay?"

"I can't tell. He dropped into forested land, and it's too thick to see." Tears clogged Nessa's voice. "He's a dragon and he's tough, but he wasn't expecting to be shot. How did they see him?"

The helicopter rose rapidly into the sky. "One thing at a time, Ness," Bear said, his voice low with command. "Send a couple of the shifters out. They can get to him quickly in bear form."

"Already did," Nessa said, sniffing. "I'll report to you as soon as I know. For now, keep heading north."

Sam leaned his head back and pushed more healing cells to the still injured parts of his body. "They'll be waiting for us," he muttered.

"They always are," Bear growled.

Sam opened his eyes. "Yeah. I have an idea."

Chapter Thirty-Seven

They landed on an island at the edge of the Sound, one Honor couldn't see until they'd actually touched down. Another young Kurjan, this one named Vero, had been waiting in the copter. He was a couple of years younger than Drake and had handed her a blanket to keep her legs warm during the trip. His eyes were a normal human blue color.

Drake opened the door and scouted the area, watching the water roll in off the side of the landing area. He tapped his ear. "Father? I'm on the island. Couldn't see anything from the air, but I'll find out what's happening." He held a hand out for Honor.

She ignored him and jumped down.

He tugged a key from his pocket and released the cuffs. "I'd bet anything there are mine traps in the water around the island, so I wouldn't attempt swimming, even if you could tell which way to swim, which I can't."

She rubbed her wrists, looking around. The island was heavily treed, with a sprawling lodge visible down a path between the pines. "How is this kept secret? Why couldn't we see it?"

"Physics," Drake said, gesturing her toward the building. "It's shielded and nicely done. Jaydon has been planning this for a while." He stiffened and grasped her arm, pulling her toward the trail. "Get out of the way."

Another helicopter landed, this one a light blue.

The back door opened, and a Cyst soldier pushed two women out. They both appeared to be in their early twenties, one blond, one dark haired with Asian features. They both fell on the asphalt and scrambled up, their hair a mess, bruises on their arms, and panicked looks in their eyes. The Cyst jumped out behind them and looked at Drake. "Prince. Hi. We've found the final two."

Prince?

Drake kept his grip on Honor. "Okay."

Honor started to speak, and he tightened his hold. "Quiet."

She pressed her lips together. Her young kidnapper didn't seem to have a full grasp of the situation. Great.

Vero cast her a sympathetic smile. "It'll be okay," he said, his voice cracking as if he was still going through puberty.

She turned with Drake and strode along the trail toward the lodge, casting looks behind her at the two shell-shocked women and trying to give them encouraging nods.

Sam and his friends would come for her. They had to. Hopefully he was awake and knew she'd been taken. God. What if he was still sleeping and healing? She tripped.

Drake settled her and drew her up the lodge stairs to push open a heavy-looking door. The Cyst soldier and two women continued onward to what appeared to be a large wooden building lacking any windows.

She and Drake walked inside what looked like a former entrance to a hotel, except all the furniture had been removed in the center to make room for a large table, maps, and weapons. A wide screen took up the entire left wall, showing green lights throughout the world.

A massively built Cyst turned around, looking at them. He wore a full black uniform with a myriad of silver metals at his breast.

Honor's legs wanted to give out. It was the same guy who'd attacked them before, and he looked even bigger now.

His gaze slashed to her, the purple in his eyes sharp as any blade. He lifted his face. "You lied. She's mated."

Drake shrugged. "Get a sample of the virus and change that. I don't care. For now, I'd like a tour of the island."

Vero flanked him, looking uncertain. "Why were those females bruised, General? We need Enhanced females for mates and want them to be healthy."

The general looked at him as if he was lower than dirt. "They put up a fight. Better to learn that lesson now, right?" He strode toward them, stopping in front of Honor. "It's a pity. You would've made a good mate." He smiled, flashing sharp canines. "We have other uses for her, now don't we?" He gave a half bow to Drake. "Prince? Come this way."

Drake turned and moved after the general.

Vero gestured her to follow them. "This way, please." The kid seemed decent and way out of his element.

Honor didn't move. "I have to get out of here."

His smile was sad. "There's no leaving. I'm sorry. The sooner you accept life here, the easier it is to live it." He gestured again.

She moved to follow Drake and the general outside to the other building, seeking a weapon as she moved. Clouds gathered high above, rolling in from the sea, dark with the promise of a storm. Thunder rolled in the distance. She shivered and moved almost gratefully into the building.

"This is crazy," Drake snapped, looking around. "How many females do you have here?"

Several women sat against the walls or milled around the wide open space, looking lost. They were all wearing the same outfit. Pure white, see-through gowns. The two bruised women they'd seen earlier were already dressed similarly, sitting near the edge, whispering quietly to each other.

Two redheaded and one blond female were shackled to a solid wall of concrete to the right. They looked emaciated and exhausted.

All three wore plain black sacks, their feet bare and dirty, bruises marring their necks and arms as if they'd taken several beatings.

Drake pivoted. "You idiot. You can't just duplicate the ritual on an island outside of Seattle. It takes place in a sacred circle between dimensions."

The general gestured toward the three chained people. "Two witches and a Fae. They can get me there." He turned and grabbed Honor. "Where are we?" he asked a guard.

The nearest one looked at Honor. "We lost two more the other night, General. After they visited you. Our healers couldn't save them."

Drake growled. "You're the one? We figured we had a rogue soldier. It was you attacking and killing Enhanced females?"

The general shrugged. "Everyone needs a hobby. I didn't take more than we could afford to lose."

Honor's gut lurched. She needed a gun. Right now.

Another guard looked up from reading a tablet, which looked small in his huge white hands. "We're at ninety-nine."

"See?" General Jaydon said, his smile chilling. "I can count. Good news. We have number one hundred right here. Get her changed." He shoved Honor toward the guard. She stumbled but regained her footing quickly.

Vero backed away. "This is wrong. This is an abomination. Only the great leader Ulric can be the Immortal One."

"Shut him down," the general said, pivoting to look at Drake. "What about you? Do I need to cut off your head?"

Drake looked at the desperate women. "No. This is an exercise in futility, General. You're going to fail, and you're going to wind up killing all of these females. We'll have to start over finding enough for the great Ulric's return." He didn't let on that he was wearing an earbud. What did that mean?

The guard grasped Honor's arm and tried to take off her sweater. She fought him, and he backhanded her, knocking her to the ground.

Vero helped her up, his pudgy hands warm and gentle. "Fighting only gets you hurt. This will be over soon. Trust me."

Honor turned her back and changed into the dress, her ears ringing. Her gaze caught on the mating mark on her right hip—a large K with swirling and dangerous looking lines around it. The sight gave her strength and hope. The males exited the door, and it locked loudly on the other side. The general had taken her clothing. Even with the mating mark pulsing on her flesh, she felt vulnerable in the light dress.

And pissed. Seriously pissed.

She turned to look at the women, some of whom appeared as if they hadn't eaten in a while. "What's going to happen?" she asked.

A thirty-something brunette with terror in her green eyes approached from the far wall. "I'm Kaisie. We're not sure, but since there are now one hundred of us, it's going to happen soon." She gestured to an older woman with bare, scratched feet. "Jenny?"

Jenny limped toward them. "We've tried to get out, but that's the only door. There are several injured here, and none of us has a weapon. They've talked about some sort of circle somewhere, and when they try to move us, we'll have a chance. It'll be our only chance."

Honor tried to dig deep for a courage she wasn't sure she possessed. "Good." She'd found the two leaders of the group, apparently. Somebody cried softly in the background, and she could understand. This was terrifying.

Jenny wiped at a scab on her chin. "Some of us haven't eaten in a few days and lack strength."

A younger woman, maybe about eighteen, kicked dirt as she walked forward. There were bruises along her neck and shoulders, visible even through the gown. "We've tried to fight and we've tried to escape." Tears leaked down her dirty face. "It's impossible. They're not even human, so we won't win. It's not worth it."

Honor touched her arm. "I'm sorry about this, but they are going to kill us. The ritual involves one hundred women being killed. So we have nothing to lose."

The woman just shook her head. "I don't care."

"I do," Honor said, looking around. "Just one more attempt? Please? We have a chance."

The two women who'd arrived when she had stood and walked toward her. The first one nodded. "We're in. We can fight."

There was such a slim chance of survival, but it was all they had. "Okay. Who's the strongest?" Honor called out. "I figure it's the newest arrivals. We should go for the strongest guards when they come back, and everyone else run and try to find weapons. Find anything we can use." She looked at Kaisie. "How long have you been here?"

"At least a month," Kaisie said, her face pale and her hair dirty in the soft light. "I'm okay to fight, though. No injuries and I really want to hurt somebody."

Honor patted her arm. "Okay. Do you want to lay out a plan?"

Kaisie sighed, looking exhausted. "My only plan is to fight until I'm dead. Do you have a better idea?"

Honor turned and looked at the women filling the space. "Even though they're armed, we have greater numbers. Some of us still have strength, so let's fan out. Everyone who thinks they can fight come forward, anybody who thinks they can run move to the sides, and anybody who's injured hang back a little."

Quietly, somberly, the women shuffled into place. Far too many of them were injured. Honor exhaled. "Okay. When those doors open, our only chance is to attack and take them by surprise. Does anybody know how to fly a helicopter?"

A forty-something-year-old woman in the runners' group raised her hand. She was blond and petite, and her eyes glowed a deep, angry brown. "I'm Alison, and I'm a pilot."

"Good. We need to clear a path for Alison to get to the helicopters," Honor said, her chest heating as anxiety flooded her. "If you could get out and find help, we might stand a chance." Some of them would die fighting. At that realization, her knees nearly gave out, but she hid the terror.

Why hadn't she told Sam of her feelings?

She threw the thought away, because right now was for survival. "I know you're tired and scared, but the bottom line is that we don't have any other options. They are going to try to kill us, so we have to do this now."

Her feet felt cold and dirty on the ground. She took a deep breath. "I'll go for the general, and everyone else rush the other soldiers. Somebody should be able to get their hands on a weapon, and then start shooting."

Kaisie pressed her cracked lips together. "No problem."

Honor gulped down air. "Shoot to kill. If you're not willing to shoot, give the gun to someone else. The faster we take them down, the better our chances will be."

Movement sounded outside the doorway. She stilled and then pivoted, making sure her feet were clear of the long skirt.

A swishing sound echoed through the air.

Kaisie frowned. "What is that?"

The room wavered, and Honor's vision blurred. Her last thought as she fell to the ground was of Sam's handsome face. Then, nothing.

Chapter Thirty-Eight

Honor was wet. Thunder bellowed and rain slammed the ground outside. Lightning zapped, and the smell of ozone filtered through the air. She seemed to be indoors, though.

She was slumped over her legs, bent at the knees. She blinked several times and then sat up, her brain foggy. "They drugged us?" she slurred. What complete cowards. She tried to focus but the room swam around her.

"Wake up," Kaisie hissed.

"I'm trying." Honor struggled, but her knees were hobbled by some odd contraption to the iron-mesh floor. Although the long white gown covered her, the stupid thing was see-through. Blood trickled to the floor on the sides of her legs. The mesh was cutting into her, but she couldn't move.

"They knocked us out. I don't know how long we've been here," Kaisie said.

Honor shook her head and finally got the room to clear. They were in a white tent, similar to those used for wedding receptions. She turned and squinted to better study the canvas walls. Except they weren't canvas. The walls were made of some sort of metal with blades pointing out every inch. Silver, sharp, deadly-looking blades. "Those look sharp," she whispered, her voice shaking.

"When the time comes, those will cut right through us," Kaisie said, her voice shaking. "I think they're on some sort of timer."

Honor partially turned her head to see all one hundred women similarly trapped by the knees on the metal floor. She tried to turn to see more, but her skin shredded. She hissed from the pain.

Kaisie was at her left. "If those knives come from every direction at the same time, we'll be cut to ribbons." She struggled uselessly in the knee hold. "Ducking won't help."

Honor partially bent at the waist, gagging. So much fear surrounded her, she couldn't think. She could only feel, taking it all in.

It was too much.

Panic grabbed her as her lungs tried to expel the drugged gas that had been used on them. "We have to get out of here."

The woman snorted. "Great plan. Those blades definitely will remove our heads. He needs this place filled with blood, and that'll happen no matter what."

"Wrong." Honor turned her head, trying to see more of the women. Some were stoic, some agitated, and some openly weeping. The blades were all around them. Tears slid down her face. There was no way out of this.

Fear tasted like metal on her tongue. She didn't want to die. Tears filled her eyes, and her body shook.

Sam's face crossed her vision. The memory of his touch, of his fire, ran through her. They'd had so little time together.

She wanted more. It wasn't fair. Where was he? What would Sam do?

He'd fight until the end. Without question. He'd also use every weapon at his disposal to do so. She pushed away the tears. She had to at least try to do the same.

Her head jerked back, and she ignored the pain in her knees. "Listen. We don't have to die. You were all willing to fight physically with me until the cowards drugged us and brought us here. That shows that they're afraid of us. Afraid of us as a group. We can use that."

Kaisie whimpered. "We're shackled to the floor."

"So what? We're here because we're Enhanced, right?" Honor struggled to turn so she could see more of the women as her brain kicked in. There was more to strength than muscle. Every single woman in that tent had a gift. An Enhanced gift. As did the Fae and the witches. "That means something. One hundred of us are Enhanced. Everyone, really quickly. What are your abilities?" Her breath sped up.

"Empath," one woman said with a sigh.

"Psychic and this doesn't look good," another groaned.

"I have no fucking clue," came a third voice.

Honor turned to the witches and the Fae, who had also been moved to the tent. They were shackled to a small area that lacked knives. Her back started to protest the twisting. "Can you three really create a circle in another place?"

The first redhead nodded, her left eye bleeding. "Aye, but that doesn't mean the ritual will be a success. We know nothing about the one that happened centuries ago. But...the general has done his research, and he was present for the first ritual, so who knows."

Kaisie shook her head. "We've already tried to escape by using our talents instead of physical strength. Empaths, psychics, and even those with telekinetic powers. We've tried to free ourselves of this place, and we've been beaten down each time."

"But I wasn't here," Honor said, her mind spinning. Oh, this might blow up her entire brain, but if it did, who cared? She was going to die anyway. "I can weave us all together. If we combine our mental talents the same way we were willing to combine our physical strength, we have a chance. Please. Let me try." She shut her eyes and lowered her chin, reaching out to every mind she could touch. A murmur sounded in the crowd.

Several snapped their minds shut and threw her out, piercing her temples like blades.

She opened her eyes. "Knock it off. Everyone open wide. I have an idea, and I think it might work. We're going to die anyway, so why not try?" She was probably going to die even if this did work. While she didn't understand how the brain or her gift really worked, attempting to reach so many people at once would have a cost. A big one. "Everyone let me in, and we'll coordinate. Time is running short. Please. Trust me. Don't let these assholes win."

"I'm in," the Fae said as the two witches nodded. "Everyone open your minds. We really have nothing to lose at this point." She sounded both exhausted and angry, but at least she was willing to help.

The tent flap opened, and General Jaydon strode inside, a whip in his hand.

Honor growled. "What? Drugging us wasn't enough? The shackles and beatings aren't enough? You need a whip? You're a coward."

He let the whip fly, and it landed hard across her cheekbone. She cried out as her skin was flayed open. Then he stalked over to the witches. "I am ready." He wore a purple robe and nothing else. Honor could see symbols etched into his skin. "Now. Start the ritual."

The two witches lowered their heads and started chanting. The Fae lady looked straight ahead but didn't seem to be seeing anything. She also wasn't doing anything, or was she? She glanced at Honor, slowly winked, and then resumed looking blank.

Power brushed against Honor's brain. Tears streamed down her face, burning in the fresh cut.

The world tilted around them. The walls morphed, and heat flashed through the tent. Fire from another place. She sucked in air and reached out to the minds around her. Seeking desperately and hoping nobody threw her out.

Most were wide open, and she glided among them, feeling each tick of terror. She had to push that away to find the gifts, and she tried to be as gentle as possible, but time was short. Her own fear slowed her down, and she had to banish it as well.

The blades clanked loudly. Something hitched. Soon they would fly.

She tried to group similar gifts together. She found the empaths and tried to knit their powers together, having them reach out and send calmness to the others. The psychics were next, holding a hint of heat in their brains. She tied them together mentally, and the air around them became electrified. Sparks jumped.

Once she had them all working as one, she latched onto the telekinetics and forced their powers toward the blades. One knife dropped out of the metal to the ground. "Keep trying," she yelled, the minor success lifting the spirits in the room. She could feel their hope as well as their fear. She could see it in the tapestries of their brains as she knitted them all together. "Empaths, more hope. Please." Brightness steadied the group.

"Shut up," the general bellowed, climbing up to a raised platform she hadn't noticed. A yawning portal opened above him, swirling a rough purple color. He held up his hands and started to chant. Fire rained down, caressing him, not burning his flesh.

Honor shut her eyes and sought the other skills, the ones she couldn't decipher easily, directing their thoughts toward the worlds beyond this one, trying to close the portal.

Metal clanked as the blades began to move toward them.

The tent swirled around them and then disappeared. Rock walls stood where it had been, right behind the wide, glinting blades, which looked as if they were hovering in space.

One woman screamed.

"Hold on," Honor yelled through the howling wind. "Just concentrate." She put all her strength into the telekinetic females, pushing them to fight the blades. She could feel their struggle as the blades sought the taste of blood.

Then she hit the witches and the Fae. Hard. Gliding into their brains, saying a silent apology, she tried to shut them down.

The wind slowed.

"No!" General Jaydon yelled.

A blade broke free.

Several women screamed, and then it halted, hovering just beyond the circle.

"Good job," Honor yelled, closing her eyes and reaching out with every ounce of energy she possessed. She touched the ones she couldn't identify, the minds full of secrets, and dug into them. Power erupted all around the circle, blowing the rocks into nothingness.

She reached the witches and the Fae female, this time lighting up their brains. She mentally knitted their power into the tapestry, and sparks flew through the air and landed all around them.

Fire lashed the air. A burst of flame, unnatural in this world, crawled along the floor. A wind keened. Something or someone screamed, high and loud, and the world spun around with an edge of ice.

Then they all fell.

She opened her eyes, back in the tent.

The knee shackles released.

She jumped to her feet and dragged up Kaisie. "Run! Everyone run."

In a mass exodus, the women surged up and ran for the one exit. Honor helped several up from the floor and pushed them toward the storm raging outside, her mind shutting down with a pain beyond any migraine.

She started to fall, and the general was there, grasping her around the neck.

His eyes swirled a furious purple, and blood flowed freely from wounds in his neck. "This is going to hurt." He lifted her by the neck, shook her like a doll, and burst out into the storm.

Chapter Thirty-Nine

Sam avoided another underwater mine and rose finally on the beach, water sliding down his body. Garrett and Bear emerged on either side of him, already striding out of the salty water. Rain poured down as if the heavens were pissed.

Females wearing flowing white robes poured out of a canvas tent, running in several directions.

A couple of Cyst guards ran after them, one with a whip.

Sam shot him between the eyes without missing a beat. "Get the women to safety. I'll find Honor."

Garrett and Bear began shooting Cyst soldiers as they rushed forward. There couldn't be that many of them.

Sam raced through the throng, his heart pounding. Where was she? He tapped the ear communicator. "Nessa? Get the Realm forces here as soon as possible. We have several injured, and at least eighty or more Enhanced females who'll need help. Maybe a hundred." The tent? Had Jaydon attempted the ritual?

If so, he'd failed. One female attacked Sam, scratching and biting. He ducked to the side. "We're the good guys," he said, continuing by. "Go to the beach. We'll get you out of here." He pushed through the throng and finally caught sight of Jaydon carrying Honor by the neck into what looked like a hotel lodge.

Panic rose up, but he batted it away.

A knife slashed into his throat.

He pivoted, swinging out and connecting with a solid jawline. Growling, he yanked the blade out, his gaze landing on a young Kurjan soldier. It took him a second, but he recognized the kid from dossiers. Drake, the heir to the throne. A second kid, this one younger, pointed a gun at him and fired. Was it Vero, a cousin to Drake? He had the oddest blue eyes. Like human eyes.

Leaping forward, Sam knocked the kid to the ground and ripped the weapon away, sending it flying across the fresh earth. Then he backflipped, facing the two. "Get out of here. Now." They were too young to kill.

"No." Drake ducked into a fighting position, drawing out a double-edged blade from his back pocket. The rain flattened his black hair to his head, and his clothing molded to his fit young body. No fear showed in his eyes, and only a glittering promise of death lurked in his green orbs.

Sam settled his stance, his neck slowly mending. Too slowly. He was nowhere near ready for a fight. "Come at me, then."

"Planning on it." Drake let his fangs drop, and they were impressive for his age. "Sorry to kill you, but we need a new Keeper."

"I really hate that name," Sam said, waiting for the kid's move.

Drake struck, dodging to the side and then coming in. He was well trained and moved fast.

Sam spun, kicked up, and nailed the kid across the cheek. Drake went down on one knee, and Sam rushed him, pulling the knife free of the Kurjan's hand. There was nothing like stabbing a guy with his own blade. "I've got decades of experience and a war behind me, kid. Don't make me kill you." To make his point, Sam slammed the blade down through the kid's thigh.

Drake bellowed, the sound high with pain. Blood burst out, splattering across Sam's hand and burning him.

Vero rushed forward, his gaze on his cousin.

Sam patted Drake on the shoulder. The kid was shuddering. "Won't kill you, but you'll remember this." Then he turned and ran into the lodge, looking for his mate. He'd worry later about the fact that the heir to the Kurjan throne had been more than happy to kill him. They must be ready for war.

Honor screamed, high and loud from down a long hallway.

Sam pivoted and ran as fast as he could, leaving a trail of blood the whole way. He shoved more healing cells to his neck, trying to stay cold when his heart kept heating his chest. He could taste her fear on the air, and the animal inside him lunged wide awake, ready to kill.

He let the beast take control.

They rounded a corner, and Jaydon turned to face him, his arm around Honor's neck, dangling her easily about a foot off the ground. "Got your female, Keeper."

"I see that." Sam took inventory, noting blood on her neck and purpling bruises on her arm. "Guess she thwarted your big ritual?" It was a good guess. He edged to the side, trying to find a way in. The general was strong enough to rip off Honor's entire head with his forearm.

Jaydon hissed, fury darkening his eyes to blood red. "Yes. Now I have to start all over." His fangs dropped, and he scraped them along her neck, drawing more blood. "So will you, Keeper."

"I really am starting to hate that name," Sam said, straightening. "I have Drake and Vero with knives to their necks right now. If I give the word, their heads will drop." The kids had probably made it to safety, but Jaydon didn't know that. "You want their blood on your hands?"

One of Jaydon's white eyebrow rose. "No, but I'm more than willing to have their blood on your hands." If anything, the bastard looked pleased by the idea. "Those kids have been in the way ever since they learned to fight."

Definite break in the Kurjan world right now. Sam would think about that later. Right now, all that mattered was Honor. He drew out a long blade from the sheath at his calf. "Stop hiding behind a female, General. I've already had the energy kicked out of me by your leader and probably can't put up much of a fight. You shouldn't be so scared."

Jaydon straightened, lifting Honor higher, taking her head back. "You met with Ulric?"

"Oh yeah," Sam said softly. "I gotta tell you, he is not happy about your plans."

Jaydon paused, and it was all the opening Sam needed. He jumped forward, knife already flashing.

* * * *

A knife sliced the air next to her ear and cut right into the general's neck. Blood poured from him, coating her skin and burning deep. She screamed, struggling against him.

Sam struck again, this time for the general's eye.

The bastard dropped Honor, and she landed on both feet, pain rippling up her vertebrae to land at the base of her neck. Gasping, wiping frantically at her burning jaw, she backed away from the two of them. Tears filled her eyes and flowed down her face; she batted them away, burning her cheeks with the blood on her hands. Her butt hit the wall, and she partially bent over, trying to catch her breath but still watching the battling immortals.

The general slammed one huge fist down on Sam's shoulder, sending him to the ground. Sam hit with one knee, denting the old wooden floor. Without a pause, he bounced up, his other foot nailing Jaydon beneath the jaw and throwing him into the opposite wall.

Sam moved so fast she could hardly follow him. His blade was brutal, slashing Jaydon from neck to groin and back.

She'd seen him fight coldly before, but this was different. Heated and intense. The marking on her hip burned hot and dug deep, warming her entire body. The pain on her face slowly receded.

She wiped her bloody hands on the flimsy white gown, looking down the hallway for any sort of weapon. There was nothing.

Jaydon performed a roundhouse kick, hitting Sam in the stomach and sending him careening into the wall. The plaster shattered, raining down and all around. The general drew a knife from his back and advanced. "I am so going to enjoy this, Keeper."

Honor lowered her head and shot every bad thought she could into his brain.

He instantly slammed it down, and she winced, pain detonating behind her eyes. She clapped both hands to her temples and went down, her butt to the ground, spiraling away to a place of no pain.

A series of grunts brought her back to the present.

She lifted her head wearily, her entire body aching.

Jaydon punched Sam repeatedly, from his head to his torso and back to his head. Sam fought back, his movements slowing. He hadn't even completely healed yet from the battle with Ulric. She fought to stand, made it to her knees, and fell sideways.

Jaydon laughed, the sound booming through the hallway. "I'm going to enjoy killing you, Keeper. Then I'm going to have all sorts of fun with your female—even if she is mated. I might have to get my hands on that virus."

Sam paused. The atmosphere heated and pulsed. Then, to put it simply, he went demonic. Fast and furious, as if controlled by a base nature she hadn't recognized, he stabbed the general in a whirlwind of rapid movements. Gut, chest, arms, hips, and face.

Honor's mouth gaped open.

Sam didn't pause. He plunged the blade deep into Jaydon's eye, taking him down to the ground. Then he lifted his arm and stabbed hard and fast to the Cyst leader's neck. Blood blew across the hallway to coat both walls. "Look away, Honor. Right now," he growled, the sound so guttural it was difficult to make out the words.

She couldn't move, her gaze locked on him and her body frozen in place.

Sam freed the knife and plunged the wicked blade in several times. The general bellowed and scrambled for the blade, but his hands were covered in blood and it slid away. Sam stabbed him again, and the knife made a terrifying clunking sound when it pierced the wooden floor beneath.

Then Sam went cold. The air even chilled. He lifted the knife and edged it in sideways, twisting and turning, pulling and plunging. Grunting, his hands coated with blood, he sawed until the general's head was severed from his body. Jaydon's eyes widened, and blood bubbled from his mouth.

Sam staggered to his feet, slid back a leg, and then kicked the general's jaw with a force that sounded like an airplane crash. The head flew away from the body, rolling end over end, bumping across the wooden floor and leaving a wide swath of pure red blood. It came to a rest with the purple eyes wide and staring down the hallway.

Honor gagged.

Sam turned and moved toward her, grasping her arm and helping her off the floor.

Her knees gave out.

He lifted her against his solid chest and strode away from the body. "Good job with the ritual," he murmured, his steps sure even as blood spurted from his ear, neck, and forehead.

"Put me down. You're hurt," she said, not sure she could stand. She looked over his shoulder at the prone body of Jaydon. "Sam. What was that?" She sounded lost, and she cleared her throat to get control over herself. Even so, her entire body trembled.

Sam pressed her head to his shoulder, holding her tight and making her feel safe. Warm and secure. "He threatened my mate, baby. Sometimes it's as simple as that." He walked her out into the storm, and she looked around.

Helicopters had landed; soldiers were rushing around, giving blankets and medical assistance to several of the women. Cyst soldiers were either down or missing, and many of the helicopters that had been there were gone. How many had gotten free?

Two soldiers jogged up, and there was no doubt the one on the left was Sam's brother.

He shifted her in his arms. "Honor? This is my brother, Zane. Zane? My mate, Honor."

Zane smiled. His eyes were a darker green than Sam's. "Welcome to the family." He tilted his head to the young soldier beside him. "This is Paxton."

Paxton smiled at her and then looked at Sam. "I'm glad you're still alive." Sincerity and power thrummed in the kid's low tone, as if there had been a doubt on that score.

"Me too." Sam nodded at his brother. "I'll call you later. Like tomorrow or the next day. After a nap. A long one." He headed back toward a silver helicopter where Bear and Garrett waited, both bloody but still standing. "You ready to go home?"

"Yes." Honor rested her face against his neck, letting him take control. It was, after all, exactly what Sam Kyllwood always did.

She kissed his neck.

Chapter Forty

Hope stirred restlessly in her sleep, her mind on how quickly her dad had left headquarters. Something had happened, but nobody would include her in the news. She had one little cold, with a slight fever, and now everyone was treating her like she was dying. She drifted off to sleep and instantly felt flickers of pain. *Serious pain. She forced her way to a dreamworld, taking comfort in the sun. A figure limped out of the pink trees. Why were the trees pink? Was this her usual world? She focused as Drake took form. She gasped and moved toward him. "What happened?"*

"Just a little battle." He grasped her hand and tugged them both to sit on the warm sand. Then he extended his legs. "Took a knife from an enemy."

She held his hand with both of hers, noting his eyes had turned a darker green. "There's a lot of that going around tonight. Tell me you weren't in a battle with the demon nation." She couldn't stand the thought of Drake and her dad fighting.

"Nope. No demon nation in this one." He grinned, looking normal again.

She smiled. "Good. We need to stay on the same side of things in this world, no matter what our people do."

He nodded, his black hair moving around his shoulders. "We are on the same side, even if things get confusing for one or both of us. You understand our path was set long ago, right?" He flattened her hand over his thigh, warming her.

She blinked. "No. I think we make our own path, Drake." She let herself brush his hair away from his angled face. "Who was your enemy today? Who stabbed you?"

He leaned into her touch, his face smooth against her palm. "Doesn't matter. He won this time, but I'll win when it counts." He took a deep breath, and healing tingles wafted through the air around them. "I hadn't realized this would be a drawn-out campaign, but it looks like that's shaping up."

She leaned back and set her hand in her lap. "The guy who stabbed you. You're going after him?"

"Yeah," Drake said softly. "Don't know when or how, but he and I aren't done. He wants to do something wrong, something seriously wrong, and I have to stop him. No matter the cost."

"Then you will." She smiled, letting the sun warm them and the ocean roll in. "Do you ever waver? I mean, do you ever worry that we don't have it all right and that we'll screw it up?" From day one, she'd felt a mantle of responsibility she wasn't sure how to handle. Wasn't sure if she'd do the right thing when the time came...or what that even meant. "Drake?"

"No." He nudged her with his broad shoulder. "I don't waver. I believe in Fate, and I adhere to the legends. It's all we have, Hope. If we let go of that, of what we know deep inside, then what are we? Who are we?" He flipped his hand over and captured hers. "You're going to have to trust me on that. Someday soon." It was as if he actually saw the future.

Or did he just believe that strongly?

"I've heard rumors," she said softly, looking up at a cutout in the nearest tree. Her book, the green and mysterious ancient book, lay open to the sun. She knew if she reached out and tried to take the book that it'd disappear. Someday she'd get to read it.

"What rumors?" Drake asked.

She glanced toward the rolling waves. "That Ulric wants to kill all Enhanced females." Her father didn't know she'd dug deep into computer files as well as into ancient books that had no names. "Nobody knows why but they say that's his plan. Is it?" She wished she'd had time to really question Ulric in his dreamworld hell, but he'd refused to answer the few questions she'd had time to ask. Her role as the Lock clearly put them on opposite sides. She understood that. Her blood, combined with that of the three Keys, could kill him. "Drake?"

Drake shook his head. "I'm not privy to that information. I can't believe that Ulric, the leader of our religious sect, would want to kill Enhanced human females. It just doesn't make sense because we need them. The only ritual we've heard about, the only one we're preparing to stop, is the one that is supposed to kill him." Drake rubbed her jawline with his knuckle. "With your blood and the three Keys. How can that be all right?"

"I don't know," she admitted. "But he did do something horrible in killing those Enhanced females in order to become immortal."

Drake nodded. "I agree. He's spent more than a thousand years in a hell prison world paying for that crime. Even humans get out of prison at some point. If he gets out, if he's done his time, why must he die?"

Hope swallowed. "What about the ritual he wants to perform?"

Drake shifted uneasily on the sand. "That might be a big lie. We discovered that our head Cyst, General Jaydon, was gathering Enhanced females for his own purpose, which has nothing to do with Ulric or bringing him home."

Hope lifted her head. "To copy Ulric's original ritual?"

"Yes. His actions were a travesty, and he's dead. My father is a powerful leader, and not even he knew what General Jaydon was planning. You need to think. Maybe there is no future ritual, so long as your people don't try to murder Ulric." Drake sighed. "We need him. He made a terrible mistake, but he's doing his

*penance and then will return to lead the Cyst. I think he might
be the only one who can."*

Hope didn't have an answer for that.

*Drake held her hand tighter. "Enough with the gloom and doom.
For now, I take it Paxton Phoenix is not sleeping in your room?"*

*She grinned. "No. It looks like I can create the dreamworlds
myself again."*

*"Good. A guy does get jealous," he murmured, his gaze dropping
to her mouth. "In a different world, Phoenix and I might be friends.
But in this one? We both want you, and you're made to be a queen.
Not a mate to an irrelevant commoner who truly doesn't matter."*

She reared back. "Pax matters. A lot."

Drake smiled. "Not right here, he doesn't. So—"

A loud bang propelled Hope right out of the dreamworld.

* * * *

Hope sat upright in her bed, her gaze on the hulking figure near
her window. "Pax," she hissed, her hair tumbling back from her
face. "What in the world are you doing?"

He moved toward her, sitting next to her, his muscled bulk
pressing the bed down. "I came to talk to you and knew instantly
you were in a dreamworld. I can't believe you keep doing this."
His large hand moved through his hair, ruffling it and giving him
a wild look. "Drake is one of the bad guys. We caught one of the
Cyst generals kidnapping a bunch of Enhanced females. What
he had planned—"

"General Jaydon?" Hope asked.

Pax's dark eyebrows rose, and his eyes glittered a silvery blue
through the darkness. "Yeah. Jaydon. I take it Drake told you?"

"Yes. He's as upset about it as you are. Said that his father didn't
know of Jaydon's plans. Jaydon is dead now, I think?" She took in
Pax's jeans and dark T-shirt. "I thought you went with my dad."

"I did. We went to take Jaydon's island and rescue the Enhanced females." Pax scrubbed his hands down his scruffy jaw. "It was a good campaign, and we were the better trained force."

She frowned. "Was Drake there? He had an injury."

"I didn't see him," Pax said. "But there were several skirmishes, so he could've been there."

Maybe Drake had fought with Jaydon or a Cyst. That would explain his injury. "I am getting really tired of people keeping me out of the loop." She turned and sneezed violently.

Paxton waited and then cupped her jaw when she turned back toward him. "We're just trying to protect you."

"I don't need protection." At least Drake had told her what was going on, even if he'd left out a few details. "You don't trust me."

Pax sighed. "I don't trust Drake, and I know you're talking to him. He's not a good guy, Hope. Even if you're meeting him in a dreamworld just like your parents did."

She didn't want to think about romance. Not right now. It was all too confusing. "What if we're wrong?"

Pax straightened. "What do you mean?"

"What if Ulric doesn't have some grand plan to kill all Enhanced females? What if Jaydon planted that idea as a front for his kidnapping all those Enhanced females so he could perform his own ritual? What if it's not true? Yeah, Ulric was a really bad guy, but he's been in a prison paying for what he did." Much that Drake had said made sense.

Pax twisted his lip. "Then we've been wasting a lot of time on legends."

She chuckled. "Right? I believe in what I see and hear and feel. The rest isn't clear enough to act on. Not yet, anyway."

"I agree." Pax held her hand. The same one that Drake had held. Pax's hand was warmer and slightly bigger. Interesting. Drake was taller. Pax was bigger. They were both…a lot. Already. "We have to go with our gut feelings. I did so recently, and I think it was the right decision. We'll see."

"Tell me more."

He tightened his hold on her hand. "I won't ever lie to you, but I'm done talking about this. For now, let's not worry about the big stuff. Well, except why the only female vampire hybrid in existence keeps catching a little human cold."

She smacked his arm. "Not nice."

"Never said I was nice." He pushed her beneath the covers and snatched the TV remote control off the table. Then he settled down next to her, a solid and warm force in a turbulent world. "We haven't watched a movie like this forever."

"You're always training," she mumbled, her eyelids growing heavy.

His words brushed over her with his heated breath. "Yeah, I am. I smell war on the breeze, Hope, and I'm going to win this one."

"*We're* going to win," she whispered, tumbling into sleep as a movie started on the screen.

"Same thing," Pax whispered. "You just don't understand that yet."

Chapter Forty-One

Honor held tight to Sam's hand as they stepped out of the truck and walked to their cabin, where several males were busy pounding nails and making a new deck. "You sure you're okay?"

"I feel great," Sam said, standing tall and looking over the cabin. "Well, almost great." He rubbed his chin and turned her, putting her rear gently against a tree. "There's something I forgot to do."

Her eyes opened wide. "Back at the island?"

"No. Here." He kissed the top of her nose, sending sweet tingles through her entire body.

She looked around. The deck was coming along nicely. What had he forgotten?

One of the men saw them and turned around. "Hey. Doc Honor. I was wondering if we could talk." He was a monster of a male at about seven feet tall, and even in human form had the eyes of a grizzly.

"Sure," she said, noting Sam's stiffening. "In a few minutes, okay, Burt?"

The mammoth clapped his hands together. "Great. I mean, it's no big deal, but I was kind of hurt Bear didn't want me on the run. Sure, I know that we needed cover here, and I'm good at scouting, but still. My feelers are kind of hurt."

Sam's chin dropped. "Feelers?"

"Yeah," the bear snapped. "Feelers are normal, right Doc? I mean, I'm not wimpy."

"You're not wimpy, Burt," Honor agreed. "Feelings are good, and it's wonderful you want to explore them. That's healthy." She nudged Sam's shoulder. "I'll be over in a few minutes."

Burt ambled happily away, swinging the hammer hard enough to rock the whole deck as he put another board in place.

"Sorry about that," Honor said, looking up at Sam. "I've created a support group for some of the bears, and I'll make sure to invite him next time. For now, what's wrong? Can I help?"

"Yes," he rumbled. "There's a lot you can do to help."

When he used that tone, all she wanted to do was get naked. At least she'd been able to change into jeans and a sweater in the truck and get rid of the bloody white gown. "I would love to help you," she said, leaning toward him.

"Good." He slid his hands down both of her arms to take her hands. "Here's the deal."

"Hey. Honor." A tall woman with stunning blond hair strode by. "Jasper is coming back to visit Nessa again about witch business, and I took your suggestion and texted him, so I'm on his mind. What should I do next?"

Sam growled.

Honor tried to hold up a hand, but both of hers were captured in Sam's. "Um, let's talk about it after dinner, okay? We can have dessert and mull it over."

"Great," the blonde said, moving toward the food tent.

Sam watched her go, looking as if he was going to throw something.

"Sam? What did you forget?" Honor asked. If it was a knife or sword or something like that, maybe she could get him one for his birthday. Once she found out when he'd been born.

He took a deep breath. "See—"

"Honor." Bear rounded a corner with Nessa on one side and Flynn the other. "There's something wrong with Nessa. Or one of the babies."

Honor freed her hands. "What?"

Nessa shook her head, and her dark hair tumbled over her shoulders. "He's being silly. There's nothing wrong. I was just really tired and slipped on the muddy walk." Mud covered her right leg. "Honest. Nothing is wrong."

Bear yanked her up against his side, his honey-brown eyes flashing wildly. "Check. Her. Out."

"Sure." Honor moved toward them, right by Sam, and placed both hands on Nessa's belly. Then she closed her eyes and just felt. Slow and smooth, not causing any disturbances. Three essences, all content. She leaned back. "Nessa and the babies are fine. The witch is going to be a handful, just by the way."

Bear beamed and then frowned. Nessa rolled her eyes.

Flynn visibly relaxed and shook his head.

"You okay, Flynn?" Sam asked, gazing at the dragon shifter.

"Yep. Took a fall, rolled, and am fine now. No worries," Flynn said, still eyeing Nessa with concern. "Maybe we should just put bubble wrap all around her."

Bear looked at him and then at Nessa. "That's not a bad idea."

"No," Nessa exploded, fire billowing down her arms.

"Fine," Bear said just as Flynn stepped back, nodding wildly.

Sam took Honor into his arms again. "As I was saying—"

"Hey, Honor. I was thinking you could start reading women before I date them." Garrett loped from the food tent with a huge sandwich in his hands.

"That's it," Sam bellowed, causing everyone to stop in place. "That is completely it. I wanted this to be private, but no. You bears are just too…involved." He grasped her arms, his grip firm as his green gaze landed on her with possession and intent. "I love you. Needed to say it. Will probably never have another chance since everyone is determined to get your attention, but I realized I hadn't told you." He settled. "I love you."

Everything she'd ever be burst wide open inside her.

Garrett rolled his eyes and moved back toward the food tent.

Bear drew Nessa away. "Man. Those hybrids sure get emotional sometimes. Geez." They kept walking with Flynn right behind them, his hands out as if he needed to be ready to catch Nessa in case she fell.

The group working on the deck cast Sam sympathetic glances and moved away toward the beer tent.

Honor smiled, her life complete. "I love you too. Have since the first time you kissed me, I think."

He kissed her again, pouring everything into it that she'd ever want or need. They were both breathing heavily when he lifted his head. "So. Want to live here for a while, cover Garrett's back, and shrink the heads of a bunch of crazy grizzly bears? I'll build you a bigger cabin and an office space *far away* from that cabin."

If her heart got any fuller, it'd burst. "Yeah. I want that." She'd planned to create her own clinic to help people, and this was even better. She leaned up and kissed his chin. "So long as we're together."

"We will be." His green gaze, as usual, was focused directly on her. "I always knew if I did the best I could, I'd get to keep my Honor."

Please read on for a snippet of GARRETT'S DESTINY, the next exciting Dark Protectors novel!

Garrett Kayrs settled his bulk in the booth, reaching for a glass of beer from the iced pitcher on the table. Raucous laughter poured through the diner as motorcycle clubs converged on the way to a festival. Not one he and his brothers were attending, but they were along for the first part of the ride.

"Would you stop frowning?" Sam Kyllwood snapped from across the booth, his green eyes irritated.

"I'm not," Garrett growled, frowning.

Honor Kyllwood, Sam's mate, slapped him on the arm. They'd been mated for more than three years, and she was definitely one of the best-natured people Garrett had ever met. "You two behave. Garrett, I'm sure you'll find somebody to play with when we get to the symposium, and Sam, give him a break. It's the first time in years when we've gone on a ride and he hasn't had a date on the back of his bike. He's lonely."

Sam grimaced. "The last female he dated tried to rob you—at knifepoint."

Honor chortled. "Yeah, but I kicked her ass. Those training sessions have gone well."

Garrett hid his grin. Plus, she was correct. He'd been searching for the right female to ride behind him for years—had been consumed by the quest—yet he hadn't found her. She was supposed to be dangerous, even deadly, and would probably try to kill him. All he knew was that she was a buxom immortal, maybe a shifter or a witch who would try to take him out. Perhaps she was a demoness. Either way, it was time to get on with it. For now, he had a job to do. After lunch.

The door opened and a vision walked in. Well, more like the girl next door. A human one. She wore a frilly green blouse, white capri jeans, and sexy tan wedges that showed off her pink toenails. A laptop bag looked heavy over her fragile shoulder. Her auburn hair curled down her back, and an air of pure irritation surrounded her.

Looking like an indignant kitten, she stomped right into the middle of the diner without seeming to realize she'd walked into a den of wolves.

The man behind her definitely noticed. He was young, with slick brown hair, pressed beige-colored pants, and thousand-dollar loafers on his feet. He looked around at the various motorcycle club members sitting in different areas of the diner, all hungry, all possibly dangerous. "Let's get out of here," he muttered.

The kitten turned, her hands going to her waist. "You just don't understand." She leaned toward him, anger turning her peaches and cream complexion into cherry-blossom pink. "The answer *was* no." She swept out her arms. "The answer *is* no." She clapped her hands. "The answer will always and forever, until the time of the rapture, *be no.*" She threw her arms up. Then she shook her head. "I quit."

The man reared back. "You don't even have proper documentation. You can't quit."

"I just did," she said with a sigh. "Right now, I'm out. I'm not finding what I need in this job, anyway." She nodded, her shoulders stiff in the flimsy blouse. "I'll send your father a nice email later today tendering my resignation. Tell him I'm grateful he gave me a chance, but life is too short to waste time." She turned away from him.

The man made the mistake of grabbing her arm.

Garrett was up in a second, towering over them both. "Let. Go."

The man drew back as if he'd been scalded.

A slight gasp came from the kitten.

Probably one of pure terror. Oh, Garrett knew what she saw. He was six and a half feet of raw muscle in a torn black motorcycle club jacket with shaggy hair to his shoulders, a couple of bruises across his jaw, and cracked knuckles he hadn't bothered to heal after a fight the night before.

He cut her a look and then rocked back on his heels.

Her greenish-blue eyes were full of delight...and wonder. "You," she whispered, reaching to touch his whiskered jaw. Her tongue peeked out to lick her luscious bottom lip. "It's *you*." She tilted her head, adoration in her gaze.

The touch shot straight to his balls, making him throb in a way he hadn't in years. He growled low.

Then she withdrew.

"No." He didn't know what he was denying, but he didn't want her to stop looking at him like that. Nobody in his entire life had looked at him like that.

The pink blossomed into full-on rose, and she clapped her hand against the laptop bag. "I, ah, um, I'm sorry." She frowned. "That was, well, that was..." She looked around, no doubt seeing that every gaze in the room was on her. She shrugged and looked back at him. "Sorry."

"Let's go," the man said, backing away.

She frowned at him. "No. Leave me be, Aster. I'll find my own way home."

Aster looked around, paling.

Then the asshole left the kitten in the den of wolves.

Her hands fluttered together. "Oh. Well." She caught sight of the empty row of barstools at the counter and started to move that direction.

"No." Garrett angled his body just enough to stop her. "How do you know me?" There were many bounties on his head right now, but there was no way the kitten was a bounty hunter. He could read people better than that.

She glanced down at his monstrous boots and took a deep breath before looking up and meeting his gaze. "I don't know you." Then she smiled, and sure as shit, it was like the sun had appeared over the mountains after the rainy season. "That was weird and I apologize. There's no way I could know you, right?"

"Right." He grasped her arm, careful not to bruise her. "You're sitting with us."

"No, I—"

He nudged her into the booth, putting his body between her and the rest of the bikers in the place.

It was time for some answers.

Printed in the United States
by Baker & Taylor Publisher Services